THE TESLA LEGACY

Sweet Black Waves

Wild Savage Stars

The Myth of Morgan la Fey

THE TESLA LEGACY

K. K. PÉREZ

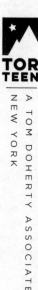

TOR
TEEN

NEW YORK

A TOM DOHERTY ASSOCIATES BOOK

This is a work of fiction. All of the characters, organizations, and events portrayed in this novel are either products of the author's imagination or are used fictitiously.

The experiments performed by the characters in this book are not intended to be replicated by the reader. Do not try this at home!

THE TESLA LEGACY

Copyright © 2019 by K. K. Pérez

A Tor Teen Book
Published by Tom Doherty Associates
175 Fifth Avenue
New York, NY 10010

www.tor-forge.com

Tor® is a registered trademark of Macmillan Publishing Group, LLC.

The Library of Congress Cataloging-in-Publication Data is available upon request.

ISBN 978-1-250-08489-7 (hardcover)
ISBN 978-1-250-08490-3 (ebook)

Our books may be purchased in bulk for promotional, educational, or business use. Please contact your local bookseller or the Macmillan Corporate and Premium Sales Department at 1-800-221-7945, extension 5442, or by email at MacmillanSpecialMarkets@ macmillan.com.

First Edition: March 2019

Printed in the United States of America

0 9 8 7 6 5 4 3 2 1

For Ruby Jane

*Our virtues and our failings are inseparable,
like force and matter. When they separate, man
is no more.*

—Nikola Tesla

THE TESLA LEGACY

OPPOSITES ATTRACT

"Wait, let me explain. *Please.*"

Cole grabbed her naked elbow. It was such a mild late-March day that Lucy hadn't bothered with a jacket. Big mistake. Cole knew his touch made her hair stand on end mad scientist–style. Metaphorically speaking.

Lucy jerked away. "I suppose this is the part where you tell me what I saw isn't what it looked like," she said, and started unlocking Marie Curie—her dependable two-wheeler—from the fence that surrounded Eaton High. God forbid her parents should trust her behind the wheel of a car.

"Aren't you going to hear me out?" Cole exhaled a frustrated breath.

Shifting closer, he rounded to Lucy's side of the bike, sliding an arm around her waist, then threaded his fingers through her tangle of black curls. His fingertips were magic as he gently massaged her scalp. A tiny, traitorous sigh escaped her.

Lucy fidgeted with the lock's dial, beginning to lose focus. The combination was the date of their first kiss. Of course it was.

She remembered each excruciating detail. She'd spilled her chocolate milkshake down her shirt, and was calculating the fastest escape route from Casey's Diner when Cole leaned across the table to steady her hand. He licked a dab of chocolate from her chin and plunged his delectably edible tongue into her mouth.

"Lucy Phelps," he'd declared. "You taste delicious."

Lucy never told Cole that he'd been her very first kiss. She had some shame. But hey, it wasn't like she'd met a ton of guys being home-schooled until junior year. She should be grateful that after some hardcore lobbying on the part of her neurologist, her parents had agreed to let her attend regular school at all. She'd already garnered enough AP credits to start taking college courses online—their distinct preference—but Lucy craved a semblance of normalcy.

"All right," Lucy relented, flicking her gaze at Cole. "Explain."

She pocketed the bike lock and turned to face him. Lucy loved his floppy brown hair, chestnut-colored, and the way he pushed back his bangs when he was agitated. Like now.

"We're *seniors*, Lucy. I didn't think it would matter."

"You didn't think it would matter that you were selling test answers?" The image of Cole handing over her notes in the middle of the hallway flashed through Lucy's mind. "Answers I gave you in the first place!" She winced as her voice reached a pitch only dogs should hear.

Cole's brow puckered. "Megan won't tell," he said lamely.

"I'm sure."

Megan Harper was one of the many girls who orbited around Cole, waiting for him to realize that he was way out of Lucy's league. Cole had also come to Eaton at the start of junior year, a track star from California with a lithely muscled runner's body and easygoing charm, who immediately took his rightful place at the top of the high school food chain. Nobody was more flabbergasted than Lucy that Cole gave her the time of day, let alone asked her out.

Cupping her cheek with his hand, he protested, "There's nothing between Megan and me."

Lucy lowered an eyebrow. Not twenty seconds ago, she hadn't thought there *was* anything going on with Megan.

"This isn't about me being *jealous*, Cole." She shook him off. "I only agreed to help *you*." And she shouldn't have.

A cheater, that's what Lucy was. It had started with help on his chemistry homework, taking her payment in kisses, and then letting him look over her shoulder on a calculus quiz. Harmless. She enjoyed physics experiments. Why shouldn't she do his take-home assignments?

It wasn't like Cole wasn't smart, he was just always so busy with track. The team depended on him to set new long-distance records at the state championships, and his athletic scholarship was riding on it; it wasn't fair to expect him to have time to study like everyone else.

Opposites attract, he was always saying: the manga-hot geek and the homecoming hero. The first time Lucy laid eyes on him, Cole was slouched on a worn tan love seat in the school administration office like he belonged there. He had a talent for belonging anywhere, Lucy figured out later. At the time, he was waiting for the orientation tour when she stumbled in, quite literally, much to her dismay.

Her book bag banged against the doorjamb, and Cole had glanced up sharply.

"I'm Lucy," she'd told him, as if maybe she wasn't sure.

"Cole." He coughed into his hand. "I'm new."

"Me too."

A mischievous smile slipped over his features. "Then we'd better stick together."

"Like magnets," Lucy had chimed in, mentally eye-rolling at herself for not being able to get through the first fifteen minutes of official school—ever—without revealing her inner dork.

He'd laughed, bemused but not unkind.

"Yeah," Cole had agreed that crisp September day. "Opposites attract."

She hadn't bothered asking him how he knew they were opposites.

"*Luce.*" Cole breathed her name, bringing her back to the present, and aimed his ultramarine gaze at her like a bull's-eye. It was the finest weapon in his arsenal. "You're blowing this out of proportion. No harm, no foul."

Ultramarine: beyond the sea. That was where Cole's eyes transported her. Always. Especially the night of Lucy's eighteenth birthday. Another first.

Such vivid blue was the result of an unpaired electron. Which was the kind of nerdtastic factoid Lucy had gleaned during a life of near isolation, helicopter parenting, and being prodded and poked to divine the root of her migraines and seizures—although they never had. The fact that plenty of other people with epilepsy didn't know what had caused theirs, either, did nothing to make Lucy feel better.

Being with Cole carried her away from all that, beyond herself, but . . . *but . . .*

He leaned within kissing distance. "I did it for us."

"Oh, really?" Lucy leaned back.

"Prom night. It's expensive."

Sure, she'd been fantasizing about a certain dress at Neiman Marcus, and a matching corsage, and all the rest of it, but where did Cole get off implying that this was somehow her fault?

"Then I'm not going," Lucy told him. "You're not putting this on me. Just give Megan her money back."

"I can't." He jutted out his lip.

"Of course you can."

"No." A pause. "I spent it."

"Since sixth period? On what?" Continuing to stare into his eyes, she realized. "This wasn't the first time. Was it, Cole?"

He shook his head.

"How long? How long has this been going on?"

Cole shrugged. "Since Christmas, maybe?" he said, like he couldn't remember when he'd started selling her out. "I didn't mean to hurt you."

He chewed his bottom lip. She wished his lips weren't so perfect, wished she didn't know how soft they were, or the taste of his Chap-Stick.

"No, you just didn't mean for me to find out!" Lucy said, voice breaking.

He didn't deny it. Tugging her in close, teasing his nose along her temple, Cole murmured, "I'm sorry. I love you, Luce."

Lucy started to shake, the whole world started to shake, and she saw flashes in the sky. "You don't use someone you love."

"Calm down. You know you're not supposed to stress. It's not good for you."

Hell no. She yanked away from him. "Don't you dare!" she yelled, her anger blazing white-hot. "Don't you dare treat me like my parents do!"

Lucy could take anything but that.

Cole's eyes went wide. She'd never allowed herself to be so furious around him before. He'd never given her a reason.

"You know what isn't good for me, Cole? *You.*"

Thunder boomed in agreement. Lucy jumped on Marie Curie and pedaled full steam ahead without looking back. Rain began to pelt her maliciously, camouflaging her tears like in every pop-song cliché.

Cole didn't chase after her.

By the time she made it home, Lucy was soaked, freezing, and alone.

An unpaired electron.

LIBER LIBRUM APERIT

"It's just you and me, Schrödinger." Lucy sighed and ladled Fancy Feast into his bowl as the tabby cat wended himself between her ankles, rubbing against her legs with a plaintive yowl. Raindrops tapped against the window, marking time.

As Schrödinger purred louder, Lucy muttered, "I'm feeding you, I'm feeding you." She realized she should probably fear for her mental state—and her social life—being home alone on a Friday night, talking to her feline companion.

At least Schrödinger wasn't talking back.

And really, the tabby treated Lucy better than she deserved, considering she'd named him after an Austrian scientist whose most celebrated thought experiment left a cat sealed in a box with a flask of poison and a radioactive agent, simultaneously alive *and* dead. Lucy scratched her Schrödinger behind the ears, releasing another sigh. Alive and dead was precisely how she felt this evening.

She slanted a surreptitious glance at her cell phone for the umpteenth time.

Still no text from Cole, just a message from her bestie, Claudia, asking if she was going to make an appearance at the swim-team party. Odds were Cole would be there. Cole never missed a party. Overzealous stereo systems pushed Lucy toward a migraine and she didn't drink because of her meds, but she'd usually go with him just to feel the comfort of his hand in hers.

Not tonight. If Cole wasn't coming to her, Lucy sure as hell wasn't going to him. Especially after he pulled the "don't stress" card. The way he'd doubted her this afternoon made her as angry as the cheating.

She wasn't a glass figurine that would shatter.

Schrödinger vibrated, begging for more. "Finish what you've got first," she admonished. Yikes, Lucy sounded just like her mother.

She opened the fridge, rummaging around for a little guilty pleasure. Normal parents would leave money for pizza; Professor Elaine Phelps had prepared a kale and quinoa salad before taking off for some departmental wine-and-cheese evening at the college where she taught. Her mom was a walking epilepsy-trigger encyclopedia, and because there was a possible correlation between foods that caused energy spikes and seizures, Lucy wasn't supposed to eat sugar or carbs or anything fun.

Both her parents handled her like a live grenade despite the fact that she hadn't had a seizure for two years. No amount of browbeating, begging, or cajoling would convince them to sign the permission slip for driver's ed. The bicycle itself had been a huge compromise when she hit the twelve-month seizure-free mark.

Lucy huffed as her eyes snagged on a can of Coke. Her dad possessed a finely honed sweet tooth. How had he slipped that past her mother?

Hello, sugar rush.

Schrödinger traipsed after her as Lucy flung herself onto the sofa in the living room and began scrolling through her Netflix queue—mostly vintage sci-fi. Shockingly enough, the parental locks hadn't been enabled. Her mom's profile was comprised entirely of History Channel programs about the Roman Empire, while her dad's was a mix of stand-up comedy, TED talks, and science documentaries.

Before her father sold out and became a banker, he'd done a Ph.D. in quantum mechanics. A few years ago, he converted the garage into a lab, where he and Lucy would run experiments together. Einstein Time, he called it. Between his business trips and her college prep, however, there hadn't been much Einstein Time lately. She actually missed it.

Restlessness coursed through Lucy that had nothing to do with the sugar high taking hold. *Scroll, scroll, scroll.*

She and Cole never fought like this. They never fought. Period.

Picturing Cole enjoying the party without her, Lucy tossed aside the remote control, pushed to her feet, and began to pace. She padded into her father's office, which was just as messy as her bedroom.

Slovenliness must be genetic.

Her eyes panned around the room and caught on the Gilbert College diploma framed on the wall beside his desk—another family tradition.

Gilbert was where her parents had met, and Lucy would be starting there in the fall. Her chest pinched. She should be thrilled. It was an excellent small college with a lauded physics department and she should feel honored to have been admitted. She did. But it was only a forty-five-minute drive from Eaton.

Lucy's parents hadn't allowed her to apply to college anywhere more than two hours away by car. That perimeter included New York City, where her dad worked at a venture capital firm, but her parents had vetoed the Big Apple because they said it would be too overwhelming for her.

She took a long slurp of Coke. If they had their way, Lucy would spend her entire life dressed in bubble wrap.

Schrödinger scampered into the office and pawed at Lucy's calf. Only catnip would pacify the little beast when he got in this mood.

Her pocket buzzed. Claudia again.

Do U need a ride? I'll let U practice ☺

Claudia had been giving Lucy driving lessons on the down-low. She didn't know what she'd do when Claudia moved halfway across the country to the University of Chicago. Claudia had lived a few houses over from Lucy for their entire lives. She'd been her best friend—her *only* friend for a while there—since the day she beat up Tony Morelli for calling Lucy "Helmet Head."

This was especially impressive seeing as Tony grew up to be Eaton High's fiercest linebacker and Claudia capped out at five-foot-nothing. And Tony wasn't wrong. Lucy had worn a helmet outside for most of her childhood in case a seizure struck. That one act of heroism—and to six-year-old Lucy it was truly heroic—had elevated Claudia to *I'll-help-you-bury-the-body-no-questions-asked* status forever.

Schrödinger upped the ante to whining as Lucy texted Claudia back, begging off the party. But she didn't text fast enough.

The tabby vaulted his ample derrière onto the desk, landing in the middle of haphazardly strewn manila folders, and sending them flying. Along with a photo of toddler Lucy missing most of her teeth.

"Schrödinger!" she yelled. The cat mewled in contrition, but it was too late.

And because the fates had conspired against her, Lucy heard the distinctive sound of a key turning in the front door. Perfect. The office looked like a bomb site.

Dropping to her hands and knees, Lucy desperately tried to gather the files as her dad called out, "Lucy? Lucy! We're back!" She reached for the photo frame—the glass had cracked, of course, and the black backing had popped open, exposing the blank side of the photo. Except it wasn't blank.

Liber Librum Aperit was scrawled on the back.

Thanks to her mom's Latin lessons, Lucy did a quick translation: *One book opens another*. She scrunched up her nose. Her mom was the Classics professor in the family but it wasn't her handwriting. Or her dad's, for that matter. Weird.

"What's going on in here?"

Lucy darted her eyes toward her dad, who hovered in the doorway.

His tie was already loosened and his suit rumpled. He looked exhausted. Harried.

"Tidying?" she replied, more question than answer, and continued trying to make some kind of order out of the chaos Schrödinger had unleashed.

"Uh-huh."

Over her dad's shoulder, Lucy spied her mother, brow creased in concern.

"Did you have an episode?" she asked.

Elaine Phelps was tall, blond, and patrician. The opposite of Lucy with her black curls and gray eyes. She possessed what Lucy referred to as "monastic composure." Her mom allowed herself one cigarette every day. Rather than the habit being an example of relatable human imperfection, Lucy saw it for what it was: an exercise in discipline.

Her mother's gaze zeroed in on the telltale can of Coke next to Lucy on the floor.

"I've warned you that sugar can be a trigger," she said in a placating kindergarten-teacher voice, and Lucy's temper flared.

"It wasn't the *sugar*, Mom. It was Schrödinger." Although the feline had conveniently vanished.

"Don't snap at your mom, Luce," her dad said, an edge to his words. *Sheesh.* Two on one was not fair. "Sorry," she mumbled, and lowered her eyes to avoid his glare. "Long day." She shuffled a few folders into a pile.

Her dad stepped forward, resting a conciliatory hand on Lucy's shoulder.

"I hear you, kiddo. And I've gotta head back to the office first thing in the morning."

"On a Saturday?" she said, head flicking up.

The tension in his jaw relaxed into a tired smile. "No rest for the wicked."

"Victor, why don't we get you a beer?" Lucy's mom suggested. He nodded, adjusting his rimless glasses; dark circles shadowed his brown eyes, making his pale skin almost vampiric. To Lucy, her mom said, "Leave the files. I'll take care of them."

Her mother couldn't stand disorder. If she noticed even the smallest speck of brown discoloring a single petal, she would discard an entire flower arrangement. Narrowing her eyes at the picture frame, she said, "You didn't cut yourself, did you?"

"Nope. Got all my digits." Lucy stretched out her hands and wiggled her fingers as proof.

Her mom's lips thinned into a patient smile. "How about some tea? To help you sleep?"

Sleep deprivation was another potential trigger.

"No, thanks." Lucy forced up one corner of her mouth. Now didn't seem like the right moment to ask her parents about the Latin quotation.

Once they'd gone through to the kitchen, she gingerly picked up the broken frame and slid the photo out, examining the scratch across the swath of blue sky. She bet she could repair the scratch on her computer and replace the photo before her parents even knew it'd been damaged.

Lucy also took the Coke on her way out. As rebellions went, it was pretty pathetic—but it was hers.

Schrödinger was curled at the foot of the staircase, eyes mournful.

"Nice try," she said. "No catnip for you."

He swished his tail.

A mixture of frustration and curiosity swirled through Lucy as she retreated upstairs to her bedroom.

She pulled out her phone again.

Her great textpectations were for naught. *Fine.*

Lucy might not be able to fix herself—or her love life—but she would fix this damn photo. *Liber Librum Aperit*, indeed.

Let's see what book this opens.

CURIOUSER AND CURIOUSER

Lucy swung open her bedroom door too fast and a framed poster of the periodic table of elements rattled over her bed, which was still unmade. It had been unmade since Wednesday. But really, what was the point of doing and undoing the same thing every day? Lucy reasoned that, like Schrödinger's cat, her bed could be both concurrently made and unmade.

Her mom wasn't buying it.

Lucy picked up a bra from where she'd flung it on her desk chair, tossed it onto the bed, and sat down at her computer. Okay, she was a slob. Everywhere except in the laboratory. She felt most free there, and most in control. Science thrilled Lucy like nothing else. Not even Cole.

She drained the last of the sugary goodness from the aluminum can as she scanned in the picture and launched the math software that Santa had brought her at Christmas. Only Lucy would ask the man in the red suit for a better way to model pendulums. She'd also produced some pretty cool animations of cannonball trajectories to simulate the laws of motion—if she did say so herself.

Toothless Lucy materialized on the screen. The photo must have been taken around the same time she experienced her first seizure. How differently would her parents have treated her if she'd never been diagnosed with epilepsy?

She wiggled the Coke can—*empty*—and pushed it to one side.

Tilting closer to the monitor, Lucy determined that since the scratch was mostly on the blue of the sky, the best method for repairing it would be to separate the image into layers. Lucy had been taking things apart to see how they worked since before she could talk. Toasters. Toy helicopters. Nothing was safe.

She loved anything to do with stripping a machine down to its basic components and building it back up again. She could build the perfect computer brain, an operating system that would never malfunction like hers.

Her fingers flew over the keyboard and the image divided into four channels: cyan, magenta, yellow, and black—the standard for most printers.

Lucy squinted at the cyan channel. She'd already been using the software to distort images from the web, creating formulas to make them bigger or smaller, *Alice in Wonderland*–style. All Lucy needed to do was determine the right equation to repeat the colored pixels over the scratched area.

She gave the image a horizontal x-axis and a vertical y-axis, like she would to solve a geometry problem on graph paper, and as she moved the four windows of the color channels side by side on the screen, her eyes caught on something odd in the yellow window.

Nearly three-quarters of the image was covered in irregularly spaced dots.

When she leaned back, Lucy realized they formed a gridlike pattern. It resembled braille or Morse code, but not quite. Strange.

One book opens another. It couldn't be a message, could it?

A knock came on the open door, and Lucy jumped.

"Mom!"

"Didn't mean to startle you." Her mom extended a mug in Lucy's direction. Peppermint tea was her mom's cure-all. Lucy had far too many memories of waking up from a seizure to the fresh, wintry smell. "Here, I thought you might change your mind," she said.

Professor Phelps wasn't accustomed to taking no for an answer. Like mother, like daughter, Lucy supposed.

Relenting, she leapt up to accept the mug and block her mom's view of the computer screen. "Thanks," she said.

"Everything okay? I thought you'd be out with Cole or Claudia."

"You *want* me to go out partying?"

"That's not what *I*—"

"I know, Mom." Grinning, Lucy took a sip of tea. "Everything's okay. Swear." She certainly couldn't tell her mother that Cole had gotten her caught up in a cheating scam. "I just wanted to veg out tonight."

Her mom nodded. "We're heading to bed now. Need anything else?"

"I'm good."

"Good," she repeated. "Don't stay up too late."

"I won't. Would you mind closing the door?"

Her mom hesitated a moment, lips pursed. "Sleep well, honey."

"You too." She took a big gulp of tea as guilt swirled in her chest. Lucy's mom wasn't effusive as a rule, but *honey* was the term of endearment she reserved for Lucy. Sure, her mom was overprotective and controlling, but it was only because she cared.

As soon as the door clicked shut, however, Lucy abandoned the tea on a bookshelf to go cold. She interlocked her fingers, stretching out her arms. Her knuckles cracked. Sitting back down, Lucy enlarged the yellow-channel window.

Could the dots be some kind of binary code?

Her eyes zigzagged across the screen. She needed a working hypothesis. *Hmm*. She drummed her fingers against the mouse pad.

If Lucy gave the dots a value of 1 and the blank spaces a value of 0, what did that give her? She opened up another text window and began transcribing the sequence of 1s and 0s. An hour ticked by but Lucy hardly noticed.

She pulled up a binary-to-text converter and input the string of numbers and . . . strikeout. Gobbledygook.

Maybe she needed to reverse the values?

Biting her tongue between her teeth, Lucy pasted the reversed text into the translator.

More gibberish.

Lucy rolled back in her desk chair, then rose to standing. Treading back and forth in the space between her desk and her bed, she nearly burned a hole in the carpet.

What was she missing?

She swiped the mug from the bookshelf and chugged the tepid tea. She rubbed her eyes, glancing at the clock. It was after midnight. Maybe she should give it a rest. *No.* A scientist didn't quit in the middle of an experiment.

Lucy's eyelids fluttered. Focusing on the screen once more, she noticed something about the dots she hadn't seen before.

Some of the dots were a darker shade of yellow than the others.

Could that have any significance?

Lucy parked herself back in the desk chair and logged into a computer builder and programmer forum where she often whiled away the hours.

Starbuck01: hey night owls, anyone know about encrypting data into images?

Less than a minute passed before Lucy got a response.

phlebas: what kind of encryption?
Starbuck01: in the yellow channel of a photo—lighter and darker dots
phlebas: you're looking at the metadata?
Starbuck01: no. not a digital photo. a scanned photo
phlebas: sounds like standard steganography but I've only seen it in digital images. sorry
Starbuck01: no problem

Lucy stood, pulling her shirt over her head to change for bed. The dots were just a red herring—something to distract her from Cole's lack of communication. She didn't need a psychologist to tell her that. Had he forgotten their fight already? Had he forgotten *her*? Lucy swallowed a lump in her throat.

Suddenly a new message appeared on the board.

Lovelace: human eyes are least sensitive to yellow
Starbuck01: huh?
Lovelace: don't mind if I butt in?
Starbuck01: no! be my guest!
Lovelace: ;-) thanks. so if you wanted to send a message that no one would notice, you'd use the yellow channel in a photo

Unless you pull the image apart, Lucy thought.

Starbuck01: even in a scanned photo?
Lovelace: could be. like a QR code. if you took a picture of the photo with a digital camera—or scanned it in—the coded message would become visible
Starbuck01: sounds like spy stuff

And who would go to so much trouble?

Lovelace: or clever marketing lol. to get people to enter a competition or something
Starbuck01: huh. wouldn't have thought of that.

Lucy's dad was the least likely person she knew to get sucked in by an advertising campaign. And, anyway, this was a photo of *her*, not a billboard.

Starbuck01: what's with the darker and lighter dots?

She tapped her foot on the caster of the rolling chair at an increasingly frenetic rate.

Lovelace: it looks like a grid, yes?

Starbuck01: yeah

Lovelace: ok, so if the square to the right has a higher level of yellow than the one to the left, it's=0. if the square to the left has a lesser level of yellow=1

Oh! Lucy hammered her fist onto the desk in excitement. The mug bounced. *Crap.* The last thing she needed was to wake her parents.

Starbuck01: how do you know about this?

Lovelace: i could tell you but then I'd have to kill you . . .

LULZ, Lucy typed back as she took several steadying breaths. Cole wasn't wrong about stress, annoyingly. It could bring on a seizure. But it hadn't for two years, Lucy reminded herself.

Lovelace: pro tip: check the center of the squares for the level of yellow. that's where the data will be

Starbuck01: thanks

Lovelace: someone sent you a coded picture?

Lucy stiffened. My boyfriend, she wrote, unsure why she felt the need to lie to a total stranger she would never meet.

Lovelace: sounds like a keeper.

Starbuck01: yeah. thanks. night

Lucy logged off, a knot forming in her stomach. Cole wouldn't have the slightest inkling how to encode a message. Was he a "keeper"? She'd thought so until this afternoon.

With a shake of her head, Lucy pushed thoughts of him from her mind and zoomed in even farther on the yellow color channel. She opened a new window and transcribed the dots according to Lovelace's advice.

Tap, tap, tap went her foot.

When she was finished, Lucy exhaled, her shoulders curling inward, and plugged the binary sequence into the converter with nervous fingers.

```
01010100 01101111 00111010 00100000 01010011 01100001
01110000 01101001 01100101 01101110 01110100 01101001
01100001 00100000 01000111 01110010 01101111 01110101
01110000 00001101 00001010 01010011 01110101 01100010
01101010 00111010 00100000 01001110 01101001 01101011
01101111 01101100 01100001 00001101 00001010 00110011
00110100 01110100 01101000 00100000 01100001 01101110
01100100 00100000 00111000 01110100 01101000 00101100
00100000 01110010 01101111 01101111 01101101 00100000
00110011 00110011 00110010 00110111 00001101 00001010
```

Holding her breath, she pressed Enter, and closed her eyes. Just for a moment.

When Lucy peeked at the screen again, her jaw fell open. She didn't know what she'd been expecting, but it certainly hadn't been this.

To: Sapientia Group
Subj: Nikola
34th and 8th, room 3327

A shiver raced down her spine.

The Sapientia Group was the name of her dad's venture capital firm. But Lucy's name definitely wasn't Nikola.

Who had sent this photo to her dad? And, why?

Thirty-fourth and Eighth must be an address. Eaton wasn't big enough to have streets or avenues ordered with numerals. She typed it into Google. *Bingo.*

The New Yorker Hotel, smack-dab in the middle of Manhattan.

Was it the location where the photo was taken? Lucy had no recollection of ever visiting that hotel. But why would she? She'd only been two or three years old at most.

Nikola.

Why would anyone call her Nikola? Unless she had an evil twin . . . *Stop, Lucy.* That made no sense. Although it also made no sense that her dad would have been sent a photo of Lucy encoded with a message that called her by a different name.

Why had he kept it?

Questions whizzed around her brain.

She let out a monumental yawn as the clock in the corner of the screen blinked 12:59 A.M. *Sleep.* Lucy should sleep. She would need all her wits about her tomorrow.

Tomorrow, her father was going to have some serious explaining to do.

TO BOLDLY GO

Lucy looked up at the turquoise expanse of star-washed sky. Only these constellations were backward. The Vanderbilt family, who commissioned the mural on the ceiling of Grand Central Terminal, would never admit their painter had confused the plans. They pronounced the mural depicted the heavens as seen by the gods, and that suited New Yorkers just fine, since they considered themselves their equals. Or that was how Lucy's mom put it anyway.

She dismissed a twinge of remorse. She'd left a note on the kitchen counter saying she was hanging out with Claudia (texted Claudia to cover for her), disabled the GPS tracker app her parents had installed on her cell (in case of emergencies, they said), and pedaled Marie Curie to the Eaton train station.

Lucy's dad had headed into the office before she woke up—schoolgirl error—and Lucy was determined to confront him about the photograph before she worried her mother.

Forty minutes south on the Metro-North, and here she was in the center of it all, looking down at the stars.

Adrenaline coursed through her. Lucy had never been so daring before.

Her favorite part of the station was the Whispering Gallery. On one of her childhood trips to see yet another specialist at New York Hospital, her dad showed Lucy its secrets. Standing at one corner, you could whisper a secret that was telegraphed across the surface of the two-thousand-square-foot chamber, landing in a faraway nook of the vault. Her dad said nobody knew whether it had been built that way on purpose.

Lucy's heart cramped. Her father always shared secrets with Lucy—he didn't keep them from her. He would have a reasonable explanation for the message encoded in the photograph. He *had* to. The alternative was . . . Lucy wouldn't think about that. A scientist dealt in facts, not fictions.

Double-checking her phone, Lucy proceeded through the Main Concourse in all of its Art Deco glory, exiting on Forty-second Street and was immediately greeted by the wail of a police siren. She rubbed her temples as they started to throb.

"You can do this," she said aloud, setting her shoulders. A pigeon cocked a disapproving head at her. *Jeez*, even the birds in this city were critics. "Stop talking to yourself." *Gah!* She'd done it again. Not a sophisticated New York thing to do.

Compressing her lips, Lucy headed uptown. The Sapientia Group was located in an office building nine blocks north on Lexington Avenue.

Bzzz. The phone in her hand vibrated.

U went to the city? Why?

If Lucy told Claudia she was braving all of the sights and sounds of the Bad Apple (as her mom called it) to chase down a string of numbers, her bestie might think Lucy's last remaining screw had finally come loose.

Needed space. Planetarium, she texted back instead.

Claudia would believe that. Lucy had been talking about visiting the Dark Matter exhibition for ages. Still, the lie made Lucy squirm.

OK . . . Cole was asking for U at the party. Seemed sad. What's up?

If Cole was so broken up, he could call her, text her, DM her. Evidently he hadn't broken each and every one of his fingers, so he had no excuse. Not that Lucy wasn't tempted to break them for him.

Nothing important. Will explain later.

Another lie. Claudia wouldn't make a beeline for the principal, but Lucy thought the fewer people who knew about the cheating, the better. Three people can keep a secret if two of them are dead, and all that. Lucy also felt foolish. Renewed fury gripped her that she was now lying to her best friend for her boyfriend.

She stormed through gaggles of out-of-town shoppers carrying Big Brown Bags and arrived at the entrance of her father's office building in no time. She craned her neck as her eyes drifted up the fifty stories to the top of the forbidding tower. Its thorny crown was meant to resemble medieval stonework and it was almost enough to make Lucy believe the city really was Gotham.

She threw her shoulders back.

Carpe diem. Wasn't that the wisdom that'd been disseminated by guidance counselors and valedictorians since the dawn of time?

Before she could talk herself out of it, Lucy seized the day, striding into the elegant, marble lobby, and approached the reception desk.

"H-hi. My father works here. At the Sapientia Group. I need to see him."

A fortysomething man wearing a navy suit looked up from the sports pages of the newspaper. His skin was a deep brown and he had a friendly smile.

"What's your name?" he asked.

"Lucinda Minerva Phelps," she said formally. *Face-palm.* Why had she given her middle name? She hated it. Minerva was what you got saddled with when your mother studied ancient poetry for a living.

The man huffed a small laugh. "Phelps? Dr. Victor Phelps's daughter?"

"The one and only," Lucy answered, smiling awkwardly. Then a disturbing thought struck her. What if the evil-twin scenario was right?

"I'm afraid you just missed him."

"I did?"

"He jumped in a cab for JFK about fifteen minutes ago."

The airport?

"Oh," said Lucy. Why hadn't her dad mentioned he was going on yet another business trip? "You're sure it was Dr. Phelps?"

"'Fraid so. His March Madness picks are terrible," said the man with another laugh, and indicated the sports page. Drawing his brows together, he said, "Your dad didn't know you were coming?"

"No, um, I wanted to surprise him." She shrugged to mask her nerves. "I guess the surprise is on me."

"Shame. Try him on his cell?"

"I will. Thanks." Dejected, Lucy turned on her heel and walked back out onto the street. She stared blankly at the passing traffic.

It wasn't totally out of the ordinary for her dad to drop everything and hop on a plane, but today of all days it galled her. She'd come into the city for nothing. Lucy could call him, of course, but this wasn't a conversation she wanted to have over the phone.

She needed to look her father in the eye.

Someone leaned on a car horn, and Lucy flinched. She clenched her fists.

Maybe her trip didn't have to be for nothing. There was another clue contained in the photo, after all.

Thirty-fourth and Eighth: the New Yorker Hotel. It was only about a mile away.

Lucy glanced at the entrance to the subway on the opposite corner and heard her mother's litany of potential seizure triggers loop at the back of her mind. But she wanted answers, and she wanted them now.

The sun was shining; Lucy would walk. She pulled up a map on her phone and retraced her steps toward Grand Central, kept going past the terminal until she hit Thirty-fourth Street, and then turned west.

She was so busy following her own blue dot on the map that she nearly missed it: the Empire State Building. Lucy sighed.

Gazing up with a goofy grin was a stupid, touristy thing to do, but she couldn't help herself. The midmorning light hit the spire at the top so that it glowed like burnished silver. Another sigh. The romantic in Lucy saw it as a lighthouse, a beacon drawing all the fearless dreamers to the city.

Slam!

Lucy toppled to the sidewalk, bracing herself with her left hand, and sliced her palm on a sliver of glass. The phone in her right hand took the brunt of her weight.

"Hey, watch it, lady!" snarled a preteen on a skateboard sporting a backwards Yankees baseball cap.

Lady? Did Lucy look like a *lady*? She was eighteen, not thirty-five!

"You watch it," Lucy called after him, but the brat was long gone, sailing down Fifth Avenue.

And her cell phone was smashed beyond repair.

Expletive. Expletive. Expletive.

This wasn't Lucy's first cellular mishap. She was plagued by nonexistent battery life and power surges—although they mostly remained in one piece. Her parents would simply take this as further evidence of her helplessness.

Go home, taunted a turncoat voice. *This is no place for you.*

Rage bubbled up in Lucy's chest. She'd already come this far; she wouldn't back down now. Wiping her bloody palm against her jeans, she continued down the long crosstown blocks that led toward the Hudson River.

As she reached Eighth Avenue multiple towers rose before Lucy's eyes, stacked on top of one another like a LEGO set; the architecture looked to be from the same era as her father's office building and the Empire State.

What was so special about the New Yorker Hotel? It couldn't be as simple as her father having an affair, could it?

Only one way to find out.

Lucy crossed the street, barely avoiding a taxi that might as well be racing in the Indy 500, and was sucked into a whirlwind of frazzled tourists checking in and checking out, carts of luggage, and screeching children. She rubbed her temples again and surveyed the lobby. Admiring the gilded ceiling and mammoth crystal chandelier, Lucy got on line for the concierge. She tried not to eavesdrop on the Midwestern couple ahead of her who were arguing about the exorbitant price of theatre tickets.

Where had her dad jetted off to? Lucy wondered. Did her mom know?

"Can I help you?"

An irritated voice cut into her stream of consciousness. "Um, hi," Lucy replied. She hadn't noticed the other couple walk away.

"Hi." The concierge was a woman in her mid-fifties with dyed-blond hair shellacked to within an inch of its life, overly tweezed eyebrows, and a grimace that said she had no time to waste.

Lucy hadn't thought through what she was going to say but "3327," flew out of her mouth before she could stop herself.

The concierge raised a pencil-thin eyebrow.

"The Tesla Suite."

"Tesla? Like the car?" Lucy wrinkled her nose. Was Elon Musk a frequent guest?

The woman gave Lucy a once-over. "Tesla as in Nikola Tesla, the famous inventor who lived in room 3327." Her words dripped with disdain.

"Right." Of course. Lucy had heard of him but . . . "Wait," she blurted, stomach flip-flopping. "His name was *Nikola*?"

"That's what I said," the concierge said flatly, and Lucy willed away the tension traveling from her shoulders to her neck. She'd known the electric cars had been named in his honor but she'd forgotten his first name.

Could the Nikola in the message refer to Tesla rather than Lucy? But that still didn't explain the connection to her father.

"I'd like to see the room, if that's okay," she said.

The concierge twitched her nose as she tapped on her keyboard. "The Tesla Suite is available. How would you like to pay?"

Pay? Lucy had fifty bucks in her wallet and she doubted that would cover it.

"Could I just take a look around? See if I want to book it in the future?" She refused to be intimidated by a woman with alien eyebrows. "My father does a lot of business in the city," she added. Yeah, that sounded plausible.

The concierge canted her head, smiled broadly, and enjoyed saying, "No." Then she looked straight through Lucy to the elderly woman behind her. "How can I help you, ma'am?"

A flush worked its way from Lucy's cheeks down her neck. Unceremoniously dismissed, she retreated toward the elevator bank to consider her options.

ACCESS CARD REQUIRED declared an officious sign.

Fantastic. Lucy needed to get into that room. She needed to understand the link between her dad and a long-dead scientist.

In her peripheral vision, Lucy spotted a bellhop helping a large family with their bags into the elevator and, with a sudden burst of moxie, she darted into the center of them. She was tired of playing everything by the book, always asking permission, never stepping out of her comfort zone.

"Thirty-three, please," she called out as the elevator doors slid shut, hazarding a guess that Room 3327 would be located on the thirty-third floor.

A long moment passed.

With a huff, much to Lucy's relief, the bellhop swiped his card and hit the button.

Her thundering heart slowed.

What was the worst that could happen?

BRAVE NEW WORLD

The elevator dinged to announce Lucy's destination.

Like any good scientist, she accepted that she lived in an uncertain universe, but whatever she discovered in the Tesla Suite might turn hers completely on its head. As Lucy hesitated, the doors started to swish closed.

"Thirty-third floor," said the bellhop with a hint of irritation, shooting out a hand to block the sensor. The doors jolted open again, and a shudder passed through her.

Be brave, Luce.

"Thanks." Her reply was sheepish as she wedged herself through the grouchy, probably jet-lagged family, to the front of the elevator.

The bellhop gave her a perfunctory, "Enjoy your stay," as the doors closed once more, whisking them onward and upward.

Lucy stepped onto a hideous brown carpet. The diamond pattern was enough to make her head spin. She very much doubted she would enjoy her stay.

Steeling herself, she glanced around the corridor. All was quiet except for the humming elevator banks.

Sleuthing wasn't exactly a specialty of Lucy's—nothing worth investigating happened in the town of Eaton—so she would approach the situation like one of her experiments. She had already completed step one by gaining access to the thirty-third floor; step two was getting into the room.

Strawberry suddenly coated her tongue.

This could *not* be happening now. Lucy was *not* having the beginning of a sensory seizure in the middle of a Manhattan hotel hallway.

It had been exactly eighteen months and twenty-one days since she'd smelled or tasted anything that wasn't real. Ever since her neurologist had switched her onto a new medication. Lucy knew the precise date because she kept her own detailed records. She'd started her "Brain Journals" when she was eight (hence the imaginative title) and they allowed her the illusion of control.

Lucy's symptoms had never conformed to any standard type of epilepsy but that didn't stop her from trying to catch something the doctors had missed.

Sweat beaded across her hairline. *You can do this.* It was almost convincing.

Methodically, Lucy put one foot in front of the other. The white walls and cognac-colored carpet made the narrow corridor appear tunnel-like: a journey to the center of the earth. As she propelled herself to the end of the hallway, the taste of strawberries mercifully faded.

The door to Room 3327 was adorned with a brass plaque.

The Tesla Suite.

Embedded into the shiny metal were two black-and-white photographs. A mustachioed man in his thirties stared out of the first, stark angular cheeks leading to lips lifted in a barely discernible smirk. His expression intimated that he was in on some cosmic joke—and you weren't.

In the second photo to the left of the engraved room number, bolts of lightning surged toward an enormous cylindrical coil. The streaks writhed in the air like the tentacles of a humongous sea creature. The sort Captain Nemo would battle.

Here lived Serbian inventor Nikola Tesla from 1933 until his death in 1943, read the inscription on the plaque.

Lucy perused the list of Tesla's achievements embossed in brass. He was the inventor of AC electrical power as well as the generator and motor. Not to mention designing the electrical power plant at Niagara Falls and patenting wireless communication.

What could be the link between Tesla's inventions and her father's company?

The Sapientia Group invested primarily in tech start-ups. It scoured the globe looking for the next Steve Jobs working out of his basement in Kuala Lumpur or Johannesburg. Surely any patents Tesla held were long-since outdated? He had died before the Cold War even started.

And why encrypt an address that was public knowledge? Especially in a photo of Lucy?

She had to get onto the other side of that door.

Lucy jiggled the knob. Another electronic keycard was required. If only she'd brought a Taser with her instead of pepper spray for protection in the Bad Apple, she could fry the circuitry. She slapped her palm against the plaque with a grunt of frustration.

Footsteps. *Crap.* Her entire body tensed. They got closer. Keeping her breathing as calm as possible, Lucy pressed herself into the opposite doorframe and tried to calculate whether the angle would be sufficient to obscure her from view.

Ten seconds. Twenty. Thirty.

A housekeeper pushed a cleaning trolley toward her. In a stroke of luck, the woman wore massive headphones, dancing the way you do when no one's around, while her eyes remained simultaneously glued to the screen of her cell. On autopilot she grabbed a handful of mini-toiletries, parked the cart, swiped a card, and shook her moneymaker right into a bedroom a couple doors down.

Exhale. Lucy's shoulders sagged.

The housekeeper hadn't noticed her, but she did leave the master keycard dangling from the handle of the cart in plain view. The phrase "low-hanging fruit" came to mind.

Was Lucy really considering what she was considering? Breaking and entering would make a Technicolor addition to her college transcript.

Taking a page from Cole's book, Lucy lunged for the cleaning cart, nabbed the keycard, and brushed it against the swipe pad before she could consider the consequences.

A satisfying click filled her ears as the door unlocked. Lucy tossed the card in the direction of the cart. It landed soundlessly on the carpet. Close enough. Hopefully the maid would think it had simply succumbed to gravity.

Eyeballing Tesla, Lucy turned the handle and stepped inside.

Here went nothing.

GILDED CAGES

And nothing was what Lucy found.

Light streamed in through gauzy curtains, slicing the suite in two. The interior was a cornucopia of beige—from the velvet armchair to the drapes to the headboard—that screamed corporate chic, but there was nothing suspicious about that. The immaculate bedroom would delight her mother to no end.

Lucy's heart began to sink.

What had she been expecting to find? Some conspiracy nut's cat's cradle of red string and newspaper clippings webbing the walls?

With a sigh, Lucy crept toward the window. Pulling back the curtain, she pressed her nose against the glass, and wings flapped angrily, rattling it. A pigeon glared at her before flying off.

Judgmental rats with wings.

Down below flowed a river of yellow cabs and Teflon-coated New Yorkers charging purposefully toward their destinations. Even from up here, Lucy could feel the thrum and buzz of the city in her bones. Her eyes drifted along the façade of Madison Square Garden and the Corinthian columns of a stately building that reminded her of a Greek temple, before landing once more on the spire where King Kong made his last stand.

Reluctantly, she turned her back on the cityscape.

There was no mystery here. Yes, it was weird that there was a message hidden in a photo of Lucy on her dad's desk, but the Nikola it referenced clearly wasn't her.

It was Tesla.

Maybe the picture was a test balloon? Some kind of trial for an encryption program that the Sapientia Group had financed? Lucy's father wouldn't invest in anything without a demonstration. When her dad got back from his business trip, she'd just ask him.

Although she'd omit her flirtation with a life of crime.

She looked over her shoulder to catch once last furtive glimpse of the Manhattan skyline. Time to resume her regularly scheduled programming. This entire escapade had effectively distracted Lucy from the fallout of her fight with Cole, but she couldn't avoid the blast radius forever.

As Lucy pushed her way out of the curtains, she spied something in her field of vision that didn't fit with the rest of the business-executive décor.

Sitting on the desk beside the window was a lamp. But not just any lamp. The base was brass, vintage, like something that belonged in the Victorian-themed Cozy Café on Eaton's main street. Resting atop the narrow shaft was no regular Philips lightbulb or shade. Instead a large glass sphere balanced in a precarious-looking manner. Lucy might have mistaken it for a crystal ball if not for the copper coil inside.

Another plaque, similar to the one on the door, was affixed to the base.

This prototype for his Incandescent Electric Light belonged to Nikola Tesla himself. He invented the plasma lamp after experimenting with the reaction between high-frequency currents and noble gases.

Lucy understood the basic concept of the plasma lamp. She'd seen something similar in the Natural History Museum once. She bit her lip, excited, the way she did when she was in the final stages of conducting an experiment.

Plasma was created by pumping a gas full of energy, and it was one of the four fundamental states of matter, making up most of the universe, the stars, and the sun. If Lucy placed a conducting object—like her hand—near the globe, light tendrils would extend toward her as she attracted the current from the inner electrode. In this case, the copper coil. It was like a mini version of the photo showing Tesla surrounded by lightning.

The idea that matter, like plasma, could be transformed was comforting to Lucy. It meant she could be transformed too.

Could the Sapientia Group be interested in Tesla's lamp? Maybe as part of a new green technology? Her dad believed alternative forms of energy were the wave of the future.

Lucy waggled her fingers, fighting an odd compulsion to touch the glass orb. The prototype didn't have a power cord, and it needed electrical current to work, but she wanted to touch the globe anyway. She'd never been so close to a tangible piece of scientific history without a display case.

Feeling like a kid about to blow out her birthday candles, Lucy placed her palm flat on the lamp.

As expected, nothing happened.

"Crap." When she removed her hand, Lucy saw a smear of blood across the glass. The cut must have been deeper than she'd thought.

She was about to wipe it away when something *did* happen.

Blue-white snakes of light connected with Lucy's smeared blood.

Which was impossible.

The lamp needed a power source. The copper coil could only supply a current if it was plugged into the mains.

Her knees began to quake. She'd never experienced a full-on visual hallucination before a seizure. *Why now?* If her parents found out, she could kiss college goodbye.

Lucy jammed her eyes shut. *You're okay, Luce.* When she opened her eyes again, the light would be gone.

Pulse skyrocketing, she opened one eye, then the other.

The tendrils of blue-white light continued to dance.

Her brain was not her friend.

Lucy dropped to a squat and checked for an outlet or a transformer or anything that would explain the reaction of the Tesla lamp. Anything besides her nervous system choosing the worst possible moment to go completely haywire.

Don't panic. You're a scientist. You can figure this out.

Could she? The simplest explanation would be that she was about to have the mother of all seizures.

She needed to get out of here. She needed to call for help—even if it meant being arrested. Lucy leapt up at a sudden cracking sound and bashed her forehead against the desk. *Ouch.*

She blinked, mouth falling open.

No way. A small recess had appeared in the interior wall beside the doorway, running from floor to ceiling. Was New York due for an earthquake Lucy hadn't been aware of? If that was a structural wall, the whole building might be on the brink of collapse. Her eyes did a quick sweep of the room. Nothing else was out of place. On closer inspection, Lucy realized the line of the recess was perfectly straight.

In fact, it was a door.

Curiosity beat out fear and she stepped closer.

Lucy swung her gaze back to the Tesla lamp. It was dark. No thin fingers of light. Dormant.

Pressure began to build at the front of her skull. Had she just hallucinated? But the door was real. Right?

Put your hypothesis to the test.

Objective. Rational. Calculating. Those were the attributes Lucy needed now.

Tentatively, with two fingers, she pushed against the opening. It deepened. *Down the rabbit hole or bust.*

Darkness enveloped Lucy as she crossed the threshold. There was no longer carpeting beneath her feet, just concrete. She could feel the hair on her arms begin to rise. A faint buzz filled her ears like television static.

The noise increased with each step she took. Overhead lights flickered. Lucy's seizures had never been provoked by strobing, and she crossed her fingers it wouldn't start now. The flickering ceased and she saw a few bare bulbs hanging from the ceiling.

They must have been motion activated. Nothing exceptional *about*—

Lucy's train of thought stopped short as she studied her new surroundings. She was standing inside a time capsule. A thick layer of dust covered everything: an antique wooden swivel chair. An old-timey radio—the kind from World War II movies. The equally vintage-looking worktable covered with metal coils, pliers, and other spare parts. In the center of the table was a large glass dome. The bottom had been carved from wood and wrapped with yet more copper wire.

All of this stuff looked like it had been around long before motion sensors were invented. And the room looked like it hadn't seen the light of day since.

This was way more than Lucy had bargained for when she boarded the train this morning.

Could her dad know about the hidden room? Was *this* the real reason the address had been encrypted in the photograph? Lucy refused to believe that she of all people might actually have uncovered Tesla's private laboratory. But if her dad were aware of its existence, it didn't seem like he—or anyone else—had been inside for decades.

She should leave. Really. She should leave right now. The pressure behind her eyes and the annoying gnat-like noise in her ears became amplified every second she remained. And yet some part of her was urging her to stay.

A weakening self-preservation instinct forced her eyes to seek out the exit.

Oh frak. All at once Lucy realized she wasn't standing inside a room. She was standing inside a cage.

Copper mesh lined the walls and ceiling. Maybe Lucy hadn't been so far off about finding a conspiracy-theory nut. The mesh would prevent any electrical signals from getting in or out, making it the ultimate defense against hackers.

A member of Lucy's computer forum—Snowden4Ever—had been building a cage like this because he thought the NSA was spying on him. It was known as a Faraday cage after the Englishman who pioneered the field of electromagnetism. Hackers were a digital problem, however, and the tech in this room was analog.

What had Tesla been trying to protect?

The buzzing in Lucy's cranium intensified until her teeth chattered. Her black curls floated up from her shoulders, haloing her face like a model in a music video, but not in a good way. More like Medusa.

She did the opposite of what logic dictated.

Gripped by curiosity and something more—more than fascination, more like something she had lost that was desperate to be found—Lucy zigzagged her forefinger down the dome, drawing a lightning bolt in the dust. Sparks zipped from her fingertip up her arm. These sparks were different from her typical pre-seizure prickles.

They made Lucy feel alive. Invincible.

A strange kind of peace settled over her as she lifted up the glass to reveal a copper egg. *An egg?* Lucy frowned. This had to be the most messed-up Easter-egg hunt ever.

Lucy found it increasingly difficult to think straight. Sparks transformed into tingles throughout her body. The floor rocked beneath her. She reached toward the egg, unable to stop herself, and it began to spin. Faster and faster, until it was totally upright.

Somewhere in the back of her mind it occurred to Lucy that the egg shouldn't be able to spin without an active electromagnetic field. And an electromagnetic field couldn't be created without a power supply.

Her body relaxed in a way Lucy had never known. She was floating. Hovering outside herself. Which might be why Lucy wasn't terrified when she saw the egg rise off the platform, levitating to eye level.

Faster, faster. She wanted to hold it in her hand.

The instant she made contact, a green flame engulfed Lucy's hand, spreading to her elbow, then her shoulder.

There was no pain. She watched herself burning but she felt nothing. Release: Years of constant worry and agony burning off her. Evaporating like mist.

She smiled as the emerald fire coated her cheeks.

Bringing the egg toward her heart, Lucy's entire body convulsed as if she'd been struck by lightning. Sparks flew behind her eyes. She *became* the lightning.

Darkness fell.

OMG

"*Bozhe moy.*"

Lucy's eyes flipped open, a stranger's face looming above her. It took a moment for Lucy to focus. Why did she look so familiar? Oh, she'd stolen her key card. Techno blasted from the headphones around the maid's neck. Not what Lucy needed. Her head pounded like she'd been on a bender.

"*Bozhe moy,*" the maid repeated. Was that Russian?

Lucy sat up like a shot as panic hit. She was on the floor. She was on the floor of the New Yorker Hotel.

Holy crap. Her days as a free woman were over. Charges of destruction of private property would be added to burglary. Not that she'd stolen anything. She twisted her torso in the direction of Tesla's secret lab. How would she explain that to the NYPD?

Lucy gasped. The door was gone. As if it had never been there. *Had* it?

She panned her gaze across the walls—the seamless beige wallpaper—and anxiety rose in her chest like a tsunami.

A gentle hand grazed her brow; Lucy rocked backward.

"You . . . okay?" the maid asked, face pinched with concern, crow's feet gathering around her shock-filled eyes. "I thought you . . . dead. *Bozhe moy.*"

Lucy forced an inappropriately cheery smile. "Not dead," she said.

Although her parents would kill her if they ever learned what she'd been up to.

Pulling back her hand, the other woman's attitude grew more leery. "Fever?"

Lucy sensed the relief the maid felt at the strange girl on the bedroom floor still having a pulse was dissipating and rapidly being replaced with well-founded suspicion. She needed to come up with a credible story to keep the woman from calling hotel security. Fast. Unfortunately, two heavyweight champions had just gone ten rounds inside her skull.

"No fever," Lucy replied.

She hated to do this, it went against every fiber of her being, but she raised her left arm slowly. A silver bracelet dangled from her wrist. From a distance it looked like a regular charm bracelet: a tiny Eiffel Tower, a shooting star, a four-leaf clover. On the center charm, however, there was no mistaking the bright-red lettering.

MEDIC ALERT. EPILEPSY.

Claudia added the charms as a surprise right before Lucy started at Eaton High. Wearing the bracelet had been one of her parents' conditions for letting her attend. Her bestie understood better than anyone Lucy's need not to be defined by the label that already determined too much of her life. Claudia had done such a clever job at camouflaging it that most of the time Lucy could forget it was anything but a charm bracelet.

She had promised herself she would never use her condition as a get-out-of-jail-free card. But that was precisely what she was doing now.

The familiar combination of pity and a trace of fear flitted through the other woman's eyes.

"I'm sorry," Lucy said, talking a mile a minute. "The concierge let me in. I must have had a seizure." She rubbed her temples for emphasis. "I'm so embarrassed." When had lying become so easy for Lucy?

Before the maid could answer, she continued, "Could I borrow your phone, please?" Lucy pointed at the phone peeking out from her apron pocket. "I need to call someone to meet me."

"*Da*." She handed over the phone as gingerly as if Lucy were an un-exploded bomb.

To be fair, her hands were trembling. She inhaled a deep breath and dialed.

It seemed like forever before anyone answered. Lucy's eyes strayed toward the window. The sun was much lower in the sky.

"Hello?" came a skeptical voice on the other end of the line. Warmth spread through Lucy at the sound. Claudia always made her feel like things would be all right.

"Clauds, it's me. Lucy."

"Luce? Why are you calling me from this number?"

"Broke my phone."

"Again?" Claudia laughed. "Where are you?" she asked.

"Still in the city. I'm gonna catch the next train. Could you get me at the station?"

There was a pause. Claudia could read Lucy too well. If she was calling for chauffeur service it meant something was wrong. Lucy was fiercely stubborn about riding her bike everywhere.

"Are you okay, Luce?"

No. Not at all. "Just a little lightheaded."

Lucy could picture Claudia's head bob. She never judged Lucy or made her feel limited, which was why Claudia was the only person she opened up to about her condition.

"Okay," replied her friend. "The Mystery Minivan will be waiting. With bells on."

Only Claudia could make Lucy smile at a time like this. Claudia had a thing for *Scooby-Doo*. She had also inherited the minivan from her three older brothers, so the mystery was how it could still be in one piece.

"Love you, Clauds." Lucy tried to keep her tone breezy as she hung up. Glancing at the maid, whose expression was still panicked, she said, "Thank you," and the phone slipped from her sweaty fingers.

"Welcome," the woman mumbled, brow furrowed.

Lucy scrambled to her feet. She needed to skedaddle before the woman changed her mind and decided to alert the authorities.

Her hand was on the doorknob when she heard, "Wait—"

Lucy froze. She pictured the disappointment on her mother's face as she received a call from the police.

"Your bag?"

The maid held out a beat-up messenger bag branded with an OMg (oxygen, magnesium) bumper sticker. Like everything else, it had totally slipped Lucy's mind. She wouldn't get far without her wallet.

Cheeks sizzling, Lucy thanked the woman again, shouldered her bag, and hightailed it out of there.

After making her way downstairs, she stepped out onto the chaotic city street and rubbed her bracelet, unable to suppress a smile. Lucy's shoulders curled forward as she exhaled.

She'd made a clean getaway.

GREASED LIGHTNIN'

The high from Lucy's great escape didn't last. As the Metro-North chugged along, the skyscrapers becoming pinpricks against the rose-colored horizon, a sick feeling settled over her. She laid her head back on the pleather seat and tried to sort through what the *frak* had just happened.

Lucy divided the events into what she knew to be true and what she hoped wasn't.

True: She had successfully broken into the Tesla Suite at the New Yorker Hotel.

Possibly true: There was some kind of link between her father's company and Tesla's inventions.

All her life, Lucy's dad had taught her the history of science, regaled her with tales of the first great thinkers. Thales of Miletu, who'd accurately predicted a solar eclipse in 585 BCE. Copernicus, who challenged an Earth-centered model of the universe. Aside from Claudia, these were Lucy's heroes. She had clung to dates and facts for safety when she couldn't even trust her own body not to betray her.

So why had her father always treated Tesla like a footnote?

Hopefully not true: Lucy's brain had just misfired at Mount Vesuvius levels. There was no way she could tell her parents what happened or the light at the end of the tunnel—college—would wink out of existence. They'd never let her leave home and she really *would* become a cat lady.

Couldn't possibly be true: Lucy's blood had activated a plasma lamp designed by Tesla to open a door to a secret laboratory, which was further shielded by a Faraday cage because Tesla wanted to protect its contents from prying eyes. Chiefly, perhaps, the bronze egg that spun of its own accord due to an unspecified electromagnetic field.

Hopefully not true: When Lucy touched the egg it triggered a seizure—possibly a stroke—and Lucy passed out.

True: Lucy couldn't remember anything between touching the egg and waking up on the hotel-room floor.

True: The room looked spotless and no one would ever believe there was a laboratory hidden within the walls of the New Yorker Hotel.

Really couldn't possibly be true: Both the Tesla lamp and the Tesla Egg needed a power source to activate but neither had one. Both remained inert until Lucy made contact.

If there was no other power source . . . then *Lucy* was the power source . . .

She bolted from her seat, ducked into the toilet at the back of the carriage, and promptly tossed her cookies. Actually, not cookies. Breakfast had been a cappuccino and half a bagel. No lunch. Mostly, she dry-heaved. Lucy slumped against the grimy wall, quivering, and slid down to the even filthier floor. She tucked her knees into her chest and let the train rock her in the fetal position.

Lucy's logic had morphed from the improbable to the truly ridiculous. A human body couldn't generate electrical power like that. It used electrical signals in the nerves and the brain. These *conducted* electricity but were fragile. Too much or too little, and the nervous system went on the fritz: heart attacks, seizures, strokes. Lucy knew that all too well. The mere suggestion was ludicrous. What she was considering would short-circuit her heart, and barbecue her brain—whatever was left of it anyway.

She snorted. Lucy was inventing a fantasy because she didn't want to admit to herself that the new medication might have stopped working. That this could be the harbinger of things to come.

Don't catastrophize, she scolded herself, edging her way upright. This could have been a one-off. It *could*.

A meager trickle dribbled from the faucet as Lucy turned the tap. She cupped her hands and brushed the cold water across her face.

Lucy's reflection in the vaguely warped mirror stared back at her in accusation. Her hair looked like she'd walked through a wind tunnel and then been tumbled-dried for good measure. Her skin was zombie white and her red-rimmed irises were more lead than silver.

What was she going to tell Claudia?

Shakily, she shut off the tap. *Pull it together.* Giving herself a final look in the mirror, Lucy raised her chin and returned to her seat just as the conductor announced Eaton was the next stop.

She would put this whole "Lucy Takes Manhattan" misadventure out of her mind. She would forget she'd ever deciphered the message. *Liber Librum Aperit*: It was probably nothing more than an in-joke between her dad and his colleagues anyway. They were all still nerds, even if they wore expensive suits. Lucy would close this particular book.

If the security guard at her dad's office building ever mentioned Lucy's visit, she would be in enough trouble with her parents as it was.

Digging around her bag for a comb or tissues or maybe Tic Tacs, her hand closed around cold, smooth metal. Heat raced up her arm and she dropped the egg into the abyss of her book bag with a shock.

It was real.

The Tesla Egg was real, not just a product of Lucy's fevered imagination. The Tesla Egg was real and she had stolen it.

At least it wasn't levitating in the middle of a commuter train.

"Eaton Station!" the loudspeaker blared.

A scream battled its way up her throat, but Lucy wouldn't let it out. She didn't know if it was a scream of joy or terror. While the Tesla Egg was proof that she hadn't hallucinated the entire afternoon, it was also proof that something far stranger than a seizure was going on.

But proof of what exactly?

Could her dad truly have known about Tesla's secret laboratory? Lucy didn't see a way to ask him about the Sapientia Group's connection to the scientist without revealing what had happened to her. And she didn't know for a fact that it was anything in Tesla's lab that had triggered Lucy's response. It could be coincidental, not causal. *Why was this happening?* She already lived her life under her parents' high-intensity microscope; she didn't want to make it worse for herself.

Breathe, Luce.

Lucy spotted the Mystery Minivan already idling in the parking lot beside the train tracks and made a beeline from the platform. She also couldn't miss Claudia's Orphan Annie–red hair or supernova of freckles if she tried.

Claudia didn't give Lucy a chance to buckle her seat belt before crushing her into a bear hug. Well, given her friend's size, it was more like a teddy-bear hug.

As Lucy squeezed her back, energy crackled between them, and they broke apart.

Claudia giggled. "It's *electrifying*!" she said, waving jazz hands.

Lucy wheezed a breathy laugh. *Grease* had been this year's musical. "Totally shocking," Lucy agreed.

Static. Completely run-of-the-mill static electricity. That was it. The separation of positive and negative charges. Electrons moving from Lucy's Eaton High sweatshirt to Claudia's hot pink sequined cardigan. Nothing more. Absolutely explainable by the laws of physics.

Absolutely.

With a crooked grin, and a glint in her hazel eyes, Claudia nudged her lightly. *Zap.* Lucy's chest spasmed as if she'd been shot in the heart.

"Wow," her friend teased. "You really are "Greased Lightnin'," Luce. Must be a storm coming."

Invisible fingers tightened around her neck. Lucy had never put much stock in gut feelings—the same way she didn't believe in Bigfoot or Ouija boards—but she couldn't shake the feeling that a storm *was* coming.

And the storm was her.

POKER FACE

No actual storm hit that weekend, but every time Lucy closed her eyes, lightning flashed.

When she'd gotten home on Saturday night, her mom had no reason to suspect Lucy hadn't been with Claudia all day long, and Lucy pretended to be surprised to learn that her dad had caught a last-minute flight to Tokyo. Even so, she avoided her mom on Sunday, convinced she would be able to discern something was wrong with her only child.

Thankfully the security guard didn't seem to have Lucy's mom on speed dial.

Now Monday morning had dawned too soon. She'd slept fitfully last night and remained utterly exhausted. Groggy, Lucy stretched her back like Schrödinger (who hadn't scratched on her door for his requisite petting) only to discover a golden nimbus glowing around her hands.

Sunlight. It was only sunlight.

Lucy hadn't become a human torch quite yet.

"Don't be pathetic," she muttered.

Lucy browsed indecisively through the limited wardrobe choices in her closet. Lacking Claudia's natural flair, Lucy stuck to safe, classic options: sweater twinsets, jeans, ballet flats. She designated her various fandom T-shirts—*Battlestar Galactica* and *Blade Runner*—strictly for sleepwear.

The only rebellion to her preppy uniform was her nail polish. She liked a little bit of glitter. Teaching herself to paint her nails was a not insubstantial triumph. It required a steady hand. Whenever Lucy gave herself a manicure it was incontrovertible evidence that she could control her condition instead of letting it control her.

Picking absently at chipped purple sparkles, Lucy settled on a jean skirt and a mauve scoop-neck shirt that was lower cut than what she ordinarily wore. It would be a lie to say she didn't want to make Cole see what he'd been missing all weekend. She side-eyed the varsity track windbreaker hanging on the back of the closet door but opted to leave it there, selecting a corduroy jacket instead.

The world clock on her night table told Lucy it was 12:45 P.M. in London and 9:45 P.M. in Sydney, which meant it was 7:45 P.M. in the great state of Connecticut. She liked imagining what people were doing in other time zones and promised herself one day she'd live farther than two hours' drive from her parents' house. That wasn't her immediate problem, however. She was going to be late for first period.

Lucy had never been late to class. Ever.

Slinging her book bag on one shoulder, she flew down the stairs, nearly drop-kicking Schrödinger. The fur ball hissed at her for all he was worth and scurried in the opposite direction. Strange. Schrödinger never hissed at her.

As she rushed past the kitchen, Lucy's mom called out, "If it isn't Rip Van Winkle! Breakfast?"

Her mom was seated on a stool, spine totally erect, sipping her tea from a china cup. A portrait of refinement. It was easy to see why Professor Elaine Phelps made freshmen quake in their boots.

"Can't," Lucy said. "Late." But man, did she crave caffeine.

Eagle eyes scrutinized her.

"Do you feel all right? You slept most of yesterday."

"Being a teenager isn't a medical condition, Mom."

A wounded look crossed her mother's face and her cheeks hollowed in a resigned sigh.

"If you say so."

Lucy immediately regretted snapping at her mom when she was already lying to her. "Sorry. Just late," she said more quietly, then dashed down the hallway and ran out onto the front lawn.

Hurrying to unlock Marie Curie (whom Claudia had rescued) from where she rested against the garage door, Lucy was too preoccupied to notice Cole's Jeep parked beside the curb.

A hand dropped onto Lucy's shoulder, sending a jolt straight through her. She lost her footing and tipped backward, landing on her butt. *Graceful.* At least the grass provided a cushion.

"Lemme help you up," said Cole, his shadow falling over her.

Lucy nearly resisted but, to her irritation, she *did* need help.

Her wrist was stuck to the bike lock. Or, more specifically, her silver Medic Alert bracelet. Just as if it'd been magnetized.

"Thanks," she murmured, and Cole pulled her upright. *Ow.* It felt like Lucy's shoulder was being ripped from its socket as her wrist detached from the lock.

She darted a glance at her book bag, which had also dropped onto the lawn.

Could the Tesla Egg have magnetized her bracelet?

Lucy probably should have hidden the egg somewhere in her room, but she was afraid her mom would find it and ask her questions she couldn't answer. Lucy wasn't sure herself what—if anything—she was going to do about the discovery she'd made at the New Yorker Hotel.

"Luce?" said Cole. She'd almost forgotten he was there. Their gazes met as he tugged her toward him.

Lucy took a step back. Much as she might want to fall into her boyfriend's arms, he hadn't apologized yet.

"You can't ghost me in person, Luce." Cole shoved his hands in his pockets.

"Ghost you?"

He made a *come on* face. "I've been texting you all weekend." He blew out a hard breath, mussing his bangs.

Oh. "My phone broke," she explained, a tad guiltily. Maybe she should have let him know.

"Really?"

"Really." She didn't want to go into the details.

After a beat Cole nodded, accepting her excuse, and a small, relieved smile formed on his lips.

"My absentminded professor," he said.

Lucy squared her shoulders, dodging his attempt to steal a kiss. "Just because I wasn't ghosting you doesn't mean I'm not still mad."

His smile died, brow creasing, and he hung his head.

"I mean, you could have come over if you couldn't reach me online," she said.

"Luce, what do you think I'm doing now?"

Touché. She shifted her weight.

"You not talking to me has been tearing me up," Cole continued, a raw quality to his voice. "I know I was a dumbass. I just wanted us to have an amazing prom. A night we won't forget when we're off at college."

"We don't need money for that, Cole."

"I know, and I'm sorry. I didn't think it through. Please, Luce. Tell me how to make this better."

His pleading look pierced her heart. It wasn't made of stone, after all.

"Okay," Lucy acquiesced. She didn't have the energy to stay angry. She wanted to rewind her life back to Friday night, before Schrödinger had knocked that stupid picture off her father's desk.

"Okay?" repeated Cole.

"I'll forgive you on two conditions."

One corner of his mouth lifted, brightening his face. "And those are?"

"First, you can't keep the money. You need to give it to charity or something. And second, you need to study for finals on your own."

His features crumpled. "The second I can do. But I told you I already spent the money—I paid for a room at the White Hart Inn in Dorset. Clauds agreed to cover for us."

It was Lucy's turn to sigh. He'd remembered. She loved that place.

Her parents stayed there for their anniversary. Lucy didn't normally get too excited about interior design, but each room had a fireplace and a wrought-iron canopy bed and it was all very romantic. Although if Claudia knew what Cole had done to pay for the room, she wouldn't be down with it. At all. Lucy hated making her an accomplice.

"What about the money Megan gave you on Friday?" she countered.

He showed her a sly grin, reached into the back pocket of his jeans, and withdrew a mesh bag containing poker chips. Sunlight caught on the foil. Chocolate poker chips.

Cole had been playing poker the first time they had a real conversation. More comfortable on the sidelines of any kind of socializing, Lucy had drifted to the edges of a party thrown by one of Claudia's many friends and her interest became piqued by the poker game Cole was playing with some of the other jocks. To be completely honest, her interest had already been piqued by Cole but she'd concluded he was someone she'd only ever know from a distance. That one time she was glad to be wrong.

Poker was a game Lucy understood. Mostly it had to do with probability and Lucy could calculate odds in her sleep. As she tracked the rounds of betting, it became clear Cole was bluffing. He had a losing hand. She'd thought she was being discreet in her observation, but Cole's head snapped up when she laughed under her breath.

Smiling wide, he'd challenged, "Hey, Opposites Attract Girl, think you can do better?"

Lucy had amazed herself by saying, "I do."

And she did. She cleaned out half the football team. They called her a ringer and wouldn't play with her again. Didn't matter, though. Lucy had won her first date with Cole along with all their money.

He watched the memory of that night pass through her eyes.

"I love that you still call my bluff, Luce."

That did it. Lucy snatched the bag of candy and planted her lips on his. He tasted like Aquafresh and Cheerios and him. A normal high school boyfriend. This was what Lucy wanted—to be back on solid ground.

A ground with totally normal polarities.

As Cole deepened the kiss, however, encircling her with his arms, a peculiar feeling flooded Lucy. She swayed on her feet, nearly as nauseated as she'd been on the train back from the city. She clung more firmly to Cole's neck, telling herself that she was imagining it and that she definitely wasn't about to have another seizure. And yet her pulse continued to climb.

Lucy panted short breaths against Cole's mouth between kisses, not caring for once that the whole neighborhood had a front-row seat to their PDA. Desperation tightened her skin as she fought the queasy feeling overtaking her senses.

It wasn't possible to become allergic to kissing, was it?

The sparks throbbing in her lips suggested maybe it was.

"Wow. You're supercharged," Cole teased, rubbing his mouth. *Yikes.*

First Claudia, now Cole. Lucy pushed him away before something worse could happen.

"So I'm forgiven?" he said. Uncertainty lingered in his voice.

"You must have bought an awful lot of chocolate with Megan's money."

"Luce, I'll buy you *all* the chocolate." Beaming, Cole snatched Lucy's book bag from the grass, shouldered it, and slid his other arm around her waist. "And I'll drive you to school. Deal?"

"Deal." That seemed like a good idea. Lucy didn't trust herself on Marie Curie right now. Then she remembered how late she was.

"Crap! We're gonna miss roll call."

Her boyfriend laughed. "I know. Look at you. Lucinda Phelps, walking on the wild side. PDA and late for class on the same day."

"You're a bad influence."

He steered her toward his Jeep, still laughing. As he opened the door for Lucy, he took advantage of their proximity to wend his finger along her collarbone.

"I missed you." His breath tickled Lucy's ear. "So much."

When she returned the sentiment with a kiss she felt sick to her stomach again.

Lucy slipped into the shotgun seat, pressing a hand against her middle. Cole didn't seem to notice her discomfort. He smiled at her as if all was right in the world, and she forced a matching smile right back.

Lucy's decision had been made for her. Ignoring what had happened in Tesla's lab was no longer an option. She needed to get to the bottom of this. She wasn't about to let her kissing privileges be revoked.

Lucy would fix this. She had to.

And she'd better do it fast.

AC/DC

White noise. Lucy basked in it. The library was almost as much of a sanctuary as the laboratory. A good researcher never relied on speculation; she needed evidence. Which was why Lucy had come here as soon as she'd apologized—for the twentieth time—to her first-period history teacher for being late.

She needed answers. Facts.

Although her gag reflex had calmed down on the ride to school, she seemed to have developed a new symptom.

Cole let Lucy choose the radio station—he liked '90s grunge, she was more Ella Fitzgerald—but when she touched the dial, the radio went berserk, blasting static. As if Lucy or the Tesla Egg—or both—were interfering with the radio.

Except that didn't make sense. It would take a big electromagnetic field to disrupt a radio, and human beings couldn't produce anything on that scale.

The welcome window for the library's electronic-resources search engine flashed up on her computer screen.

Nikola Tesla, she typed.

Lucy could have Googled Tesla at home, but she knew better than to trust everything she found online. In her downtime, she often edited inaccuracies on *Wikipedia*. Plus, she didn't want to leave a digital footprint. And yes, she knew that was paranoid. Not that, to her knowledge, her parents went through her browser history. Still, she'd rather be safe than sorry.

5 matches.

Lucy tapped a finger against the mouse, perusing the list. One title jumped out at her.

AC/DC: The Current Wars.

During her homeschooling, she'd learned that Thomas Edison invented DC—direct current—but that alternating current was gradually introduced because it was safer. Lucy's father had never mentioned that Tesla was the one to invent AC, however, or that there had been a war. AC power was superior to DC because it could safely travel long distances, and it powered every home in America.

If Tesla had won the war over electrical current, Lucy wondered, why wasn't he as much of a household name as the inventor of the lightbulb?

She scribbled down the call number for the book and bounded toward the stacks. When presented with the impossibly improbable, Lucy was determined to approach the problem the way her father had trained her. She would research and experiment, and discover a way to undo whatever had happened to her in the Tesla Suite so she could stop lying to her best friend and go back to kissing her boyfriend.

Once she found the tome she was looking for, Lucy ensconced herself in an especially secluded corner of the library.

Time lost all meaning as she devoured the life of Nikola Tesla.

Before she could blink, the bell rang for next period. Feeling unsteady on her feet—which was getting old fast—Lucy closed the book and gathered her things, walking at a snail's pace toward the checkout desk. She'd left the Tesla Egg in her locker for safekeeping, so Lucy knew this tilt-a-whirl feeling was all her.

Disturbing fact number one: Tesla was born on the stroke of midnight during an electrical storm.

So was Lucy.

Born on two days, Lucy's younger self used to demand two birthday cakes: one chocolate, the other red velvet. Never mind that she didn't have enough guests at her birthday parties to finish one. It was a rare indulgent act on the part of her otherwise pragmatic parents.

Disturbing fact number two: Tesla was plagued by ill health and visions—flashes of light behind his eyes throughout his entire life. He believed these symptoms were prophetic, but they sounded like seizures to Lucy.

On their own, neither fact was more than a random, bizarre parallel to Lucy's life.

But then there was disturbing fact number three.

The Westinghouse Electric & Manufacturing Company had paid the rent on Tesla's New Yorker room from 1934 until his death. The same company that funded her father's Ph.D. research and had just built a state-of-the-art physics lab at Gilbert College.

That seemed a little too coincidental.

Could her father's doctoral work have been connected to Tesla's experiments somehow? Would he know how to reverse whatever had happened to her? Asking for his help, of course, would require Lucy to *admit* what had happened. And that would very likely end her college career before it had begun.

Not wanting to be late for another class, Lucy cleared her throat impatiently when she discovered the librarian's desk empty.

"Wait a sec—" came a muffled voice before a blond head popped up from behind the desk.

"Oh. Hi, Lucy." Megan Harper said her name like she'd just swallowed a bug.

The other girl was gorgeous: long, perfectly tousled hair and legs that went on for days, making her the star hurdler of the track team. Thinking of Megan in her uniform sidling next to Cole at practice, it had never frustrated Lucy more that she couldn't play on a team because of her condition. The fact that he'd sold Lucy's test answers to Megan of all people only made it worse.

"I need to check this out," she said, handing over the book.

The other girl wriggled her nose as she glanced at the title with the natural disdain of those who'd always belonged to the in-crowd.

"Extra-credit project?"

"No." Lucy shrugged, cheeks heating. "Just fun."

"We all have to make our own, I suppose." Megan brandished a sugary-bitchy smile. "Student ID."

Begrudgingly, Lucy forked over the laminated nightmare. Why hadn't she let Claudia style her hair for the photo like she'd offered? Megan barely stifled a snicker at Lucy's unruly black curls. Lucy had invested in a straightening iron soon after the photo was snapped. Not soon enough, as it turned out.

The computer beeped twice as Megan scanned in the barcode of her ID and then the book. "Speaking of fun," she purred at Lucy, slanting forward like they were co-conspirators. "We missed you at the swim party. I kept Cole entertained, though."

Blood roared in Lucy's ears. *Don't rise to the bait.*

"I bet," she replied shortly. It didn't matter if nobody else at school understood why Lucy and Cole were together.

Megan raised her eyebrows. "I'm glad you don't mind sharing . . . your homework, I mean."

Lucy leaned across the desk, panic surging in a cold sweat across her back. "*Shh!* Keep your voice down."

"I thought that was *my* line." Nonchalantly, Megan tapped the sign on the desk that read: LIBRARIAN, and slid the scanned book toward Lucy.

"The cheating was a one-time thing." Lucy's voice was tight.

Megan's lips parted in a supermodel pout. "Is that what Cole told you?"

"I mean it," Lucy ground out. "He could get expelled. So could you."

The other girl flipped her hair, unperturbed. "And you."

Mutually assured destruction. How could Cole have jeopardized his scholarship and Lucy's college plans?

In an oh-so-innocent voice, Megan said, "I'd never rat Cole out." The implication wasn't exactly subtle.

"Glad we're clear." Lucy clutched the book to her chest as if it could provide a protective force field.

"Of course. Cole's an amazing guy. I mean, he's even willing to over-look your . . ." She glanced pointedly at Lucy's charm bracelet.

Sucker punch. Cole was one of the only people at Eaton High be-sides Claudia who didn't see Lucy as Helmet Head. Lucy would always be supremely grateful he'd moved to town after that phase in her life. Megan, however, had been one of the kids cheering on Tony Morelli.

"Hold on to him—if you can. Not everyone is so open-minded."

Tears pricked at Lucy's eyes and then something strange happened. The tears evaporated, replaced with rage. Pure, hot rage. It swam from Lucy's heart through her veins. Her body sang with it. Time became too fast and too slow at once. From the corner of her eye, she spied the stapler on the far side of the desk rise from the tabletop and fly toward them.

Not them.

Megan.

Megan's head to be precise.

"Watch out!" Lucy yelled. She plunged forward, pushing Megan out of the stapler's trajectory. *Thwack*. It crashed against Lucy's temple and clattered to the floor.

Megan shrieked. "What the hell?"

"*I*—" Lucy had no words. Only fear. Fear because the rage, and the power that came with it, had felt so good. Electric. And hers.

The other girl's expression changed from fury to apprehension.

"Shit. You're bleeding."

It was true. A cold, wet trickle dripped down her cheek. Lucy hadn't even noticed.

"*I*—" she tried again, but broke off. Lucy needed to get away.

"Freak," she heard Megan mutter as she ran from the library.

This time Lucy didn't have a comeback.

QUIS CUSTODIET IPSOS CUSTODES?

Lucy couldn't decide if the cherry on top of her craptastic morning was watching a twelve-year-old merrily pick his nose or the Wonder Woman Band-Aid adorning her eyebrow. Both were the result of the junior high field day taking place on the football field. The nurse's office had been littered with skinned knees and was fresh out of flesh-toned bandages. Lucy had opted for Wonder Woman over the Flash but, either way, she was sure the universe was mocking her.

Nurse Díaz had given Lucy the third degree while patching her up. A millimeter deeper and the cut would have required stitches. The prospect made Lucy go stiff. Stitches would definitely send her parents' Lucy Watch to DEFCON 1. The nurse had barely been convinced by Lucy's "I lost a fight with my locker" excuse.

For the first time in Lucy's life she'd wished what happened in the library *were* an ordinary seizure. She highly doubted Nurse Díaz would believe her if she told the truth: "I made a stapler fly at a would-be boyfriend stealer with the power of my mind." Lucy had no idea what Megan thought had happened either. She would waste no time embellishing the incident for the known world—but what would she say?

Lucy's heels clicked on the linoleum as she hurried to the physics lab. The sound reverberated in the empty hallway, further straining her nerves.

There was no rational explanation for the flying stapler. The non-rational explanation was that it had been attracted to her. Not the Tesla Egg—which remained safely stowed in her locker—but Lucy herself. As if her emotions had given the metal a charge. Maybe the same thing had happened when Cole had surprised her? The shot of adrenaline could have attracted the bike lock to her bracelet.

Which was all well and good, except that inanimate objects couldn't read emotions and emotions weren't electric or magnetic.

Lucy scowled and scratched at the Band-Aid. The one person she wanted to discuss all of this with was the one person she couldn't: her dad.

Putting aside logic, if Lucy somehow generated electrical currents and fields, then might it not also stand to reason that they would become more intense when her body's temperature and heart rate increased? And those things *did* occur when emotions were heightened. It was the same story for seizures.

Given that everything Lucy had seen and experienced since Friday would earn her a one-way trip to a place devoid of sharp objects, she had nothing to lose by testing her outlandish theory.

Glancing at her watch, she picked up the pace. Physics class was her haven. Lucy needed it more than ever now that her world had been turned inside out.

Slam.

"Crikey!" said a male voice straight out of a *Masterpiece Theatre* costume drama.

It took Lucy a moment to recover enough to reply. A flush crawled up her neck as a prickling sensation swelled throughout her body. Unlike the spun-in-a-blender reaction she'd had to kissing Cole, these tingles were pleasant.

Daring to lift her gaze, she repeated "Crikey?" as a question.

Amusement glittered in his brown eyes, which were captivating even from behind the square, tortoiseshell hipster glasses.

Hold on, it wasn't like Lucy to notice another guy's eyes. Or that his smooth-looking skin was a few hues darker than his eyes; his hair midnight black, closely cut, almost military.

"Sorry, didn't see you there," he said without a trace of irony. Did he really think the collision had been his fault?

"Yeah, me neither."

The stranger chuckled and it had a different cadence from American laughter. Something about it coaxed a wry smile from Lucy. She couldn't resist giving him a quick once-over: tweed blazer, chinos, and a *Doctor Who* T-shirt. *Definitely not from around here.*

"Are you new?" Lucy asked for lack of something more original to say while showing off her evidently acute deductive reasoning skills. There was the faintest hint of stubble on the stranger's jaw. She didn't think he could be younger than her, but why would a senior transfer in so close to graduation?

He quirked his lips. "If I don't answer, will you rope me with your Lasso of Truth?"

Lucy just stared.

"Wonder Woman." His smile faltered and he touched his index finger to the Band-Aid.

When no sparks flew, Lucy let out a short, relieved breath.

"Oh. Right. Justice League aficionado?"

"I like comics." A casual shrug. "Although *Watchmen* is more my speed."

"*Quis custodiet ipsos custodes*, huh?"

"Good question. Who *will* watch the watchers? And they say Americans have less culture than yogurt." He pronounced it *yah-gurt*, which made the dairy product sound infinitely more sophisticated than it was.

Lucy laughed. "I suppose I should be offended on behalf of my countrymen."

"As well as friends and Romans?" he said.

Was the Brit flirting with her? And wait, was Lucy flirting back?

"If I've offended you," he began, clenching a fist to his chest. "I sincerely apologize because I need a favor."

"What kind of favor?" She arched a brow.

"I was looking for the physics lab."

Physics! Argh! "I'm headed that way. Let's go."

He grinned. "I'll follow your lead."

Lucy was careful not to graze him with a hand or shoulder as she navigated them down the corridor. She couldn't begin to understand the different kinds of tingles he'd provoked. She only knew she couldn't control it.

The droning of teachers from behind classroom doors provided an awkward soundtrack. After a few moments of walking in silence, she said, "Don't worry about being late—Mrs. Brandon is a total softie. I'm her student aide."

"Oh, really?" He smoothed the lapels of his jacket, considering the tip. Catching her eye, he said, "To answer your question, I *am* new. Just arrived from Cambridge. Near London, not Boston."

"You don't say." A smile tugged at Lucy's lips. "One day I'd like to see Newton's apple tree." He was probably their most famous alumnus. Next to Stephen Hawking.

"It doesn't really exist, you know. There's a tree outside Trinity College—but that's just for tourists."

"Then I guess that'd be perfect for me."

He laughed and gave her a long, curious look.

Lucy was kind of sad to bring their conversation to an end, but they'd arrived at the lab. The Brit had provided her with two whole worry-free minutes.

"Here we are."

He broke eye contact. "Right-o. Here we go," he said, opening the door for Lucy like a gentleman—not the instinctive behavior of American high school boys—before his expression transformed into something far more earnest.

"Hey, I forgot to ask," Lucy started. "What's your name?"

Mrs. Brandon answered for him.

"Ah, there you are!" said the teacher from the front of the lab, smiling brightly. "Class, this is Ravi Malik. He's a final-year student at Cambridge University and he's on an exchange program at our very own Heron College." That was where Lucy's mom taught. "Ravi will be my teaching assistant for the rest of the semester. Please make him feel welcome!"

Teaching assistant?

The Brit wasn't a new senior. He was a *college* senior.

And Lucy had been flirting with him. The fact that he'd been polite enough to humor her only made her want to curl into a ball and die.

This was definitely the cherry on top.

SPEAKEASY

Caffeine, like duct tape, fixes nearly everything.

Lucy took a gulp of her triple-shot gingerbread latte, closed her eyes, and sank into a plush turquoise sofa at the café where Claudia worked after school. Since she had an in with the barista, Lucy ordered Christmas concoctions all year-round. Claudia made up a few of her own, like the Sugar Plum Fairy, just for Lucy.

The Gallery—which displayed works by local artists in addition to being a coffeehouse—was located on the other side of town near the Heron College campus. It was relatively slow this afternoon because most of the college kids were off spring breaking. The Eaton High crowd tended to hang out at Casey's Diner or the fast-food restaurants closer to school. Lucy was happy for some distance from her classmates—and from Cole.

His smile was tinged with hurt when she'd rejected his offer for a ride home in favor of accompanying Claudia to the Gallery, but Lucy was afraid of what might happen if they were together in a confined space. How could she tell her boyfriend that his kisses made her want to hurl? She took another sip and heaved a sigh.

At the register, Claudia was laughing while providing service with a smile to a lone patron, probably a Heron student. The girl had spiky blond hair, an eyebrow ring, and sported one of those *Ceci n'est pas une pipe* T-shirts.

Just Claudia's type. She loved a good tortured artist—on canvas or in the flesh. Lucy would rather "solve for x" every day of the week than try to interpret a Monet. Art was her bestie's department. Claudia would be spending the summer interning at the Art Institute of Chicago before freshman orientation began.

Overhead, the mellow stylings of folk rock about star-crossed lovers streamed from the speakers. Not what Lucy needed.

Megan had pierced her with ice-pick glances throughout the entire double-period physics lab while shamelessly flirting with Ravi, calling him Mr. Darcy, and asking, "Is it true bodies rest in motion?" *Ugh.*

Not that Lucy could entirely blame the other girl. When Mrs. Brandon had asked Lucy to stay after class with Ravi, her insides had performed an ambitious trapeze act. Her physics teacher said it would be a great experience for Ravi to take over supervising Lucy's independent-study project and hoped Lucy wouldn't mind.

Mind?

With a warm smile, Ravi told Lucy he was keen—he'd actually used the word "keen"—to work together. So was Lucy. Which made her the lowest of the low. Worse than Megan.

It's just because things are weird with Cole, she told herself.

She finished her latte in record time and decided she needed another shot. Or five. Thank goodness caffeine wasn't one of her triggers or Lucy wouldn't survive high school.

"Earth to Minnie Mouse?" asked Claudia as Lucy approached the counter.

Lucy faux glared. "You know I hate that nickname."

Long ago, her friend had decided that Minnie Mouse was a fitting substitute for Lucy's middle name. It beat Minerva, anyhow.

"Yep." Who could resist her friend's impish smile? Not her. Lucy doubted the Heron girl could either, from the way her eyes meandered back in Claudia's direction.

"More caffeine, please."

Claudia waved her hand across the menu board with a flourish. "Any specific variety?"

"Strong."

Drawing her eyebrows together, her friend's reply was unyielding. "One more and I'm cutting you off. *Capisce?*"

"*Capisce.*" Lucy tried to keep a straight face as Claudia vanished behind the enormous chrome espresso machine. Immediately the rumble of the coffee grinder and whir of the frother drowned out another folk song about being done wrong.

"I'm still waiting for you to dish about your fight with Megan," Claudia shouted over the din. Fortunately the café was empty except for the Heron girl, who was now sprawled in an armchair next to the bay window completely absorbed—or pretending to be completely absorbed—by a dog-eared copy of Sartre. The Existentialists had never interested Lucy. She found all the reason she needed for existence in the laws of science. Until this past Saturday, that was.

The grinding stopped and Claudia reappeared with two mugs in hand.

"Hurling office supplies is no way to get out of library fines," said her friend with a wink. Lucy sucked in her cheeks. "Come on, Minnie. I'm due for a break." Obediently, she followed Claudia back toward the sofa, and they melted against it side by side.

Growing up, most of the neighborhood kids were afraid to touch Lucy. No doubt her parents had provided their parents with a laundry list of dos and don'ts that made offers for playdates dry up like the Sahara. While the likes of Tony Morelli and Megan thought they could catch Lucy's "seizure cooties," Claudia never once shied away from holding her hand.

Froth covered Claudia's top lip as she took a swig of her hazelnut cappuccino. Lucy loved that she knew how Claudia liked her java, that she preferred curly fries to regular, and that the spaghetti-and-meatball scene in *Lady and the Tramp* always made her cry. She would miss this, just spending time together, so much next year.

Lucy took her hand now and gave a squeeze.

"Why so glum, chum?" Claudia asked, her over-the-top *Oliver Twist* accent a marked departure from Ravi's.

Lucy shrugged. "I'm not."

"Liar."

"Did Megan really claim I threw the stapler at her?"

"If you did, you have extraordinarily bad aim." Claudia smirked, nodding at the Wonder Woman Band-Aid. Interrogation wasn't really her style. She never prodded too hard until Lucy was ready to talk, but her concern was plain.

Lucy laughed her trademark self-deprecatory snort-chuckle. "It's nothing so dramatic," she said. "My locker holds a grudge is all." In reality, the flying stapler had demonstrated perfect aim—something the pre–Tesla Suite Lucy could never have pulled off.

"If I need to kill someone, just tell me which tools to bring," Claudia offered, dead serious despite her smile. "I can make 'em suffer."

"I know you've got me covered, Clauds."

"Damn straight."

Lucy's chest caved as she exhaled. Claudia scooted closer, smile fading, and placed a hand on her knee. There was no static electricity this time but a sensation similar to when she had collided with Ravi flared at the point of contact.

Lucy was confident she wasn't attracted to her best friend in the same way she was to the Brit. (And okay, she *was* attracted to him, but that was beside the point.) But maybe the tingly feelings had nothing to do with an ill-advised crush. That would simplify things. She wasn't sure what it meant, but it was promising.

Claudia's eyes never left her face as Lucy put this together.

"Did something happen . . ." she began gently, "like, in the city?"

Lucy hadn't offered up any details beyond telling Claudia she'd felt lightheaded, and Claudia hadn't pressed her on the ride from the train station. Now, though, Lucy saw genuine worry—maybe fear—in her friend's eyes. She hated herself for putting it there.

"No. Really. It wasn't . . . *that.*" Lucy met her friend's pained gaze. She hated herself even more for lying. "I would tell you, Clauds." And yet there was no explanation Lucy could give Claudia that didn't *sound* like a lie.

"You promise?"

A vise twisted her heart. Lucy needed more time. Once she had figured out what was happening to her, she'd tell her friend everything.

"I promise," said Lucy, and she hoped it was a promise she could keep.

"Good."

The tension broke as Claudia grinned, although it lacked some of her usual vigor. "Is there anything else I should know? Have you and Cole kissed and made up?"

"More or less." Lucy plunged a hand into the book bag at her feet, knowing Claudia wasn't blind to her evasion tactics. "Look!" She twirled the poker chips in the air. "A very sweet apology. Want one?"

Her friend extended an open palm. "Hit me." As Lucy pressed a green-and-black chip into her hand, Claudia mused, "I don't know what Cole would do without you."

Lucy pursed her lips.

"What? He'd never win a hand."

"That's not *tr*—"

"He might actually have to pay a mechanic to fix his Jeep when it breaks down," Claudia continued.

"I *like* fixing his Jeep." Lucy plunked a piece of chocolate in her mouth as an act of protest. She had strategically learned everything she could about cars in the hopes that her parents might let her drive one someday. Not happening. But she enjoyed putting her skills to good use.

Claudia graced her with a half eye-roll. "I know, I know. It *relaxes* you."

"It does!"

"Anyway, enough boy talk," announced her friend, grabbing another poker chip. "There are more pressing matters at hand."

Truer words had never been spoken. "Hear, hear."

"We need to discuss the lighting for prom. Is your iPad handy?"

Internally, Lucy groaned. Prom was still a sore subject. Regardless of her feelings, however, she'd agreed to run the lighting and sound system. Letting Claudia down wasn't an option.

The student council had chosen the Roaring Twenties for the theme and put the stage crew in charge of the decorations. As themes go, it wasn't bad. Lucy needed to design a lighting scheme to show off the backdrops Claudia was creating.

Lucy had been roped into stage crew when the spotlight blew halfway through the fall musical a year earlier. She'd been in the audience to admire Claudia's set design and saved the day with duct tape and ingenuity.

She passed her friend the iPad as cheerily as possible.

"I had a few thoughts," Claudia said, starting to swipe at the screen. A deep V formed on the bridge of her nose. She always got this intense look on her face when she was thinking about art. "Me and Stew and Cate want to transform the gym into a speakeasy."

Stew and Cate were the other two-thirds of the set-design triumvirate and the only other people at Eaton who made Lucy feel truly welcome.

"So we're thinking dark, moody lighting," her friend said.

Lucy rested her shoulder against Claudia's so she could hold the iPad while Claudia swiped through a clipboard of images. Lots of gangsters in pinstripe suits hefting tommy guns, DO THE CHARLESTON! posters, feather boas, and the Empire State Building under construction.

"Could the budget stretch to a smoke machine?" Claudia asked.

"I don't know. I'll have to run the numbers. Dry ice would probably be cheaper—and just as effective."

"You're a genius, Lucy Phelps!"

"I don't know if I'd go *that* far *bu*—" She paused mid-thought as her eye snagged on a small black-and-white photo at the edge of the digital board. "Can you make that bigger? Zoom in?" There was a rough edge to her voice.

As Claudia complied, Lucy cringed. She touched the screen with her forefinger, not believing what she was seeing.

In the center of a white-tie affair in some Art Deco ballroom, dressed exceedingly dapper, stood Nikola Tesla. In his hand was a tiny, oval-shaped object. A speck. You wouldn't notice it unless you knew what you were looking for. It was the same shape as the object in Lucy's back-pack.

And if you squinted hard enough you'd see that the egg wasn't *in* Tesla's hand—it was floating above it.

Hot chills blistered beneath Lucy's skin and adrenaline tightened every muscle in her body. The iPad scorched her hands like burning embers and the screen blipped to black. Yelping, she dropped the device onto the wooden floor. The screen cracked as smoke rose from the top.

"*Damn*," exclaimed Claudia. "Hope you've got a warranty on that thing." She poked at the smoking ruins. "Must be faulty wiring."

"Must be," Lucy agreed, but she wasn't listening. She was transfixed, like a deer in headlights.

She had done this. Her adrenaline had spiked. It was her fault.

Was Lucy actually dangerous? Could she have *hurt* Claudia?

Before Lucy could react, her best friend was on the ground, trying in vain to collect the jagged shards of the shattered screen. Out of no-where, the Heron girl dropped to her knees beside the sofa.

"Let me help," she said, eyeing Claudia eagerly. Guess she'd found her conversation starter. Lucy would have smiled if she weren't so pet-rified.

The skin turned rosy beneath her friend's freckles. "It's cool. I work here."

"I don't mind," the girl replied. "Pay it forward, you know."

Claudia's eyes did a swift lap of the deserted café.

"If you insist." A coy smile. "The dustpan is behind the muffin display."

"On it," the girl said with an equally coy smile.

"Thanks, *um*—"

"Jessica—Jess." The Heron girl held Claudia's gaze for a moment be-fore launching herself toward the register. Right. Now that Lucy's heart-beat was returning to a steady rhythm, she realized, "I should go."

"What? No."

Lucy tilted her chin in Jess's direction. "Yes. Don't want to salt your game."

"There's no game." Her friend slapped her playfully. "She's a *customer*."

"I believe the lady doth protest too much."

Claudia couldn't conceal her delight. "But . . . what about your iPad?"

"Toss it. It's toast."

"Literally." They shared a grin. "I still have another hour on my shift, though," Claudia said, frowning. "How are you gonna get home?"

"I can call Cole."

Claudia was about to say something else when Jess returned, dustpan in hand, flashing her an inviting grin. Lucy chugged the remnants of her latte and grabbed her book bag.

"Text me later!" Claudia called after her.

The door to the café clicked shut and, to her chagrin, Lucy realized she couldn't text Cole even if she wanted to because she was still phoneless. But Lucy *didn't* want to. Not after she'd nuked her iPad. She could use the long walk home to devise an excuse for how another expensive piece of technology had bitten the dust.

The breeze outside was summerlike but she hugged her jacket closer. How long before Lucy short-circuited herself?

A PETER PARKER EXPERIENCE

Classical music filtered down from the attic as Lucy opened the front door to her house. That could only mean one thing: her mom was elbow-deep in writing her book. While Lucy and her dad were jazz connoisseurs—"Take Five" was known to blare from his office—her mom, predictably, hardly ever listened to anything composed after the invention of the automobile. Vivaldi if her research was going well; Beethoven if it wasn't. Sounded like his Ninth Symphony. Uh-oh.

Schrödinger perched on the bottom step and assessed Lucy warily.

"Had a manic Monday too?" she teased, approaching him with unfamiliar trepidation. Lucy dropped her book bag to the carpet and stooped down to stroke him. As her hand hovered above his mottled black-and-auburn fur, it began to stand on end. Schrödinger emitted a low-frequency growl that escalated to a full-fledged howl when Lucy's hand made contact.

A spray of bright, white sparks traveled from his head to his tail. Alarmed, she lurched backward, tiny pops bristling along her skin. The cat launched himself at her, claws extended for mortal combat. Lucy ducked and he crashed into the brass umbrella stand beside the doormat.

I'm sorry, she mouthed because she couldn't get the words out. Lucy's breaths came in short bursts. Schrödinger recovered quickly and dashed into her father's office, still hissing.

The percussion of kettledrums and vigorous violins came to an abrupt halt.

"Lucy? Is that you?"

Gulping down a lungful of air, Lucy rasped out, "It's me," because she didn't want her mother to think there was an intruder in the house. Even if Lucy had recently added breaking and entering to her résumé.

"Can you come up here?"

Tremors pulsed through Lucy's body. Not seizure tremors, she didn't think. Standard-issue freaked-out-to-the-nth-degree tremors.

Lucy crept up the stairs like she was walking the plank. She tried to divide the incidents into some sort of order. Categories. Classes. Schemas. That was what a scientist would do.

The sparks she'd produced petting Schrödinger were attributable to static electricity. As was hugging Claudia the other night. If it weren't for everything else, she'd be able to laugh it off.

Those were the first electricity-related phenomena to occur since Lucy discovered Tesla's secret lab.

The second kind were the tingly sensations provoked by Cole, Claudia, and the Brit. Kissing Cole was equivalent to sticking her stomach in a centrifuge, whereas contact with Claudia and Ravi had been warm, pleasant—ticklish, even. It wasn't strictly electricity-related but definitely a result of her experience in the Tesla Suite.

The more disquieting phenomena were Lucy's seeming ability to magnetize metallic objects, cause them to levitate, interfere with radio transmissions, and electrocute iPads. The first three in the list suggested that Lucy possessed an electromagnetic field and should therefore be classified together, while the latter suggested that Lucy transformed that field into electricity.

Megan was right. Lucy was four different kinds of freak.

As for the Tesla Egg, it didn't seem to be a power source in and of itself. The expression on Tesla's face in the photograph had been one of smug mastery. He'd been in complete control. Lucy suspected he'd been aping—in a suave manner—for the camera. Daring people to notice. The way it'd been levitating made her think of a maglev train. Was Tesla's magnetic field *that* powerful?

Her pulse kicked up. Would that happen to Lucy too?

She reached the second-floor landing and wiped her sweaty palms against her jean skirt. A ladder had been lowered from a trapdoor in the ceiling leading up to the attic, and buttery light shone down, illuminating the dusk-darkened hallway. Lucy had always viewed it as a place of mystery. For years she hadn't been allowed to climb the ladder to her mom's study in case she injured herself. Now that she could, it retained the allure in Lucy's mind.

There was a combination of irritation and concern as her mother repeated, "Lucy?" Evidently she still worried her daughter couldn't handle the ladder.

In this instance, she might just be right.

Her mom swiveled in her desk chair to greet Lucy as she emerged through the trapdoor. As always her mother sat with prima-ballerina posture, silhouetted in the tangerine haze of a Tiffany lamp, although her French knot was slightly askew. The aroma of her one daily cigarette lingered in the air. Odd. As a rule, she saved it for after dinner.

"How was your day?" her mom asked, distracted, glancing back at an enormous leather volume open on the desk. "Picked up a new phone for you." She gestured at a shopping bag but her gaze remained fixed on the book.

"Thanks. And, uneventful," Lucy lied with a shrug, her eyes shifting toward the tome preoccupying her mom. Drawing closer, she could tell it was actually a facsimile of some old manuscript too valuable to remove from a library. Greek alphabet letters that she recognized were sprinkled among strange symbols and pictographs that looked like an archaic version of emoticons.

"Translating?" Lucy surmised.

Her mom gave a tired laugh. "Translating would be generous." She pulled the clip from her hair before hastily rearranging it into a tighter knot. "I need to stick at it, though. Hope you don't mind eating alone. There's an organic squash and roast-chicken salad in the fridge."

"Sure." Lucy had zero appetite. She hadn't even been able to bring herself to finish the chocolate poker chips on her walk home.

She bent over to collect the shopping bag from where it rested by her mom's feet and heard a gasp.

"Oh, honey. What happened?"

Lucy's mom smoothed the Wonder Woman Band-Aid over her eye. Instantly, she tensed—then, nothing. Only the reassuring touch of the woman who had soothed hundreds of her bruises over the years.

"It's no biggie. Had a fight with my locker."

Their eyes met. "Lucinda," her mom said, low, a warning tone.

"Really." Lucy fiddled with the handle of the bag because she couldn't lie while staring her mom in the eye.

"Maybe I should call Dr. Rosen? I'm sure he'd fit you in."

"I don't need to see Dr. Rosen!" So much for making up for snapping at her this morning. In a more appeasing tone, Lucy said, "The school nurse already looked at it. I'm good to go."

Her mother exhaled a long breath.

"All right. But you haven't skipped your pills, have you?"

"Of course not," she replied automatically. Then it hit her.

Lucy *had* forgotten to take her meds. All weekend. A fleeting hope kindled inside her. Could that be it? She wanted to believe the solution could be that easy. Take her medication and all her freaky abilities would vanish.

Her scientific mind couldn't accept that hypothesis. Either way, Lucy wouldn't miss any more doses. She needed her brain as stable as possible at a time like this.

Lucy circled her gaze around the study. It was a total contrast to her dad's. Neat rows of IKEA bookcases were stacked against the walls, the titles organized by subject and then in alphabetical order. Atop the filing cabinets were neatly arranged figurines, reproductions of ancient Greek and Roman statues: the Winged Victory of Samothrace, the Elgin marbles, the Venus de Milo, as well as an Egyptian scarab.

Finally she dragged her eyes back to her mother. Her careworn face made Lucy ache. "You don't have to worry, Mom. I'm okay."

"I'm your mother—it comes with job." She squeezed Lucy's elbow. "Don't forget to eat something with your pills."

"I won't." Lucy pivoted in the direction of the trapdoor.

"And Lucy?"

She craned her neck over her shoulder.

"Try not to break the phone. It's your third since school started."

Lucy swallowed. "Okay," she said, beginning to descend. Definitely not the best time to mention the French-fried iPad. *Oh.* She paused midstep.

Oh no. Lucy gripped the ladder for dear life as her mother's words replayed in her head.

She could blame the latest busted phone on the acne-prone skater boy, but the one before that had mysteriously died. Kaput. Refused to turn on one day—the day Lucy first slept with Cole. She'd nearly jumped out of her skin in anticipation. Surely that resulted in a surge of adrenaline.

Was it possible she'd seared her phone like she had the iPad?

But that was months ago. Lucy felt the distinct yank of a rug being pulled out from underneath her. Again.

She also had yet to formulate an adequate explanation for the reaction of the plasma Tesla lamp. It fell under the fourth category of freakiness she'd established, but it occurred *before* Lucy found the egg or the lab.

She was willing to—maybe—accept that she'd had a Peter Parker radioactive-spider experience in Tesla's lab. She was unwilling to entertain the idea that she'd possessed any of these abilities prior to entering the room.

Fisting her hands, Lucy dismissed any further speculation.

Time to put on her virtual lab coat.

Tonight, she would put her theories to the test.

SNAP! CRACKLE! POP!

The last time Lucy had poked around the kitchen, Cole's misguided financing of prom night was her biggest problem. Ah, to be young again. Was it only Friday?

Squash and chicken salad definitely didn't appeal.

When she'd activated her new phone, all of Cole's messages from the past weekend came flooding in. He must have sent the first right after her phone smashed.

I miss you. Followed a couple hours later by: *I want to hear your voice.*

Nothing on Saturday night, but the texts on Sunday grew progressively more frustrated and sad, ending with: *This has been the worst weekend of my life.*

Hers too.

Lucy had hoped he would text her this evening. So far, nothing. She hadn't texted him either, though. She didn't know what to say. She couldn't tell Cole why she was acting so distant and she had reached her daily quota of lies. The only messages she'd received were from Claudia, brimming with excitement that Jess had asked for her number. Lucy was glad that at least Claudia's love life wasn't in free fall.

She slammed the fridge door with more force than necessary and huffed. Not even ice cream—sugar-free and organic, obviously—tempted her. Lucy grabbed a package of Jiffy Pop from the cabinet above the sink but didn't plan on eating it. The instant popcorn was for experimental purposes only.

Lucy's dad wasn't nearly as health conscious as her mom and he said making popcorn on the stovetop reminded him of his college days when he survived on ramen and nearly set his fraternity house on fire with his culinary pyrotechnics. This didn't convince her mother as to the logic of stovetop popcorn, but she'd relented.

Removing the paper wrapper, Lucy listened for the *it-was-a-dark-and-stormy-night* chord progressions of Beethoven.

Check. Safe to proceed.

When Lucy was eight, her dad had turned his unhealthy eating habits into a science lesson. The popcorn kernels came in a frying-pan-shaped aluminum container filled with oil. When heated on the stove, the aluminum conducted the energy necessary to cook the kernels. Leave it too long and the expanding aluminum explodes. Lucy's dad would do that sometimes because she liked it and her mom would complain about the mess while nibbling on the end product.

Lucy didn't plan on using the stove.

She set the pan on the countertop, then carefully removed her Medic Alert bracelet and shoved it in her pocket. She didn't want anything interfering with the parameters of the experiment.

Her fingers twitched as she placed her right hand flush against the cold, smooth aluminum.

The test was simple. Empirical.

The incidents with the bracelet, the stapler, and the iPad all seemed to suggest that Lucy was creating large electric and magnetic fields, and that they were somehow tied to her emotions. In physics, one of the most fundamental laws was that energy couldn't be created or destroyed. Almost two hundred years ago, Michael Faraday—the same guy who designed the cage in Tesla's lab—had discovered that changing a magnetic field induces electric current.

Therefore, if Lucy really was generating her own magnetic fields, and if she could control them, she should be able to induce electricity in any handy piece of metal: such as the popcorn pan. By running this current through aluminum, which, like all metals, had a natural resistance, it should produce the heat required to pop the kernels.

It was a totally straightforward, totally illogical experiment.

Lucy closed her eyes and drew in a steadying breath. The aluminum crinkled beneath her fingertips.

Concentrate.

When she'd toasted the iPad, she'd been alarmed. Panicked. And when Megan had taunted Lucy about Cole, she'd been afraid the Mean Girl was right. Lucy needed an adrenaline jolt and because she was clearly a masochist, she focused on re-creating those conditions.

One by one, she scrolled through her catalogue of fears. She conjured the memory of standing alone on the playground, the other kids laughing and pointing at her helmet. Her body tensed with the phantom throbbing in her temples that preceded a seizure.

Not enough.

She pictured the blanket of blackness that covered her mind when a seizure gripped her. That paralyzing moment before her conscious mind gave up the fight while she knew what was coming. The inevitable surrender.

Still not enough. Maybe surrender had become too familiar.

Dig deeper.

Lucy forced herself to relive the fear that had plagued her for months after she started dating Cole: the potential humiliation of succumbing to a seizure while having sex for the first time. He hadn't pushed the issue; Lucy had been the one to suggest it. Their one-year anniversary and Lucy's eighteenth birthday had been fast approaching and she'd told Cole he could do better than an Amazon gift card.

The Coke he'd been drinking nearly spurted through his nostrils.

I love you, Lucy Phelps, he'd said.

Nevertheless, the thought of messing up their first time together had terrorized her. She was too embarrassed to talk to Dr. Rosen about sex, but she reasoned if she couldn't play sports because of her heart rate, then sex might also be a trigger. Nor did Lucy want to tell her parents she and Cole were taking things to the next level. Yes, they were East Coast liberals but even they had their limits.

Lucy screwed her eyelids tighter, pulse accelerating, and thrust herself further into the memory.

Shortly after Cole's declaration, they'd picked a night to be "The Night." He often had the house to himself because Mr. Hewitt was a software sales rep and Cole's mom traveled with him to wine and dine clients. Claudia had been in on the plan, of course, providing the cover of a sleepover for Lucy's parents. Lucy would've disabled the GPS tracker on her phone that night, but it didn't matter because her phone conked out hours before the big event.

Standing in the kitchen, perspiration began to dot Lucy's hairline. She recalled sweating all through the romantic dinner Cole had made as well. He burned the steaks but it was the thought that counted. There were candles and a bouquet of pink carnations on the table. He watched her avidly, sensing something was off as Lucy had grown quieter and quieter.

By the time Cole served up a Sara Lee chocolate cake, he dragged his chair next to hers, resting his hand on top of hers and saying, "We don't have to do anything you're not ready for." His tone was relaxed and Lucy knew he really would be okay to wait, but she confessed, "It's not that."

What had really scared Lucy was the possibility that if she told Cole she might seize during sex, he wouldn't want to touch her. Ever again. But in that moment she decided if she trusted him enough to sleep with him, she had to trust him with the truth.

His response couldn't have been more perfect. He tucked a hair behind her ear, and looked her directly in the eye. "I want to be with you," he said. "All of you. I'm not scared." The words convinced Lucy that what she'd been feeling for Cole really was love. It was why she'd forgiven him for selling the test answers.

So why couldn't she trust him with the truth about this?

A faint crackling noise filled the kitchen. It grew louder by the second and her heartbeat skittered.

Lucy didn't want to tell Cole the truth because now she really might be something he *should* be scared of—something that scared her too.

Warmth spread from her hand to her elbow as the aluminum wrapping began to unfurl.

It was working. *Holy crap*. It was working!

Dread iced her from within as heat surged from her fingers. She didn't want to open her eyes but there was no avoiding it.

Ouch! Hot. Lucy lifted her hand so it hovered just above the Jiffy Pop. Apparently her skin wasn't fireproof. Inconvenient.

The aluminum swelled, larger and rounder, until it became a balloon.

Lucy's hand was glowing. But not with sunlight like this morning. An emerald-green aura comprised of thin, radiant streaks of light. Jellyfish-like tentacles. She had a distinct sense of déjà vu.

The aura continued to burn more intensely but the temperature in Lucy's hand remained constant. As long as she didn't touch the metal, it didn't hurt. In fact, it felt good. The zap that killed the iPad had been a short burst of energy, a shock. This was different. The slow burn was making her giddy.

The bag stretched to bursting.

All the fear at what she was capable of vaporized and Lucy laughed.

Popcorn suddenly sprayed everywhere and the bang made Lucy lurch, jolting backwards, bashing her skull against the cabinet. *Double ouch*. There was only so much head trauma she could take in one day.

Her gaze returned to her hands. The green glow was gone.

If she wasn't mistaken, the glow had been St. Elmo's fire—a greenish-bluish light that appeared around the masts of ships before a storm due to the electricity in the air. During the age of Columbus, sailors viewed it as a bad omen because it could disrupt compass readings. Her mouth fell open.

Lucy had interfered with Cole's car radio in the same way.

St. Elmo's fire was an incandescent plasma, like in the Tesla lamp, caused by an electrical discharge adjacent to a metal conductor. The aluminum foil had probably done the trick. *Oh no*. What if Lucy had made the stapler glow in the library this morning? What rumor would Megan have started then? Lucy had never believed in the paranormal, but . . . how else could she explain what had just happened?

The only person who might have an explanation had been dead since 1943.

In. Out. *Just breathe*, she commanded herself.

The strains of Beethoven ceased and Lucy heard footsteps on the stairs.

There was no explaining this away. The kitchen looked like a junk-food war zone.

A second later, her mom appeared in the entryway.

"Oh, Lucy." Her name became a lament. More than annoyance, there was sympathy in her mother's eyes.

"Sorry," Lucy choked out.

Her mom sighed. "You and your father."

"I'll clean it up."

Nodding, her mother shuffled back toward the living room and Lucy noticed her withdraw a pack of cigarettes from her sweater pocket.

Acid churned in Lucy's gut as she gauged the damage. Popcorn she could clean up. Her life? Not so much.

DARK STAR

Lucy's last few days had gone something like this: she slipped off her Medic Alert bracelet as soon as she was out of her mom's view in the morning, stopped wearing earrings altogether, and gave cutlery the fisheye, afraid it would pull a *Fantasia* on her.

She'd also added another fib to her expanding repertoire, telling Claudia that Marie Curie had a punctured tire. She hated lying but she couldn't risk the ten-speed developing a mind of its own in the middle of traffic. Her best friend didn't mind shuttling Lucy back and forth in the Mystery Minivan because it provided her with ample opportunity to relay the details of her nightly text exchanges with Jess.

As Lucy had suspected, Jess was a sophomore at Heron, double-majoring in art history and psychology. Her family was Irish like Claudia's; she had an unhealthy obsession with Sriracha sauce (she even put it on her cereal); and dabbled in BASE jumping. Lucy wondered how anyone could "dabble" in BASE jumping without becoming roadkill, but she kept mum because she'd never seen Claudia so gaga.

When the final bell rang on Friday, relief, nerves, and excitement warred inside her. Approaching the office at the back of the physics classroom, Lucy's right thumb twitched instinctively against the inside of her opposite wrist, searching out the charms that usually dangled there. She couldn't believe how naked her skin felt without the bracelet she'd once loathed. The clinking sound as she flicked the silver charms together was always soothing, and soothing was what she needed now.

She blinked away the image of Cole's bewildered face as she turned down the offer of being his cheerleader at track practice today. Most of the time, Lucy was more than happy to cheer him on from the sidelines, but this afternoon what she needed more than her boyfriend was physics. Science. Laws that made sense.

Lucy took a deep breath, straightened up, and rapped twice on the office door. Mrs. Brandon had given Lucy her own key, free to come and go as she pleased, but she didn't want to be presumptuous with Ravi.

She knocked again with a little more force.

Mass times acceleration. Lucy rolled her eyes. What a nerd. And yet there was something reassuring about reciting formulas. They were constant. They always worked correctly. Unlike her. Even pre–Tesla Suite. And now—now her life was anything but formulaic.

Her hand hovered mid-knock as the door shuddered open.

Ravi's face was creased beneath his glasses, demeanor harried. He pulled out his earbuds, draping them on either side of his neck.

"Lucy," he said. His eyes brightened and his soft inflection made her go soft in the head. Fiddling with the wires, he added, "Didn't hear you."

Looking anywhere but his eyes, Lucy spotted an origami unicorn prancing in the rain across his black T-shirt. She owned the exact same one.

"Do you dream of electric sheep?" she said, grinning in spite of her erratic pulse.

He returned it. "*Blade Runner* is a classic."

"I'm surprised to hear you say that. Since Americans have less culture than *yah-gurt.*" She dared to lift her gaze and he chuckled. "But here's a really high-stakes question for you: book or movie?"

"Those *are* high stakes."

"The best kind." Lucy double-checked her hands weren't glowing with emerald fire. *Phew.* The sudden sass was entirely homegrown.

Ravi tapped his chin as he considered. "Generally, because I'm a purist as well as a pedant, I would have to go with Philip K. Dick's short story."

"I know it's a short story."

"I didn't doubt it." He laughed again. "On the other hand, the movie does have Rutger Hauer. No one does menacing quite like him."

"Fair point," she conceded.

Turning the tables, Ravi said, "I have a high-stakes question for you." He folded his arms, exposing the leather patches on the elbows of his jacket. "Which is more authentic, human or Replicant?"

"That *is* a high-stakes question."

"The best kind."

Their eyes met and her mind went blank. Lucy and Cole never bantered like this. *That's right: Cole. Your boyfriend!*

Forcing herself to focus on the question at hand, Lucy smooshed her lips together and mulled over her response. The classroom became intensely quiet. In both the movie and the short story, Replicants were androids nearly indistinguishable from humans except they couldn't experience true human emotions or dreams that weren't preprogrammed. At least, that's what the humans thought.

She hugged herself as a wintry blast rushed through her. Did Lucy's post–Tesla Suite symptoms make her less than human? There was no way she was some kind of sophisticated android—right?

Ravi tilted his head, still waiting for an answer.

"Hmm," she began eloquently. "I guess that depends on your definition of authentic."

"Agreed. How would you define it?"

"Being true to yourself."

"I like that," he told her, and slouched against the doorjamb. "So, which is it? Who's more true to themselves: humans or Replicants?"

Lucy just barely resisted swaying towards him. Mirroring his body language, she folded her arms and replied, "Replicants. Because they try harder to know themselves."

"Nice." A broad smile swept across his face, which shouldn't have made Lucy as giddy as it did. "Do I spy a budding philosophy major?"

"Hardly. Science all the way."

"You have a talent for it. Speaking of which, time to get down to business." His face smoothed into something more serious. "Do you want to talk me through your experiment?"

Hands clammy, she mumbled, "Sure," and followed him inside.

That's the reason Lucy was here, after all. The *only* reason: Science and nothing but science.

Once the components of the experiment were arranged carefully on the black countertop at the front of the classroom, Ravi asked Lucy to describe her objectives.

"Right. So." She chewed the inside of her cheek. "The experiment I devised was to re-create the first battery invented by Alessandro Volta in 1800, and then to use the battery to power an iPod." It had actually been her dad's talks about alternative power that inspired Lucy's project.

As Ravi's eyes drifted to the tabletop and back to her, Lucy dug her fingernails into her palms. The experiment must have seemed incredibly elementary.

"I'm also writing a paper," she told him. "Explaining the significance of Volta's invention in the history of science. He lent his name to the volt, after all. But of course you know—"

Ravi cut her off. "Talk me through it."

The earnest quality of his voice quelled her doubts. The laboratory was Lucy's domain. Here—if nowhere else—she knew what she was doing. She inhaled through her nose, her restlessness draining away.

You've got this.

Lucy pointed at the alternating zinc, copper, and cardboard discs stacked on top of one another like some kind of electrical s'mores.

"Volta was a student of Luigi Galvani. Galvani theorized that animals create their own electricity. He conducted an experiment in which a dead frog's legs were connected to two different pieces of metal. When the legs twitched, Galvani concluded the electricity came from the frog. But Volta deduced it was the touching of the metals—brass and iron—that caused the frog's legs to twitch, rather than the frog itself."

Leaning toward her, Ravi asked, "Was Galvani completely wrong about animal electricity?"

"Of course." Lucy's pulse thudded in her throat.

"Think about how a thumbprint is used to unlock a smartphone," he pressed her. Ravi had no idea how close to an uncomfortable truth he was getting. "It's not just the fingerprint. It's the body's conductivity to electricity that allows it to be read."

"The nervous system, you mean."

"Precisely." His half-smile made him look almost boyish and it delighted Lucy, yet she couldn't shake a sinking feeling.

"It's not the same, though." Her words were labored. "Our nerves send electrical impulses around the body but they can't power anything."

Liar. Liar. Liar.

Lucy's lower lip quivered because she wanted it to be true, and she was immensely grateful when Ravi said, "All right. Back to the Voltaic pile. How does it work?"

Fighting her unease, Lucy replied, "The battery has a negative charge at one end and a positive charge at the other." She cleared her throat, and her voice grew stronger. "Volta discovered that a single juncture between two metals doesn't produce much electricity. When he multiplied the junctures and joined them with saltwater-soaked cardboard, however, he could generate enough electricity for a mild shock."

"What does the saltwater do?"

"The saltwater allows for the flow of electricity without the metals touching each other."

Ravi murmured a noise of assent. "And how do you determine how much voltage is required to power the iPod?" he said, his question laced with encouragement.

"Well, Volta used himself as the conductor—adding more discs to his pile and letting his body receive increasingly large shocks." Lucy laughed. "Lucky for me, I have a voltage meter."

Ravi laughed along. "Yeah. Let's not do it Volta's way. Otherwise I'll have the shortest teaching career in history."

"So, you're eager to mold young minds, then?" Lucy's mouth ticked up. "Physics is your major, I'm guessing."

"Actually, it's maths. Or *math*, as you Yanks say. Really. It's mathematics plural. I don't get it." He offered her a smirk. "Barbarians."

Lucy snorted as her belly flipped. *Stop that.*

"Why come to the land of barbarians?"

Ravi regarded her a beat, shifting his jaw back and forth.

"A change of scene. Less rain."

Classic non-answer. Still, instinct told her not to push the issue. Scrambling for a safer, less personal topic of conversation, Lucy sputtered, "Alessandro Volta also invented the first remotely operated pistol."

"I didn't know that."

"Yeah. Newton and the Royal Society in London were very interested. So was Napoleon."

"I can only imagine. The precursor to the modern drone. War is always profitable—for someone."

Lucy coughed. She'd been so impressed by Volta's technological achievements that she hadn't thought about the other implications.

After an awkward lull, Ravi asked, "What about you?"

"What *about* me?"

"Would you want to teach—one day?"

Standing in front of a class and trying to tame a horde of teenagers made Lucy want to run for the hills.

"No. I think I'd rather be a researcher. Tucked safely away in my lab."

"Sounds like hiding to me."

Her insides contorted into a pretzel. "Not a fan of crowds," she said.

"Is that why you've never entered any science fairs?"

Ravi had a worrying way of making Lucy want to spill her darkest secrets. She tried to maintain an inscrutable expression.

"I saw in Mrs. Brandon's progress reports that she'd encouraged you to enter," he went on.

He'd read her file?

Lucy's lips lemon-puckered as a million conflicting thoughts whirled around her mind. She didn't want her medical condition to be the only thing Ravi saw when he looked at her. "Um, yeah," she hedged. "My parents thought the attention would be too much stress for me."

She had fought them on it when Mrs. Brandon first nominated her. Eventually, though, Lucy came to the conclusion they were right. She hadn't wanted to jeopardize all the strides she'd made controlling her seizures before college.

"You don't strike me as someone who caves under pressure, Lucy."

The breath caught in her throat. No one—absolutely no one—had ever said that to Lucy before. Their gazes merged and the quiet began to roar.

Or maybe it was just her.

Switching back into scientist mode, Lucy resumed her explanation. "Anyway, the voltage generated by Volta's battery is determined by the kind of electrolyte used—saltwater or something else—as well as its concentration. Volta used a combination of saltwater and sulfuric acid but Mrs. Brandon suggested I try copper sulfate instead. Less likely to blind myself."

"Cracking," Ravi agreed with a grin. Lucy shot him a quizzical look. There was another hint of a flush on his cheeks. "I mean, good thinking."

"'Cracking'? That's not English."

"I think you mean it's not *American*, because it most certainly *is* good English."

They reached for the iPod resting next to the battery at the same moment and as Ravi's hand extended from beneath the sleeve of his jacket, Lucy's eyes landed on a tattoo that spread across the underside of his wrist and up his forearm. She wouldn't have pegged him for the tattoo type.

On closer inspection, it was a symbol Lucy recognized. An eight-pointed star that made her think of a blossom unfurling. She'd seen it the other night in the manuscript her mom was translating.

Lucy brushed her hand unthinkingly over the dark star and pleasure catapulted through her, followed by searing humiliation. Ravi tensed as he exhaled. *Oh no.* Had she zapped him?

"It means creation," he said without inflection.

No zap. Thankfully.

"Sorry, *I*—" Lucy stammered, but he didn't seem upset. "In which language?"

"It's not a language. Not as such."

Then why was her mother translating it?

Lucy's eyes were drawn back to the outlines of midnight ink overlapping on his skin. She counted the triangles that comprised it without meaning to. It was almost mesmerizing.

In a soft voice, he offered, "It's alchemy."

"Alchemy?" She released a strained laugh.

"Alchemy gets a bad rap. But a lot of ancient—and not-so-ancient—scientists were also alchemists."

Lucy made a *hmm* noise. Her dad regarded alchemists as quacks, trying to turn anything and everything into gold. She couldn't imagine what interest her mom would have in them either. Her mother's research generally revolved around the depiction of women in the *Odyssey* or something equally arcane.

"What does it mean to you?" she asked.

The question just slipped out, and Lucy recoiled. Yet she did want to know.

His eyes were steady on hers as he replied.

"I like the idea that nothing is ever completely destroyed. That it's just transformed into something else."

"You're talking about energy."

"And other things." There was a longing in his answer that made Lucy want to pry further but Ravi tugged down the sleeve of his jacket, covering the tattoo and effectively ending the conversation. "Right, then, let's see what kind of energy your battery can create."

Taking the hint, Lucy reached for the two wires on either side of the Voltaic pile and connected them to the iPod. A ghostly glow illuminated the screen as the track listing appeared: Miles Davis. "So What."

"Not a fan of crowds, but a fan of jazz." He arched a brow. "Me too. I like the—"

"Controlled chaos," they said together.

Lucy's heart jackhammered and Ravi seemed equally taken aback, muttering "Great minds," but garbling the words, a wary set to his shoulders.

They pressed the Play button simultaneously. A ticklish sensation surged from Lucy's forefinger like wildfire down her arm and across her chest. She swayed on her feet as the tickles morphed into sparks. It felt like someone was chiseling her brain.

She didn't realize her finger was still pressed to the iPod until it began to smoke.

The riffs of a trumpet floated over Lucy as her eyelids fluttered, her knees turning to jelly, and she slumped toward the floor.

Lucy only had time to think, *Not frakkin' again*, before the world smeared to black.

SCHOOLGIRL
FANTASY, INDEED

She had no sense of how long she'd been down for the count when her eyes opened on Ravi's face.

I've got to stop waking up like this.

Lucy expected to feel cold linoleum beneath her. She didn't expect to feel scratchy tweed against her cheeks. *Oh crap.*

Ravi was crouched beside her and Lucy was cradled in his arms. The scent of cedar, and something peppery, teased her nose. And she liked it. Way too much.

He surveyed her in an analytical manner, relief washing over him. With a cautious smile, he asked, "Did you dream of electric sheep?"

From this perspective, Lucy could see the beginning of his five o'clock shadow. Would it be downy or bristly? *So beyond the point.*

She blamed the non sequitur on her wooziness. She quickly dabbed at the corners of her mouth, checking for drool.

Phew. Small mercy.

Lucy forced a halfhearted laugh and tried to sit up, but her limbs flopped like overcooked spaghetti.

"Steady," warned Ravi. He gripped her shoulders firmly. Lucy wasn't complaining. Not really. In fact, she stifled a sigh.

"Thanks. Um, did I fall?"

"I caught you."

Lucy peeked up at him. If he was uncomfortable holding her, he didn't show it. Why would he be? He was simply trying to prevent her from getting a concussion.

Each and every one of Lucy's toes curled. She was developing a recklessly rich fantasy life.

"Are *you* okay?" she asked him. Electrocuting the teaching assistant was no way to get an A.

Ravi scrunched his dark brows together, his entire demeanor becoming haggard, like a world-weary soldier.

"You don't have to worry about me, Lucy." Then his lips quirked and the storm clouds vanished. "Your iPod, however, has gone to the great Apple Store in the sky."

She groaned. Not another one.

"You must have miscalculated the concentration of the electrolyte solution," he said. "We can recalibrate and try again. I have an old iPod we can sacrifice to the cause."

"I *didn't*—" Lucy halted her self-defense midstream. She knew the experiment worked perfectly because she'd already run a successful demonstration for Mrs. Brandon. She had calculated the 5 volts necessary to charge the iPod without incident. The electrolytes weren't the problem—*she* was. But how could Lucy explain that? She couldn't exactly tell Ravi it was his touch that sent her pulse soaring.

Sitting up more slowly, Lucy said, "Okay. I'll look at my calculations again. Sorry for . . . sorry."

"No need to apologize. That's science. I have faith in you."

Still squatting by her side, Ravi's face was dangerously close to hers. In Lucy's mind, anyway. She caught another whiff of pepper and cedar, which didn't do anything to help clear her head.

"The nurse is probably still around," he said.

Ugh. Twice in one week and Nurse Díaz would definitely tattle to her parents.

"I'm fine. Just hazard-prone."

His mouth curved upward in a wicked way. Feather-light, he tapped the scab that had formed above Lucy's eyebrow from the stapler incident.

"Maybe you're a daredevil."

"I thought I was Wonder Woman?"

"You could be both."

She scoffed. "Or neither."

"I doubt that." His voice was low and it sent a shiver straight through her. A completely natural, completely inadvisable shiver.

He must have noticed—*dammit*—because he offered Lucy a hand as she pushed to her feet.

"Are you certain you don't want to see the nurse? Seemed like a nasty shock."

"It was nothing," she lied. "Don't want to set the record for most visits to the nurse's office."

"Oh, it would scarcely be a record. I more or less lived in the infirmary at boarding school."

Lucy widened her eyes in question and he gave a self-deprecating laugh.

"I was on the small side for rugby." Given that Ravi was now over six feet tall, it was hard to believe. Reading her expression, he added, "There were other reasons I was an easy target, but at least my growth spurt kicked in before graduation." His voice faded out and the tips of his ears changed color.

Lucy wanted to say something nice but couldn't think of anything that wouldn't reveal her ridiculous crush. And, okay, it *was* a crush.

"Can we, um," she began, "keep this between us? Wouldn't want people to think I'm some kind of swooning Southern belle."

"Absolutely. Your secret is safe with me."

Her heart skidded to a stop. If only it could be. If only she could trust him with her preposterous abilities. He *did* like superhero comics. Maybe he could help her figure out a cure?

No. As much as Lucy wanted to, she couldn't get anyone else involved. This was her problem to solve.

Her gaze was pulled toward the botched experiment. The iPod was charred, as were the wires attached to the Voltaic pile.

"I guess I should clean up," she muttered.

"I'll do it," said Ravi. "You take it easy. Get some rest. If you still feel fuzzy later, promise me you'll see a doctor."

"I didn't intend to *actually* use Volta's method, you know."

"That can be our secret too."

"Shortest teaching career in history?"

"Precisely." He grinned.

Lucy needed to go home. Really. Before she could say anything she might regret later, she scooped up her book bag from another desktop.

"See you next week!"

"Have a good weekend, Lucy."

They both made awkward half-wave gestures as Lucy walked carefully out the door and down the hallway. If she wanted, she could probably catch the end of Cole's track practice. A few weeks ago, Lucy had surprised the team with her secret recipe brownies (M&Ms and peanut butter) and Cole had told everyone within earshot that he had the best girlfriend in any of the multiverses. Then he'd winked at her and said, "See, I *do* pay attention." Lucy had been pretty sure he'd zoned out when she told him about Schrödinger's multiple simultaneous universes theory. Schrödinger the scientist, not Schrödinger the cat. Obviously.

Lucy considered heading to the sports grounds for another thirty seconds but she wasn't in the mood to deal with Megan's passive-aggressive BS, and who knew what another kiss from Cole might do to her in her current state? All Lucy needed was for someone to video her puking in the bleachers.

Besides, she had a new hypothesis to test. There was a voltage meter stashed in her garage and Lucy intended to measure the amount she produced under different conditions. Volta must have been a few slices short of a loaf to use himself as a shock absorber, but the logic also worked in reverse.

Cole's hurt face wavered in the back of Lucy's mind again. Her gut pinched and she reached into the pocket of her jeans to send him a good luck text for his meet tomorrow.

Empty. No way. Her mom was going to kill her.

Right as Lucy started to panic, she heard someone calling her name.

Ravi waved an iPhone at her as he took a couple of long strides to meet her.

"*Thankyouthankyouthankyou*," she gushed.

"I found it on the floor."

"You're a lifesaver." She swiped the phone from his outstretched hands. "I just got this. It's my third this year. Like I said, hazard-prone."

The Brit gave her an enigmatic smile.

"Wonder Woman."

And then he walked away, leaving Lucy wondering if there were an alternate universe in which he could be right.

ELECTRIC SLIDE

The backyard was rain-washed, silvery in the dull morning light. There was something lonely about the sight, which matched Lucy's mood.

Cole had never responded to her *Good Luck! X* text.

Her sneakers made a squelching noise as she crossed the lawn toward the garage. In the end, Lucy had been too tired after frying the iPod to run any further experiments. Maybe she should have done more than text Cole.

Could he really be so upset she'd missed his practice that he was giving her the cold shoulder? That wasn't like him. But then, Lucy hadn't been herself lately either.

Her eyes traveled over the frosted blades of grass, sucking her back into the dream she'd had last night, and it wasn't about electric sheep. Nor was it about a certain Replicant lover, although he may have flitted through her consciousness as she nodded off.

In the dream, Lucy had been around the same age as in the photo from her father's desk—the photo she still hadn't fixed. Her three-year-old self had scampered through a garden, lush and tropical, not like anything on the East Coast. As far as Lucy was aware, she'd never left the Northeast but the flowers in her dream were so vivid she'd been able to scour the Internet upon waking for their phylum and class. Star-shaped jasmine, climbing lilies brighter than flame with bladelike petals, and rambutan fruits that resembled hairy hacky sacks.

The breeze had been sticky on her face as Dream Lucy ran, hands outstretched, to the roll of thunder in the distance. Lightning lanced the sky and she giggled. This was what she'd been waiting for. Her skipping turned into a gallop.

No one could catch her.

Lucy didn't know what it was like to feel so unfettered. She couldn't remember not constantly being afraid of her own body.

Dream Lucy stuck out her tongue with delight to catch the raindrops pelting the blossoms all around her. She watched the water collect and drip from their petals. Another boom of thunder, another giggle. Jagged streaks lit the clouds as if they were showing off just for her.

Her name carried on the wind. Someone was searching for her, urgently. Someone was worried. Not Dream Lucy.

She raised her hands toward the golden bolts, not caring that her sundress was soaked. At that moment, her mom rounded a coconut tree and discovered her hiding spot. Lucy's dream mother looked the same only younger, her long blond hair loose around her shoulders, wet and windblown.

"Lucy, come in from the storm!" she called, and Dream Lucy was confused by her distress.

Proudly, she told her mother, "I can make lightning too!"

There was a blinding-white flash as a stream of light jumped from her tiny hands to a magenta orchid plant.

The petals started to burn, and Dream Lucy smiled.

With a sigh, flesh-and-blood Lucy unlocked the door to her garage lab. She didn't put much stock in dreams. Or, she hadn't before she could pop kernels of corn with her fingertips. Her scientific instincts told her that dreams were simply wish fulfillment, a way to process the fears and desires of the conscious mind. This was nothing more than a manifestation of her fear of being found out as . . . whatever she was.

But why did it feel so real?

Switching on the overhead lights, Lucy smothered the memory of wanting more—more of the lightning, more of the power. The only other time she'd felt that humming beneath her skin was when she made a stapler fly at Megan's head. She wished she understood the difference between when her post–Tesla Suite symptoms made her feel invincible and when they caused her to pass out.

Doubt everything.

One of her dad's maxims clanged around her brain as she rummaged in a drawer for the voltage meter and plugged it into the mains. If you wanted to seek out the truth, he insisted, you needed to doubt everything. He'd been paraphrasing René Descartes, the French mathematician, which seemed like an odd choice for someone who always seemed so certain about everything.

Lucy pulled the Tesla Egg from the pocket of her hoodie and set it beside the voltage meter. Next, she retrieved her phone and walked it to the opposite side of the garage for safekeeping. Before she stowed it next to her model of the solar system, she took a quick peek at Cole's Instagram feed. Ill-advised. Megan was sitting thigh-close to him on the bus to the track meet, making a pouty duck face, while his head was thrown back in a genuine rack-your-body chortle.

Lucy huffed. *Get to work.* She twirled her black locks on top of her head, tying the bun sloppily with a rubber band she found lying around.

First order of business was to test the electrical energy of the Tesla Egg. Pinching it between her thumb and forefinger, she gave the copper egg a little spin. Lucy had theorized that it didn't generate electricity independently, but she needed to be sure.

The meter resembled an antiquated scale with a red needle. Lucy clicked the On switch and twisted the knob so the meter would give its readings in volts rather than amps or ohms. Since her dad was as big a geek as she was, he'd splurged on a swanky meter that was rated for a kilovolt. Lucy figured there was no way her experiments were in danger of exceeding 1,000 volts.

She connected the red and black test leads to the jacks, leaving the metal tips exposed, and checked that the needle remained at the leftmost position, indicating an open circuit. The power created by any electric circuit was a result of the voltage multiplied by the current. Voltage was potential, like a difference in height between the top of a hill and the bottom. Her dad once explained it to Lucy in terms of a waterfall.

The farther the top from the bottom, the greater the drop, or voltage. The greater the drop, the faster the water would rush and the water's speed became the current.

Licking her lips, she touched the metal wire tips to either side of the Tesla Egg. As predicted, the needle didn't move across the scale. So far, so good. The copper was uniform, at least on the visible surface, so there was no possibility of a voltage. In the Voltaic pile, it was the difference between the two types of metals that allowed for a voltage to be created.

Lucy released another sigh and removed the wires. If the Voltaic pile she'd designed delivered exactly 5 volts to the iPod—and she knew she hadn't made a mistake in her measurements—then the question was how many additional volts had she caused to course through it?

Electric eels could produce 600 volts, but Lucy was further up the evolutionary ladder from the slithering sea creatures. Wasn't she?

Lucy rolled the exposed end of the red lead between her fingertips. Normally, she shouldn't make the needle on the voltage meter move either. The human body could produce up to one-tenth of a volt, which wasn't enough for the meter to register on its current setting.

Okay, lay it on me, Descartes.

She gripped the black wire with her other hand and took a deep breath.

2 volts.

More than normal, but not as much as she'd anticipated. Two extra volts seemed a little small to short-circuit the iPod. It also didn't explain what had happened to the iPad at the Gallery. Lucy had zapped that without the help of a Voltaic battery. Like with the popcorn experiment, she needed to elevate her heart rate.

Did she dare check on Cole's track meet?

Lucy retrieved her phone and, as her damp fingers slipped across the home screen, she realized she'd forgotten a crucial factor.

Sweat acted like the electrolyte in a battery. When Lucy had touched Ravi, the thrill—yes, thrill—had caused her pulse to race and her palms to grow moist. Skin naturally resisted the flow of electrical current, but getting it wet decreased that resistance. If she plunged her hands in water and then touched the leads, the current through the meter would increase.

Dream Lucy flashed through her mind: she'd been soaking wet when she set the flower on fire.

Stop. "It was just a dream," Lucy mumbled out loud, and choked on a breath as she opened up Cole's feed again.

In the past fifteen minutes, he'd posted a photo of Megan painting a green E on his cheek, another of her kissing it, and yet another of her green lips pulled back in a very eel-like smile.

Was this it? Were she and Cole done? Anger ripped through Lucy. If he wanted to end things, he should at least tell her to her face.

She dropped the phone before she could incinerate it. Returning to the voltage meter, Lucy wrapped her hands around the wires. Sure, she wouldn't deny how much she liked getting to know Ravi, but Lucy would never humiliate Cole. She squeezed the leads until her knuckles turned white.

10 volts.

Her lips parted in a smile. That was more like it. A blink-and-you-miss-it emerald glow outlined her hands.

She released one of the wires and reached for the Tesla Egg.

When Lucy had first seen the photograph of Tesla at the ball, she'd thought he exerted enough magnetic pressure to keep the egg airborne. Now it occurred to her that the egg might be an amplifier of some kind.

She closed her right hand around the egg and continued holding the lead with her left. She waited. Brow growing damp, she urged her heart to beat more furiously.

50 volts.

"Come on," she groused. Lucy wanted to feel the same elation as in her dream. She didn't want to be scared anymore. Of herself. Of anything.

55 volts. She tightened her grip on the Tesla Egg.

Show me what you can do.

The faint evergreen glow became a blazing fire, consuming her forearms, traveling to her shoulders, and then her head. The world became tinted in shades of green.

Lucy's limbs quaked but she didn't let go. Exhilaration suffused every nerve ending.

300 volts.

More. Her teeth ached but she wanted more. Outside, the sky darkened, another storm rolling in.

The needle swung toward the edge of the scale but Lucy could no longer focus her eyes sufficiently to get an accurate reading.

Don't hold back.

An acrid smell filled her nostrils. Plastic. Scorched plastic.

Thunder shook the garage at the same instant and sparks rained down from above. The lightbulb had burst. Lucy crouched down instinctively, dropping the wires to cover her face. She panted against her knees, back aching. She hadn't wanted to stop.

Holy frak. Had she just blown the fuse box?

After a minute or two, Lucy recovered enough to push to the balls of her feet. Her gaze targeted the voltage meter.

Melted.

But that would mean . . . Lucy and the Tesla Egg had produced a lot more than a thousand volts. She struggled to catch her breath.

Lucy truly *was* dangerous.

And the most dangerous thing was that part of her didn't care.

THAT GIRL IS POISON

When Lucy woke up the following day, the power was still out.

She hadn't just blown all the fuses in her house—she'd caused a streetwide blackout. In a lucky break, the storm had provided the ideal cover for the surge that fried the mains.

With a yawn, she finger-combed her hair and pulled her unicorn dancing in the rain T-shirt over a pair of leggings. Although a DANGER: HIGH VOLTAGE sign would have been more appropriate. She tugged a loose thread from the seam.

Why hadn't Lucy experienced a seizure or lost consciousness with a thousand volts rushing through her? Biology dictated that not only should she have seized, her heart should have stopped, and Lucy should be very much dead. Not that she was looking a gift horse in the mouth. But she had a theory.

When Lucy was holding the wires, she'd had this sense of pushing the energy outward, like water spraying from a firehouse, and her whole being quivered with what she could only describe as euphoria. By contrast, the two previous incidents when Lucy had lost consciousness— at the New Yorker Hotel and in the physics lab—it had felt more like the energy was trapped, burning her up from the inside.

Somehow Lucy had to learn how to control the direction of the energy, push it out of her before the inevitable happened and it boiled her alive. But how was she going to do that on command? Now would be the time for some kind of wizened electrical Merlin to show up. That's what would happen in the fantasy novels Claudia loved so much.

She yawned again. Lucy could go for one of her bestie's highly caffeinated concoctions in a major way. Opening her bedroom door, a parcel blocked her path. Hmm.

Lucy crouched down and removed the gift card attached to the front. *Sorry I left without saying goodbye. See you soon, kiddo. Love, Dad*

She sucked in a breath. Her father's handwriting was crisp and clipped. The script of someone who'd spent decades taking lab notes. What would his reaction be if he knew his daughter had caused a neighborhood blackout?

Lucy thought back to the writing on the back of the fateful photograph. Those letters were also square but more slanted. Her mother always wrote in cursive: elegant, controlled loops. Who had written on the back of that photo? And why? She'd been so focused on understanding her new symptoms that she'd nearly forgotten about what had sent her to the New Yorker Hotel in the first place.

Lucy dropped her gaze to the rectangular box and, curiosity piqued, ripped off the blue wrapping paper. A picture of a robot dog wagging its tail greeted her. The cardboard was covered in Japanese kanji.

Lucy's mouth pulled upward. She'd wanted one of these for a while. Flipping the box over, she found instructions in English. It was a DIY kit.

Dr. Victor Phelps subscribed to the "teach a man to fish" philosophy and believed if you made something yourself, you appreciated it more. She doubted Schrödinger would truly appreciate an animatronic Fido running around the house, but she'd seen neither hide nor hair of the cat for days. Her former feline companion had detected there was something seriously off with Lucy even if nobody else could.

Would it ever be possible for Lucy to turn a metaphysical dial and zap the robot dog just enough to bring it to life without liquefying its circuits?

Wait. What was she even thinking? She should be focused on trying to get rid of her electrical freakiness, not trying to master it.

There was only one avenue of experimentation she hadn't yet explored: medical science. Most of the time she dreaded them, but maybe she was due for a checkup with Dr. Rosen. If her new abilities had a physical manifestation in her brain, an EEG—electroencephalogram—should pick it up. She couldn't risk an MRI scan, however, because that was basically a giant magnet.

And so was Lucy.

Before she considered spilling the beans to her parents, she wanted to be in possession of all the possible evidence, present them with a complete data set. As well as a cohesive argument as to why she should still be allowed to attend college.

"Lucy? Are you up?" Her mom's voice carried down from the attic, cutting into her speculation.

She set the box down on her bed, then padded down the hallway and hoisted herself up the ladder to the study. At the top, she was overpowered by a peppermint fog. Uh-oh. There was no Beethoven today because of the power outage, but there was a steaming mug of peppermint tea on her mother's desk next to the battery-operated kettle they brought on camping trips.

Definitely not her first mug of the day.

Lucy skimmed her mother's profile. A pencil was gripped between her teeth, her cheeks were sunken, and she was wearing the same clothes as the day before. She'd seen her mom hyperfocused on a book deadline before, but not like this. Strategically positioned on a bookshelf was an industrial-strength flashlight aimed at the manuscript over which her mom was hunched.

Had she been up all night?

"Mom?" Lucy said, hesitant.

Her head snapped in Lucy's direction and she spit out the pencil.

"Oh. It *was* you," said her mother as if she hadn't summoned her. Who else would it be? "You found the gift?"

Lucy nodded. "Not sure Schrödinger will approve."

"Perhaps not." A weak laugh. "Your dad thought you'd like it. He's going to be in Tokyo at least another week."

"Another week? This is a record. Even for him."

Her mom made a dismissive hand motion. "One of their investors is being difficult." She took a sip from the mug on her desk. "But don't worry, your father can be very persuasive."

"I'm not worried," Lucy said, crossing toward her. Not exactly. Her father's prolonged absence couldn't be connected to her discovery of Tesla's lab. He had no way of knowing what she'd found before he left. Nobody knew. Still. Her pulse quickened.

"Do you know what the project is they're trying to fund?" she asked, snatching the scarab figurine from the filing cabinet. She began turning it over between her fingers, and her mom stiffened. Lucy put it back where she found it.

"You know your father," said her mom. "He has so many deals in the works. It's hard to keep track."

"Anything to do with alternative energy?" she persisted.

"Maybe. Why?"

"Oh, no reason. Just interested." Lucy twisted the hem of her T-shirt. If she pushed this line of questioning any further, her mother would ferret out her secrets. A diversionary tactic was required.

"How's *your* work going, Mom?" she asked, pointing at the facsimile open on the desk.

Professor Elaine Phelps lowered a perfectly sculpted eyebrow.

"You're not usually interested in my research."

"That's not true," Lucy protested. Okay, it was mostly true. She'd adopted her father's anti–liberal arts prejudice long ago. It wasn't like Lucy didn't enjoy literature; it just didn't have the same capacity to change the world as science.

She perched against her mother's desk to take a closer look.

"This is alchemy, isn't it?"

Her mom sat up straighter than if Lucy had sent several hundred volts through her, gaze sharpening to a knife-point.

"What makes you say that?"

Lucy pitied the student who claimed the dog ate his homework. She squirmed on the spot. "I just . . . some reading I've been doing for my independent-study project. There was a chapter about alchemy. I recognized some of the symbols from your manuscript . . ." She trailed off. Lucy hated lying to her mom but it seemed like a bad idea to mention her new teaching assistant had a tattoo. Or that she'd seen it.

"Oh, of course." Her mother's shoulders relaxed. "Which symbols?"

Lucy swallowed. "Um, one was an eight-pointed star."

"And what did you learn about it?"

Crap. Neither of her parents was the type to spoon-feed her the answers. She wished she'd been brave enough to ask Ravi more about it.

"Creation. It means creation," Lucy replied haltingly as she recalled brushing her fingertips against his wrist.

Her mom leaned back in the swivel chair and crossed her arms.

"Creation, yes. More specifically, transmutation."

"Transmutation? Like turning lead into gold?" Lucy snorted. "Dad always says alchemists were charlatans."

"Does he? Charlatans? That sounds like your father." A low laugh rattled in her mother's throat. "He's very practical minded," she said with fondness. *He's a scientist,* Lucy wanted to defend him, but decided against interrupting. "Alchemists weren't just interested in goldmaking. They were interested in all chemical processes."

"So you're translating a textbook?"

Another low laugh. "Not quite." Lucy scooped up the scarab from the cabinet once more and her mother took it from her hands. "The scarab represents creation. The alchemists were interested in the transformative processes of life." She gave the turquoise stone an indulgent smile.

Funny how Lucy had seen the beetle for years and never given it a second thought. There had been a wistfulness in Ravi's voice when he'd spoken about transformation. What had happened in his life that drew him to alchemy?

"Why the scarab?" Lucy asked.

Her mom glanced up from the stone beetle, a faraway look on her face, and Lucy watched her put on her professor cap.

"As I imagine you read, alchemy originated in Egypt, where the scarab was considered a sacred animal." She paused, and Lucy nodded. "The scarab was revered because the Egyptians erroneously believed female beetles could reproduce on their own, like their god Atum."

She passed the figurine back to Lucy. "Alexander the Great conquered Egypt and the oldest extant alchemical texts are therefore of Greco-Egyptian origin. However, they only survived because of Arabic scholars who translated the ancient texts when they conquered Alexandria."

It always amazed Lucy how long her mother could lecture without taking a breath.

"I didn't think you were interested in science," she said, and her mom responded by pressing her lips into a line.

"The Ancient Greeks didn't distinguish science from philosophy."

Hmm. Tapping the corner of the manuscript, Lucy said, "So this is philosophy?"

"This is the *Pharmakon of Kleopatra*." Her mom sighed, scrubbing the heels of her hands against her eyes. They were red and tired. "A fool's errand. Worse than fool's gold."

"*The* Cleopatra?"

Exhaustion bled through her mother's laugh. "No, not the femme fatale. The alchemist. She lived in the third century and was said to be one of the four female alchemists who could create a philosopher's stone."

Lucy had never heard of female alchemists, but it would be impossible to grow up with a Potterhead best friend and not know the philosopher's stone was the mythical transmutation agent that would transform base metals into gold.

"And a *pharmakon*?"

"*Pharmakon* is a fancy word for medicine—or poison. I'm inclined to view it as a poison at this point."

Lucy dashed her mom a quizzical glance.

"The *Pharmakon of Kleopatra* is her only remaining text. In theory, it contains the secret to her philosopher's stone, except no one has ever been able to successfully translate it. Even Newton tried and failed."

"Wow."

Lucy hadn't realized Sir Isaac Newton, the father of modern physics himself, was so interested in alchemy. Apparently, Ravi was right about proper scientists being alchemists. And the transformation of plasma wasn't so different from transmutation, she supposed.

Inching closer, wetting her lips, Lucy began flicking through the facsimile. Half of the pages were filled with hand-drawn illustrations of the cosmos or the ocean bordered in gold leaf. She couldn't fathom the number of hours it must have taken to complete the excruciating detail of each miniature, from the scales on the fish to the tails of the shooting stars. The facing pages were scattered with the Greek letters and hieroglyphs Lucy had spotted the last time, as well as what she presumed were other alchemical symbols. She zipped her eyes across the lines but failed to deduce any patterns. It was totally random. Almost as if . . .

"It needs a cipher!" Lucy exclaimed, getting the same buzz in her chest as when solving a tricky calculus problem set.

Her mom touched Lucy's elbow in a rare show of emotion, a smile spreading across her face.

"Exactly. Part of the cipher was discovered within a different Medieval Latin text from the thirteenth century. Regrettably, it's not enough."

Liber Librum Aperit. Lucy bit her lips together. Hard. Her mother was literally trying to use one book to open another. It had to be a coincidence.

Keeping her eyes trained on the folios, Lucy said, "This doesn't seem like your usual research."

"You're not wrong. I blame too many glasses of wine at the last annual Antiquities Congress."

Lucy afforded her mom a disbelieving side-eye. Professor Elaine Phelps would never lose a modicum of composure at an academic conference, and they both knew it.

"I like a challenge," her mother admitted. "In Greco-Roman Egypt, chemistry was dominated by women, most of whom created perfumes and cosmetics. I became interested in the role of women in science in the ancient world."

She sipped her tea and allowed her attention to wander back to the manuscript. "Once a colleague showed me the *Pharmakon*, I was enthralled." There was a gleam in her mom's eyes that made her seem not girlish, but definitely younger, less worn-out. "A linguistic Rubik's Cube. I couldn't resist."

For once, Lucy saw the appeal of her mother's research. She swallowed again, chest growing tight.

"Why would Kleopatra turn her formula into a riddle?" she wondered aloud. "Scientists normally want their students to be able to replicate their experiments."

Her mother regarded Lucy with a sphinxlike expression, listing her head to the side. "Professional rivalry, perhaps," she suggested after a moment or two. "Also fear of persecution. In Kleopatra's time, the emperor Diocletian—and many after him—persecuted the alchemists, burning their works. Sometimes burning the alchemists as well, accusing them of witchcraft."

Lucy shuddered. She probably would have been tied to a stake right beside Kleopatra.

Her mom leaned her face close to Lucy's as she turned the page. "Some scholars believe the cipher is hidden in the manuscript illuminations," she continued. "Many alchemists hid their formulas in allegorical dreams or visions. Often they took the form of a dreamer wandering around a garden."

"*Garden?*" Lucy choked out, glad her mom couldn't see her face.

There was the soft shushing of paper on paper and then Lucy was confronted with an intricately painted jungle garden scene. Jewel-green palm fronds, tangerine blossoms. And in the center, looming over the page, was a supernaturally large orchid plant. The exact same shade of magenta as in her dream.

"The Flower of Life," her mother explained. "Six symmetrical petals, like a hexagon. It features in many alchemical texts. They believed it was part of a sacred geometry that revealed the secrets of the universe."

Lucy lurched back, afraid to set the book on fire. Her heartbeat stampeded in her ears. How was this possible? How could Lucy have dreamed something from a book she'd never seen? And if Lucy had set the Flower of Life alight—did that mean Lucy brought death?

"Lucy?" Her mom launched to her feet. "Are you feeling well? You're white as a sheet." She reached out to check her daughter's temperature but Lucy staggered farther back, out of her grasp.

"I . . . I think I must have eaten something funny."

Her mother took another step, hands on hip. "*Lu—*"

"Really, Mom. Stop. I'll go find some Tums."

A resigned huff. "All right, honey. I'll check on you later."

"Thanks." Guilt pricked Lucy as she rocketed down the stairs.

She needed space to breathe. To think. Unlike Kleopatra's *pharmakon*, however, Lucy was coming to the conclusion that she was a code without a cipher.

STRANGE FREQUENCIES

Saturday morning at the Gallery was like rush hour at Grand Central Station.

Lucy might need a spyglass to spot her friend among the throng of hungover coeds getting their java jolts, gym rats indulging in a post-workout carb fest, and grumpy old men hiding behind copies of the *New York Times*. Eyes peeled, Lucy picked her way around a slapdash cushion fort constructed by a pair of bored but highly sugared middle school boys. *Ugh.* This whole week had been one long obstacle course.

Ravi had asked Lucy several times to give him new calculations for the Voltaic pile and to schedule another trial run, but she'd managed to put him off. Meanwhile, she and Cole had only exchanged furtive glances across hallways and classrooms since she'd seen his Megan slideshow.

She didn't know if that meant they were officially broken up or what, but she was also too afraid to ask. Afraid for Cole. Lucy didn't want to hotwire her boyfriend.

Much.

She was more angry than sad when she thought about the ambiguous state of their relationship, and she didn't know what that meant. Or how she felt about it.

Plus, she had bigger problems.

Lucy's gaze skidded to a halt as she took in the new exhibition lining the walls of the café. Huge black-and-white flowers taken with a macro lens loomed in front of her. Hauntingly beautiful. Especially the ones flecked with crystalline raindrops.

Message received, universe.

Hard as she tried, Lucy couldn't ignore the fact that her mom was decoding an almost two-thousand-year-old manuscript whose illuminations resembled Lucy's dreams. Which would be strange enough if Lucy hadn't also become a human Taser.

Not that she truly believed the universe was taking an interest in her. Tesla would have, though. Lucy had stayed up into the wee hours of the night finishing the *Current Wars* book. Later in life, Tesla became obsessed with the notion that everyone and everything on the planet had its own unique frequency, like radio waves. If you could tune yourself to the same frequency, he believed you could receive psychic messages.

It was sad that such a genius had clearly gone senile.

A Mommy & Me group had laid siege to Lucy's preferred velvet sofa, forcing her to shimmy her way through a barricade of strollers. She rubbed her temples. Lucy suspected the alchemists would also have believed in Tesla's strange frequencies.

She'd done a little Googling on Kleopatra's manuscript herself and, by falling down the black holes of New Age websites, she'd discovered the Enigma code breakers had taken a stab at it and that Leonardo da Vinci explored the Flower of Life in his work.

How much of it did Ravi actually believe?

Lucy patted her pocket, ensuring the Tesla Egg was still there. As long as it didn't make direct contact with her skin, it seemed harmless, and she'd started carrying it around like a security blanket. Maybe because it was the only tangible proof that, unlike Tesla, Lucy hadn't lost her grip on reality. Yet.

She couldn't be late for Dr. Rosen.

Elbowing her way to the counter, she deflected death glares from other customers.

"Claudia?" she asked when she finally caught the eye of a harried barista wearing a paint-speckled baseball cap. His answer was a gruff, "Out back," glancing at the caffeine-starved horde with true fear. The café was about to be overrun. It wasn't like Claudia to abandon ship.

Lucy thanked him and edged away slowly toward the side exit. Yes, she could have simply texted her friend to cover her but, truth be told, Lucy was more nervous about her visit to Dr. Rosen than she wanted to admit. What she wanted was a best-friend hug.

As the door opened into the parking lot, Lucy saw that Claudia hadn't abandoned ship. Not quite. Pressed against the Mystery Minivan, fingers tangled in Jess's vaguely porcupine-esque hair, Claudia had a blissfully content smile on her face.

Lucy hated to interrupt, but . . . *Cough, cough.*

It took a few moments to penetrate their love bubble.

Finally focusing, Claudia's eyes lit behind heavy lids. "Minnie Mouse! What's my favorite person doing here?" Then she squeezed Jess's waist. "Second favorite." She dropped her voice, pretending it was a secret, and Lucy dismissed a prick of jealousy.

Jess pivoted to face her, taking Claudia's hand. Possessive much?

"Hey," she said. "I'm Jess." Today she was dressed in a 1950s-style cocktail frock accessorized with strands of chunky green beads. Claudia sported the *Ceci n'est pas une pipe* T-shirt that Jess had been wearing the day they met. Oh my. Things were moving fast.

"Best friend, meet girlfriend," Claudia said with a giggle. "Girlfriend, best friend."

Girlfriend? Already?

Without thinking, Lucy whipped out the egg and started flipping it over in her hand. "Hey," she said back, smiling as big as she could. "Lucy. No mouse ears or anything." She cast a fake glare at her friend.

"You here for a Frosty or a Rudolph?"

Jess arched an eyebrow and Claudia explained about Lucy's Christmas coffee predilections. "Never fear, I'll make you a Mrs. Claus," Claudia assured her with a smooch.

"What's that?"

Claudia whispered something in her ear and Jess grinned a mile wide.

Lucy had been on the outside looking in plenty of times in her life. Just never with Claudia. She clutched the egg tighter.

"Anyway," Lucy interjected. "I'm headed to the city. Could you cover with my mom if she calls? I should be back by dinnertime."

"No problemo. Whatcha up to?"

She cut a glance at Jess. No reason to divulge all her secrets in front of a stranger.

"There's a new exhibition at the Natural History Museum."

"I hope you've got a membership card." Claudia wrinkled her nose, observing Lucy shrewdly enough to make her fidget. "Fine, fine," her friend said, backing off. "I just hope you've had time to work on your lighting designs."

Oh. *Crap.* Lucy had totally blanked.

"I'm sure I'll be inspired at the planetarium."

"Meeting's next Thursday."

"I hadn't forgotten," Lucy lied smoothly.

"Cutest dictator ever," Jess said with affection, dashing Claudia a kiss. Claudia gazed back adoringly. Despite herself, Lucy appreciated the save.

"Hey, you don't survive with three older brothers by being demure."

"You could never be demure, Clauds."

"Amen," Jess agreed, and winked at Lucy.

"I didn't introduce you two so you could gang up on me."

"Too late," Lucy said. She relaxed her grip on the egg and tucked it away. "Well, I'm going to miss my train."

"Have fun," Jess told her. This time her smile was genuinely friendly. She pressed a warm hand to Lucy's shoulder, gracing her with European-style kisses on either cheek, and a wave of guilt swept over Lucy. Her initial claws-out approach had been unwarranted. Jess seemed nice, even if Lucy was intimidated by her stylish, artsy ways.

"You too." Lucy would give her the benefit of the doubt. If she hurt

Claudia, however, she'd make her pay. The Best Friend Code mandated no less.

"Oh, we will."

The lovebirds exchanged a from-here-to-eternity glance and Lucy's goodbyes were lost as they disappeared back into their bubble. Maybe Tesla hadn't been entirely wrong. Those two were definitely on the same wavelength. And the upside to Claudia walking on air was that she wouldn't be wondering too hard about where in Manhattan Lucy was really going.

Or why.

WE'RE ALL MAD HERE

Rushing to catch the 6 train at Grand Central, Lucy had passed by the Whispering Gallery. *Give me an answer*, she'd pleaded.

But Dr. Rosen didn't have any.

Lucy should have been glad he'd found nothing out of the ordinary during his examination. She wasn't. Crossing the avenue from his office, a feeling of helplessness pervaded her as she entered Central Park. At least there was still time to walk to the West Side and catch a show at the planetarium. That way the trip wouldn't be a total bust, and Lucy wouldn't be a total liar.

She strolled past the Metropolitan Museum of Art and her gaze was attracted to the sunlight glittering off the glass wall that encased the Temple of Dendur. One advantage to being homeschooled was that her classroom could be anywhere and everywhere. Lucy had spent many hours in the Greco-Roman and Egyptology wings of the Met with her mom. She remembered that the Temple of Dendur had been built by a Roman governor of Egypt. Had he ruled at the time of Kleopatra?

There was probably as much chance of deciphering the *Pharmakon* as figuring out what was wrong with her. Lucy might as well ask a Magic 8-Ball. Although with her track record, the answer would be *Try Again Later*.

Dr. Rosen had performed the standard EEG to analyze the electrical signals produced by her brain. Since she was little, Lucy had undergone hundreds of them. They didn't make her anxious, but today was different. As the electrodes were connected to her scalp, Lucy had dredged up all of her most painfully awkward experiences, part of her hoping to short out the EEG machine.

Nothing.

Could her ability to produce electricity be directly related to touch? Skin contact? Or was the machine simply not sensitive enough to note the changes taking place in Lucy's brain?

She should have charbroiled her gray matter when she'd shot a thousand volts from her fingertips. The fact that she hadn't must mean that her brain waves were functioning in an abnormal way. Hypothesis: however the waves were behaving wasn't detectable by a machine designed for normal human brain patterns. Conclusion: Lucy no longer possessed a human brain?

She exhaled, feeling wrung out.

The only unusual thing about her trip as far as Dr. Rosen was concerned was the fact that she'd come alone.

"Is your mother in the waiting room?" he'd asked, pushing his wire-rimmed spectacles up the bridge of his nose.

"No. I came on my own." Pause. "Dr. Rosen, since I'm eighteen now, doesn't that mean you don't have to share my medical reports with my parents?"

He'd slanted forward, resting his elbows on his leather armchair.

"That's right. Although if you're still on their insurance, they'll see you've been for a visit. And which tests were ordered."

Lucy nodded. She'd deal with that later. For now, her dad was MIA and her mom was neck deep in hieroglyphs.

The doctor had dismissed her with a grandfatherly smile, instructing Lucy to up her medication by half a tablet, and said he'd see her in six months.

Which left her feeling more lost than ever. Lucy trudged downtown toward the Alice in Wonderland statue that overlooked the sailboat pond. If only there were a magic potion she could take to turn back the clock so that she'd never entered Tesla's lab.

Lucy circled the pond slowly, watching the ripples left by the toy ships. If she jumped into the water and swam across, she'd leave a similar pattern in her wake. The formula that explained the waves was constant. Physics was supposed to be constant. *Her* constant.

And yet, here she was, defying all of its laws.

Her eyes shifted back toward the gleaming bronze Alice surrounded by her posse: the Mad Hatter, the White Rabbit, the Cheshire Cat. A single tear welled at the corner of her eye and she was powerless to stop it.

"Lucy?"

She pivoted toward the voice. "Ravi?"

Frak my life. Discreetly, she dabbed away the tear.

"We've got to stop meeting like this." He laughed, closing the short distance between them and, for a moment, all Lucy could concentrate on was his smile. A ray of light fell across his lips. Solar flares burst on Lucy's cheeks as he came to a stop beside her.

"What are you doing here?" she asked, her question almost an accusation.

"I like the boats."

Lucy focused intently on a boat with a yellow sail bobbing up and down, but her body was acutely aware of his proximity.

"My boarding school was by the sea," said Ravi. "Sometimes I miss the crash of the surf." His voice was steady. And yet something about his lilt made his words intimate, almost a confession. The ten million other people in New York City ceased to exist.

"I like the ripples," she told him. "There's something calming about them."

Ravi tilted his head and the way he looked at her reminded Lucy of a scientist with a puzzle to solve.

"Something on your mind?" he asked.

Her heart stuttered. Maybe it was the lack of answers provided by Dr. Rosen, or the fact that her life already seemed to be spinning out of control but Lucy found herself unable—or unwilling—to deflect the question.

"I came into Manhattan to see my neurologist," she began. "I have epilepsy. It's why I didn't enter any science fairs. Stress can be a trigger. It's also why my parents homeschooled me," she continued in a rush. "The doctors have never been able to give me a complete diagnosis. I don't fit the mold of any standard syndromes. I guess I broke it." Lucy snorted. "*I'm* too breakable."

The admission left her breathless.

What seemed like an eternity of silence followed. Then Ravi put a hand on Lucy's shoulder, and the most extraordinary feeling of melting consumed her.

"I think you're a lot of things, Lucinda. Breakable isn't one of them."

She peered up at him. *Lucinda*. Ravi made her sound like someone else. A fierce, strong woman.

"Did you get bad news today?" he asked. "From the doctor?"

"No news."

"No news is generally good news, right?"

"Right." She glanced away.

"When you passed out—" Ravi started and Lucy cut him off.

"It wasn't a seizure." Oh, how Lucy wished it were that simple. "But if my parents found out, my chances of *ever* driving a car would disappear."

"Your parents are very protective."

Lucy exhaled through her nose and rolled her eyes. "You don't know the half of it. I had to beg them to let me attend high school—to just let me be normal for once. Although I guess I'll always be an outsider."

At that moment, Ravi seemed to realize his hand was still on Lucy's shoulder and he dropped it to his side. *Smooth*. Why had she said that?

"I'm not sure normal exists," Ravi said softly. "But I do know something about being an outsider."

"You mean here in the land of barbarians?" Lucy said with a half smile, trying to dig herself out of the conversational hole.

"No." Swift shake of the head. "No, I mean at school. It wasn't easy being the only brown kid in my year." He set his jaw. "I still can't hear the words *Slumdog Millionaire* without cringing." There was an unfamiliar roughness to his voice as he shifted his gaze back to the boats.

Lucy inhaled sharply. "That's terrible. I'm sorry, Ravi." She didn't know what else to say. Her experience of being an outsider was completely different from his. Without her helmet, Lucy's difference was invisible. She didn't want to compare.

Ravi shrugged. "People can be wankers." He released a strained laugh. "Especially in school."

"When you said you ended up in the infirmary a lot from rugby—that was why," Lucy realized. "People really do suck." She was grateful for Claudia all over again.

"Yeah." He turned his face toward her, a faint red tinge to his cheeks. "But school doesn't last forever and, in my experience, leading the life you want to lead is the best revenge against the wankers."

"Revenge against the wankers. I like that."

The breeze picked up, whipping a curl across her eyes and Ravi brushed it away, his hand hovering right above her cheek. Lucy shouldn't be so eager for his touch. She focused all of her mental energy on not sending any non-metaphysical sparks his way.

"And are you doing that?" Lucy asked. "Leading the life you want?"

"Right now?"

She swallowed. "Here, I mean. In the States?"

Ravi coughed and shoved his hand in the pocket of his corduroy jacket awkwardly. "I suppose I am." He coughed again. "Which direction were you headed?"

Lucy had no desire to move from this very spot, but . . . "West Side," she finally replied.

Ravi checked his watch. "I have some time," he said. "I could walk you, if you want?"

"That'd be great." She tried not to let show just *how* great on her face.

He smiled. "Which way? I'm the tourist here." Lucy shrugged and then indicated where the sun was just beginning to make its leisurely descent. Ravi laughed. "Good guess," he said.

"I was never a Girl Scout. But I do my best."

They walked side by side, perhaps closer than strictly necessary, and a canopy of leaves cast them in dappled shadows. Central Park was forty miles, give or take, from Eaton High, but it might as well be the moon.

And far, far away from Cole.

"So did you come into the city to be a tourist?" Lucy asked Ravi, restarting the conversation. "It's definitely more exciting than Eaton."

"Partially, although Eaton has its charms," he said, not quite glancing at her, and Lucy felt a small hitch in her chest.

Stupid. He doesn't mean you.

"I have family visiting from the UK, actually," he said.

"Your parents?"

"*Er*, no." Ravi paused, pursed his lips. "They're dead."

Foot. Mouth. Repeat.

"Oh, *oh*—I-I'm so sorry," Lucy said, voice fading to a whisper. She touched two fingers to the back of his hand. Ravi's shoulders stiffened but he didn't pull away, and a swell of melancholy rushed through her from the point of contact.

"Thanks," he said. Shadows from the trees veiled his eyes, making them unreadable. "Didn't mean that to come out so ominous." A smile hovered on his lips, equal parts uncertain, flirty, and wistful. "It was a long time ago." He kicked a twig from the trail. "I'm meeting my godfather for dinner."

They rounded a boulder and the path narrowed, their hips bumping together.

"You'd like Professor T," he told Lucy, eyes pointed forward. "He took me under his wing after my parents were killed."

Killed? So many questions whirled in Lucy's mind. "You call him Professor?" was the one she settled on, trying not to put another foot wrong.

"It's hard to call a bloke with a Nobel anything but Professor."

"A Nobel Prize?" Awe shaded her voice. Winning a Nobel was the stuff of Lucy's wildest dreams.

Sheer pride shone on Ravi's face. "For quantum biology. Professor Tarquin Weston-Jones."

"I see why you call him Professor T."

"It's quite the mouthful, to be fair." He worked his jaw and his expression grew somber. "But he saved my life."

Lucy held her breath, waiting for him to finish the story. It had become so still that the only sound was the wind through the trees. Who knew there could be such peace in the middle of Manhattan?

"My parents were both biologists. They worked in Professor T's research group at Cambridge." Ravi tugged on his jacket collar, eyes straight ahead. "I used to do my homework in the lab after school." The muscles in his neck tightened as he explained, "I was there when the fire broke out."

"How old were you?"

"Nine."

Lucy reached out but stopped short of touching him again. She couldn't even imagine what that would be like. As much as she resented her parents' constant monitoring, she'd never want to lose them. Her troubles suddenly seemed trivial compared with being orphaned.

"I heard this blast. Then there was so much smoke. I tried to find them but I couldn't see anything." His eyes were unfocused now, as if he were watching the scene play out in front of him. "Somehow Professor T found me. Got me out."

"What happened?" she asked gently.

"No one knows for certain. It could have been an accident. It could have been terrorism."

Ravi crooked his neck at her, taking in the shock she couldn't conceal.

"They were working on gene therapy," he said. "It has its opponents." His attempt at a neutral shrug was belied by the anger in his eyes. Lucy realized she'd never seen him without his glasses before. It was almost too tempting to stroke his brow.

He scrubbed a hand over his face. "It's a beautiful day," he said, a false lightness underpinning his words. "No sense dwelling in the past."

Lucy's heart ached for him. Not being sure why your parents were killed—or by whom. Never getting answers. Being bullied and alone at boarding school.

"Thanks for telling me," she said. "For trusting me. And I'm sorry if I said the wrong thing. I hate when people act like epilepsy is my defining characteristic. I wouldn't want you to think that's how I see you."

Ravi lifted a wry eyebrow. "Poor orphan boy?"

"Yeah. I mean, *no*."

He laughed. Then, more seriously, he said, "You didn't say anything wrong. There's no right thing to say. But you didn't say anything wrong." The corner of his mouth tilted upward again. "We Brits aren't renowned for sharing our feelings. It must be your American influence."

"I'm glad. Because *I*—I like getting to know you, Ravi."

"Me too, Lucy. I hope we can try that experiment again."

She nodded as her stomach churned. Ravi was being so honest with her that Lucy hated herself a little for not being totally honest with him. Maybe he was the one person who could help her investigate her abilities without thinking she needed to be protected from herself?

Lucy was perilously close to unburdening herself when they followed another bend in the path and her breath buckled in her throat.

A postcard-perfect view of New York greeted them. Skyscrapers provided the backdrop to a lake sprinkled with couples in rowboats. Cumulus clouds hung in a pastel-blue sky, their undersides glowing with a hint of apricot.

This is where I want to be. Not Gilbert College.

Lucy hadn't realized it until this moment. She loved her parents, but they were so afraid for her to have dreams of her own.

She stole a sideways glance at Ravi. Which life *did* she want to lead?

A long, almost medieval-style bridge covered the expanse of water. Lucy was sure she'd seen it in the rom-coms Claudia streamed when it was her turn to pick their sleepover movie.

"It's not the Serpentine," Ravi noted, "but it is impressive."

"The Serpentine?"

"A lake in London. Hyde Park."

"Sounds unfriendly."

"Only if you can't swim," he said with a laugh. "Shall we?" He motioned toward the bridge.

"We shall," she agreed, and Ravi grinned at her best Mary Poppins impression.

Fighting a furious blush, Lucy admired the interlocking discs that comprised the length of the stone bridge. Her pulse skipped as her eyes caught on the flower shape at the center of each. Carefully she counted each petal. Five, not six. Only five petals. It wasn't a Flower of Life. It wasn't.

Her shoulders sagged with relief. She hadn't noticed they'd come to a stop at the midpoint of the bridge until Ravi asked, "What is it?"

"Oh, I was just counting the semicircles," she said, his scrutiny palpable. "I like patterns." Which wasn't a lie.

"So do I. Tessellation is the topic I proposed for my Ph.D."

"Tessellation?"

"Something along the lines of M. C. Escher's drawings. Repeated geometric shapes without gaps or overlaps. They occur in nature—like honeycombs."

"You're doing a Ph.D.?"

His lips tightened microscopically. "Maybe. I've been offered a place to stay at the maths department at Cambridge."

Her stomach shouldn't be plummeting at the thought of Ravi going back to England. That was where he lived. *Gah.*

"Why tessellation?" Lucy asked.

"Because it can be used to understand more than the three dimensions of our universe. There's more to everything than meets the eye," he said, catching hers.

"Like sacred geometry?" She gulped.

"That's one way to look at it. Most mathematicians call it hyperbolic geometry. It's related to the theory of special relativity."

Another gulp. "As in the space-time continuum?"

"Precisely!" The enthusiasm in his voice was infectious. It infected Lucy, anyway. He leaned closer to her and he smelled good. Musky.

Get a grip, Luce.

"Have you considered studying maths further at uni?" he asked.

"I don't know." She worried her lower lip, praying he couldn't sense her distraction. There was scarcely an inch between their mouths.

"I prefer experimental to theoretical physics," she said. "I like to get my hands dirty."

Wow. That had come out unexpectedly sultry.

Before she could babble anything resembling a retraction, a heavy shoulder knocked into her, sending her to her knees. But it wasn't the force of the collision that made Lucy lose her balance. It was the choking sensation, like toxic sludge clogging her lungs. Ravi grabbed her upper arms, searching her face, and the tingly heat he provoked battled against the sludge.

"My bag," Lucy gasped. "He's got my bag."

She jutted her chin toward a thickly muscled figure sprinting across to the other side of the park with her messenger bag.

"Stay here," Ravi commanded. His tone was far more imperious than Lucy would have thought the easygoing sci-fi geek capable. As was the flash of absolute rage that crossed his face.

He set after the thief at a pace that easily would have challenged Cole. Also unexpected. Once the choking sensation abated, Lucy pushed to her feet, calling after him to stop. Ravi's gallantry was swoon-worthy, to be sure, but her wallet and phone weren't worth getting hurt over.

Either Ravi didn't hear her or he didn't want to give up his pursuit.

She stumbled forward a couple steps. What was going on with her? She'd have to add the toxic gagging response to her list of symptoms. Fantastic.

A couple minutes later, Ravi trotted back to meet her at the far end of the bridge. He was muttering a number of British profanities like "tosser," "bloody," and "bollocks" that Lucy found highly amusing despite having been robbed.

"I wish I could say I challenged the wastrel to a duel," Ravi said, holding out Lucy's bag. "Truth is he dropped it on the ground and kept running. No heroics involved."

"I wouldn't say that."

His brow remained creased. "See if anything is missing."

Lucy raked through the bag. Phone? Check. Wallet? Check. Everything was there except . . .

Oh no.

The Tesla Egg.

She'd put it in her bag during the EEG so it wouldn't disrupt the machine.

Ravi watched her face fall. "What is it?"

"It's stupid, really. Just this . . . family heirloom." That sounded believable.

"What kind of heirloom?"

"An egg?"

He regarded her strangely. "An egg?"

"Not an actual egg. A bronze one." She blew out a breath. "Doesn't matter. It's not worth anything to anyone but me." Lucy figured that was probably true.

"I'm so sorry this happened." There was pain—no, guilt—in his voice.

"Don't be. Nobody expects the Spanish Inquisition, right?"

"Our chief weapon is surprise," Ravi quoted back at her. "Didn't realize *Monty Python* was so popular over here." Amusement laced his words. "Our indoctrination will soon be complete."

Lucy snort-laughed, jabbing him on the shoulder. Their eyes met and her laughter cut off abruptly as the intensity of his gaze became tangible. Her hand slid tentatively through the air, reaching for his cheek but changed course at the last second and landed on his shoulder.

Soberly, she told him, "I didn't care about my bag. I was worried about you."

"I thought I told you not to worry about me."

She crossed her arms, stepping backward. "Well, I *do*. I mean, I was. Worried. Not all the time. Just now."

"Thank you," Ravi said, flushing slightly, and held out an arm. "Can

I escort you wherever you're going before I meet Professor T? There seem to be scoundrels about."

"You don't think I can handle myself around scoundrels?" she said, half teasing.

"I think you can do anything you set your mind to, Lucinda. But," Ravi added, "I'm rather enjoying your company."

The tenderness in his statement compelled Lucy to accept his offer. Lightness spread through her as she looped her arm through his. The same weightlessness she'd experienced in her dreams. Right before she set the Flower of Life on fire.

Only she wasn't dreaming now.

HURTS SO GOOD

"Can we talk?"

Three of the scariest words in the English language—especially when coming from the maybe-ex-boyfriend you haven't spoken to for two weeks.

The noise of all the other students in the hallway discussing their weekend plans petered out. Cole's breath was warm on Lucy's hair, but her shoulders stiffened, waiting to see what her body's reaction would be.

Slowly she turned to face him, hands clamped to her sides.

"Talk," she said.

Cole scuffed the toe of his sneaker against the linoleum.

"You missed the last meet of the season. We won—if you care."

"Congratulations."

"We won—I even set a new personal best—and *I* didn't care." He tore at the cuticles on his thumb, one of his few nervous habits, while staring at his feet. "I didn't care because you weren't there, Luce. Because you didn't *want* to be there."

Lucy felt a twinge of guilt, almost like a paper cut. It was true.

"You've got enough groupies," she said.

Cole lifted his gaze. "You saw the photos."

"The up-close-and-personal with Megan? Oh yeah. So why are we even talking? I seem to have been replaced."

"Replaced?"

He curled his fingers around Lucy's upper arm in desperation. No motion sickness this time, but what Lucy did feel was almost worse, like dangling from a slippery cliff. She'd hoped that the thief had done her a favor by removing the Tesla Egg from her possession, hoped maybe all her weird abilities would evaporate.

Nope.

"That's not why I posted them," Cole said, half plea, half growl, while shaking his head.

"Then why *did* you?" Lucy demanded.

"I needed to see if you'd get jealous."

"You were *trying* to hurt me? I never thought you were a sadist, Cole."

"What? No. I had to know if you'd care. But then you didn't even confront me. You didn't even seem upset." His eyes traveled to where he was gripping her arm. "You barely touch me anymore."

Channeling all of her frustration at Cole, Lucy shouted, "Of course I care!" and jabbed his shoulder, proving she could touch him when she wanted. "And you better believe I'm mad."

A tiny crescent formed on his lips.

"Why are you smiling?" she said.

"Because you're mad. You care." Cole leaned into her and brushed his knuckles along her jawbone. "Please, Luce. I want things to go back to the way they were."

She inhaled all the way from her toes. Lucy wanted things to be like they'd been before the cheating and the Tesla Suite too.

"Let me make it up to you," said Cole. "Saturday. My parents will be out of town. I'll make you dinner. I'll be better." He took a breath. "I promise."

Lucy sank her front teeth into her bottom lip, undecided.

"Actually," he began, "I was hoping you could tutor me—for real this time. I'm going to fail the physics final without you."

"You mean now that you actually have to do the work?" Lucy couldn't keep an edge from her voice.

"Yes." Cole had the grace to look ashamed.

Lucy thought about what Claudia would say. She'd tell her to stop fixing Cole's messes. And yet, here he was, genuinely asking for Lucy's help. How could she turn him down flat? She didn't want to be the reason Cole didn't graduate. Besides, after her moment—or whatever—with Ravi, Lucy should maybe do some penance herself.

Cole plowed his fingertips through her curls and massaged her scalp the way he knew she liked. "So, physics and pasta. How 'bout it?"

Lucy's gaze dropped to his lips, unable to take the intensity of his stare. Misinterpreting guilt for desire, Cole hugged her closer and kissed her hungrily. Her stomach turned over.

Coming up for air, Cole smiled as he said, "It's a date." The look in his eye was less confident than his smile.

He rested his forehead against hers so their noses touched. If she were honest, things had been strained between them for a while, but was she truly ready to say goodbye to the first boy she'd ever loved?

"It's a date," Lucy agreed. She kissed him back, softer this time, but she couldn't rid herself of that nauseated feeling.

A tug came on Lucy's shoulder, extricating her from the lip lock with Cole not a moment too soon.

"Share and share alike," said Claudia, trailing her eyes from Lucy to Cole.

Cole goofy grinned. "What's up, Short Stack?"

"I need to borrow your moll, doll face," she replied in a Mafioso tone. Cole just stared. "Your better half is required elsewhere," she clarified, casting Lucy a quick glance, and Lucy tried to hide her relief.

"She is?"

"You forgot." Her friend's voice hardened. Not good. Claudia could be scarier than all three of her brothers combined when she wanted to be.

Picking up on the tension, Cole evaluated his options and wisely chose a quick exit. "Saturday," he whispered into Lucy's ear as he kissed her cheek. Claudia kept her eyes on Lucy and she had that rampaging elf look about her.

Lucy opened her mouth to say . . . she wasn't sure what, but Claudia cut her off.

"Cate and Stew are waiting. Hope the planetarium was real inspiring."

She started toward the auditorium and Lucy trailed half a pace behind, regret gnawing at her. Claudia was the most loyal, dependable person ever. She deserved better from Lucy.

"*Clauds*—" she began as her friend swung open the backstage door and announced, "Welcome to Gangland!"

Cate and Stew were perched on ladders on either side of the stage, paintbrushes in hand, working on a series of eight-foot-high backdrops. Lucy's eyes darted to a portrait of the Statue of Liberty with a mustache, holding an ice-cream cone instead of the Eternal Flame.

She nudged Claudia. "Why is Lady Liberty sporting a Movember 'stache?"

"It's Dada."

Lucy attempted a sage nod but Claudia saw right through it. "Dada was an art movement in the 1920s that criticized the commercialization of art," she explained. "Poked fun at high culture. They painted mustaches on the *Mona Lisa* and framed toilet seats—which you would know if you'd read any of the emails I'd sent you this week!"

Emails?

"Did you even glance at the sketches I sent you?" Claudia said.

"I'm sorry." Guilt spread over her like a rash. Lucy had become self-absorbed and a liar. Her eyes flitted around the auditorium. "It's a really cool concept, Clauds. Like a 1920s Occupy," she said, cajoling a tiny smile from her friend.

"It was Jess's idea. Who knew anti-establishmentarianism could be so hot?" They shared a laugh. Claudia surveyed the backdrops, then snapped her focus back to Lucy. "So, *mon amie*, are you going to make my Dada Speakeasy *electrifying*?"

"I'll do my best." That was Lucy's specialty, after all.

"Good. Let's join the rest of the worker bees."

As if on cue, Cate greeted them with a double-dimpled smile.

Over the next hour or so, Lucy studied the half-painted sets and the sketches strewn around the stage, determining which color gels she could recycle from the fall musical for the lights and what she would need to order. In addition to Lady Liberty, there was a panorama of the New York City skyline complete with King Kong in a top hat. Since there wouldn't be any alcohol at the prom (at least, not school-sanctioned), Claudia had designed a trompe-l'oeil beveled mirror lined with shelves of multicolored liquor bottles to sit behind the fruit punch stand. She'd even stenciled MOONSHINE in capital letters on empty wine bottles that would be filled with Kool-Aid.

Stew suggested they sprinkle some sawdust on the gym floor to make it feel like an authentic bootleggers' paradise. They all agreed that was genius, and Lucy added it to her shopping list for the hardware store. By the time they were finished for the day, she felt more like her old self. She clung to that feeling—with all her might.

Cate and Stew waved goodbye but Lucy was so concentrated on double-checking her notes she hardly noticed. The seat beside her whined as Claudia plopped herself down in the front row. She traced a finger along the sketch of a theater marquee Lucy was holding.

"Think we can really pull it off?" she said with an uncharacteristic quaver. This meant a lot to her friend. Lucy wouldn't flake out again.

"Definitely. We're Broadway-bound, baby."

Claudia had been thrilled with Lucy's idea to have Times Square–style billboards dangling from the ceiling, dotted with halogen light-bulbs to capture the Prohibition Era ambiance.

"I guess the stars really did inspire you," Claudia said. She pulled one of her curls straight. "I shouldn't have been so snarky."

Lucy stopped scribbling. She shifted in her seat, angling her body until their knees touched. A burst of warm energy radiated from the spot.

"Does that mean our fight is over?" she asked.

"That wouldn't even come close to qualifying as a fight in the O'Rourke household."

Lucy drilled the tip of the pen against the notebook. "It's as close as I ever want to get."

Claudia's hazel eyes searched hers out and the truth began pushing its way to the surface.

"Listen, Clauds."

Her friend listened.

"I didn't go to the planetarium."

Head nod.

"I went to see my neurologist."

Nod.

"I'm fine."

"Why didn't you want your mom to know?"

Trust Claudia to get to the heart of the matter. "I thought I might have had a seizure. I didn't want her to overreact." One day Lucy would be suffocated by her pile of half-truths.

"That's why you weren't riding Marie Curie," her friend deduced. Lucy smiled guiltily. Her bestie really did know her better than anyone else.

Claudia didn't smile back. "Why didn't you tell me, Luce? You promised."

Lucy nearly uttered the phrase *It's complicated* before deciding she would sound exactly like Cole had trying to justify his sins of omission.

"I was scared." Finally, the truth.

Nod.

Lucy lowered her gaze. "I'm sorry."

"But you're okay now?"

"We adjusted my meds." The rest of the truth cut at her insides, but she was still too afraid to let it out.

"I understand why you've been distracted. I just wish you knew by now that you can trust me." Lucy raised her eyes to Claudia and she instantly wished she hadn't. Her confusion was mirrored back at her. "I'll always have your back, Luce," she said, as solemn as any vow.

Lucy nodded because her throat was too scratchy. She drew Claudia into a tight hug and they stayed that way for a good long while. They both ignored the crackle of static in the air.

Regaining her voice, Lucy asked, "Wanna come over? Hang out?" The question was hesitant, her chest tight. "Or are you working at the Gallery? I could come with?"

Claudia pulled out of the embrace. She bit her lip.

"Jess's expecting me at her dorm. Soon."

"Right. Wouldn't want to stand in the way of young love!" Lucy said with forced cheer. Five weeks and dwindling. Lucy didn't want to share Clauds with Jess for any of them.

"I can drive you home first."

"Nah. I'm good. I could use the fresh air. And I wanna double-check the gels again."

"You sure?"

"Sure. Have fun." Lucy beamed a smile brighter than the lights of old Broadway as Claudia left for her date.

She sat in the quiet for a bit, then turned off the auditorium lights one by one.

OUROBOROS

Plodding toward home, Lucy peered down at Tesla's enigmatic expression on the cover of *The Current Wars*. She'd renewed it at the library that morning.

Since experimental science and medical science had so far yielded unsatisfactory results in explaining Lucy's freaky symptoms, she'd decided to return to the source. Perhaps the clues to what had happened in the Tesla Suite were hidden in his life story?

Tesla's light-blue eyes seemed so alive to Lucy, brilliant, like they contained the solution to a thousand riddles. He claimed that his eyes had once been a darker hue but employing his intellectual faculties so heavily had diluted them.

As if being a brainiac could change your eye color!

For every one of Tesla's incredible innovations, Lucy discovered there was an equally untenable belief. By the end of his life, Tesla had shunned human company, and New York society shunned him. His most frequent visitors at the New Yorker Hotel were the injured pigeons he rescued and nursed back to health.

If Lucy couldn't find a way to control or rid herself of her symptoms, would she wind up a recluse like him?

A honking horn wrested Lucy's glower from Tesla. She swung it toward a black Land Rover with tinted windows that had pulled up alongside her. The passenger-side window slid down to reveal the one person Lucy couldn't keep at a distance. Although she really, really should.

"Hi, Ravi." A ridiculous smile overtook her face. "I wouldn't have pegged you for a *Men in Black* car, blacked-out windows and every-thing."

"You never know when you need to go off-roading. Or outrun the paparazzi. Besides, it belongs to Professor T." He raised an eyebrow. "Need a ride?"

Yes. No. "Sure."

Without stopping to consult her conscience further, Lucy jumped into the shotgun seat.

"Don't worry," Ravi said as she fastened her seat belt. "I've almost got this driving-on-the-wrong-side-of-the-road thing down."

"Gotcha. I'm taking my life in my hands."

The cadence of his laughter made Lucy's heartbeat trip over itself.

"Where to?" he asked.

"Take a right at the end of the street. I'll guide you."

"Where I'm from, you're the one in the driver's seat."

If Lucy were a romance novel heroine rather than an observer of ob-jective fact, she might be tempted to call his gaze a soul-searching stare. She also might add double-entendre to the catalog of auditory hallucinations that preceded a seizure. Either way, Lucy looked away first, dropping her gaze to her lap.

The car edged away from the curb. "What are you reading?" Ravi asked.

All Lucy's senses went on high alert. As if she'd been caught in a trap, her fingers splayed taut across the book. The crunching of wheels on the badly paved road resounded in her ears.

"Did you know Nikola Tesla invented the alternating-current sys-tem?" Her voice hitched up an octave. "Edison was already heavily invested in direct current, so he tried to convince the public that alter-nating was unsafe. Launched a smear campaign. Even publicly elec-trocuted an elephant to prove his point."

Eyes on the road, Ravi murmured, "Sounds dramatic."

Shaky laugh. "Yeah, I've been reading up on the Current Wars." She tapped the title. "Getting more context for my final paper. It's almost done, by the way." *Put that shovel down, Luce.* "Anyway, I'm just surprised Tesla isn't on the syllabus. He's never been in any textbook I was assigned, for that matter. Not even when my dad homeschooled me."

"Hmmm." Ravi hit the turn indicator. "I suppose there's limited room in any curriculum, and Tesla's inventions are more about technology, about exploiting science, rather than the laws of science themselves."

Huh. Lucy hadn't made that distinction before. She wondered if her dad would agree. Could that be why he'd barely mentioned Tesla to her?

"Also," Ravi continued, "a lot of Tesla's projects were more theoretical than what's required for a sixth form—er, high school—understanding of physics." He dashed her a cheeky grin.

"Still getting the colonial lingo down?" she teased, matching his grin.

"Studying my vocab every night. Although I might be considered a colonial as well."

"Oh, right. Of course." *Idiot.* Lucy flushed. "Americans aren't great at world history, but I do know that much. Sorry." She cringed in her seat.

Ravi glanced at her sideways. "I was born in London. I'm as British as they come, really. I still have relatives in Rajasthan, but I've never met them. I kind of lost touch after . . ." His voice trailed off. "One of these days I'm going to pick up Hindi. Or a Rajasthani dialect, maybe."

"Did you speak that with your parents?" Lucy asked.

"Not really. Mostly when my mum was telling me off." His laugh held a tinge of melancholy.

"I'd like to learn another language. I only know dead ones." Ravi raised an eyebrow, and Lucy elaborated, "My mom is a classicist. She taught me Latin and Greek while I was homeschooled."

"So your mom covered arts subjects and your dad taught you science?"

Lucy nodded. "And maths," she said in the British way. Ravi smiled. "He did postdoctoral research before going into finance. He invests in tech firms now. Westinghouse funded his Ph.D. research—the same guys who bankrolled Tesla." Okay, she was bragging. Was it wrong to try to impress him? Ravi's godfather had a Nobel to his name, after all.

"Interesting," he said without inflection. "What's your father's field?"

"Quantum mechanics."

Half his face lifted in a crooked smile. "I see why you like to get your hands dirty in the experimental side of things. Who did you say he worked for?"

She hadn't. "The Sapientia Group."

From the corner of her eye, Lucy noticed a muscle twitch in Ravi's jaw as he nodded.

"I'm sure Professor T knows of them. He launched his own biotech company a few years back. When he retired as chair of the department."

"Why'd he retire?" Lucy asked.

"Fancied a new challenge, I suppose. He's still a fellow at Trinity College."

Like Newton. "Must be nice. You wouldn't rather work with him than teach American high schoolers?" Lucy teased.

Ravi's posture grew rigid and she knew she'd said something wrong. They were saved by a stoplight. "Which way from here?" he asked.

"Another right," she said. "Onto Salisbury Street."

His face crinkled more and then he laughed to himself. "I almost forgot—if you're dead into Tesla, you should check out one of my favorite graphic novels." To her questioning eyebrow, he replied, "*The League of Extraordinary Gentlemen*," as the light went green. "He's this mad, steampunk fantasist."

"Thanks. I'm not sure if I'm *dead into* Tesla, but I will." Lucy would leave no stone unturned in her elusive quest. "Although I don't think 'fantasist' is a fair way to describe him."

"Go on. I do enjoy our debates."

So did Lucy. Too much.

"Take Niagara Falls, for instance. The idea may have come to Tesla in a boyhood dream—but it doesn't automatically make him a fantasist. He was the first to harness hydraulic power. Not that I believe in dreams."

"Why not?" Ravi captured her gaze.

Because she didn't want to. "Do you?" she countered.

"I don't discount anything. And I never said there was anything wrong with being a fantasist."

Was that Lucy's problem? Was she too logical to be an innovator? To find a way to fix herself?

"The alchemy thing again," she said.

Amusement framed his next words. "The alchemy thing?"

"Yeah, um, the eight-pointed star. Creation and transmutation. Your tattoo, it . . . intrigued me."

This time Ravi went quiet for so long Lucy considered flinging herself from the moving vehicle to avoid further awkwardness.

"One the all," he breathed at last. It was prayerlike, reverent. "The eight-pointed star represents the alchemical principle of the Ouroboros—the snake eating its own tail." He laughed. "Doesn't sound appetizing, I know."

"You can say that again."

"Alchemists believe that one thing can be transmuted into another because at the deepest level they're all the same. Just like the snake perpetually consumes and regenerates itself. It's a constant. The Ouroboros always was and always will be."

Lucy wished she could believe in something constant.

Ravi's grip tightened on the steering wheel. "I got the tattoo on the fifth anniversary of my parents' deaths."

When he was fourteen. A pang of sympathy constricted Lucy's chest. "Does it make you feel closer to them?"

"Sometimes." His knuckles bulged on the wheel.

Lucy touched his elbow and his hold loosened. Why had she done that?

"The Ouroboros sounds kind of like a renewable energy source,"

Lucy said, trying to direct the conversation to something less fraught. "Right up Tesla's alley."

"Why would you say that?"

"Oh, just some of the things he said . . . like how he designed the induction motor—they sound a little, um, mystical."

She flipped through the book in a frenzy. "Here! Tesla would recite poetry to himself as he walked around in Budapest. It's a passage by a German poet named Goethe." Lucy was no expert in dramatic readings—that's why she hid backstage—but she gave it her best shot.

"*The glow retreats; done in the day of toil; It yonder hastes, new fields of life exploring.*" Her breathing became more rapid as she spoke, her heart nearly flying out of her rib cage. "*Ah, that no wing can lift me from the soil, Upon its track to follow, follow soaring!*"

Sparks coursed through Lucy as Ravi watched her from the corner of his eye. Metaphorical sparks.

"Tesla recounted the verses while admiring the retreating sun and the motor just designed itself in his head," she continued. "I like sunsets as much as the next girl, but they've never revealed the secret to using alternating current to create mechanical power to me."

Ravi laughed. "I see your point. Mystical. I've heard the passage before. It's from a play called *Faust*. Have you read it?"

A blush straggled across Lucy's cheeks. How could she think she'd be telling him anything he didn't know?

"In the legend, Faust is a scholar who makes a pact with the devil," Ravi said. "Faust trades his soul for infinite knowledge."

"You think Tesla traded his soul?"

A hearty laugh rumbled in Ravi's chest but that didn't prevent the chills from racing down Lucy's spine.

"I'm interested in alchemy. Science. Not Satanism."

Lucy swallowed in response. The cookie-cutter houses of Salisbury Street whizzed by in a blur. She sensed Ravi's eyes on her but kept hers trained on the automatic sprinklers and crocus-adorned window boxes.

"Those verses have always reminded me more of Icarus, actually," he said.

Lucy knew the Greek myth well. Icarus's father, Daedalus, was a master craftsman who fashioned two pairs of wings from feathers and wax. Daedalus warned Icarus not to fly too high or the blazing sun would melt the wax. Icarus didn't listen. Drunk on flying, he soared higher and higher until there were no feathers left. He plunged into the sea. Lost forever.

A new tide of chills deluged Lucy. "You think Tesla flew too close to the sun?"

With a shrug, Ravi replied, "He did fall from grace."

Lucy had read how Tesla lost all of his investors—and his social standing—because of his obsession with man-made lightning. But what had happened to her in his lab seemed to suggest he'd succeeded.

"Maybe that's why he's left out of textbooks," said Lucy.

Ravi made a noncommittal noise. "Maybe."

"Stop!"

He slammed on the brakes. "You okay?"

"Yes. Sorry. *Sorry*. It's just—we passed my house."

"Bollocks." He readjusted his glasses. "You gave me a fright."

Mortification fizzed through Lucy as Ravi cautiously performed a U-turn and she indicated her front lawn. Lucy should have hurled herself from the Land Rover when she'd had the chance.

When he'd come to a full and complete stop, she said, "Thanks for the ride. Sorry for almost getting you killed."

A short laugh. "Never a dull moment with you. Cheers for the debate."

Lucy freed herself from the seat belt, face still hot. "Well . . ." She trailed off and reached for the handle.

"Wait—I meant to give this to you after class." He shut off the ignition. "Hold on." He reached into the inside pocket of his jacket. "I felt badly I couldn't retrieve your family heirloom from that rapscallion."

Rapscallion. It was unfairly sexy when he used words like that.

Her eyes widened as he withdrew an oval stone the color of midnight, about the size of a quarter. It was smooth, its surface cut so that it resembled interlocking diamonds.

"Tessellation," she said.

Ravi flashed her the knowing smile of one geek to another.

"It's not an egg, but it is an oval—from the Latin *ovum*, or egg."

Lucy had thought of that too, and it was so, so wrong that her next thought was that Cole never would.

Her cheeks were sore from smiling. "It's beautiful," she gushed. "But totally unnecessary. *I can't*—"

Oh. He placed it in the palm of her hand and the cool surface provided instant relief—to what exactly, Lucy wasn't sure.

"I did some research of my own," he said. "About seizures."

Lucy's fight-or-flight response most often kicked in during these kinds of conversations but all she felt was calm.

"I thought this might help—like worry beads. It might relax you if you feel one coming on."

She doubted the stone would do any good—her parents would have figured it out years ago if it would—but the gift was incredibly sweet, and she loved the fact that he'd been thinking about her. She didn't want to refuse it. Not really. Even if that was the smart thing to do.

"I'll give it a shot," she said, closing her fist around the stone, gazing into his dark eyes.

And now what? She should get out of the car, that's what. But . . . she became transfixed by his lips, and she felt herself leaning forward . . .

Ravi jerked back in his seat and Lucy fell headfirst like Icarus into a sea of embarrassment. *Frak.* The spell—if it had affected anyone but Lucy—was over.

Turning the key in the ignition, Ravi gunned the engine.

"See you in school," he said in a monotone.

Lucy launched herself out of the car faster than a speeding bullet. Her pulse should have been supersonic, yet as she clung to the stone, it stayed completely even. Maybe Ravi hadn't been so off-base?

That was a definite plus, but watching the Land Rover vanish around a corner, she had no idea how she could ever face him again.

Yep. Roadkill would have been preferable.

REACH OUT AND TOUCH SOMEONE

It was Claudia's fault that Lucy owned a bikini at all. Lucy abdicated authority over major wardrobe decisions to her more sartorially gifted best friend. Last summer, Claudia had proclaimed it was about time for Lucy to show off her curves properly, and Cole had been most appreciative.

She heard him splashing around outside in the hot tub as she examined herself in the mirror of his pool house. As promised, they had the place to themselves. Lucy had insisted on tutoring before dinner and Cole had insisted on hot-tubbing afterward. Most teenagers would be ecstatic. Lucy clipped her curls on top of her head as a knot formed in her exposed stomach.

She snatched the stone Ravi had given her from where she'd thrown her clothes on the floor. Squeezing it in her palm, she released a shuddering breath. To her utter astonishment, over the past couple of days, the stone had helped Lucy keep a lid on any magnetism or static electricity.

Actual magnetism, that was. Lucy couldn't help her eyes from being drawn to Ravi during her physics lab, although he'd barely acknowledged her. She knew it was for the best that he was ignoring her crush. Very polite of him, in fact, to disregard all knowledge of what a fool she'd made of herself.

"Lucy! I'm getting lonely out here!"

"Coming!" she called back, pressing the stone harder into her flesh. This was what she needed: a romantic evening with her boyfriend to push any ill-advised notions about handsome Brits from her head.

Please let me have one night of normal.

Reluctantly, Lucy relinquished her grip on the stone, and Cole wolf-whistled as she stepped onto the patio.

He was illuminated from below by the watery lights of the Jacuzzi. Smooth jazz whistled from the outdoor speakers. It might seem like Seduction 101 but Lucy knew better. Cole was genuinely trying to make her happy, trying to make amends—from the jazz to the lasagna he'd baked because he knew Italian was Lucy's favorite.

Goosebumps broke out along her skin from the chilly air. Seeing her shiver, Cole launched himself toward the edge of the Jacuzzi.

"Get in, I'll warm you up."

His eyebrows did a gigolo wriggle and Lucy laughed, nerves settling somewhat. She wished she could have hidden the stone in her bikini, but the silver pieces of string left very little to the imagination.

Cole gathered her into his arms as soon as she hit the water, nuzzling the nape of her neck. "Remind me to thank Short Stack again for her fashion tips."

Lucy did her best to relax against his chest. Cole's muscles were slippery against her back, and she'd have to be dead not to want to wheel around and trace them with her fingertips, painted Dorothy ruby red for tonight. Frustratingly, Lucy still wasn't able to kiss Cole without feeling queasy. It had absolutely nothing to do with Ravi. Absolutely nothing.

She teased Cole with a splash, doing a variation on the hula out of his arms, and settled on the bench that ringed the inside of the hot tub. He followed her over, pressing in close, thighs touching. The soft material of his swim trunks floated against her skin, raising tiny hairs all over Lucy's body.

Everything was quiet except for the sound of the bubble jets.

Cole stretched his arms around the edge of the Jacuzzi, leaned his head back, and closed his eyes.

"Tonight's been perfect, Luce."

"Yeah." Lucy listed her head back too, allowing her body to float like a ragdoll.

"Like before," he murmured, eyes still shut.

Except it wasn't. She gazed up at the night sky and the inverted constellations of Grand Central twinkled in her mind. There was so much Cole didn't know, so much Lucy didn't know how to tell him.

But if Lucy really loved Cole, didn't she owe him the truth?

"Do you ever"—she started, searching for the right words—"do you ever wish you could do things differently? Make different choices?"

"About what?"

Lucy swallowed. "About . . ." Suddenly saying, *Decoding a hidden message*, or *Breaking into the secret lab of a dead scientist* sounded beyond farfetched. Cole would assume she was pranking him.

"Luce?" He knocked his knee gently against hers.

"Oh, you know, life," she deflected, losing her nerve. "College. Everything."

"Everything is a lot to worry about."

When Lucy didn't respond, Cole rolled onto his side, propping himself up on an elbow. He stroked her jawbone with his thumb.

"I know I made the right decision about you."

His eyes were nearly black in the dim glow of the Jacuzzi lights.

"What about next year?" she asked.

He shrugged. "It'll work itself out," he said. But Cole's future was set. A straight line from graduation to college. Lucy couldn't share his confidence.

"I guess."

"Trust me. You think too much, Luce."

Cole might be right about that.

He wrapped a wet curl absently around his index finger. "Let's just get through finals," he said in a low voice, and walked his fingers up her thigh. Lucy dropped her feet to the bottom of the tub, needing support. She concentrated on the ridges of tile sliding along her soles.

Snapping the sliver of bikini at her hip, Cole said, "Besides, when you're wearing that I can't think about anything except the laws of motion."

Lucy snorted. "Using physics to turn on your girlfriend?"

He grinned. Half-lopsided, half-wicked. "I know what she likes."

"Oh, do you?" she teased.

In a playful almost football tackle, Cole grabbed her around the waist and swung her onto his lap, her knees straddling him. Water surged over the sides. Lucy inhaled sharply, battling the queasy feeling in her gut as he began kissing her neck. They bumped against the aluminum guiderail.

One of Cole's hands danced along her spine while the other cupped her butt, tentatively at first, drawing her closer. "Is this okay?" he whispered.

Remembering their first night together, Lucy reassured him by taking his earlobe between her teeth. She wanted to feel that magic again. She would *not* let the seasick feeling defeat her. This was her body, and Lucy was in control.

"More than okay," she told him. Cole groaned.

"Man, I've missed you." He started fumbling with the clasp of her bikini top. "We haven't—you know—since . . ."

Lucy finished his thought by reaching behind her back and unhooking the plastic easily.

"Girl magic," her boyfriend declared wondrously, smiling.

Cole was so distracted by peeling away the slip of silver that he didn't notice the lights at the bottom of the Jacuzzi flicker.

No. *No.* It was just Lucy's imagination.

She wrapped her hands behind Cole's neck, molding herself against him. Skin to skin. Her stomach staged a revolt but Lucy ignored it.

I'm in charge.

When he tried to kiss her on the mouth, however, she dodged and nibbled his earlobe again. Throwing up would be a mood killer.

Another flicker. *Stop*, she commanded the lights in vain.

Cole's hand slid down the crease of her breasts toward her belly button, followed by his lips.

Was the water bubbling more than before?

Lucy dug her fingers into his shoulders as her temples throbbed. Cole toyed with the edge of her bikini bottom. She wanted it to feel good. It did feel good. Partially. But she couldn't stop the whirlwind building in her veins.

A shudder wracked her body that she couldn't suppress. She grabbed the handrail for balance.

Eyes glazed, Cole pulled back. "Should we stop? Are you seizing?"

"I'm not seizing," Lucy snapped, and hurt rippled across his brow. "Sorry." She gentled her tone. "I'm okay."

"Sure?"

This was the moment. This was the moment she should tell him the truth.

"Don't stop," she rasped instead, shoving her tongue forcefully into his mouth, desperately, as her body quivered, and Cole matched her kisses.

Lucy bucked in the water. Where her toes had brushed against the metal casings of the lights, heat seared her. *Frak.* Her gaze dropped to the volatile, horror-movie lighting before rising back to the hand that gripped the handrail.

Green flames burned against the night sky.

She stared in awe for a few moments as tendrils of St. Elmo's fire began circling her forearm. Then fear knocked Lucy back to her senses.

Water and electricity didn't mix for regular humans.

She thrust both her hands against Cole's chest, slamming him back against the wall of the Jacuzzi.

"What's *go*—" he started to shout just as the bulbs blew beneath their feet. Cole's scowl transformed to shock, and maybe a shred of fear. "Holy mother of—did you feel that?" he spluttered. "I think I got an electric shock."

Lucy propelled herself to the opposite side of the hot tub.

"We should sue," he said. "That shit's dangerous."

Lucy could only make out his silhouette in the faint rays of light shining from the pool house and she was glad Cole couldn't see her properly either.

She quaked from head to toe. How could she be so reckless? Selfish? Lucy had deluded herself into believing she could control her symptoms. What a joke. This was a whole magnitude more serious than shorting out an iPad.

"You okay, Luce?"

Water sloshed as he moved toward her.

"Stop!" she screeched, hands flying outward. "Don't touch me."

"What the *fu*—?" Cole raised his voice, frustration punctuating his question. "What's wrong?"

But she couldn't tell him. Emptiness spread from her core as the realization dawned. Cole would never understand—and Lucy didn't want to try to make him. She didn't love him enough to try.

She didn't . . . she'd fallen out of love.

"I'm trying here," Cole pleaded. "You're hot, you're cold. I don't understand what's going on with you."

Lucy scanned his creased features, exasperation tensing each muscle. One way or another, tonight wasn't going to end without her hurting him.

"I'm sorry, Cole." Lucy was grateful that the darkness she'd caused masked the tears welling in her eyes. "I don't think we get each other anymore."

"But . . . but everything seemed like before."

"It did, but *I'm* not." It would never be like before.

Cole let out a monumental sigh. "So where does that leave us?"

"I think—I think we should take a break."

He smacked the surface of the water with his palm. Hard. Regret stirred in Lucy's chest.

She had used Cole too. Not for the solution to quadratic equations, but to pretend she was a normal all-American high school girl. Pretending had almost gotten Cole electrocuted.

"Prom?" he asked.

"I don't think it was meant to be." Lucy couldn't use Cole as a shield.

She was who she was. And if she was totally honest, she'd been hiding behind Cole long before she ever entered the Tesla Suite.

"Then let's call this what it is, Luce. We're graduating soon. This is a *breakup*. There's no going back."

She nodded, tears flowing more freely, finding it hard to speak.

Cole scoffed. "I never expected you of all people to break my heart."

Lucy didn't know how to take that, so she remained quiet, reattached her bikini top, and got out of the hot tub with as much dignity as anyone could manage half-naked.

She had reached the door of the pool house when Cole's voice carried to her in the still night air.

"I guess opposites don't really attract."

SHAKEN, NOT STIRRED

Nearly deep frying your newly ex-boyfriend gave anyone the excuse to lose their minds just a bit. Which was Lucy's justification for her present cyberstalking.

On her long, lonely walk home, she had decided two things.

First, she needed help getting answers. Second, if anyone in her life deserved the truth from Lucy, it was Claudia. Lucy could trust her bestie not to judge her, and she didn't want to lie anymore. She didn't want to hide.

Lucy's fingers slipped over the keyboard, water dripping from her messy curls. She hadn't bothered changing yet. Her skirt showed the outline of her bikini bottoms and her desk chair was growing soggier by the second. The night-hued stone rested beside the mouse.

Ravi Malik. Malik, Ravi. R. Malik.

Where was he?

The all-seeing eye that was Google had no clue.

Nothing but his very uninformative profile on the staff page of the Eaton High website. It gave his school email but Lucy couldn't say what she needed to say by email. And she couldn't wait. She was well aware that tracking him down where he lived was outside the bounds of what was socially acceptable.

But at this moment, Lucy didn't care.

She jammed her eyes shut, trying to summon the numbers and letters of the Land Rover's license plate. *Nada*.

How could Ravi have no social media presence? He didn't seem like the type to give a running commentary of his breakfast on Twitter (he probably ate something British like crumpets), but any self-respecting fanboy would have a Tumblr or participate in some kind of online forum. Nothing popped up on the Heron College website either.

Lucy rocked back in her chair, clutching the ebony stone and lifting it to her heart.

Think, Luce. She clicked her mouse.

Ravi's face stared back at her from the Eaton staff page. He looked on the brink of the laugh she liked too much. Bright sunshine splashed across a green lawn in the background. Lucy squinted. And . . . was that a river?

A trick she'd picked up from the coder forum struck her.

She right-clicked on the photo and copied the URL while opening a new browser window. If Ravi had used this photo for any other online account, then a reverse image search should find it. A ripple of unwarranted jealousy passed through Lucy just thinking about finding a dating profile.

It took less than a second to produce a result.

Ravi's face had been cropped from a larger photo. An older gentleman with a white beard and gunmetal eyes had his arm around him, beaming a paternal smile. He looked like the actor hired to play "distinguished professor" in a movie.

Clicking on the photo took Lucy to the website for a newspaper called the *Cambridge Evening News*. The article was talking about some bicentenary at Trinity College, but that wasn't what made Lucy's blood run cold. What iced her to the core was the caption beneath the picture.

Professor Tarquin Weston-Jones, left; Dr. Ravi Singh, right.

Ravi *Singh*! No wonder she couldn't find a Facebook account. He'd lied about his name. And hold the phone, he was *Dr.* Ravi Singh?

Which meant he already *had* a Ph.D. How was that possible? Why would he conceal his identity?

Lucy bit down on the inside of her cheek until she tasted a coppery tang. She'd never felt paranoid before.

You're not paranoid if someone's really after you.

She rubbed her temples. She couldn't afford to panic any more than she already was.

Why would Ravi lie about his name but not about Professor T? If he already had a Ph.D., why was he pretending to be a college student? Didn't he think Lucy would work it out? No, Ravi probably didn't think she'd be playing detective on the Internet.

Well, too bad.

Ravi Singh, Cambridge, she tapped with fevered fingers. There were too many results. She refined the search. *Ravi Singh + Cambridge + Mathematics*

Jackpot.

Heart pounding, she pored over matriculation and graduation records. Lucy was torn between wanting to get to the bottom of his deception and wanting to make plausible excuses for him.

She spun the stone in her hand, light from the computer screen glimmering off its diamondlike ridges.

Ravi must have cared about her to give her something like this. But why? *Why* did Ravi care about Lucy? She'd been too flattered to question it.

Returning the cursor to the search results, she swept toward the bottom of the page, where there was another link to the same newspaper. Only, this article was dated from 2007.

TWO UNIVERSITY SCIENTISTS KILLED IN FIRE, read the headline.

Lucy skimmed the first couple of paragraphs.

Two university geneticists were killed yesterday afternoon when a fire broke out in the Old Cavendish Laboratory on Free School Lane. Dr. Seema Singh, 39, and Dr. Amit Singh, 42, a married couple working together on a cure for Alzheimer's succumbed to their injuries at Addenbrooke's Hospital.

They are survived by their son, Ravi Singh, age 9, who was treated for smoke inhalation by paramedics at the scene along with Professor Tarquin Weston-Jones, 59, of Trinity College, Cambridge, who rescued the boy.

Witnesses reported hearing an explosion before flames engulfed the second floor of the building. No immediate source of the blast was confirmed. The Cambridgeshire Fire Brigade is investigating the electrical wiring of the 133-year-old structure as a possible cause.

The article went on to discuss the Singhs' research and questions of fire safety in the laboratory, but nowhere did it mention terrorism or foul play. What would make Ravi think that? Who could possibly be against a cure for Alzheimer's?

Lucy was relieved Ravi's story about being saved by Professor T checked out. And yet, it didn't explain why he would be using a false name. If he was so traumatized by his parents' deaths that he wanted to forget all about it, surely he would have changed his name years ago?

Be a scientist. Drawing down a lungful of air, Lucy began to type up a list of indisputable facts.

1. Ravi Malik does not exist
2. Ravi Singh received his Ph.D. in mathematics from Trinity College last December
3. Ravi's parents were killed in a fire (Accident? Arson?)
4. Ravi was saved and mentored by Professor T

What was she missing? It didn't add up.

Her gaze skittered back to the photograph. What did she know about Professor T? Biologist. Nobel Prize winner. Started his own biotech firm. Shouldn't be hard to find.

A few keystrokes led Lucy to his company's website.

The logo appeared and her adrenal gland worked overtime.

"Ouroboros," she muttered under her breath, despite the fact that no one could hear her. They couldn't, could they? *Stop, Lucy.* She wasn't about to start believing in an omniscient, omnipresent *they.*

A sleek, digital serpent encircled the company name: Chrysopoeia Tech.

Lucy played another round of hyperlink leapfrog and found the definition of *chrysopoeia*: transmutation.

That explained how Ravi had been exposed to alchemy. Of course he'd take up his godfather's interests. From their body language in the photo they seemed close. She moved her cursor to the *About Us* link on Professor T's website.

Chrysopoeia Tech was founded in 2010 by Professor Tarquin Weston-Jones, Fellow for Life at Trinity College, Cambridge. Professor Weston-Jones became a Nobel laureate for his pioneering research in the field of quantum biology, specifically DNA mutation. Perhaps the world's most renowned proponent of biophysics, Weston-Jones launched Chrysopoeia Tech to strengthen the links between science, medicine, and industry. Recognizing the paucity of university-level departments for the interdisciplinary field of biophysics, Chrysopoeia's privately funded laboratory is a haven where neuroscientists, mathematicians, physicists and biochemists can work together for the advancement of technology and the eradication of genetic diseases.

Lucy thought back to her botched Voltaic pile experiment. The way Ravi had challenged her about Galvani's theory of animal electricity suddenly made sense. Galvani was probably the grandfather of quantum biology.

She lurched away from the computer, afraid to cause another power outage.

Ravi knew. He must. Or at least suspect.

How? She gripped the armrests of her chair so hard she thought they might snap. Mentally, she added to her tally of facts.

5. Ravi somehow stumbled upon her in the middle of New York City
6. Ravi chased after a mugger without a second thought
7. Ravi showed up at Eaton High right after Lucy broke into the Tesla Suite

Burning plastic wafted through the air as molten puddles appeared beneath Lucy's fingers. *Ow!*

8. Ravi had come to Eaton for Lucy

She didn't know why, but Ravi better believe Lucy was going to find out. Before she risked exposing Claudia to whatever was going on, she needed to confront him.

It would just have to wait until Monday.

AMBUSH

Lucy's eyes were ringed with shadows. She'd been too keyed up for more than a couple hours of sleep. She'd needed to arrive at school before Ravi so she risked riding Marie Curie and, miraculously, arrived without incident.

The hallways were freshly mopped, the tang of Lysol in the air, and she skidded a few times over the linoleum on her way to the physics lab. The door to the classroom had already been unlocked by the janitor and she turned the handle gingerly, as if expecting an ax murderer to jump out from behind the blackboard.

She rooted around her bag, jangling the keychain at the bottom. In any other situation she wouldn't even consider breaking into a teacher's office. But needs must.

Thank you, Mrs. Brandon.

Lucy flipped through her house keys, garage keys, spare key to Claudia's house for emergencies . . .

No science-office key.

Weird.

She couldn't remember taking it off her Death Star keychain. Not that Lucy hadn't been distracted lately. *Dammit.* She should have double-checked before she left home. Her eyes cut to the wall clock: 7:55 A.M. No time to go back now.

Arms at her sides, Lucy stood sentry-straight, counting the seconds.

She didn't have to wait long.

Ravi ambled in a few minutes later, head bopping to whatever was blasting from his earbuds. He had his phone in one hand, a thermos in the other. Stubble was scattered along his jaw. She liked the scruffiness.

Lock down those hormones. Lucy had to stop thinking there was anything cute about him. He had lied to her—to everyone at Eaton High. She ignored the voice reminding her that she was no better.

His eyes lifted from the screen. When he recognized her, he grinned in an endearing way.

No, not endearing. Ingratiating. Weasely.

"Morning," he said, taking out the earbuds. He gestured at her *[Fe]male* T-shirt, chuckling. "I like it. Apropos."

Fe was the chemical symbol for iron and it seemed appropriate to Lucy that all females were inherently iron men.

When she didn't laugh or smile, Ravi furrowed his brow.

"Did we have an appointment?"

"No."

"Okay." His face gave nothing away. Hooking an ankle around one of the stools that lined the rows of desks, he took a seat. Lucy remained standing.

"What did you want to talk about?" he asked, and took a sip from his thermos, totally relaxed. He had no idea what was coming.

Now or never.

"I want to talk about what you're really doing at Eaton High."

The thermos slipped from his grasp but he caught it again with quicksilver reflexes. Lucy had been hoping for shock, indignation, recrimination. What she got was eerie composure. Ravi set the thermos on the desktop and met her disbelieving gaze.

"You're not going to tell me I'm wrong? That you're not a liar?" She attempted to copy his emotionless façade but incredulity saturated her voice.

He tipped forward, took her hand deliberately, and interlaced their fingers. Lucy should have resisted. She didn't. The moment their skin made contact she felt like she was flying.

"The only thing I lied to you about was my name," he said, his voice strained.

"What about your Ph.D.?"

He glanced down, setting the thermos on the desk. "And my Ph.D.—it was on tessellation, though." Looking up again, he said, "Everything else was one hundred percent me."

"How do you expect me to believe that?"

"Because you feel it. I know you do."

His eyes pulled her in like a homing beacon.

"I don't know what I feel," she protested.

Ravi reached toward her. "Lucy, believe me when I say I'm here to help." He glanced toward the door, then swept his gaze across the windows as if he were doing reconnaissance. "We can't speak openly here."

She snorted. "You think Eaton High is bugged?"

His demeanor said he did. "Meet me later."

"So you can make me disappear? Or whatever you Area 54 types do?" Lucy may have watched more space operas than spy thrillers, but she knew this scenario didn't typically end well for the unsuspecting schoolgirl.

Forcing a laugh, Ravi said, "You're not an alien, Lucinda."

She hated how much she liked the way he said her full name.

"But you know what I am," she countered.

"Meet me and I'll explain."

Lucy raised an eyebrow. "Like where no one can hear me scream?"

"Anywhere you want," he said. Then he added a caveat, "Somewhere outside and private would be better."

Meeting a guy with a secret identity somewhere secluded was mind-crushingly stupid.

But what choice did she have?

"After school. There's a popular hiking trail. Bear Mountain. I'm going to let my friend know where I'll be," she told him as imperiously as possible. "If I go missing, people will know."

Darkness passed over Ravi's face and he took a labored breath.

"I would never hurt you, Lucinda."

"That remains to be seen. Three fifteen P.M., sharp. If you're late, I walk."

Chin high, Lucy strutted from the physics lab hoping he didn't notice the trembling of her lips.

THE BODY PIEZOELECTRIC

An overcast sky swirled above Bear Mountain. Lucy had hiked it count-less times with her dad. She'd had many a lesson on flora and fauna in these woods.

It must be three or four o'clock in the morning in Tokyo right now. How was her dad doing? Lucy couldn't remember ever going so long without seeing him in her entire life. Her mom didn't seem worried but she'd barely lifted her head out of the *Pharmakon* over the last few weeks. All she said was that he'd be home as soon as he could.

A twig snapped and Lucy teetered forward, hopping up from the boulder on which she was perched. Her muscles tensed as if expecting a body blow.

"Hiya." The late-April breeze mussed Ravi's hair as he patted it down, testing out a lukewarm smile.

Lucy would not be charmed. "Two more minutes and you would've been talking to yourself. So spill."

He took another few steps toward her, hands outstretched in sur-render, as if Lucy might bolt at any moment. Which was pretty accu-rate.

"That's close enough," she warned him.

Ravi scratched his temple, coughed into his hand.

"I was going to tell you the truth, Lucy. I was working up to it."

Been there, done that, she thought. First Cole, now Ravi. Were all guys the same?

"*I*—I can't imagine how confusing this all is for you." His mouth twisted in agitation, his words sandpaper. "You shouldn't have found out like this." He clenched his fists.

"The cat is out of the bag, so quit stalling."

"You have a right to be angry."

The way Ravi studied her made Lucy feel like a lab specimen. She'd had a lifetime of doctors looking at her that way. She was sick of it.

"Thanks very much for your permission." Sweat beaded her hairline and she willed the simmering beneath her skin to cease.

"If you have the stone I gave you," he said. "I suggest you take it out."

"Why? It didn't stop me from nearly roasting my boyfriend alive!" she shouted, losing her cool. Was Lucy hallucinating, or did Ravi wince at the word "boyfriend"?

"Black tourmaline is piezoelectric. That's why it helps keep your condition in check. Just try it." He fidgeted with his glasses, making his statement half entreaty, half academic lecture.

"What do you know about my condition?" Lucy huffed. "And don't pretend to be a concerned citizen."

Annoyance streaked Ravi's face. "I care about you, Lucy." He moved forward, taking two long strides. "I care about your . . . welfare. And I know more about your condition than you do."

Lucy laughed in his face.

"I know you don't have epilepsy, for one."

Her knees went weak. She wanted to yell at him, tell him he was totally off his rocker. But something stopped her. She sagged against the boulder, the fight leaching from her.

"Why would you think that?" Her question came out frustratingly childlike. She watched as Ravi's face smoothed, shoulders relaxing a fraction.

"The tourmaline wouldn't affect you if you had standard epilepsy." His tone was patient. "You only experience similar symptoms."

Ravi might as well be positing that night was day, and day was night. Her whole life was built on the simple fact that she had epilepsy; that's the way her parents had built it.

"Then what am I?" She wished she didn't sound so broken.

He dipped his head, a quarter-smile teasing his mouth.

"Wonder Woman."

She straightened up. "I'm leaving."

"*Wait*—" Ravi grabbed her elbow. "Tell me what you feel. Right now."

Ticklish. Like a thousand fireflies were lighting her up from the inside.

"Nothing."

He frowned. "Have you been getting queasy feelings around anyone lately? Maybe something worse?"

You could say that again. "Why? What does it mean?"

"Your powers allow you to read people's emotional states."

Lucy ripped her elbow from his grasp and folded her arms.

"I do not have *powers*."

"You and I both know that's not true." Ravi spoke in deadly earnest and it was enough to wipe the sneer from her face. "What you register as motion sickness, for instance, is actually internal conflict. You're reacting to the other person's state of mind."

"Uh-huh. And how am I doing that?"

"By tuning in to their frequencies."

Her stomach cartwheeled. "That's what Tesla believed."

"Yes, precisely." Ravi's eyes sparked with excitement. "Eventually you'll be able to read people's minds. Brain waves are just another form of electricity, so it makes sense."

"Nothing about this situation makes sense," she countered. Especially since it had been Lucy who had hurt Cole on Saturday. His kisses might have made her feel sick, but she was the one feeling conflicted about him.

"I understand it's a lot to take in," Ravi told her.

"Understatement of the millennium."

Ravi shifted his hip against the boulder so that there were only a few inches between them. "You're strong, Lucy." His gaze panned over her. "If anyone can deal with this, it's you."

She didn't know about that. What Lucy did know was that *she* was the one asking the questions here.

"Answer me this—how do you know about my . . . *powers*?" Was she really using that word? "About *me*? Why did you come to Eaton under-cover? How do you have a Ph.D.? How old *are* you?" The questions came out rapid-fire, Lucy's frustration mounting with each one.

Ravi's expression remained neutral. "All valid questions." Clearing his throat, he said, "As for the last two, I sort of bypassed high school and went straight to Cambridge at fifteen. I just turned twenty-one."

Wow. Ravi was a hand-to-god prodigy. Lucy shouldn't have been so glad he was only three years older than her. He had still deceived her.

"As for your other questions, can we walk a little first?" He adjusted his glasses.

Lucy nodded and led him toward a trail she knew well. She won-dered if Ravi was aware of the message she'd decoded, but she didn't want to show him all of her cards.

Silence stretched between them, pierced occasionally by chirping sparrows. Finally, Ravi began, "The answer to how I know about your powers is: my parents." Acorns and wildflowers crunched underfoot as he spoke. "They were studying your condition when they died."

"I thought they were researching Alzheimer's."

He cut her a startled glance.

"There's this handy thing called the Internet," she explained, a mite haughtily. "Just full of information."

A crooked grin. "So I've heard."

"It's how I figured out you weren't who you claimed."

Ravi's grin faded. "Out of curiosity, how did you find me out?"

"Reverse image search of your photo on the Eaton High website."

He held Lucy's gaze until it became uncomfortable.

"What?" she demanded.

"You just keep impressing me."

Do. Not. Smile.

"I'm sorry about the deception," he told her. "Perhaps it was a miscalculation. I needed a way to approach you that wouldn't raise any red flags with . . . certain parties."

"Again with the vague," Lucy shot back. "*Why* did you want to approach me? Exactly how long have you been stalking me?"

Ravi came to a dead stop and she jostled into him. He reached for her hand. She shoved it in the pocket of her jeans instead, fingers closing around the tourmaline.

"Look at me, Lucinda," he implored. Like she could look anywhere else. "The first time I saw you was at the New Yorker Hotel."

"You were there?"

"No. I saw the surveillance footage." Lucy had thought she'd gotten away clean. Ha. "The people I work for," he continued, "they own the hotel. Only someone with your abilities could have opened the door to Tesla's lab."

"And by the people you work for, I presume you don't mean Eaton High," Lucy said. Ravi shook his head. "Chrysopoeia Tech?"

"That's part of it," he replied. "They want to meet you."

"Who is *they*?" Lucy couldn't believe there really was an omniscient, omnipotent *they*, after all.

"Professor T, for a start."

She drew her brows together. "And I'm just supposed to go blindly to meet with the members of your shady organization?"

He laughed. "Professor T is hardly shady."

"But he *is* an alchemist."

"You two will get on swimmingly."

"Swimmingly." Lucy couldn't resist mocking his accent despite her erratic heartbeat. Alchemists wanted to meet her. This was all too much. "If you wanted me to trust you, Ravi—you shouldn't have lied to me." Lucy squared her shoulders. "What about Mrs. Brandon? Is she part of your organization, or are your sketchy friends blackmailing her?"

Ravi grimaced. "We're scientists, Lucy. Not mobsters."

"Scientists who commit identity fraud. Why should I believe anything you have to say?"

"Because what I'm saying rings true to you. But if you want to be sure: hug me."

What? "Are you serious right now?"

"As a heart attack."

"That could be arranged," she informed him, and he gave another soft laugh. "Why on earth would I hug you?" Never mind that Lucy might have fantasized about it once or twice.

Ravi's Adam's apple bobbed. "The hug would work in the same way as the tourmaline." His eyes roamed her face.

"Which is?"

"The Greeks discovered that certain crystals, when placed in hot ashes, attract the ash and then repel it. These crystals, or piezoelectric materials, have a natural frequency at which they resonate."

"Like a tuning fork?"

"That's one way to think of it. The harder you strike a tuning fork, the greater the oscillation of the sound waves. The same holds true for your electric field, Lucy."

She gulped but she didn't deny it. "Is that what happened—what happened with Cole?"

Ravi took off his glasses and began fiddling with them.

"May I ask what you were doing when the incident occurred?"

"We were in his hot tub, um, we were—" A heat wave broke out across Lucy's skin as she rambled.

"I think I've got the picture." Ravi clicked the stems of his glasses together more rapidly. "As your heart rate increases, or you have a hormonal surge—cortisol, adrenaline—there's a corresponding increase in the frequency and amplitude of the oscillation of your electrical field."

"I figured out that much already."

"I'm not surprised. Well, the increased frequency makes you prone to—"

"Knocking out the power grid?"

He caught her eye. "I thought that might have been you."

"Guilty."

"Because human skin is also piezoelectric, when you hold the black tourmaline against it, the stone couples your electrical field's oscillations to the vibrations of the tourmaline. The tourmaline will interrupt any increase in your oscillations due to any, er, outside factors. It will anchor your field to the resonant frequency of the tourmaline."

"Basically, you're saying it acts like a dampener?" she said, and he nodded. "Will it make me less dangerous?"

"You're not dangerous, Lucy."

"I think Cole would disagree."

Ravi replaced his glasses on the bridge of his nose. "Right. In future, you might avoid any . . . water sports with Mr. Hewitt. At least until you've gained control over your abilities. Water, as you know, decreases the resistance to electricity."

"Yep." She hiccupped a tired laugh. "It's a moot point, anyway. I doubt I'll be participating in any *water sports* with Mr. Hewitt again."

"Oh?" His eyebrows shot up before he regimented his features back into a neutral mask. "Be that as it may—"

"Ravi," she interrupted. "What does this have to do with giving you a hug?"

Red rose in his cheeks as he explained. "When you touch someone, Lucinda, you're able to sync with the oscillations of their nervous system. Just as you do with the tourmaline. Those oscillations are then re-created in your own brain—a shadow, if you will, of what's happening in theirs." He coughed. "The more . . . intimate the contact, the fuller the picture you receive."

"The more accurately I can read people's emotions."

He nodded.

"So all I have to do is hug you and I'll feel what you're feeling?"

"The more you practice, the better you'll get at identifying specific emotions. But for now, you'll be able to recognize that my feelings towards you are . . . concerned." He swallowed. "Protective." Another swallow. "That I mean you no harm." He dropped his hands to his sides. "But only if you want. The choice is entirely yours."

Ravi stood scarecrow still. He wouldn't initiate anything. She needed to go to him.

Lucy took a step forward, releasing her grip on the tourmaline in her pocket. She couldn't believe that she was entertaining the notion that the universe had supplied the answers she needed when she needed them, but she wanted to believe Ravi.

He was taller than Cole. Lucy had to reach higher to slide her hands behind his shoulders. He shivered, making her hesitate.

"You're not scared?" she whispered.

"I trust you."

He might live to regret it. Or . . . not.

Gently, she laid her head against his chest and she wanted to laugh from the feeling of floating. Was this Ravi's frequency? She glanced up at him and the blush on his cheeks was distinctly satisfying. Slowly, his arms encircled her waist. Was it possible he'd imagined holding Lucy too?

She grazed his cheek with her hand, the texture of his halfhearted facial hair delighting her. Lucy giggled. She would have sworn she was flying, and yet she also felt peaceful.

"Do you feel that?" she asked.

"Yes." Barely a whisper.

She should let go. Her instincts—or powers—were telling her that Ravi was on her side. There was no reason to continue the embrace. His arms tightened around her. No reason at all . . . except she wanted him closer.

Pushing onto her tiptoes, Lucy pressed her mouth to Ravi's, parting his lips, exploring. They were as soft as they looked. Her mind filled with the hot-pink tendrils of a breaking dawn.

She savored the taste of him as sunlight filtered behind her eyes.

Ravi pulled back. "That wasn't supposed to happen," he said in a low voice.

"You didn't want to?"

"I did. I do. But I'm here to train you."

"Meaning?"

Ravi released her and Lucy instantly missed the feel of him.

"Meaning this . . ." He indicated the space between them, "will only confuse matters."

Talk about being doused with cold water.

"Please don't take it the wrong—"

"Whatever," she cut him off. "You got what you wanted. I'm on board with your conspiracy theory."

"*Lucinda.*"

"I'd stand back if I were you." She withdrew the tourmaline and tossed it from one hand to the other, daring him to cross her.

"There are people who would hurt you for being who you are." His expression grew severe. "I came to teach you how to defend yourself. If we could find you, so could they."

"Again with the *they*?" she said irritably. "You've heard of smoke and mirrors on your side of the pond?"

"The threat is real," he ground out.

"Gee, five stars for terrifying the young ingénue."

Lucy turned on her heel.

"I'm only telling you because I know you can handle it."

"You don't know me at all. And I obviously don't know you, Ravi Singh."

"Tomorrow. We start training."

"Whether I like it or not?"

"I'm sorry, but yes." His tone was cool, determined. "And you can't tell anyone about your abilities—for your own safety. As well as theirs."

"Right." Over her shoulder, she said, "I'll make my own way home. You'll probably be watching me anyway. But if you think I'm done asking questions, think again."

His voice followed her as she stomped away.

"I'd be rather disappointed if you were."

INTO THE WOODS

Lucy refused to turn around, but, as she sent Claudia an *AOK* text, she began to think her dramatic exit might have been a pyrrhic victory.

There were still so many questions left unanswered.

For instance, could her father be connected to these so-called alchemists? And what was he *really* doing in Tokyo all this time?

Lucy found it hard to believe that if her dad had any inkling that piezoelectric materials would temper her seizures and other neurological symptoms he wouldn't have tried it years ago. Her parents did everything they could to protect her—so much so it was often suffocating. If they'd known tourmaline would help manage her condition, surely they would have made Lucy a suit of armor from it.

She swallowed a lump rising in her throat.

The truth was so much more *X-Files* than Lucy could have imagined. Would her parents even believe her? She put the chances at slim to nil.

Lucy reached the student parking lot and unlocked Marie Curie, heaving herself on top as exhaustion rippled through her. Sloth-like, she began pedaling toward Claudia's house to study for the American lit final.

She touched two fingers to her mouth in an attempt to extinguish phantom flames.

Don't think about his lips.

To kiss or not to kiss was not the most crucial question at hand. Far more important was how the mysterious *they* Ravi worked for had tracked Lucy down after she fled the New Yorker Hotel? Why did they own it in the first place? How long had Ravi's employers been waiting for someone to open the door to Tesla's lab, and what were they hoping to find inside?

And, perhaps most pressingly, why had Tesla gone to such lengths to conceal it?

Lost in her maelstrom of thoughts, Lucy was knocking on Claudia's front door before she knew it.

"Jess?"

The other girl smiled as she pulled it the rest of the way open.

"Hey, Lucy. The dictator is kicking me out so you two can study."

"*Oh*–uh . . ." Lucy stuttered, trying to remember to be socially competent. "You don't have to leave."

Jess fidgeted her eyebrow ring. "It's cool. I should be studying myself." She flashed another smile. "Plus, I wouldn't dream of interfering with best-friend time."

She sounded totally sincere. "Thanks," Lucy replied, uncertain whether it was a polite thing to say, but some alone time with her best friend was what she needed right now. Desperately. Only Claudia could anchor Lucy back into something resembling reality.

Pursing her lips, Jess said, "You okay?"

Lucy must look as blindsided as she felt. She didn't get a chance to answer before Claudia came rushing down the stairs.

"Minnie! Here safe and sound, I see." She laughed. True to form, Claudia hadn't asked Lucy why she felt compelled to hike a trail this afternoon.

"Yeah." Lucy forced a weak smile. She was safe. Sound was a completely separate matter.

Jess looked between them. "That's my cue." She squeezed Lucy on the shoulder. "Good luck with the studying," she said, and guilt swelled inside Lucy at being glad to have her friend to herself.

"What about me?" Claudia teased her girlfriend. "Aren't you going to wish me luck too?"

Jess stepped toward her, grinning mischievously, and drew Claudia in close. She planted a scorching hot kiss on her lips. "Will that do?"

"For now."

Laughing, Jess shook her head. "Thank you, Supreme Leader. I'll text you later." Moving back toward the door, she said, "Bye, Lucy."

Lucy responded with a small wave. As soon as the door closed behind Jess, she turned to her beaming bestie, commenting, "Things seem to be going well," and her friend made a faraway *Mmmm* noise.

"How about you?" Claudia asked. "Fresh air clear your head?"

If only. Lucy couldn't stop her face from creasing. In an instant, Claudia had thrown her arms around her in a fierce hug. Warm tingles washed over Lucy and she recognized them as Claudia's energy: her love and concern.

Lucy stiffened. Ravi had described her ability to read other people's emotions like it was a *good* thing. Hugging Claudia now, Lucy's powers seemed like an invasion of privacy. Unethical. Wrong, even. She stiffened further.

"Oh, babe," said her friend. "Let's head upstairs."

A virtual forest slid its shadowy branches across Lucy's face as she entered Claudia's bedroom and she had to remind herself she wasn't back in her dreamscape. Lucy had helped Claudia to wire up the chandelier constructed from mesh, twisted bicycle spokes, and other found objects. When the single bulb glowed, it cast fairy-tale impressions on the seafoam-green walls.

Claudia plunked herself down on the bed. "Cole asked me to return this to you," she said, scooping something up from the comforter.

A wink of metal. Like an SOS. The key to the science office lay in Claudia's outstretched palm.

How could Lucy have misplaced it? *Ugh.* "Thanks," she said.

"Wanna tell me why I'm playing messenger, doll face?"

"We broke up." Lucy slid onto the bed next to her friend. She stared up at the weathered ballerina ornament Claudia had recently added to the scraggly aluminum branches, its legs frozen in a pirouette.

Claudia stroked Lucy's cheek and another surge of happy, ticklish goosebumps prickled beneath her skin. Was it a violation if she already knew her best friend loved her?

Lucy licked her lips. "Cole and I have been drifting apart for a while now. I think it was inevitable."

Claudia bobbed her head.

"Everyone knows long distance is the kiss of death, anyway," she carried on. "I didn't see the point in keeping up appearances for the last few weeks of school." She blew a hair from her face. "The good news is that I'll be totally focused on the sound and lighting at the prom— you and Jess can enjoy yourselves."

A frown briefly gripped Claudia's face; Lucy realized her mistake too late.

"Oh, Clauds. I didn't mean long distance *never* works. I'm sure you and Jess will be fine. It's only, well, Cole and I already had problems . . ." Lucy trailed off.

What were the seasick feelings she had picked up from him on Saturday? she wondered. She already knew about the test-selling scam. Maybe Cole's own feelings for Lucy had been more conflicted than even he realized.

"Don't sweat it, Minnie," Claudia assured her. "I know what you meant." She rolled onto her back. "Jess and I haven't talked about it yet. Things are still so new, you know? Although my parents would be thrilled if I had a reason to visit Eaton more often next year." She hooked Lucy's pinky with her own. "I just want to make sure you're okay. I'm always up for a good ol' tar and feathering in the town square if Cole's done you wrong."

Lucy snort-laughed. "Same goes for Jess. But no, the breakup was my idea."

"If you're okay, I'm okay."

Lucy covered Claudia's hand with her own, a lifetime of memories flooding through her. Claudia was the sister she'd always wanted. When she was younger, Lucy had been jealous of Claudia's rambunctious household since there were no siblings or cousins to keep her company.

Both of Lucy's parents were only children and her grandparents had all died long before she was born. But Claudia was enough.

Her pulse jackhammered knowing she would soon be so far away.

Claudia yelped as electricity crackled between them. Lucy snatched her hand back, scouring Claudia's skin for any burn marks.

"Sorry, I'm so sorry," she stammered.

"Hey, *hey*. I'm fine." Claudia patted Lucy's arm. "Just static. Nobody died."

Lucy grit her teeth together. The first thing she would demand Ravi teach her tomorrow was how to show affection without supercharging the people she loved. He might have come to Eaton to train her, but that didn't mean he was calling all the shots.

She looked her friend up and down, fighting back tears. There was so much Lucy wanted to tell her. But Ravi's warning echoed in her mind, and she didn't want Claudia on his employers' radar.

Instinctively, Lucy felt for the tourmaline in her pocket. As she flipped it between her fingers, relief spread through her chest, a sensation she now recognized as her electrical field coupling with the stone's. Her breathing returned to normal.

"What's that?" Claudia jerked her chin at the stone.

Lucy handed it over. "Tourmaline."

Rubbing her hands together, Claudia said, "*Preeeeecious*." Her Gollum impersonation was eerily spot-on, and Lucy laughed. Her bestie raised the stone up to the light, its edges shimmering in the woodland shadows.

"It's something new I'm trying," Lucy offered, "to keep my seizure symptoms at bay."

Claudia cocked an eyebrow.

"It's supposed to relax me if I'm starting to feel stressed . . . or something."

"Mercury must be in retrograde or the end times are coming if empirical method—only Lucy Phelps is trying out alternative healing."

Coming from anyone else, Lucy would have been offended. Since it was Claudia, she snorted. Her friend was right. Lucy was beginning to believe in a lot of things she wouldn't have a month ago.

"Where'd you get it?" Claudia asked.

"Ravi gave it to me." *Gulp.* Why had she let that slip out?

"Ravi?" She traced the diamond ridges of the tourmaline. "The new teaching assistant?"

Lucy's flush was all the confirmation her best friend needed. She wanted to protest that he wasn't *really* a teaching assistant, she wasn't really breaking any rules, and he'd given her the stone for a very scientific reason. Mind-blowing kiss notwithstanding, there was nothing going on between them.

"Riiiiight," Claudia said. "He's cute, I suppose. If you swing that way."

"Mrs. Brandon asked him to supervise my independent study. That's all," Lucy replied defensively. "He read up about my condition. He suggested I try it."

Claudia splayed on her front, propping herself up on her elbows, and her expression turned serious.

"If you talked to him about your medical stuff, you must really trust him."

The insight gave Lucy pause. Claudia knew better than anyone how much she hated drawing attention to her condition. How much Lucy hated pity. And yet, Lucy had felt comfortable enough to confide in him that day in Central Park.

"Maybe I do," Lucy admitted. But it still burned her that Ravi had allowed her to ramble on about her epilepsy that day when he knew it was a lie. Why couldn't he have just come clean with her then?

Claudia watched Lucy, eyes intent. "Is Ravi the reason for the demise of Cole?"

"You make it sound like the *Desolation of Smaug.*"

"Aha! I knew you'd appreciate Tolkien eventually."

"*Pshaw.* Give me the USS *Enterprise* over the Shire any day."

"I like my Shire," her friend retorted. "But seriously. I get it. I've succumbed to the allure of a college girl myself." Lucy jabbed her playfully in response. "Would it get you more psyched for prom to learn Ravi has signed up for chaperone duty?" Claudia said.

Lucy's heart did skip a beat. Stupid heart. Ravi had probably been instructed to attend the prom to keep an eye on her.

"I'll be there to man the battle stations, Clauds. But that's it."

"*Nuh-uh*. No way. I'm not letting you skulk in the background, Luce." She narrowed her eyes. Damn, Claudia knew her too well. "You can be my date."

"Isn't Jess your date?"

The corner of Claudia's mouth hooked up in a crafty grin.

"We'll make it a threesome. Eaton High won't know what hit it."

Laughter wracked Lucy's body and she thanked the nonexistent gods above once more that Claudia's family had moved in next door.

"I mean it," Claudia protested.

"I know you do."

"Jess found this costume shop on Etsy that makes replica flapper costumes, tassels and all. Who doesn't love tassels? There's still time to order another one."

"That's really sweet, but—"

"I'm not taking no for an answer."

Lucy sighed. Resistance was futile. "If you're sure Jess won't mind a third wheel."

Claudia waved dismissively. "And you know what?" she said, pinching the tourmaline between her fingers. "I could make this into a pendant. It would look totally '20s."

Gratitude suffused Lucy and the breath rushed from her.

"You're the best, Clauds," she said, hoarse. "I don't know what I'd do without you."

Claudia beamed a cherubic smile.

"Then it's a good thing you'll never have to find out."

TIME FOR A MONTAGE

Lucy had found it less than shocking when she received a text from Ravi naming the time and place for their first training session—without ever having given him her number.

Anticipation flitted through her as she pedaled Marie Curie to the rendezvous point. Which had next to nothing to do with seeing him again.

Lucy had always dreamed about having mastery over her body, of making it follow her commands rather than the other way around. And despite her reservations about the alchemists' agenda, this elusive possibility seemed to be just what Ravi was offering. She didn't know what he wanted from her, but what Lucy wanted from Ravi was knowledge.

That was it. She'd just extricated herself from one romantic complication and she didn't need another.

Lucy's hair rose from her shoulders, her anxiety mounting, as she arrived at the old boathouse by Lake Windermere. She understood why he'd chosen the spot. This side of the lake was rarely traversed since the Eaton Recreation Club had been built on the opposite bank. Only the odd hiker or two. There were unlikely to be any witnesses to whatever Ravi had planned.

He was focused on the horizon where Sunfish cut through the middle of the lake. From the minute tensing of his posture, Lucy could tell that he was aware of her presence for a few moments before he swiveled toward her with a welcoming smile.

"I'm glad you came," he said.

"I didn't think I had a choice."

Lucy wasn't sure why she'd expected him to morph from a tweed-wearing, *Doctor Who*–loving, bespectacled (if hot) mathematician into GI Joe (or whatever the British equivalent was) overnight. Well, he hadn't. The only difference in Ravi's appearance was the lack of blazer, and without said blazer she couldn't help but notice his well-sculpted biceps. He didn't get those researching tessellation. Her gaze skirted the eight-pointed star and she felt her expression soften at everything it represented.

When she stopped less than a couple feet from him, Ravi asked, "Ready?" but not like it was really a question.

The little girl who could make lightning flashed through her mind.

"More than ready for my training montage," she assured him.

"Then let's get started."

Lucy's montage, however, had apparently been shot in slow-mo.

No orders to run laps, do push-ups or pull-ups of any kind. A tad disappointing. Rather, Ravi motioned for Lucy to follow him up a mossy trail that led to a better vantage point over the lake below. The phrase *And she was never seen again* sped through her mind, but Lucy decided to trust her powers.

They were basically augmented intuition, right?

An early summer breeze kissed the surface of the water and sunlight burnished the ripples. Ravi lowered himself onto a flat rock near the edge of the ridge.

Peering at the long drop down to the water, Lucy said, "I can already tell you that if you push me, I'm not going to fly."

His lips arced in amusement but his shoulders remained tight. Since he'd been unmasked, Ravi's demeanor had changed, become more guarded, as if prepared for an assault on all fronts.

"Today we're going to start with defense," he said evenly.

"Because it's the best offense?"

"No. In time, you'll have a much better offense. But before you can do anything else, you need to be able to block out other people's frequencies. Otherwise they might become overwhelming."

The way Ravi's voice became quieter on that last word chilled Lucy's heart.

"How do I do that?" she asked.

"It will take discipline."

Lucy snorted. What a surprise.

"You can come closer," he said. "I won't bite."

So far she'd avoided touching him at all. If she did, Lucy was worried that her resolve to see him as a platonic Yoda might falter. Why couldn't he be old, bald, or the slightest bit green? Steeling herself, she took a seat on the opposite end of the rock.

"Yesterday," he began, less poised, "when I, *er*, convinced you to believe me. What precisely did you experience?"

"A lady never kisses and tells."

"I'm not trying to embarrass you. This is an objective question."

Okay, Lucy could do this. She wasn't twelve. She was a scientist.

Lucy proceeded to rattle off her list of observations in a clipped, emotionless tone: "Ticklish. A kind of floaty feeling. But also a sense of calm." Ravi nodded at each statement, his eyes trained on hers. "It wasn't the first time you made me—that I experienced those phenomena when I made contact with your skin," she added, as indifferently as possible.

Ravi sucked in a short breath. "Why are you surprised?" Lucy asked.

"I should have done a better job at shielding myself."

"Shielding yourself?"

"Have you noticed that you may be picking up readings—good or bad—from some people more than others?"

"Stop answering a question with a question," she snapped, but then she thought about it. As soon as Lucy had seen Cole after her visit to Tesla's lab, the seasickness had started. The next person to provoke a reaction was Ravi. And Claudia. Nothing from her mother. *Huh.*

After another few seconds, Lucy admitted, "Yes. My best friend and my *boy*—ex-boyfriend." She spied a tendon tic in Ravi's jaw at that piece of information, but she ignored it.

"That follows," he said. "People who are more emotionally involved with you will be easier to read." Lucy wondered what that said about her mom. "Also, some people just repress their true thoughts and feelings as a matter of course." Well, that explained her mom.

"So why did I feel those tingles the first time I bumped into you in the hallway? We'd never even met."

Ravi rubbed the knuckles of his left hand across his tattoo.

"I suppose I was a little apprehensive about meeting you. About pulling off the whole charade." He paused. "As I said, I should have shielded myself better."

"But you were lying right to my face. Shouldn't my powers have picked up on that? Seems like a design flaw to me."

Ravi leaned forward, grabbing her gaze. "Lucy, I'm sorry about the deception. Professor T thought you might respond better to being approached by someone closer to your own age. But I see now I handled it wrong."

Thinking about being discussed like the invasion of Poland, Lucy huffed.

"You never did tell me how you hunted me down."

He bristled. "We weren't *hunting* you." Lucy put a hand on her hip as if to say, *Well?* "We intercepted the phone call you made to Claudia O'Rourke. From there it was a process of elimination."

Static electricity immediately filled the inches between them.

"I don't want Claudia mixed up in this," Lucy said.

"We're the *good guys*. We would never hurt you. Or your friend. Please, believe me." His eyes grew troubled. "I swear, I just want to help."

"What about the threat you promised me was real?"

Ravi toed the pebbles at his feet. "We have no reason to believe that they know where you are. Or that it would serve their purposes to hurt your friends or family."

"It's just me they want."

Lucy let her gaze bore into him until he confirmed, "Yes."

Her shoulders deflated as she let out a sigh of relief. "Okay. I can handle that." She laughed shakily. Not that Lucy wasn't scared for herself, she was, but she'd rather have the target on her own back than on anyone she cared about.

"They're alchemists too," Lucy surmised. To which Ravi answered grimly, "They started out that way."

"All right." She straightened her spine. "Let's see if I've got it so far. Some people's frequencies are easier to tune into than others if they're wear-their-heart-on-their-sleeves types or if we're emotionally involved. I can tune into those frequencies through touch, and the sensation gets stronger through more . . . *intimate* contact."

"Precisely."

"What about the static electricity that occurs around certain people?"

"That's the result of your own heightened emotional state. The tourmaline should help control it."

Lucy scooted back on the rock and dragged her knees to her chest.

"Why did all this start after I visited the Tesla Suite?" She tried to keep her voice from trembling. This was what she'd wanted to know for weeks.

Ravi twisted his torso so that he was looking at Lucy straight-on.

"It didn't."

"Of course it did!"

"The seizures—and seizure-like phenomena—you've been experiencing are side effects of your underlying condition."

"Which is *what*?" she wanted to know.

He rocked closer. "My parents nicknamed it the lightning gene; they were studying its mutation."

Fear skittered down Lucy's spine. "I'm a *mutant*?" There was no way Ravi could know about her dream, was there?

"You're not a mutant, Lucy." He attempted a reassuring smile. "You have a mutated gene. Nothing more."

Nothing more?

Throat hoarse, she forced out the words, "Tesla had the lightning gene too, didn't he?"

"We believe so."

"That's why you needed someone like me to unlock the lab," she realized, her chest constricting. "The plasma lamp—when I touched it, I had a cut on my hand." *Breathe, Lucy.* "It recognized the genetic mutation in my blood."

"Yes," he confirmed. "We're working from that assumption."

It was also incredibly sophisticated technology for 1943. Not that anything could truly astonish Lucy when it came to Tesla anymore.

"This lightning gene is what's been causing my brain to misfire, making doctors misdiagnose me with epilepsy?" she said. Ravi nodded. "Then why haven't I had a seizure for two years? The meds seemed to be keeping everything under control until I stumbled upon the lab. How is that possible? I hadn't been tuning into anyone's frequency either."

Ravi smiled sympathetically. "I don't have all the answers. A lot of my parents' research was lost in the fire." He waved a hand in the air. "If I were to hazard a guess, I'd say that your seizures were linked to normal changes—like puberty. You could simply be more stable than when you were younger. It could also be that the medication you've been taking targeted some of the same neural pathways. The interaction with the plasma lamp may have triggered your dormant abilities."

His shrug was elegant but his gaze was laser-focused. "I promise we'll figure it out together, Lucinda."

Lucinda. She really wished she didn't love it when he called her that.

Could Tesla's Egg have been the trigger? The way it had reacted to her presence, levitating, spinning, almost like an excited puppy—it would make the most sense. Somehow it had undone the stability established by her meds. And she'd already determined it amplified her powers. Fabulous.

She was about to tell Ravi about the egg, but she stopped herself. Not yet. She needed to know more about the alchemists first.

"In the meantime, it would probably be safest to stop taking the medication," Ravi said. "We don't know how it will interact with your nervous system now that your abilities have been triggered."

Lucy nodded. He was probably right. Guilt deluged her again at how hard her parents had tried to help her over the years, even when it was smothering.

Ravi dropped a hand onto Lucy's knee. No tingles. She looked at him, questioning.

"I'm shielding," he replied. "Now you try."

"How?"

"Look at the lake. The size of the waves increases as the wind's strength increases."

"Thanks for explaining how waves work, Ravi."

He disregarded the barb. "Close your eyes," he instructed, and, despite her irritation, she did. "Visualize an enormous sandbar against which the waves crash, never reaching the shore."

Lucy cracked one eye open. "I thought no man—or woman—was an island."

"Very droll." Ravi smirked. "But just give me the benefit of the doubt."

"Isn't that what I'm doing?"

"Fair enough."

Lucy interlaced Ravi's fingers with her own. Still no tingles.

"Okay, I'll try," she told him.

She shut her eyes once more, hyperaware of his scrutiny.

"Maintain the image of the sandbar in your mind." His voice was scarcely more than a whisper. "I'm going to slowly lower my defenses and you're going to raise yours."

Since this was Lucy's fantasy, she replaced Lake Windermere with the turquoise waters of a tropical island somewhere exotic like Thailand or Zanzibar. Someplace her parents would never let her visit. She conjured a glittering white-sand beach, grains like diamonds.

Ravi's shield lowered gradually, his energy tantalizing. Lucy gripped his hand more firmly as a breath shuddered through her. On the horizon, gilded waves gained momentum. The whitecaps multiplied and coalesced into a tidal wave. Euphoric laughter echoed on the breeze.

Don't give in.

Lucy evoked an enormous sandcastle wall protecting the shore. She was a fortress. She wouldn't allow anyone to scale her walls.

The wave surged closer. She squirmed, tingles tickling the soles of her feet.

I am a fortress. I am an island.

Lucy knew the instant Ravi relinquished the last shred of control. The sky over her sandbar lit the same fiery pink as when they'd kissed. Was Ravi's frequency pink? Did everyone have a frequency that corresponded to the color spectrum?

Part of her wanted nothing more than to dive into the tidal wave, let herself float, let it lift her higher and higher. Then Lucy remembered the three-chili-dogs-on-a-roller-coaster feeling that Cole had provoked, and the choking toxic sludge from the thief in Central Park. Could the choking sensation be aggression? Or anger? Either way, she didn't want to go through that again.

Lucy added another mental layer to the ramparts of her castle. And another. And another until it scraped at the sleeping stars.

The tidal wave broke and Lucy, and Lucy felt . . . nothing.

Her eyelids flipped open. "Did you put your shield back up?"

Shaking his head, Ravi wore a proud expression. Lucy's gaze darted to their interlocked hands. "That's all you," he said, and a smile blossomed on her face.

Victory was sweet. So sweet her limbs became weightless, gravity a stranger. The smile evaporated. Cursing at herself, Lucy withdrew her hand from his.

"That didn't last long."

"Rubbish. You did well. You'll get the hang of it. Soon enough you won't even have to think about it—it'll be like breathing."

Lucy rolled her eyes.

Ravi showed her an open palm. "Again," he insisted. She squared her shoulders, glaring at his authoritative tone.

What did she have to lose? Other than everything.

She took his hand.

INK OF A SCHOLAR

Eat. Finals. Train. Sleep. Repeat.

For the past week, Lucy had done nothing but study, work with Ravi, and adjust the sound and lighting system in the gymnasium. Prom was in two days and she couldn't wait to get it over with. Although she had to admit the smoky gray flapper dress and sparkling tassels really did match her eyes.

Lucy's father had sent her a model airplane with a note saying, *I'm sure you'll soar through your exams*, and the promise that he'd be home soon. The airplane had to be assembled, of course. There hadn't been any *gotcha!* questions, so Lucy was actually feeling pretty confident about her results.

The only nausea-inducing moment was right before the physics final started, when Megan showed her a ferociously feline smile. Cole couldn't even look in her direction. Lucy supposed she deserved that.

She stole a surreptitious glance at Ravi, who was keeping time to Herbie Hancock on the wheel of the Land Rover while navigating midtown Manhattan traffic. Her last exam had been this morning and if her mom emerged from her writing cocoon, she wouldn't wonder where Lucy was until dinnertime. A perfect chance for a road trip to meet Professor T.

Her eyelids were heavy as they passed Madison Square Park, which was littered with office workers ducking out for a quick snack from one of the many food trucks. Lucy hadn't had to feign napping on the drive to the city. Meeting a Nobel laureate and alchemist would be daunting enough if Ravi hadn't been running her ragged to boot.

Weightlifting and crunches would have been highly preferable to the pneumatic-drill headaches Lucy got trying to break through Ravi's shield. Once she'd become relatively proficient at blocking him, he taught her to visualize a battering ram to shatter other people's defenses. The ability seemed morally dubious to Lucy but he'd assured her it was only a precautionary measure.

She didn't mention her throbbing temples to Ravi because she didn't want him to put the kibosh on their training sessions. As bone-tired as she was, Lucy needed to learn as much as she possibly could. She doubted he'd be sticking around as her personal Jedi master forever.

Besides the frequency jamming, Ravi had Lucy practicing how to control her electromagnetic field with and without the help of the tourmaline. So far she'd had less success without it. She'd shared her theory with him about pushing her electrical current outward versus trapping it inside and he had listened without judgment. With great interest, in fact. Lucy couldn't deny how much she liked the way Ravi crinkled his nose while he listened or considered a problem.

If they were going to work together, however, as colleagues of sorts, she needed to keep her own defenses in place.

The car stopped.

"Lucy," he said gently, with the faintest touch to her shoulder. "We're here."

Her eyes bugged.

The façade of the mansion on a cross street off Park Avenue South was, in a word, imposing. The ornate metal scrollwork around the entryway reminded Lucy of her father's office building. Beautiful and Gothic. Very *Abandon All Hope Ye Who Enter Here.*

"Professor T *lives* here?" Lucy marveled.

"When he's not in England," Ravi said. Where did Professor T live in England? A palace?

She counted at least four stories, each level demarcated by a cornice ornamented with gleaming golden gargoyles. It couldn't be real gold, could it?

The gargoyles nestled between lustrous foliage, palm fronds with liquid lines. Lucy's chest squeezed as she realized the head of each gargoyle was ringed by petals. Six petals. *Gulp*. She still hadn't revealed her dream to Ravi. It seemed too ridiculous. Even for an alchemist. Or an alchemist's apprentice. How did that work, anyhow?

"You planning on getting out of the car anytime today?" Ravi teased.

Smothering a blush, Lucy opened the door and stepped out onto the mansion's private driveway, then trailed him up an incredibly grand stone staircase. Her eyes raked the sculptures comprising the balustrade. Women in flowing robes, like togas, peered back at her. Their lips were upturned as if they had a secret.

Ravi rang the doorbell on the first-floor landing and her fingers grasped for the missing charm bracelet. A doorbell seemed too pedestrian for an abode such as this. She would have expected a mischievous enchanted knocker.

On either side of the doorway stood two marble columns like she'd never seen. Chiseled into the buff stone capitals were overlapping, repeating motifs: an Egyptian ankh, a crown, and an eagle. It was hard to say where one ended and the next began, yet each symbol was distinct.

Lucy met Ravi's sideways glance. "Tessellation," she said.

He grinned. "No need to be nervous."

Says you, she told him with a flick of her eyebrow. She gave her outfit a quick up and down. Lucy wasn't sure what one wore to meet a world-renowned scientist, but she wanted to come across as serious, professional. She'd chosen a creamy satin blouse, a navy-blue skirt, and a patterned cardigan. Ravi had swapped his usual geek-chic T-shirts for an Oxford shirt, which reassured Lucy she'd made the right call.

He gave her hand a quick squeeze just as the door swung open. Ravi had lowered his shield on purpose. If only his frequency didn't feel so damn good.

"Ravi!" boomed a friendly, very British voice from inside, although his accent was different, thinner somehow.

The owner of that voice appeared a second later.

Professor T's broad shoulders filled out a tailored linen suit that looked like it cost a million bucks. A few thousand, in any case. And as he embraced Ravi, Lucy noted that he was an inch or two taller, and almost as fit despite his age. He was someone who commanded respect.

Stepping back, he shifted his focus to Lucy.

The bushy, snow-white eyebrows that matched his beard did nothing to soften his penetrating stare. Lucy shifted her weight. Professor T's slate eyes held a hint of blue to them, and although they glowed warmly at her now, she was positive they could cool to ice.

"You must be Miss Phelps."

He took her hand, grip firm. No sensation. Of course, he most likely taught Ravi all of his tricks.

"*Pr*-Professor Weston-Jones," Lucy stuttered. "It's an honor to meet you."

"As it is to meet you." His eyes twinkled and he let out a chuckle reminiscent of Ravi's. "Now, come in, come in, the tea is steeping. And you must call me Tarquin—or Professor T, as Ravi is wont to do." He winked at his godson, putting an arm around Lucy's shoulders to shepherd her into a stately foyer.

"Thank you, Professor T," she managed.

"I hope you like Moroccan mint," he said, peering down at her. "It's perfect for the season. Refreshing. Cleanses the palate."

Lucy was only half listening because her gaze had drifted upward to the fresco gracing the ceiling of the entrance hall. A man with winged sandals hovered in the clouds above them. Hermes, the Greek messenger god. Since meeting Ravi she'd become infinitely more indebted to her mom for imparting her knowledge of classical mythology.

If Lucy thought the foyer was lavish, however, it was nothing compared with the library.

Magnificent, oak-hewn bookshelves towered above her, twenty or thirty feet high. The stacks reached toward a dome-shaped roof comprised of tinted glass. Natural light streamed onto Lucy's face. A swift scan of the room told her she was standing at the heart of the mansion. It must have been designed like a Roman villa, only instead of a court-yard there was a library at its center.

Between the stacks on this floor and those on the surrounding, second-story balcony, the library easily contained twenty thousand volumes. Probably more. She inhaled their musty but delicious scent.

A spiral staircase cast from brushed steel and copper connected the two levels, another tessellation of triangles like those on the Chrysler Building adorning its length, creating a feathering effect. Along the sides of the first-floor reading room were long tables for research, Tiffany lamps and lecterns placed at intervals, and in the middle of the room was a sofa, several armchairs, and a mosaic coffee table. The perfect researcher's respite.

"Please make yourself comfortable whilst I chase up the tea." Profes-sor T gestured for Lucy to be seated on the leather sofa. She hesitated, afraid to damage it, unconsciously counting the brass buttons studding the armrests.

"I'll get the tea," Ravi offered. Lucy fired him a panicked look. *You're fine*, he mouthed. She grimaced. "Back in two ticks."

The butterflies in Lucy's stomach got jet packs.

Professor T settled into an armchair opposite the sofa, leaving her with no choice but to finally sit while her eyes roved the bookcases. Her mom would sell a kidney for a private library like this.

"The ink of a scholar is more holy than the blood of a martyr," he said, and Lucy wrested her gaze from the filigreed spines. "From what Ravi tells me of your academic prowess, I'm confident you'd agree." His lips quirked as she nodded mutely, both self-conscious and elated that Ravi had paid her such a compliment.

"I can't take credit for the sentiment," Professor T continued. "That honor belongs to Caliph Harun al-Rashid, who ruled Baghdad in the eighth century. He brought scholars together in his fabled House of Wisdom, a library to rival Alexandria, commissioning translations into Arabic from treatises collected in Greece and India."

"He preserved the alchemical texts."

"Indeed." His tone held approval and a thrill of triumph zipped through Lucy. Professor T crossed his legs in a deliberately casual manner. "This is my humble and unsatisfactory imitation of the caliph's great house," he said, waving a hand around the cavernous space. "Feel free to consult its knowledge at your leisure, Miss Phelps."

Her jaw dropped. All she could think to say was, "Lucy. Call me Lucy."

He smiled, leaning toward her. "You're welcome here anytime, Lucy. *Liber librum aperit.*"

"*Wh*-what did you say?"

"*Liber librum aperit.* An old alchemist's motto. It means—"

"One book opens another," Lucy interrupted, too dazed to cringe at her own rudeness. Whoever had written on the photo in her father's study must know about alchemy. But the handwriting didn't belong to either her mother or her father. And whoever it was also knew about the Tesla Suite.

Did that someone know about Lucy's powers?

How could a stranger know and not her own parents?

"I wasn't aware that Latin was still part of the curriculum at most American schools," Professor T commented, intruding on Lucy's speculation.

Distractedly, she replied, "Oh, my mother taught me. She's a classicist."

He steepled his fingers, evaluating her.

"A classical education is extremely useful in the sciences as well as the arts. I understand from Ravi that your father is a physicist."

"Yes. Quantum mechanics. Although he's mostly a businessman these days."

"Nothing wrong with wedding science and industry."

Lucy's cheeks burned. "Of course." Where *was* Ravi? She wasn't sure how much more of this small talk/cross-examination she could handle. How long could it possibly take to brew tea?

"Quite an accomplished family," Professor T said. "What is your mother working on at the moment?"

Her heart thumped. She wished she hadn't lent Claudia the tourmaline to make her necklace on today of all days.

"The role of female scientists in the ancient world," Lucy answered after a beat. It was a partial truth. She worried how Professor T would react if he learned her mom was trying to decipher the *Pharmakon of Kleopatra*.

Lucy's parents might not think she could take care of herself, but she would still try to take care of them.

"A rich topic." Professor T inclined his chin. "I'd love to read her work."

Who was the colleague who had shown her mother the *Pharmakon*? Could he or she be an alchemist too?

Lucy let her eyes fall to the carpet. Antique, like everything else in the place, alchemical symbols woven into a royal-blue base. She picked out the astrological sign for Mercury. Like Lucy, it was a volatile, potentially lethal chemical.

Time to gather her courage. She had come here for a reason.

"Professor T, I've read about your research into DNA mutation online. That's why I'm here, isn't it? The lightning gene." She lifted her gaze and pinned him with it. "Can you help me?"

"I think we can help each other, Lucinda."

TEA AND SYMPATHY

Ravi picked that moment to return with a silver tray. Lucy sucked down a sigh, her bravery faltering.

He poured a pale, apple-green liquid into three porcelain teacups. The sterling-silver teapot, engraved with a pastoral scene, would have been right at home in Queen Victoria's drawing room.

Ravi positioned himself next to Lucy on the sofa, extending a cup, which she accepted with trepidation. She avoided anything precious out of habit since her parents hadn't trusted Lucy with breakable things growing up. Most of their dishes at home were still made from melamine.

Two pairs of eyes watched Lucy sip her tea.

"Heavenly, is it not?" Professor T mused, taking a sip from his own cup. "I have a friend at the souk in Marrakesh who couriers it to me."

"Delicious," she agreed.

The professor shifted back in his armchair, balancing the saucer on his knee. Something about his posture, even sinking against the leather, resembled a fighting stance. Ravi must take after him.

"What can you tell me about Archimedes?" Professor T asked her, bringing the cup to his lips, his eyes never leaving hers.

Talk about a non sequitur. Lucy's mind raced, dredging up her father's history lessons. "Archimedes was an ancient mathematician . . ."

Think, Lucy. "He discovered that a floating object displaces its own volume in liquid."

"Do you recall the story of his discovery?"

"Not entirely."

Professor T set his cup on its saucer and the *clink* reverberated through the library.

"Archimedes was the chief scientist of Hieron II, king of Sicily," he began. "King Hieron had commissioned a new golden crown but when it arrived, he suspected the smith had mixed silver into the gold. He tasked Archimedes with determining whether or not he had been swindled. Archimedes promptly went to the public baths to contemplate the problem, as you do."

Professor T exchanged a conspiratorial smile with Ravi, who obviously knew how the story ended. "When Archimedes submerged himself, water sloshed over the sides. *Eureka!*" The professor jabbed a finger in the air. "Archimedes realized that he could test an equal weight of gold to see if it displaced more or less water than the crown. If it did, the crown was not pure gold."

"And was it?" asked Lucy.

"No, indeed. That was the end of the goldsmith's career. As well as his life." Another laugh. "Archimedes also invented great war machines. The catapult, for instance. Once, he defended his homeland from invading Roman ships by arranging a series of mirrors on a cliff and harnessing the power of the sun to set them on fire."

Lucy hadn't known that. Goosebumps irritated the back of her neck.

"I suppose you're wondering what Archimedes has to do with why you're here," said Professor T. "Ravi?" An arched brow was all the prompt he needed.

Ravi put down his teacup and turned toward her, a distant look in his eyes. Lucy chewed her lip. Way to drag out the tension.

He rolled up the sleeve of his shirt to reveal the eight-pointed star.

Then Professor T did the same.

"We belong to the Order of Archimedes," Ravi said. He weighted each word, speaking reverently as he always did about the alchemists.

"And like him, we believe that science should be used in the service of the state, or the people as a whole."

Lucy flashed back to the crown on the columns outside. Hieron's crown.

"Was Archimedes the founder?" That would make the Order thousands of years old.

Ravi shook his head. "We were founded by John Dee, an adviser to Queen Elizabeth the First. He was an alchemist, philosopher, mathematician. A true Renaissance man. He thought Archimedes a fitting tribute."

"Right," Lucy said, unsure where he was going with this. Apparently she hadn't been totally wrong to think the teapot could have served the British royal family.

Five hundred years ago.

"The alchemists had reached a crisis point in the Middle Ages after being persecuted for generations," Professor T explained.

Lucy kept her expression placid as he talked. She didn't want to let on she'd already learned this from her mother.

"They were divided into two camps. Those who wanted to hide, squirrel their knowledge away. And those who wanted to find a way to work with the great rulers of Europe for the benefit of everyone."

"I take it John Dee belonged to the latter camp."

"Just so. He demonstrated to Queen Elizabeth that scientific progress was not something to be feared but rather essential to good governance."

"Also maintaining power," Lucy added. Immediately, she felt Professor T's gaze land on her.

"John Dee laid the foundations for the Invisible Colleges and the Royal Society that followed." There was a hint of defensiveness in his tone.

"Are you saying Sir Isaac Newton belonged to the Order of Archimedes?"

A rare smug smile from Ravi. "Him and many more. Edison. Roger Bacon." The smile deepened. "Even your Volta."

Disbelief washed over her. "Why haven't I ever heard of you?"

It was Professor T who answered. "While we believe in sharing our knowledge, we do not like to advertise ourselves."

"But you've told me." She paused. "Are you going to kill me now?"

His laugh was meaty. "On the contrary, we believe you'd make an excellent recruit."

The room seemed to spin. Was Lucy really being offered the opportunity to join a secret society to which all of her scientific heroes had belonged?

"Because of my lightning gene," she inferred.

"Not only that. But yes, we believe it is the key to completing the research I had been conducting with Ravi's parents." Professor T regarded his godson with true fondness.

Lucy's gaze returned to Ravi. She felt a prickle in her heart. As an aspiring researcher, she could think of nothing worse than leaving her work unfinished, her legacy uncertain. He must not have told her because he didn't want her to feel obligated.

She inched her hand toward him on the sofa, then stopped herself. "How would I be able to help?" she asked.

"We believe that your mutation might provide answers to the cause of a variety of neurological conditions," Ravi said, meeting her eyes.

"Like Alzheimer's," she said, thinking back to the article about the fire, and he nodded. "Then why am I in danger? Who could have an issue with curing disease? And what does it have to do with Tesla?"

"There are always those who fear progress," Professor T answered.

Something worse than darkness shone from the professor's eyes. Bleaker. Lucy was very, very glad he wanted to be her ally rather than her enemy.

"The other alchemists?"

"They're called the Order of Sophia. They believe that the general public should be protected from technological advancement." Lucy thought the professor might spit. "Craven zealots."

His enraged response stunned her into silence.

More quietly, Ravi said, "The Sophists consider your genetic mutation to be dangerous."

"To whom?" she demanded.

"Humanity."

"Humanity? And that means what, exactly?"

"The ignorant seek to destroy that which they do not understand," replied Professor T. "But we won't let that happen."

Destroy?

Lucy's guts twisted.

"*Lucinda.*" The tenderness infusing Ravi's voice pulled her from her spiraling thoughts. "We'll protect you. *I'll* protect you."

Which was all well and good, but he wouldn't always be around.

"I need to be able to protect myself."

"Yes, you do," Professor T agreed. "Come work with us. We will study your powers together, hone them. The Sophists will have much more to fear from you."

Lucy didn't think that sounded any better.

"There's no way to get rid of my powers?" she asked with a trace of desperation.

He frowned. "Lucinda, they're part of who you are. I'm sorry we didn't find you sooner. That you have lived your life until this point believing you were damaged. Somehow less. You are far from damaged." The compassion in his statement matched the ferociousness moments before.

How did he know that was how she'd felt? The way her parents treated her?

As if he hadn't rocked her world enough, Professor T let slip, "We believe you are the next stage in evolution."

Holy. Frak.

"If that's the case, why aren't there more people like me?" Lucy asked, a strange calm descending on her. Shock, she guessed. "Why are we so hard to find?"

Neither of them answered. The quiet became oppressive. It weighed on her chest. Ravi and Professor T exchanged a glance.

Of course. They weren't responding because the answer was blindingly obvious.

"They're dead, aren't they?" she said in a hush.

Professor T slid to the edge of his seat. "The abilities caused by the genetic mutation can be unpredictable."

"Unpredictable," she repeated. "You mean maladaptive." Lucy knew enough about biology and evolution to know that species with maladaptive traits went extinct. "The nervous system can't withstand so much electricity."

The human brain wasn't built to cope with the amount of electricity she could produce. Eventually, her mental faculties would be compromised, and she might even stroke out.

Lucy looked from Professor T to Ravi. Ravi coughed.

"Tesla's mutation is to blame for his increasingly erratic behavior, right?" she persisted. "Will the same thing happen to me?" Shock transformed into panic.

"We want to make sure it doesn't," Ravi told her firmly. She dropped her eyes to the floor.

Lucy's thoughts whirled, searching for some kind of solution. "But, but . . . Tesla was in his eighties when he died. How did he survive so long?"

"We believe Tesla discovered a method to diminish and amplify his powers at will," Professor T told her. "Perhaps even replicate them."

Hope kindled inside her. "How?" she asked.

"We don't know," Ravi said apologetically.

Wait a minute. The Order of Archimedes might not know how Tesla had amplified his powers, but maybe Lucy did. An egg-shaped amplifier.

"Lamentably, Tesla was eliminated before he could share his findings with my predecessors." Professor T released a sigh. "His research stolen."

Lucy's head snapped up. "Tesla's death was an accident. He was hit by a taxi."

"Right after he'd sent an ecstatic telegram to the Order saying he'd made a substantial breakthrough." He spread his hands. "What are the chances?"

Another realization hit Lucy like a brick.

"Tesla was murdered. Because he was like me."

She raised her chin, daring—*wanting*—them to contradict her.

"So, let me get this straight," Lucy said. "These Sophists killed Tesla and stole his research—research that allows carriers of the lightning gene to live to a ripe old age." The words gushed out of her, and she felt ill. "And you haven't been able to replicate Tesla's discovery. Whatever it was."

Ravi grabbed her hand. "We've found you now," he said, eyes blazing. "Everything will be okay."

Everything was pretty damn far from okay. She was living on borrowed time.

"You can't promise that." Lucy turned to Professor T. "I should be getting home soon. My mother will start to worry."

"Of course." He glanced at Ravi. "Continue working together in Eaton until you graduate. Afterwards, I can offer you a summer internship at my company."

"In England? My parents would never let me go." Lucy didn't even have a passport.

Professor T's brow creased in a momentary scowl. "I can be quite convincing."

She didn't doubt it, but, "*I*—I need to think about it," she told him.

A month ago an internship at Chrysopoeia Tech would have been her dream come true. But now . . . maybe Lucy didn't want to know more. She'd come here for answers and they'd turned out to be more terrifying than she could have imagined.

"Naturally. I don't want to pressure you," the professor replied. "Just remember, you're not in this alone. Not anymore."

Lucy released Ravi's hand and pushed to her feet.

"Thank you for inviting me to your home, Professor," she said, remembering her manners.

"You're always welcome here, Lucinda." He smiled. "This place belongs to all Archimedeans. We take care of our own."

YOU WOULDN'T LIKE ME
WHEN I'M ANGRY

As Lucy hurried to the principal's office the next morning, she had no clue what he might want with her. She'd never received a summons before.

She had only come into school at all to sort out the last of the colored gels for the spotlights. If she were being hunted by assassin alchemists, she would at least make sure Claudia's speakeasy was illuminated in living color before she took the long dirt nap.

Sheesh. Her bestie's mobster talk was rubbing off on her.

Lucy's palm was slick on the doorknob. Why was she so uneasy? She hadn't done anything wrong. A small green flame appeared where her skin made contact with the brass. *Crap*. She concentrated on steadying her breathing and willed her nerves away.

Mrs. White, Principal Petersen's secretary, didn't smile at Lucy as she entered. She was an older woman, late sixties, known for her seasonal collection of brooches. Today's was an enamel cherry blossom.

"He's waiting for you," Mrs. White said, her voice nasal and disapproving, and pointed a finger toward an inner door branded PRINCIPAL GEOFFREY PETERSEN in black letters.

"Um, thanks." For nothing.

Exercising caution, Lucy used the sleeve of her sweater to twist the doorknob. No need to alarm the secretary with her superpowers.

The last person she expected to see as the door creaked open was Ravi. Or Mrs. Brandon. Her physics teacher smiled sympathetically.

Principal Petersen, on the other hand, glowered from behind his desk. Not good.

Oh no, had he found out about the kiss somehow? Was *Ravi* in trouble?

"Miss Phelps," said the principal. "So glad you could join us. Have a seat." Who knew he could bring the snark? Lucy had hoofed it as fast as humanly possible when she'd received the note. Although she might not be entirely human.

Don't think about that.

The chair scraped against the linoleum as she pulled it out and slanted a questioning gaze at Ravi. He simply adjusted the cuffs on his tweed jacket. Mrs. Brandon folded her hands together.

Really not good.

"It has come to my attention, Miss Phelps, that you and your fellow students have done exceedingly well on this year's physics final." Principal Petersen smiled condescendingly, tipping his head in Mrs. Brandon's direction. "In fact, there were numerous perfect scores. Some might call that miraculous."

Lucy's brow crimped in confusion, her interest briefly drawn to the glass apple on his desk. She doubted any of his students had given him that.

"Miss Phelps?" the principal snapped, regaining her full concentration. "Do you know why I asked you here?"

"No, sir."

"We take the honor code very seriously at Eaton High."

An anvil dropped in Lucy's stomach. Had Megan made good on her threat to turn her in? Why now? Ravi noticed her chest rise and fall rapidly, and he rubbed his thumb against the inside of his palm.

Lucy got the message: *Use the tourmaline. Don't sauté the principal.* But Claudia was still fashioning the necklace for tomorrow night.

"Having consulted with Mrs. Brandon and Mr. Malik, the only

explanation for the perfect scores is that the students had access to the examination ahead of time." Principal Petersen rested his elbows on the desk. "Neither of them distributed the exams, which leaves only one other person with access to the science office. Mrs. Brandon's student aide. *You.*"

He made the pronouncement as if he'd solved the murder of the century.

Lucy would have snorted if the situation weren't so dire. Her parents would flip if they found out. She'd be grounded until she was forty.

The words *I would never!* died on her lips because she'd helped Cole cheat one too many times. But Lucy hadn't done this.

"Mrs. Brandon trusted you when she gave you a key to the office," the principal said gravely.

Oh. Frak. The key. Lucy hadn't simply lost it. Cole must have swiped it.

"Principal Petersen," she said as calmly as she could. "I have no need to cheat." Which was the truth. She'd become an expert in sins of omission.

Mrs. Brandon nodded in agreement.

He sighed. "Your academic and disciplinary record have thus far been exemplary, Miss Phelps. Which is why this behavior is so very disappointing. These are grounds for expulsion." The word echoed in Lucy's cranium. "And of course," he continued, "I would have to notify Gilbert College. It would be up to their admissions office whether or not to withdraw your acceptance."

College. Freedom. Everything Lucy had worked for. It couldn't just all be yanked out from under her like this. It *couldn't.*

Lucy's gaze darted from Ravi to Mrs. Brandon, pleading.

Her fingers latched onto the edge of the desk. "But I didn't do it! And you don't have any proof!"

The principal's nostrils flared. That had clearly been the wrong tactic to use.

"I will give you the weekend to rethink your position. On Monday

I expect you to do the honorable thing and either turn yourself—or the other responsible party—in."

Lucy trembled in response. Not with fear.

With rage.

"You're dismissed, Miss Phelps."

She stormed from the room, clenching her fists at her sides, before she could turbocharge any of the office supplies. She wouldn't mind melting Principal Petersen's god-awful woodpecker tie clip and see what he had to say about *that*.

Damn you, Cole Hewitt.

She should have known a leopard didn't change its spots so easily. How gullible was she? Actually believing Cole wanted her to tutor him! Did he steal the key from her purse before or after their study session?

Typical Cole. No thought for consequences. No thought for how it might affect the girl he professed to love. That must be the internal conflict she'd been picking up from him in the hot tub that night.

And she had blamed herself! She should have listened to her instincts.

Lucy was near the front lobby when she heard a loud bang.

She twirled around to see one of the locker doors hanging off its hinges.

Her hands shook. From the other end of the hallway, Ravi saw it too.

This time Lucy did run. She needed to be where other people—and metallic objects—were not.

RED SKY AT MORNING

"Sorry about the ambush."

Lucy's gaze traveled from the lake toward Ravi's soft, lilting voice. She'd booked it to their training spot without thinking. Well, maybe some part of her wanted him to find her. The drive back to Eaton yesterday had been awkwardly silent as Lucy tried to process everything she'd learned.

Ravi dropped down next to her on the boulder. The breeze ruffled his sable-colored hair and Lucy sat on her hands so she didn't smooth it back.

"I know you wouldn't steal the test, Lucy."

She blew out a shaky breath. "It's hard to prove a negative."

It was also hard to feel anything but defeated. After she'd hulked out at the school, Lucy's rage slowly burned off. Assassin alchemists, deterioration of her mental faculties, ripping a locker from its hinges with an electromagnetic field she wasn't supposed to possess . . . all of these things were more terrifying than being expelled. Objectively. But it was the possibility of being denied college—the chance to strike out on her own—that scared her most.

Taken together, Lucy was emptied out.

Ravi touched a hand to her cheek in a debatably more-than-friendly move. "What do you think happened?" he asked.

Without her permission, Lucy's body leaned into his touch. His shield was up, so there were no ticklish tingles, only his warm, steady presence.

Sighing, Lucy covered his hand with hers, and gently removed it from her cheekbone. "I didn't steal the exam," she told him. "But I think it's my fault."

"How so?" His face was open, no judgment in his eyes, just the intensity that was quintessentially him.

"My ex-boyfriend. I'd been helping him with his homework a bit too much." Lucy smoothed her palms against her thighs before daring a glance at him. Ravi's expression remained unchanged. Clinging to the denim, she finished her confession. "I found out he'd been selling my work to other students. I put an end to it," she hastened to add, "and said I wouldn't do his work for him anymore. He must have stolen the key from me."

"Cretin."

Lucy shrugged in resignation. "I don't have any proof, only a theory. And I was also in the wrong. Two wrongs don't make a right, right?" She gurgled a faint laugh. It was a good thing Lucy had never told Claudia about Cole's scheme, or she might be considered an accomplice.

"Do you think you could get him to confess?" Ravi asked.

She wiggled her fingers tauntingly in the air. "With my own form of electroshock therapy?"

He laughed. "By appealing to his sense of decency?"

Considering Lucy had already texted Cole multiple times and he'd ignored her? Unlikely. Cole wasn't an evil mastermind, but he *was* selfish. And he didn't take responsibility for his actions. It was part of why she'd fallen out of love with him, after all.

"You don't think less of me?" she whispered. Despite Ravi's secret-agent routine, his opinion had come to matter to Lucy. A lot.

His eyes pierced her as he said, "I think we all make mistakes when it comes to people we care about."

Lucy shifted her body so that her knees met his. "You know, it's funny," she mused. "If I hadn't been fighting with Cole, I might never have ended up at the hotel." *I might never have met you.* Her gaze dropped to their legs. Ravi hadn't tensed or moved away.

"How *did* you find your way to the Tesla Suite? I didn't want to press you before," he said.

"You mean you don't know?" Lucy replied, and Ravi shook his head.

Static began to fizz between them as her thoughts whirled, and Lucy was the one who pulled away, facing forward to admire the lake.

If she told him the truth, he might know who had sent the photo. But she also might be compromising her parents somehow.

She felt Ravi's posture stiffen beside her as he waited for her answer. She sighed again.

"Lucy?" he prompted.

"This is probably going to sound ridiculous," she said, cutting him a sideways glance. "It started when Schrödinger—that's my cat—knocked over a picture frame."

The corner of Ravi's mouth lifted in a half-smile. "Is the cat alive or dead?"

"Both. Zombie cat." Lucy gave a small laugh and drew a circle on the craggy face of the rock. "Anyway, the glass cracked, damaging the photograph. I scanned it into my computer to see if I could use some math—*maths*—software to repair it."

"Clever. Sounds like you," Ravi said, and Lucy felt herself flush. "What was the photo of?"

"Me. Well, toothless me. Trust me, I look better with teeth."

He laughed. "No career as a prizefighter for you?"

"Doubtful. Although, if I'm going to end up with brain damage, I might as well go a few rounds, I guess."

"Don't say that."

At Ravi's unexpectedly gruff tone, Lucy went quiet. It was the only logical deduction. She watched the rainbow of sails glide on the wind. Sailing away from her problems would be nice.

"How did the photo lead you to the Tesla Suite?" Ravi asked. His expression was curious, and something else. Something like fear.

Lucy swallowed. She didn't want to lie to him, but she also needed to protect her parents. She picked her words very carefully.

"Steganography," she replied. "I discovered a binary sequence encoded in the yellow channel of the photo. It contained the address for the New Yorker Hotel, Room 3327."

Ravi pushed to his feet and began to pace. Lucy decided to leave out the part about it being addressed to her father's company—and the alchemist's motto that had been written on the back.

"My dad's not an Archimedean, is he?" she asked.

"Not to my knowledge, no." His tone was brusque. "Do you know when the photo was sent?"

She shrugged. "It's been in my house for as long as I can remember." From everything Professor T had told Lucy about the Order of Sophia, if they knew about her existence, they would have darkened her door long ago.

But if it hadn't been either of the Orders, who else could have sent it?

"Have you told your parents what you found?" Ravi asked, quizzing Lucy the way she imagined the professor would.

"No. My dad's been away on business, and my mom—I didn't want to worry her with my new symptoms." Or wind up under house arrest.

"Good, good," Ravi said, mostly to himself.

"I'll have to tell them the truth at some point, though," Lucy said, and she realized she actually meant it.

Ravi stopped, pivoting towards Lucy, lips flat. "I don't think that's a good idea."

"They're my *parents*."

"I know." A shadow crossed his face. "But it's not safe. Not yet." He closed the space between them. "If you could bring me the photograph, I can do further analysis."

Lucy gulped. "Sure." But then Ravi would know she wasn't being entirely straight with him. She would have to find a way to stall.

"In the meantime," he implored, "please don't go anywhere without your mobile."

She liked the way he said "mobile" instead of "cell phone." Still, she asked, "Why not?"

"So I know where you are." Ravi raked a hand through his hair, and Lucy's rage began to simmer again.

"How would you know that?" she demanded.

"I installed a GPS app in your phone," he replied sheepishly—but not nearly sheepishly enough.

"For my protection, right?" Lucy leapt to her feet, getting in his face. "That's how you just *happened* to bump into me in Central Park!" Exactly like her parents! *Hiss.* Her rage approached a boil. "I am so tired of other people deciding who and what to protect me from!" The full-throttle freak-out she'd restrained last night came roaring to life.

"You *do* need to be protected from the Order of Sophia, Lucy." Ravi gripped her shoulders, both of them breathing hard. "You still don't understand."

"I understand you're a bona fide stalker," she said. "You put me in virtual handcuffs!"

Instantly, he released her. He stepped back.

"I'm sorry, Lucinda. Truly I am, but—"

"But *what*, Ravi?"

From low in his throat, he told her, "The Sophists murdered my parents."

Lucy blinked. "Oh, Ravi. I . . ." She placed a hand on his shoulder and pain came off him in waves. His shield was cracking. She felt it bleeding through his natural frequency. Pain like Lucy had never experienced.

"Why didn't Professor T say anything?" she said in a hush.

"It's my story to tell." Ravi squinted into the mid-distance. "They're ruthless. Powerful. Connected." Far beyond what Lucy could have conceived.

The Order of Sophia was behind the fire in his parents' lab. It made sense. They wanted to stop the research into the lightning gene. They'd been prepared to kill people to achieve their aims. And they'd gotten away with it.

"If something happened to you, I wouldn't be able to live with myself," he told her.

Softly, she said, "I'm not your responsibility, Ravi."

He exhaled a hard breath. "I don't want to lose anyone else I care about." His gaze skimmed her face, lingering on her lips, then dropped to the ground.

She was still angry about him tracking her without permission, but the fact that he was putting himself in the cross hairs of the people who killed his family for her sake . . .

"I care about you too," Lucy admitted.

The pain emanating from Ravi dissipated but he said nothing. He'd probably already said too much. The wind rustled the leaves. His breathing steadied.

Lucy spoke first. "The mugger in Central Park—you think that was them?" There was a quaver to her question.

He lifted his eyes, and she pretended not to notice that they were watery.

"I don't know," Ravi said. He frowned. "It doesn't seem like their MO."

"They're more 'annihilate first, ask questions later'?" Lucy said, keeping her voice breezy.

"That's not funny."

Maybe not. But if she didn't laugh, she would cry. She shifted her weight from one foot to the other.

"Ravi, I lied to you about what was stolen from my bag," Lucy said, deciding she owed him at least this much honesty. "I didn't think it mattered at the time . . . it was something I took from Tesla's lab. A bronze egg. I wasn't lying about that."

"What does it do?" he asked calmly. Too calmly.

"I can't say with absolute certainty. But I conducted a few experiments, and . . ." She chewed her lips guiltily, then met his stare. "It amplifies my powers. I think it might have been what Tesla used."

"Bloody hell, Lucy."

She looked away. "I'm sorry."

Ravi snaked his fingers through her curls, drawing her closer. Not the reaction she'd anticipated. "We'll sort this," he promised. "We will."

He rested his forehead against hers and Lucy closed her eyes, seeing a red dawn in her mind. *Sailors take warning.*

Slipping her arms around his waist, she hugged Ravi back. For this stolen moment, nothing existed but the warmth between them. Heartbeats and breath and heat.

Tomorrow, she would get back to training. Tomorrow, she would deal with Cole. Not right now.

Right now, Lucy just wanted to be held.

THROUGH THE LOOKING GLASS

She didn't recognize the girl in the mirror.

Lucy belonged to another time. Tesla's time.

The slip dress was a waterfall of gray—pearly at the top, gaining momentum to dove, oyster, and gunmetal at the bottom. Tassels shimmered like breakers, light from her desk lamp winking off the beads.

Rhinestones glittered across Lucy's brow, bobby pins tined between her teeth as she skewered the headband into place. Dusky feathers tickled the shell of her ear, a hint lighter than the locks she'd swept into an updo at Claudia's insistence. She and Jess would be here to pick Lucy up soon and Lucy didn't dare deviate from her stylist's explicit instructions.

Her lips twitched in the whisper of a smile. Perhaps for tonight she could be someone else.

"Oh, Lucinda."

Her mom's reflection appeared behind her in the doorway, an almost melancholy expression on her face.

"You look stunning," she said, moving toward her. "Just like your namesake." Lucy had been named for the Roman goddess whose name meant light.

"Thanks." She fiddled with a bobby pin. "I can't take any credit. This look is all Claudia."

"Here, let me help," her mom offered. Lucy tensed as their hands met, but she didn't seem to notice.

Exhale. No odd prickles.

Deftly, efficiently, her mom double-checked and secured each of the pins. "There." She patted the chignon hanging against the nape of Lucy's neck. "Cole will have the most beautiful girl at the prom on his arm."

Lucy bit her lip. "Actually, we broke up."

"What? When did this happen?" she asked, a deep V creasing her brow.

"Recently."

"Sorry, honey. I suppose I've been in my own world lately."

The regret in her voice was unfamiliar. "It's okay," Lucy said. She couldn't think of a time when *she* had reassured her mom. "I'll have a better time with Clauds."

She scooped the black tourmaline necklace from her dresser and began fidgeting with the clasp. They'd never had the girl-talk kind of mother-daughter relationship, and Lucy didn't plan on starting tonight.

Her mom's gaze hooked on the stone. "Lovely. Let me."

Lucy handed her the necklace and she held it up to the light. The tourmaline swayed as it dangled.

A quizzical look appeared on her mom's face as she draped it around Lucy's neck. "Is this new?" she asked.

The tourmaline fit exactly in the hollow of Lucy's throat. Her heart instantly resumed a more regular cadence. It occurred to her that she, like Ravi, now had a dark star of her own. If she decided to join the Order of Archimedes, would Lucy get an identical tattoo? She didn't want to think about how she would explain getting inked to her parents.

Lucy smiled up at her mom. "Claudia made it for me." Not a totally untrue statement. And she had done an amazing job with the setting. Metallic slivers burst outward from the stone like rays of sunlight. It gleamed as brightly as if it were genuine silver. Leave it to her bestie to come up with something so original in no time.

Her mom pressed her cheek to Lucy's, always so smooth.

"It suits you."

Slam! A sudden noise jolted them apart.

"Elaine? Lucy?"

Her father's deep baritone bellowed from downstairs. Lucy scurried toward it like a little girl, pausing on the landing.

"Dad!" She couldn't help being excited to see him. Despite all her questions, she'd missed him.

He dropped his suitcases by the front door and stared at her with a bewildered smile on his face.

"When did you get so grown up?" her dad said. This was the dad who shared Einstein Time with Lucy. The dad she adored. Seeing him again, a surge of protectiveness rose up in her. After what had happened to Ravi's parents, Lucy was inclined to heed his warnings. She would have to keep her own counsel for a little while longer.

"Come here!" Her dad waved in a beckoning motion. "Let me get a better look at you."

She raced down the stairs, her mother gliding after her.

"Beautiful," he said. Glancing from Lucy to her mom, her dad sighed. If Lucy wasn't mistaken, he had a few more gray hairs than when he'd left.

"My two favorite girls." He kissed her mother's temple as she hugged him.

"Welcome home, Victor," she told him, her shoulders sagging. Lucy's mom never seemed like she needed anyone's support, but something had changed in the past few weeks. It was probably the separation.

"I'm glad to be home," he murmured, and kissed her again.

Lucy had acquired her aversion to PDA from her parents. Seeing them so wrapped up in each other was just plain weird. Weirder than having telekinetic powers.

"What are you doing back?" Lucy teased.

"I live here, don't I?" Her dad waggled his eyebrows as he stepped back from her mom, still holding firm to her waist. "And I couldn't miss such a momentous occasion."

"I'm not sure prom qualifies as momentous."

"In that case, you won't mind staying home tonight."

"*Dad.*"

He pulled a *Who me?* face. "Well, you and Cole be sure to remember your curfew."

I will. But Claudia's my date. She and her girlfriend will be here soon. I'm the third wheel."

"A lot has changed while I've been away," he commented.

Like you wouldn't believe.

He shrugged off his trench coat to reveal a business suit. He must have jumped straight on the plane from a meeting.

"Did you wrangle that difficult investor?" Lucy asked. "You must know Tokyo like the back of your hand by now."

Her parents shared a look.

"Still in the process of wrangling," he answered, jaw not entirely relaxed. "But I didn't want to stay away any longer. I've missed too much already."

Her mom rubbed his shoulder in a placating way, taking the coat from him.

"You'll prevail in the end."

"I'd better." There was a strange longing in his words. Lucy had never known her dad to get so worked up about a deal. Shifting his attention back to her, he said, "How were your finals?"

Her lips curved in a meager smile. "Um, fine. I think." She still didn't know what she was going to tell Principal Petersen.

"Don't be so modest." He squeezed Lucy's shoulder and she braced herself. Nothing. If she wanted to, she could break through his shield, although it would most likely give her a nosebleed, and that would spoil her outfit. She couldn't risk Claudia's wrath.

Her dad scrutinized her once more, lips tensing slightly. "New necklace?"

Guilt pressed on Lucy's chest. "Claudia's handiwork, Victor," her mom informed him.

A sidelong glance. "She's talented."

Just then, the doorbell rang.

"I'll get it!" Lucy exclaimed in relief.

Principal Petersen and murderous alchemists were problems for another day.

Tonight was prom.

UNDER MY SKIN

Lucy sipped her white lightning from the DJ booth. Her heart had thundered for a few beats as Claudia ladled it from the punch bowl before explaining "white lightning" was Prohibition slang for bootleg liquor. This concoction, conversely, was virgin sangria—mostly Sprite and orange slices. Not nearly potent enough to blind anyone.

She twiddled a dial on the lighting board as her classmates trickled into the gymnasium. The dance committee had all arrived early to make sure the lights on their reimagined Broadway never went dark. Lucy hadn't escaped her house without a few obligatory pre-prom photos, however. She didn't really mind. A few years ago, Lucy wouldn't have believed her parents would ever let her attend.

Although Jess looked incredibly sophisticated in black satin, her short hair sculpted in a Marcel wave, she adamantly refused to join them in the photos. Lucy had been surprised—Jess didn't seem like the self-conscious sort—but selfishly glad. Going to prom with her best friend was the way things should be. Claudia's turquoise dress had a drop-waist cinched with peacock feathers that complemented Lucy's crescendo of gray. They struck a pose gleefully. Giggling, arms around each other, huge smiles.

No matter what lay in store for her, Lucy would have these photos as proof that, at least for tonight, life had been good.

Pride swelled inside her as more students took the dance floor *ooh-*

ing and *ahhing* at the scenery. Lucy had positioned the spotlights so they hit the mirror ball in such a way that blue and purple snowflakes fell on the speakeasy patrons.

"Nobody puts Baby in a corner."

Claudia thrust out her hand, a mischievous grin spreading her lips.

"I told you I was manning the battle stations," Lucy protested.

"I wanna dance with somebody who loves me." She winked.

"Where's Jess?"

"My moll's outside yammering on the phone." Claudia shrugged. What could be so important that Jess would take a call in the middle of prom?

Lucy sighed. She had zero interest in dancing but she couldn't leave her bestie hanging. "Don't touch any of the dials," she commanded the DJ, another Heron student, with more piercings than she could count. He grunted his compliance.

"He'll be *fine*," Claudia assured her and tugged Lucy down the rickety stairs toward the center of the gym.

To her left, King Kong did a tap dance on the Empire State Building. To her right, cars beeped their horns in a vintage Times Square.

"It's incredible, Clauds."

"Thanks to you."

"Thanks to you," Lucy corrected.

Looping her arm and swinging Lucy onto the dance floor, Claudia compromised, saying, "Thanks to *us*!" and erupted into contented laughter.

Lucy tried to follow her lead as Claudia performed some kind of mash-up between swing dancing and the Charleston. If only she'd been a teenager in the '90s when moshing was cool. Headbanging Lucy could manage. Nevertheless, after a few minutes she was breathless and chortling and didn't give a damn if she was writhing like she'd stuck her hand in an electric socket.

When she spied Jess making her way back toward their vicinity, she pecked Claudia on the cheek. "Thanks for the dance, doll face. I'll cut in later."

"You'd better!" Claudia wagged her finger.

The second Jess laid her hand on Claudia's waist, Claudia smiled at her like she was her whole world. Tightness pinched Lucy's chest. They would beat the odds and make long distance work. They had to. Claudia deserved to be happy more than anyone she knew. And Lucy wanted to believe in love, believe that someone would stare at her with the same adoration one day.

If she made it that long. The deck seemed stacked against her.

Perspiration trickling down her spine, Lucy decided to get some air. She was halfway out the side door of the gymnasium when a familiar voice asked, "Leaving so soon?"

Lucy twirled on the spot.

Wow.

Ravi stood before her in white tie and tails, light bouncing off his patent-leather brogues, no glasses. He'd even slicked his hair back with gel.

"Just something you had lying around?" she said.

"A gentleman never travels without formalwear."

"I can see why not."

Lucy detected pink undertones to his cheeks even under the lavender mood lighting. He coughed into his hand.

Methodically, Ravi raised his eyes to hers, appraised the length of her body, and met her eyes again. "You look captivating tonight, Lucinda."

Captivating. He did have a way with words. There was nothing Lucy could do about the buzzing beneath her skin.

"Dance with me," she said, feeling brave. He licked his lips. She held his gaze and leaned into him. "*Ravi.*"

One second. Two seconds. Three.

He lifted his elbow to escort her. "It would be my honor."

Lucy had gone to school dances with Cole, of course, but she'd never had this same exhilaration coursing through her veins, as if someone had popped a Champagne cork inside her. They wove their way between the other couples but Lucy was scarcely aware of their existence.

Wordlessly, Ravi interlocked his fingers with hers and placed a firm hand on her lower back. It felt so right there.

The tempo slowed to a ballad as he pressed her closer, searched her face. A smooth, yearning saxophone played the opening bars to a Cole Porter song Lucy knew well. She wouldn't put it past Claudia to have provided the DJ with a set list of Prohibition Era music.

Ravi's fingertips tensed on her ribs as he led her in a box step. Mostly that involved swaying to the beat. Good thing. Lucy was positive she'd be swaying in his arms, no matter what.

"What are you thinking?" he asked.

"I was thinking the universe has a sense of humor."

"Oh?"

"This song. *I've got you under my skin*."

"I see your point." He laughed, twirling her in and out.

"You're good at this," Lucy told him.

"I've had lessons," Ravi explained. She arched an eyebrow. "The benefits of a boarding school education."

Lucy laughed as he spun her once more, then she slipped her hands around his neck, teasing the tiny hairs resting there. She felt an involuntary tremor cascade through him.

Ravi touched one finger to the tourmaline at her throat and she held her breath. "I like what you've done with it."

"Beautiful and practical," Lucy quipped.

"Like you."

Oh boy. The tourmaline could do nothing for her pulse now.

Ravi glanced at his hand as if remembering he was still technically a chaperone for the evening, and dropped it back to Lucy's hip.

"I hope the Eaton High prom doesn't disappoint," she said lightly.

"Nothing about Eaton has been a disappointment."

Emboldened, Lucy tipped forward until they were almost nose-to-nose. She couldn't kiss him in the middle of the dance floor, all of her classmates and Principal Petersen ogling them, but she wanted more.

"Let down your shield."

The song was almost over.

His eyes went wide and curious. "You don't know how hard it is for me not to let you in, Lucinda."

"Stop trying," she said.

Ravi obeyed. Tingles crashed over her and Lucy laughed in a giddy way. "I wish you could feel what I feel," she murmured into his ear.

He braced one hand between her shoulder blades and dipped her, low and deep. "Believe me, I feel far more than I should."

His gaze traced her like a caress.

"I've heard enough *shoulds* to last a lifetime, Ravi."

Lucy floated up, up, up. There was hunger to his energy tonight.

And she liked it.

Extraordinarily slowly, Ravi raised her back to an upright position and drew up his shield. That had been more intense than kissing. More intimate than anything Lucy had ever done with Cole.

"It's hard for me to keep you out too," she told him, and a pained look crossed his face.

Nearby, one of the bulbs on a floor light blew. Perfect timing.

"I'd better go check on that," she said.

"Lucinda—"

Now she really did need a breather.

Flashing him a wobbly smile, she promised, "Be right back," and dashed off before Ravi could finish whatever he'd been about to say.

Prom had been perfect. Reality could wait.

WHITE LIGHTNING

The beat picked up as Lucy hurried along the edge of the dance floor but she glimpsed Claudia and Jess still dancing cheek to cheek. No one else seemed to have noticed the burst bulb. Maybe it was just a fluke. Maybe it wasn't Lucy's mojo.

She clutched the pendant, twisting it in place.

A hand shot out from the crowd and Lucy stumbled.

Megan.

"Having a nice evening?" The other girl dazzled her with a shark-like smile. Had she been sharpening her incisors? "Glad there are no hard feelings about Cole. Who would've thought Seizure Girl would snag Mr. Darcy?"

"I don't know what you're talking about."

Megan plumped the poofy pink taffeta of her skirt. She looked like walking cotton candy. "He's quite the dancer," she said, raising a supercilious eyebrow. "Cole caught the show too. Thank you for that. Should clear his conscience about the whole overlap issue."

Lucy twisted the tourmaline so hard the chain nearly snapped.

"Overlap?"

"I knew it was only a matter of time," Megan continued blithely. "I've had my prom dress picked out for months."

As if there were a time delay, Lucy's ears picked up on the end of Megan's sentence.

"Months?" she repeated.

The razor-sharp smile widened. "Some things are just inevitable. We were celebrating our admission to the U of Northern New York—didn't Cole tell you we'll be freshmen together in the fall?—and one thing led to another . . ." Megan drummed her fingers against her chin as if she had a quandary. "It only took him this long to break up with you because he felt sorry for you."

"I am not some charity case." Lucy bared her teeth.

"Aren't you? Giving Cole the physics exam in the hopes of winning him back smacks of desperation."

Is that what he'd told her? Before Lucy could clarify a few things, including the fact that *she* had dumped him, the devil himself appeared.

Cole emerged from the crowd of glimmering, sweat-soaked bodies with two cups of fruit punch in hand. Oblivious as always.

Lucy regarded him with nothing but disgust.

"You two deserve each other."

Shoving the punch at Megan, he demanded, "What did you say to her?"

Lucy didn't stick around to hear any more of Megan's lies. Storming toward the DJ booth, she did some quick math. She'd slept with Cole for the first time *after* he'd found out about his scholarship— which meant he and Megan had already hooked up. Had he really stayed with Lucy because he held the caveman belief that her virginity was some kind of prize to be won?

"Lucy! Lucy, *stop*."

Cole raced around from behind her and planted his feet, blocking her exit path. Bass pumped out of the enormous speaker next to them.

"Lucy!" he shouted again. "Lucy, can we go somewhere quieter to talk?"

"I have nothing left to say to you."

"That's not fair."

"Fair?" she yelled back. "Using my key to steal the physics exam isn't fair! Leaving me to take the fall isn't fair!" There was a frenzied twang to her voice. "Cheating on me for months with Megan isn't *fair*!"

Cole pushed back his shaggy bangs. "I didn't cheat on you. Megan kissed *me*—once. Nothing happened before you dumped me."

"Do whatever you want with Megan. You can go to hell. Together."

"Luce, come on. I'm sorry about the exam. You were never supposed to get into trouble," he said like he was actually concerned. "But it'll blow over."

"Principal Petersen is threatening to expel me! It won't just *blow over!*"

Lucy's heartbeat strained against the pull of the tourmaline. Her energy didn't want to be leashed. "And you know what's sad? Despite everything, I would have helped you study if you'd just asked. Megan's right: I am pathetic."

He grabbed her hand. "You're not pathetic."

"Don't touch me," Lucy scolded him as a torrent of nausea struck. Cole's conflicted emotions—anger, hurt, concern—churned Lucy's stomach. She shook him off. His feelings weren't her problem.

Grimacing, Cole said, "I couldn't do it on my own. I'm not as smart as you. I needed to keep my scholarship."

"You never think about anyone but yourself." She hugged herself tight.

"You're wrong! I tried so hard to make you happy, Luce."

Lucy laughed an unkind laugh, a buzz rising inside her.

"You tried to make me happy by hooking up with Megan?"

"It happened *once*. But at least she wants me. I was never enough for you. Do you know how hard that is to take?"

Static blasted from the speaker. A horrible, nerve-rattling noise.

Cole took a step closer, not realizing he was in danger. Lucy's eyes darted toward the rafters. She couldn't tell whether the disco lights were flashing the way she had programmed them or as the result of electromagnetic interference.

Her interference.

"Stay back," she warned.

"Don't be so dramatic. I'm not going to hurt you."

I might hurt you. She lurched back, bracing her hands on the speaker. On. Off. On. Off. The lights were definitely not supposed to do that.

Some of her classmates gasped, others laughed.

"I wanted you to fight for us, Luce," he said, pleading. "But you didn't."

Searing-hot rage bubbled just beneath the surface. She wouldn't listen to any more excuses.

"What a mistake that would have been."

Cole shrunk back as if she'd slapped him. Good. Power rushing through her, Lucy was too scared to actually touch him, but she wanted him to hurt.

"Either you turn yourself in to Principal Petersen—or I will." Her nostrils flared as she lay down her ultimatum.

Doubt smoothed his features before creasing again in anger.

"Do that and I'll tell Petersen about your extracurriculars with the Brit. Being a sex offender could really put a cramp in his teaching career."

"This isn't about Ravi."

Cole scoffed. Then his eyes rounded. "Lucy?" His voice trembled. "Lucy? I think you're on fire."

She followed his gaze to her hands.

The entire speaker—as well as Lucy's arms up to her elbows—was engulfed in undulating emerald flames.

Cole staggered back in fear. For the first time, Lucy truly understood how Frankenstein's Monster felt when confronted by torch-wielding villagers.

Boom!

Sparks sprayed from overhead as the speaker combusted. Static raged from those remaining. Lucy's classmates braced their hands over their ears. A few made a valiant attempt to keep dancing.

Pop. Pop. Pop.

One by one the spotlights exploded.

Lucy was too stunned to move.

The final bulb burst and the gymnasium descended into darkness.

Boom! There went the last of the speakers.

Quiet and dark. Almost peaceful. Like the moments before the Big Bang.

Glass tinkled as it cracked and began to fall.

Then screams shredded Lucy's eardrums.

EYE OF THE STORM

"Come with me."

The rasp in her ear sounded very far away, as if she were at the bottom of a deep well. Lucy wouldn't mind staying there. Just for a bit.

"Let's get you out of here," Ravi said in a calm, efficient tone. Battle-field calm.

She didn't move. She was still glowing green.

He reached for her elbow and her heartbeat bucked.

"Don't," she barked. Lucy pushed herself away from the speaker, her thoughts in a million pieces. How could Ravi dare to touch her in that state? And, *oh God*. Cole had seen her illuminated with fire but not burning. And she had blown up the prom. Claudia's prom. *Oh, Clauds*.

Ravi tucked her hand in his and pulled her toward the exit. He wasn't taking no for an answer.

Other students raced by her, loping down the hallways with a *clickety-clack* of high heels, bumping into one another, groping in the darkness. Havoc. Total havoc. Lucy shook.

In a daze, she allowed Ravi to lead her toward the parking lot.

"Claudia. I need to find her." It was Lucy's first coherent thought.

"You can call her later. We should get you home."

"Before I can cause any more destruction?"

"To make sure you're okay." Ravi shot her an authoritative look. Lucy would be annoyed except she knew he was only worried. Possibly scared. With good reason. He'd never seen Lucy in action before.

His brow crinkled, reaching toward Lucy's nose. "You're bleeding."

Frak. "It's nothing."

"It's not nothing."

"Just let me see that Claudia's okay and we can go." Lucy hadn't been able to spot her on the dance floor when the lights shattered. She would never forgive herself if Claudia had been injured. She wiped away the rest of the blood.

Ravi nodded, realizing she wouldn't back down.

High beams momentarily blinded her. Lucy squinted, rushing toward where they'd parked the Mystery Minivan. The lot became checkered in red and white as students dove for their cars. At least it was a prom no one would ever forget.

Claudia's space was empty.

No way would she ditch Lucy. Her stomach rolled over.

Amidst the gunning engines and squealing tires, Lucy detected her "Imperial March" ringtone. *Wait.* She didn't have her phone. Huh?

With precision, Ravi withdrew Lucy's small, beaded evening bag from the inner pocket of his tailcoat.

"Full-service date," she said. "Not a date, I mean—"

He cut her off. "I should have stepped in with that wanker sooner."

There was no need to explain any further. Ravi had been watching over her, taking precautions in case she blew her fuse. Ha. Tonight she was indebted to his vigilance.

"Thanks," she said, and opened the purse. Lucy had been the one who failed him, failed to remember her training, to keep her emotions reined in.

1 new message

Her lungs practically collapsed in relief. Claudia was the sender.

Your services are required. If you wish your friend to remain unharmed you will make your way to Long Island City within the next 90 min. Further instructions to follow. Come alone.

The parking lot whirled around Lucy. Shaking, she passed the phone to Ravi.

His fingers tightened around the case as he read the message.

"It's a trap," he said.

Rage like snow settled over her and the haze of her mind cleared. "Obviously."

"You can't go."

Lucy balled her hands into fists. "Don't tell me what I can't do." Her voice was colder and more dangerous than black ice. "This is the Order of Sophia, isn't it? They've kidnapped Claudia to get to me. Well, they can have me." And if they touched a hair on her friend's head, she would make them regret it.

"*No.*" Ravi framed her face with his hands, his eyes beseeching. "You're too important, Lucinda."

"To the Archimedeans?" She couldn't care less about them when Claudia was in danger.

"To *me.*" He crashed his lips into hers, heedless of the fleeing prom-goers. This kiss was wild, fevered. Flames licked the underside of Lucy's skin. She kissed him back with forceful lips and teeth before pulling away.

"Claudia's my family, Ravi. I have to do what the Sophists say. You would do the same."

His chest rose and fell as he stabilized his breathing, regaining control.

"I don't think it's the Order of Sophia."

"Why not?"

"They wouldn't require your services," he said coolly. "They don't want you to use your powers at all."

"Who else could it be?" Lucy grabbed for the tourmaline even though the stone had failed to stop her eruption in the gym. "Who else could know about me?"

"Has there been anyone new in your life lately?"

"Besides you?"

Ravi didn't laugh. "Besides me."

New in her life? Other than Ravi, she couldn't think of anyone. It had been the same ol', same ol'. Cole, Claudia . . . *Holy crap*.

"Not in *my* life," Lucy said. "But Claudia just started dating Jess around the time—in fact, they met the same day you started teaching at Eaton High. I don't know, though. She seems so smitten, I find it hard to *be*—"

"Blast!" Ravi exclaimed. He hammered a fist against his thigh. "This Jess, if that's her name, do you have any photos of her?"

Lucy took back the phone and began to scroll. No. *Oh no, no, no*. Jess had refused to be in the prom photos for a reason—and it wasn't shyness.

"Claudia said Jess had to make a call earlier. I thought it was strange to be phoning anyone during prom." Her voice faded out as she recalled the times she'd made direct contact with Jess. Lucy had felt guilt. She'd just assumed it was her own for not wanting to share her best friend before they left for college.

Ravi cursed. "The blackout provided a useful diversion." Catching Lucy's stricken reaction, he added, "It would have happened regardless."

That didn't make her feel any better. Defeated, her head drooped. She stared at Claudia's megawatt smile on the screen of her phone.

"If the Order of Sophia didn't take Claudia, who did?" Lucy asked miserably.

"The Freelancers."

"The *who* now?" Her gaze flicked up. "You're telling me there's another faction of crackpots I have to worry about?" Reality had just taken the bullet train to the Twilight Zone. She laughed in desperation.

"The Freelancers are defectors from both Orders. Mercenaries. They contract for the highest bidder."

Could they have been the ones to send the photograph of Lucy to the Sapientia Group? Had they known about her for *years*?

"This all just keeps getting better and better," Lucy told him. "What do they want with me?"

Ravi exhaled through his nostrils. "Nothing good. Whatever it is, I'd wager it has something to do with the Tesla Egg. They must have stolen it."

Lucy smacked her forehead.

"What is it?" he asked.

"I saw Jess and Claudia before I caught the train that day. She saw me with the egg." Lucy really didn't want to believe that Jess could have been playing Claudia, but it was the only thing that made sense.

Did the Freelancers know the egg amplified Lucy's powers?

"Bollocks. Could Jess have planted a tracer on you?" Ravi asked.

"Anything's possible. My super spy skills are a little rusty." She'd meant it as a joke, kind of, but her words flew out daggered.

He ignored her tone. "We need to check." He glanced around the now mostly empty parking lot. "Not here."

"You think it's still on me?"

Ravi nodded grimly.

"But I'm not wearing the same clothes. And I've been known to take a bath."

"It would be subcutaneous."

"I think I'd remember being injected with something."

He surveyed the lot again. "It might have felt like a pinprick. Perhaps not even that."

Lucy shuddered. "'Cause that's not disturbing at all." And even more reason to do whatever the Freelancers wanted to get her best friend back. "I need to get Claudia. Now."

"I can't let you play into their hands, Lucy. The Freelancers always have an agenda."

"Not my problem." She raised a hand before he could interrupt her. "I don't care about some centuries-old feud between the Orders or the Freelancers or whoever else. I need to find Clauds."

"I can't put it beyond them to be collecting you on behalf of the Sophists."

Lucy crossed her arms. "It's a risk I'll have to take."

"You don't know what they're capable of." Ravi was shifting his weight onto the balls of his feet. If Lucy tried to bolt, he was prepared to snatch her.

"They don't know what *I'm* capable of, Ravi. Exhibit A: the worst prom ever."

"Lucy," he cautioned.

"How do they know about me? Huh?"

One hand curled into a loose fist. "We must have a mole," he said.

"A mole? Great. Just great. What's to say this mole hasn't told the Order of Sophia where I am anyway?" she huffed, power curling inside her, begging for release. "You're doing a real bang-up job of protecting me."

All emotion left Ravi's face. "The mole will be discovered and dealt with."

"While you're working on that, I guess I'm at the service of the Freelancers."

"I admire your bravery, Lucinda," Ravi said in clipped tones. "But we'll figure out another way to get your friend back. Perhaps we can offer them something else. The Freelancers are always open to a trade."

"Ravi, they want me. And I'm going. I'm not asking your permission."

"Please, be reasonable. You're already injured." He pointed at a speck of blood she'd missed on her upper lip.

She scrubbed at it. "Nothing that hasn't happened before."

"What?" Fresh alarm tightened his features.

"It happens after training sometimes. It's not a big deal." She gave an exaggerated shrug.

"*Lucy*. You should have told me."

"There are a lot of things we should have told each other, it seems. Like the existence of mercenary alchemists!"

Ravi tore at his gel-laden hair. "I didn't want to scare you."

"How about you try *trusting* me for a change? Claudia's been kidnapped—*kidnapped*—because you didn't trust me!"

Lucy spun on her heel and he grabbed her around the waist, dragging her back against his chest. His grip was tight but his energy was warm, gentle. Her powers were still telling her he was on her side. He just didn't want Lucy to get hurt. But that wasn't Ravi's choice.

"If you care about me you won't try to stop me," she said hoarsely. "What would you have done if you'd been given the chance to save your parents?"

Ravi turned her around in his arms to face him, emotions warring on his features.

"If you go, Lucy, I go."

"They said to come alone." She raised her chin stubbornly. "I won't jeopardize Claudia's safety."

"They'll never see me."

"I don't know . . ." Lucy could probably use his help, since she had no idea what she was doing, but . . .

"Come on." He stroked her cheek and smiled. "Let's pick up my toys."

GHOSTS

Ravi's apartment was barren. A one-room testament to austerity: white walls, a double bed in the corner, a small kitchenette with two stools tucked under the countertop. The only decoration was an out-dated wall calendar featuring photographs of New England birds. Lucy didn't take Ravi for much of a birdwatcher. She'd never even known there was a studio to rent over the gas station. Probably because nobody ever rented it.

Ravi watched as Lucy made a quick review of his living quarters.

"Not much, is it?" he said. He pulled his bow tie loose.

"It looks like a ghost lives here."

Stripping off his tailcoat, he showed her a half-smile, a Ravi smile. Not the hard one he'd flashed her back at school.

"A friendly ghost?" Ravi asked, unbuttoning his dress shirt. *Oh my.* Lucy skewed her gaze to a patch of mold on the ceiling, intensely aware of the fact that he was undressing in front of her.

Since this was a studio, Lucy was essentially standing in his bed-room. *Grow up.* Ravi wasn't acting like this was anything out of the ordinary. Aside from the fact that Claudia had been kidnapped and he was changing so they could go rescue her, of course.

Crouching down, he rifled through a duffel bag at the foot of the bed. He fished out a short-sleeved black shirt, Lycra, like one of Cole's racing jerseys. Lucy wrinkled her nose just thinking his name. She never wanted to hear it again.

"White tie isn't really stealth," Ravi said, sounding apologetic about the wardrobe change.

"Neither is flapper wear."

"I'm afraid I don't have anything in your size." And he sounded genuinely remorseful.

Lucy waged an internal war against admiring his abdominal muscles that had definitely not been sculpted by investigating quantum geometry.

"You never unpacked," she noted. "Is the whole Spartan aesthetic thing part of your cover?"

A whip-quick headshake. "Between boarding school, uni, and traveling for Professor T, I've learned to live with just the essentials. Ready to drop and roll at a moment's notice."

"Your essentials include white tie?"

His eyes lanced her as he rose to standing. "That was a special order," he said. "I wanted to look good for your prom."

Lucy inhaled through her nose, closing the short distance between them.

"Mission accomplished."

Ravi smiled. "I could offer you track-suit bottoms? You'll swim in them, though."

"You mean sweatpants," she said, eyeing the puddle of navy blue inside the duffel bag.

"The term 'sweatpants' is inherently uncouth." He pretended to shiver.

She laughed, releasing some of the tension that held her tight.

As Ravi discarded the dress shirt, his eyes followed hers to the scar tissue webbing the left side of his torso. The burn marks were raised, some streaks lighter than his brown skin, others darker.

A muscle twitched in his jaw, and her heart throbbed for the boy who lost his parents. The boy who carried his scars inside and out.

Impulsively, Lucy splayed her hand across them. The tissue was softer than the rest. Ravi shivered as she stroked him, air whistling through his teeth, and he closed his eyes.

Taut silence strained between them. He didn't stop Lucy's fingers from exploring, although she could sense him clinging tightly to his virtual shield.

Diffident, opening his eyes, he asked, "Not too off-putting?"

"Not at all."

Her gaze roamed his torso, then returned to his dark eyes. He slid his arms around her waist, hugging Lucy whisper-close.

"We'll get Claudia back. I promise," Ravi told her. Determination filled his voice.

Jolting into action, he released Lucy, pulled the T-shirt over his head, changed his patent-leather dress shoes for combat boots, and grabbed a toolbox from under his bed—all in one blur of motion. Lucy could only watch, dumbfounded.

Ravi held up a wand-shaped metal detector, the kind used at airports.

"Step back and hold up your arms," he ordered. "Please."

"Won't my electromagnetic field confuse the machine?" Lucy asked, raising her arms.

A measured glance. "Possibly."

Ravi started from behind, skimming the wand down her spine. Lucy's heart pounded as he examined every inch of her. His movements were performed with military efficiency. But. This was Ravi. She couldn't help the thrill his nearness inspired.

"How long have you been training with the Archimedeans?" Lucy asked to distract herself. If he noticed her labored breathing, he didn't let on.

"Since I was fourteen," he said. When he got the tattoo. Ravi hadn't had a permanent home since the Order of Sophia killed his family, Lucy realized.

"Seems like a lonely life." Hers now seemed like a cakewalk by comparison.

"Not so lonely lately."

Lucy's breath caught for a second. "So . . . in addition to getting a Ph.D., the Order has been training you to, what, be all Navy SEAL?"

"I think you mean SAS. But no." Ravi shook his head, laughing softly, as the wand traveled the length of Lucy's right arm.

"The Order has many branches, divisions, departments. It's a bit of a hydra. Too much to explain tonight." He moved on to her left arm. "Primarily, I'm a researcher. I'm attached to Chrysopoeia Tech, with Professor T. But we all have enough training to take care of ourselves."

He positioned himself so they were toe-to-toe.

"I'll keep you safe, Lucy."

"It's not my safety that worries me."

"I know," he agreed. "And that's what worries *me*."

Beep. The wand detected the necklace. Lucy's eyes dropped to the night-sky stone.

"Ravi, I'm sorry for blowing up at you back there. What I said about the mole. About this being your fault. It wasn't fair."

His brow furrowed. "You weren't wrong."

Lucy chewed her lip as Ravi continued scanning her down to the scalloped hem of her dress. Nothing. He muttered something under his breath.

"What is it?" she prodded.

"If there is a tracer, then it's most likely an isotope."

Her temper came dangerously close to spiking.

"It's in my *blood*?" Meaning there was no way to get rid of it.

"The good news is that the half-life of radioactive isotopes isn't all that long," Ravi offered. "It may have worked its way out of your system already."

"If not?"

He tossed the wand onto the bed and took Lucy's hand.

"The range for detection is also relatively short. They can't track you over long distances."

"Yay for that," Lucy said.

He interlaced their fingers. "You don't have to do this. We can find another way."

"No." She clenched her fists. "This ends tonight."

THE LION'S DEN

Ravi broke the speed limit and a plethora of other traffic laws getting to Long Island City. The Archimedeans probably had a way to skirt moving violations. A smaller, also black, duffel bag full of Ravi's toys jostled in the backseat.

Ten minutes earlier, Lucy had received another text. An address on Vernon Boulevard.

Queens whirred by in a blaze of orange streetlights.

Lucy's skin crawled at the notion that there was something inside her disclosing her location to the Freelancers at this very moment. Once she got Claudia back, she would do whatever was necessary never to let her body be used against her again.

The wheels of the SUV ground to a halt a few blocks from the designated address. Lucy surveyed the narrow side street. The odd townhouse was interspersed between old factories that had been converted into art galleries and craft-beer breweries. The neighborhood hardly screamed *Criminal Activity Takes Place Here*.

Lucy pitched her gaze at the dashboard. Two minutes late.

"I'll walk the rest of the way," she told Ravi, and reached for the door.

Shadows obscured half his face but his concern was plain as day.

"Wait." He grabbed the duffel in a rushed motion. "Two can play at the tracker game."

"Won't they just check me?" Lucy said, hesitating. "I don't want to piss them off." Or give them any reason to hurt Claudia.

"They might." Ravi pinched something clear and plastic, smaller than an earbud, between his fingers. "This is the latest technology. Undetectable."

"An Archimedean special?"

He answered with a grin. "May I?"

Lucy nodded and Ravi leaned across her, his touch gentle yet surgically exact as he planted the device inside her ear. She inhaled the sweet, mellow scent of cedar. When he was satisfied the device was secure, he lowered a hand to her shoulder but didn't lean back.

"I'll be able to hear whatever you hear. Try to get them to tell you as much as you can about what they're planning. Drop hints about what you see around you."

"Does it let you track me?" she asked.

"The range is short, but I'll stay as close as I can without drawing suspicion. The com works on radio waves. The Freelancers won't be able to distinguish it from regular transmissions."

"Okay." She nodded.

"You'll be able to hear me too. I'll be with you the entire time." Ravi tilted his face closer. "I won't leave you."

"I know you won't. Just one more thing—" Lucy tugged him toward her and planted her lips on his, fierce and sweet, before hopping onto the pavement.

"That better not have been a goodbye kiss," he said, catching his breath.

"Nah." She mustered as much bravado as she could. "I'm Wonder Woman, remember?"

"You certainly are."

Lucy felt less wondrous with every step she took toward the abandoned warehouse. Squeezing the tourmaline at her throat, her resolve hardened. She wouldn't let her fear or self-pity interfere with rescuing Claudia.

Lucy had been afraid of herself for as long as she could remember.

Tonight her abilities were a weapon and she would use them to save her best friend.

She stared up at the darkened building. A dirt-encrusted sign warned: TRESPASSERS WILL BE PROSECUTED.

"What do I do now?"

"Just wait." She hadn't realized she'd said that aloud until Ravi answered in her head. That was all kinds of weird. And yet she smiled even though he couldn't see her.

But somebody else could.

Sure enough, gears started to groan, and a peeling, rusted garage door yawned open.

From the darkness, a figure approached.

"We've been expecting you."

LASSO OF TRUTH

Lucy walked into the warehouse.

"At your service." She would do anything for Claudia.

Even so, her cocky grin wavered as the rusty door squeaked closed behind her.

The man who greeted Lucy wasn't much taller than her and there was a relaxed slope to his shoulders—the careless stance of someone confident he was the master of his surroundings. The smell of clove cigarettes wafted over her.

"Join us," he said, waving genteelly toward the innards of the warehouse. "We're on a tight schedule." A request. A command. The way he spoke made it hard to tell. His accent was also difficult to place: French—yet somehow not.

Every one of Lucy's instincts screamed at her not to budge another inch.

She ignored them.

"Don't worry, we'll have you home before curfew."

He laughed and it devolved into a smoker's cough. The dim lighting transformed the wrinkles creasing his dark brown skin into deep craters as he smiled.

Lucy matched the man's purposeful strides. It would do no good to show her fear or beg him for Claudia's release. According to Ravi, the Freelancers were mercenaries. And they needed her—for what, she didn't care. They might not hold up their end of the bargain, but her hands were tied. At least they weren't like the Order of Sophia, who hated Lucy simply for existing.

There was a worktable in the middle of the warehouse and a few folding chairs. That was it. Apparently they were also fans of Spartan chic.

Lounging in the metal chairs were several people clad in the same black attire as her host. Lucy perused their faces. Four she didn't recognize; one she did.

Anger lit inside her. She had really, really wanted to be wrong.

Jess was slumped in her seat, eyes pinned to the floor. She had changed out of her satin prom dress but glitter still clung to her cheeks. Claudia loved that damn glitter and Lucy knew from personal experience it took a few days to wash off. Only a couple hours ago, Jess had been holding Claudia close, as if she were something precious to her.

Lucy rubbed the pendant to keep from doing something she'd regret.

"Where's Claudia, Jess?" she asked, throwing her words like knives.

Jess glanced up, eyes shining. Mascara was flecked beneath them. The other Freelancers stiffened in their seats, prepared for a fight.

Lucy's host said, "Ah, yes. You know Jessica. Forgive me for not introducing myself sooner. You may call me Rick."

Fear darted through her. Kidnapping teenagers was still illegal the last time she'd checked, and Lucy could identify them to the authorities.

Did the Freelancers not actually plan to let her walk away from this?

"Rick," Lucy repeated for Ravi's benefit and, in her ear, he reassured, "Reading you loud and clear."

She stifled a sigh of relief. Ravi would help her through this. Lucy needed to control her temper and feed him as much information as possible.

"I go by Lucy," she told Rick. "But you knew that."

"*Enchanté.*" Pointing at a thickly muscled man with golden-brown skin, Rick said, "That's Pedro." Pedro ignored the introductions and continued polishing something in his lap—Lucy really hoped it wasn't a gun.

Rick continued naming the rest of the group. Now Lucy could put names to faces. *So* not good. They might be fake names but she didn't like her chances of survival.

Next to Pedro was the equally huge Mikhail who had a hawkish nose and eyes that seemed too small for his bald, white head. Both men looked to be in their late twenties or early thirties. Lucy tried to memorize the details to report to the Archimedeans later—if she made it out of this.

One of the women, Meifen, was long and lean, her straight black bangs and blunt bob framing her pale face. Lucy pegged her at forty only from the finest lines around her eyes and mouth. The woman sitting closest to Jess—Amara—seemed a few years older than Lucy, holding herself with poise. Her thin, delicately woven braids were arranged in an elegant halo atop her head. She raised an arm in a wave and Lucy noticed the sharp cut of her triceps against her warm brown skin.

Who were these people? The United Nations of criminals?

Rick observed Lucy observing his crew.

"Now that we've all made each other's acquaintance," he said, "we can get down to business."

"I'm not doing anything for you until I know where Claudia is," Lucy said, crossing her arms. True, she didn't want to get on Rick's bad side, but if she was about to break a bunch of laws, she needed to make sure her friend was safe first.

It was Jess who answered. "She's not hurt, Lucy. She's secure." The words were spoken like an apology but Lucy wasn't interested. There was no forgiving this.

"Excuse me if I don't believe a word that comes out of your mouth," she shot back.

"You want proof of life?" Rick inferred. Casually, he pulled a phone from his pocket. "*Voici.*"

He passed her the phone. It was a video.

Claudia lay on a bed, curled into a ball, fast asleep. The peacock feathers on her headband fluttered as she snored softly. Lucy studied her friend's surroundings for a clue as to where she was being held. Unfortunately, the webcam was trained on the bed. The headboard was mahogany and the silky sheets gleamed.

A hotel maybe?

Lucy could barely contain her fury. "Did you *drug* her?" She speared Jess with another heated glance; Jess couldn't meet her eyes.

"Perhaps your friend partied too hard," Rick replied.

Helpless. Claudia looked so helpless. Could Lucy have prevented all of this if she'd just been honest with her? She'd accused Ravi of keeping secrets but Lucy was in no position to judge.

"How do I know the video is live? If anything happens to *my*—" Lucy threatened and Rick cut her off.

"That is up to you. Your friend is resting comfortably. We're not monsters. Not like the Orders."

"The Orders haven't kidnapped anyone I know."

Rick raised his eyebrows, then his face became unreadable.

"So . . . you are properly motivated?"

"Yes," she spat.

"*Très bien*. Amara?" He beckoned her to his side. "We need to scan you before we go on our excursion. I'm sure you understand." He sounded totally lackadaisical. Like this were some kind of school field trip.

Lucy flashed a flinty glare at Rick as she held out her arms and allowed Amara to scan her body for bugs. The other woman used a device similar to Ravi's, and Lucy prayed the gizmo in her ear really was undetectable. She kept her eyes steady on Amara, face neutral. Amara's mouth had a similar shape to Rick's, as well as the set of their eyes— were they related?

"Where are we going?" Lucy asked.

Rick rubbed his thumb against his forefinger. He wanted a cigarette. Lucy recognized it as a tell. Wherever they were going, there was a certain amount of risk involved.

"There's an item in a secure facility that we require your assistance to obtain."

"Could you be any more vague?"

He chortled. "Perhaps."

Amara finished a final sweep and declared, "She's clean."

Rick nodded, and Lucy tried not to let her relief show.

"Take our guest to change," he instructed Amara. To Lucy, he said, "The dress is *charmante* but hardly suitable."

"If I'd had advance notice, I wouldn't have worn heels."

"*Vas-y.* Time is of the essence."

Jess leapt up. "I'll take her," she offered. Amara narrowed her eyes, but Rick just shrugged. "This way," Jess told Lucy, pointing toward the back of the warehouse.

Reluctantly, Lucy followed the other girl into a cluttered room in which the windows had been blacked out, allowing for some privacy. It must have been the foreman's office once upon a time.

Jess closed the door and immediately launched into a confession.

"I didn't know this would happen, Lucy. You have to believe me."

"I really don't." She turned away from Jess and surveyed a dusty desk where a pair of sneakers, black leggings, and a stretchy turtleneck had been laid out. "I presume these are for me."

Jess nodded, touching the cut on her bottom lip nervously. "I didn't know what they were planning, I swear," she started again in a low whisper. "I was only told to determine who had the lightning gene and then stay close."

"What do you mean?" Lucy demanded.

"That day at the Gallery. When the iPad shorted out. You were both holding it."

The explanation hit Lucy like a body blow. All this time, every day, Claudia had been in danger because of her. *Calm, Luce, calm.*

"I should've left Claudia alone once I'd determined it was you," Jess said. "I just . . . couldn't. I fell hard. Rick isn't very happy with me right now."

"But you're still here, with Rick, and Claudia is—wherever you stashed her. Pretend you're just a soldier following orders if you want to, Jess." Lucy kicked off her heels, glaring over her shoulder. "I'm not buying it."

Jess's complexion turned ashen.

"Claudia was falling in love with you." Lucy began stepping into the leggings. "My best friend deserves better."

Jess turned her back while Lucy changed. Lucy saw her shoulders heave as if she was crying, but she didn't make any noise.

"This was my first mission," Jess mumbled, voice ragged.

Lucy didn't respond. She slipped on the sneakers. They were a perfect fit.

"I tried to stop it. I would never hurt Clauds."

"You don't get to call her *Clauds*. She doesn't even know who you really are."

"I wanted to tell her. So many times." Jess dragged in a breath. "I've never been in love before."

"You can turn around now," Lucy said coldly, and crouched down to tighten her shoelaces.

Pivoting to face her, Jess dabbed at her tears with her sleeve. "Listen to me, Lucy. I know you don't trust me, but both Orders will chew you up and spit you out. If we'd found you first, things could have played out differently."

Lucy sprang to her feet. "You think I'd *ever* team up with people who would kidnap innocent bystanders?" She snorted. "You should choose your friends more carefully, Jess." And she should be grateful Lucy couldn't breathe fire.

Jess stuck out her chin even as her split lip quivered. "You don't know anything about this world. To the Orders, we're all just a means to an end."

"And what am I to you? What was Clauds?" Lucy stalked forward. "Maybe if you hadn't kidnapped the girl you say you love, I'd be more interested in what you have to say!"

"They'll destroy you," Jess warned, anger roughening her voice.

"I already know the Order of Sophia thinks my powers are an abomination or whatever."

The other girl felled her with a heavy look.

"I'm not talking about the Sophists. I defected from the Order of Archimedes."

"Why?" Lucy choked out, a fist clenching her middle.

Pain fractured Jess's face, making her look much older than her twenty years. "My brother asked too many questions. They sent him on a mission. That was a year ago." The response was robotic. "He never came back." Jess scrubbed a hand over her face. "That's why I joined Rick. To stop them. To avenge my brother."

Lucy ran her index finger over the ridges of the tourmaline. If Ravi was receiving all of this over the com, he wasn't weighing in. She studied Jess's face. Her grief was real but Lucy didn't believe for a second that Ravi would be involved with an organization that made people disappear.

And given where Lucy was standing this very second, all she could manage in response was "I'm sorry about your brother."

Jess swallowed a sob. "Claudia's the only thing that's made me feel like living again since it happened." Lucy could only scoff, but Jess dared a step closer.

"If you don't believe me, read me."

She placed a hand on Lucy's shoulder in challenge.

Lucy met her meadow-green eyes. Claudia had waxed lyrical about Jess's eyes on several occasions. Lucy exhaled and lowered her shield.

Jess's frequency immediately stung her. Sticky blackness clogged her veins, and she balked. Every muscle, every tendon elongated. Lucy's whole body wanted to snap in two. She could barely catch her breath. Darkness pushed against the edges of her skull.

Chest heaving, she swatted Jess's hand from her shoulder.

"Stop," she wheezed.

Jess's eyes rounded. "You really are what they say you are." Her brow creased as Lucy leaned against the desk for support. "Are you okay?"

A knock came at the door.

"*Allons-y!*" shouted an impatient female voice.

"Amara says we need to go."

Lucy forced a nod as her trembling thighs recovered enough to walk. The other girl's pain was suffocating. Even if her feelings for Claudia were genuine, they were buried beneath a terrifying rage.

"I'm sorry, Lucy," Jess whispered. "Just get Rick what he wants. He's a reasonable man."

"I think we must have different definitions of reasonable," Lucy told her, and propelled herself past Jess into the main room through sheer force of will.

She left all vestiges of Lucinda the captivating flapper in a glimmering pool on the concrete floor. That girl was gone. Probably forever.

Rick directed everyone to pile into a nondescript white van.

He stopped Jess at the warehouse door. "We don't need you for this part of the mission," he said. "We'll talk about our disagreement later."

Jess paled further. She dashed Lucy a pleading look.

Lucy walked on and was stepping into the back of the van when a hand gripped her elbow.

"Not so fast," Rick told her. "You're up front with me."

DOCTOR MANHATTAN

As they traversed the Fifty-ninth Street Bridge, Lucy counted the seconds between the yellow-orange swaths cutting across the dashboard to steady her nerves. The light revealed the barest hint of gray stubble scattered on Rick's closely shaven jawline. She got the distinct sense Rick was letting her stew in her own juices.

"What happens to Claudia if I can't help you?" she finally blurted.

"I never agree to take a job unless I'm certain I can fulfill my client's request," Rick replied, blasé. "It would be bad for business."

"You haven't answered my question."

He angled his head. "I wouldn't have gone to the trouble of acquiring your services if they weren't essential to my plan."

Trouble?! Rick made kidnapping Lucy's best friend sound like a chore.

The east side of the island sprawled before them: its bright lights seductive, its spires like barbed wire. Exiting the bridge, the van hooked a left and continued traveling south on the highway hugging the river.

After another moment of silence, Rick said, "You're wondering why I asked you to ride with me and not the others?"

Yes. But Lucy wouldn't give the satisfaction of the answer he wanted. She folded her arms and imagined what Claudia's reaction would be. Her friend had never been afraid to take on a bully twice her size. She had defended Lucy countless times; now it was Lucy's turn.

"I assumed you were afraid I might pan-fry the rest of your crew to a tender medium-rare." She chucked him a haughty smirk.

"Not at all. You're too smart for that. Touch my crew and Mademoiselle O'Rourke won't have a very good night. I didn't think it necessary to spell it out."

The van halted at a red light and Rick met Lucy's stare head-on.

"Because her night's been just peachy so far," she muttered in a smaller voice.

Rick hit the gas as the light went green. "I want to tell you a story," he continued.

"Do I get a cookie with that?" Lucy wasn't in the mood for story time. And definitely not from the man who had arranged Claudia's snatch and grab.

Still, she kept quiet. A simmering quiet.

"Tell me," he said. "What do you know about the Orders?"

Not nearly enough, it would seem.

"They're alchemists," Lucy responded slowly, fiddling with the lock on the door. She chose her words like weapons for a duel. "Scientists. Or the Archimedeans are. The Order of Sophia are zealots. They think I'm dangerous and should be eliminated."

Dark, masculine laughter bounced around the enclosed space.

"Spoken like an Archimedean," Rick said.

Where was Ravi? Had the signal failed? She couldn't believe he wouldn't add his two cents. Or was he too far out of range?

Or—*oh no*. What if he'd been hurt?

Suddenly the van pressed in on her. "You're a Sophist?" Lucy said.

The picture of Claudia, fast asleep and helpless, blistered the back of her eyes. If Lucy had to trade herself for her friend's release, she would. Surely the Order of Sophia would at least allow them to say goodbye.

"I have no allegiance to anyone but myself." Rick's voice held no emotion, but his knuckles tightened briefly on the wheel.

"But you *did* belong."

"I was raised to believe that knowledge must always be governed by wisdom. When Kleopatra of Egypt founded the Order, she named it for Sophia, the goddess of wisdom." He rolled his shoulders. "Wisdom above all is not a bad philosophy—in theory."

Frost settled over Lucy's heart.

"Kleopatra the alchemist founded the Order of Sophia?"

Rick glanced at her sidelong. "You've heard of her?"

She nodded.

"Kleopatra discovered the secret to the philosopher's stone—and she saw it led to greed, treachery, and death."

Which was why she'd hidden it in her *Pharmakon*. Lucy wouldn't let on to Rick she knew about that too, however. What would happen if her mom actually managed to decipher the text? The Sophists would come after *her* was what.

Rick exhaled a long breath. "Kleopatra realized that sometimes scientists must have the wisdom to prevent themselves from acquiring certain knowledge."

The founder of the Sophists would therefore have believed that scientists should be protected from Lucy—from whatever secrets of evolution were contained within her DNA.

"It sounds like you still agree with her," she charged.

"I live by no code but my own." One-handed, Rick turned the wheel.

Lucy pulled the tourmaline loose from beneath the collar of the turtleneck. If she agreed to be tattooed with the same dark star as Ravi, exactly which code would she be living her life by?

"The Archimedeans believe in progress, state-sponsored science," Lucy said. "What's wrong with that?"

"I didn't say there was anything wrong with it. I keep an open mind. Although, state-sponsored science brought the atom bomb into the world." He caught her eye. "And that was the last time the Orders worked together."

Lucy couldn't prevent her jaw from dropping.

"You're saying the Orders were behind the Manhattan Project?"

"Mostly." A careless smile. "Quite the appropriate setting for this discussion."

If nonchalance were a superpower, then Rick deserved a cape and tights.

"What happened?" she said.

"Success is its own form of defeat."

Lucy arched an eyebrow.

"You've seen the mushroom cloud. No one had ever achieved such destruction. Total. Horrendous. But scientifically glorious. Many were left disillusioned—hence the Freelancers. *Putain!*"

Rick swerved to avoid a car that had broken down in the off-ramp to the South Street Seaport. Another breath hissed through his teeth. Waving dismissively in Lucy's direction, he said, "After the Manhattan Project, the Order of Sophia became more fanatical about never letting a weapon of such mass destruction be constructed again. Not everyone has the stomach to eliminate all threats."

The indifference as he talked about threats and eliminations made Lucy wonder, "Why did you leave?" Rick didn't strike her as someone opposed to using violence or blackmail to get what he wanted.

"Each of us has a story. Mine is not for tonight."

Lucy could tell that pushing Rick to reveal his reason for leaving would get her nowhere. She didn't really care anyway. She wouldn't waste her questions on his personal history.

"Eliminating threats—is that why the Sophists killed Tesla?"

In principle, she didn't disagree with their policy of not developing WMDs. The problem seemed to be they thought *Lucy* was one.

Rick pulled the van over to the curb on a cobblestoned street.

"Tesla died before the successful detonation of an atom bomb. And he belonged to the Order of Sophia," he informed her. "Why would they kill him?"

Professor T said Tesla had telegrammed the Archimedeans on the day he died. If Rick wasn't aware that Tesla had switched allegiances, however, Lucy wasn't about to spill the beans. She imagined the Sophists dealt swiftly with traitors.

"We've arrived," he announced.

Lucy circled her eyes around colonial-era buildings. She didn't know this part of the city at all.

The locks popped and Rick exited the vehicle.

Lucy's chest expanded. "Ravi?" she whispered.

No answer. What had happened to him?

Spare change on the dashboard, a few pennies and dimes, flew toward her and she ducked. Lucy had to get her electromagnetic field under control. Claudia's life depended on it.

She closed her eyes and imagined herself dressed in a coat of armor like Ravi had taught her. No energy could get in or out. Lucy added another layer of virtual protection and the pennies stopped rattling.

A different kind of rapping broke her concentration.

"We don't have all night." Amara knocked on the window again.

"I'm coming."

I'm coming, Clauds.

DON'T LOOK DOWN

Rick's words echoing in her mind, Lucy followed the Freelancers toward their destination in Lower Manhattan. Amara flanked her so closely they may as well have been superglued. Under very different conditions, she might bring Ravi here to see the tall ships moored to Pier 17.

It occurred to Lucy that the Order of Sophia feared her genetic mutation because it could render humanity as archaic as a schooner. Given that carriers of the lightning gene were prone to premature death, however, their intolerant stance seemed like a bit of an overreaction. How much mayhem could she really cause?

Lucy's eyes flitted across the redbrick façades of nineteenth-century row houses. She'd presumed Rick would be burglarizing one of the many Wall Street office buildings within spitting distance, going after the corporate titans made from steel and glass.

Why would one of the houses in the historic district be heavily guarded?

The group turned down a dead-end alley. There were no doors or windows interrupting the brick of the row houses. If Rick thought Lucy could walk through walls, he was in for the disappointment of his life.

Shadows from the nearby skyscrapers were cold on her cheeks.

Rick made some kind of hand signal and the crew scattered, melting into the darkened corners of the alleyway. He crooked a pinky at Lucy. With no choice but to obey, she trudged to his side.

"Now what?" she said, hoping that Ravi was still picking her up through the com device.

"We go down."

Lucy followed his gaze. It was a manhole. A bronze manhole cover decorated with six-petaled flowers. Six six-petaled blossoms surrounding a word in Greek that stopped her heart.

σοφία

Lucy's eyes went wide and Rick muffled a chuckle-cough in his fist.

"Sophia," Lucy whispered, the word lacerating her throat. "You brought me straight to the Sophists' door?"

After Rick's spiel about not agreeing with the extremists, she'd allowed herself to believe he wouldn't just hand her over. She should have realized he was ruled by self-interest. There was probably a pretty penny for her head.

"*Calmes-toi.* Nobody's home." His laughter became a barking cough. "They simply have something I want."

Rick's attempt at reassurance did nothing to lift the weight from Lucy's chest.

Trying not to shake, she demanded, "What do you expect me to do? Lift the cover with the power of my mind?" A flying stapler was one thing. A sheet of metal with a three-foot diameter was quite another. "I can't do it."

He narrowed his eyes to slits, assessing her like a predator who toys with his prey before swallowing it whole.

"You can. Or you will. But we don't have time for that tonight."

"Then what?"

"Patience."

Patience was an important virtue for a scientist to possess, but Lucy had steadily been running out of hers. Every second that ticked by was another second Claudia was being held captive.

Rick clicked his fingers and Mikhail materialized out of nowhere, crowbar in hand. Where had he stashed the crowbar? Better to remain ignorant, actually.

"Won't it be alarmed?" Lucy cautioned.

Vulpine smile. "We have an inside man," Rick replied.

Of course they did. The Freelancers had moles in both Orders. Perfect.

With a couple grunts, Mikhail made quick work of the manhole cover.

As promised, no alarm sounded.

Rick performed a mocking half bow and waved his hand. "Ladies first."

Great. A mercenary who was a stickler for manners.

Girding herself, Lucy wrapped her hands around the rusty rung of a ladder and began her descent below the city. Grime slid between her fingers as a dank smell filled her nostrils. She really didn't want to know what it was. She also ignored the chattering of some kind of critter with whiskers that interrupted the trickling of water.

Rick plunged after her into the darkness, a flashlight gripped between his teeth.

Mikhail re-covered the manhole, eclipsing any streetlight filtering down.

Her insides convulsed.

The darkness was too familiar. An old friend Lucy wanted to forget. Knowing that her seizures were caused by a genetic mutation rather than a more straightforward neurological condition didn't change the reality of her symptoms. Professor T had given Lucy hope that she could learn to master them, but the darkness would always be waiting for her.

Her feet connected with a hard, slippery concrete floor. Rick reached the bottom a few seconds later and Lucy winced as the flashlight shone directly in her eyes. Shielding herself, yellow dots continued to strobe against the inky blackness.

"Where are the others?" she whispered as her eyes readjusted, roving the tunnel that stretched before them. "And where are we?"

"There are tunnels all over this city if you know where to look." He shrugged. "As for the others—they do not need to see what you can do. I am considerate, *non*?"

Rick was a lot of things. Considerate wasn't at the top of Lucy's list.

"Are you saying the Orders built a secret labyrinth beneath New York City?" she asked.

"London *aussi*. Paris. Rome. The Orders are everywhere." He circled the light around the cramped corridor and began walking. "They can't take all the credit, however. There were the bootleggers. And the Freemasons."

Rick glanced back at Lucy over his shoulder and removed something from his pocket with casual grace.

"You might need this. Catch!"

Lucy raised her hands, fumbling as the Tesla Egg landed between them.

"It *was* you!" she hissed.

He laughed as he continued navigating them forward. She stared at the egg. If Rick knew what it could do, he must know the risks of giving it back to her. He must be confident that he had enough leverage to keep Lucy compliant.

Much as it infuriated her, he was right.

A grateful, happy buzz spread through her body as her hand closed around the egg. As if a missing limb had been returned.

Emerald light illuminated the tunnel. She heard a low whistle as Rick shut off his flashlight. He didn't need it anymore.

Simultaneously the tourmaline began to dig harder into Lucy's throat, almost choking her. The stone struggled to match the boost to the oscillation of her electromagnetic field provoked by Tesla's invention. Excitement thrummed through Lucy thinking of the experiments she could perform on herself, scientific fascination momentarily outweighing fear.

"We could take your show on the road," Rick commented.

Bite me, Lucy thought. She bit her tongue instead.

They reached a crossroads.

He pointed at a ladder.

Up they went.

A WORTHY FOE

Being burned alive was not how Lucy had planned to end her evening.

Luckily, the fireplace was a fake. As Rick crawled through the firebox on his belly, Lucy wiped her dirty palms against her leggings. She had to hand it to the Sophists. The illusion was complete, right down to the chopped wood resting by the hearth. No one would ever suspect that a trapdoor to a secret network of tunnels lay beneath the chimney.

Lucy twirled on the spot, observing her surroundings by the forest-green glow radiating from the Tesla Egg. She wasn't sure how far they'd walked underground, perhaps only a block or two, but it appeared as if they'd stumbled through a wormhole into the early 1800s. And they were standing in someone's living room: a pair of claw-footed armchairs were positioned on either side of the fireplace; in the far corner of the room was a Jane Austen–era pianoforte. Oil paintings of battles and portraits of women with Marie Antoinette powdered wigs were staggered along oak-paneled walls.

Her eyes completed their circuit and settled on the mosaic inlaid across the mantel. Rose-colored tiles were once more arranged in six blossoms containing six petals each. At the midpoint of the mantel, three flowers on either side, lay a beetle.

Crackling filled her ears. The com device. Something must be jamming it. She shook her head like a wet dog and the static dissipated.

"The scarab," Lucy said, taken aback, praying that if Ravi could hear her he might recognize her location.

Rick traced his finger along the tiles. The Freelancer might have abandoned the Order of Sophia, but he admired the insect with the same expression Ravi wore when he talked about the Ouroboros. What was it her mom had told Lucy about the scarab? The Egyptian alchemists believed it to be a sacred animal, possessing the power of creation and transmutation. But surely the Sophists knew that wasn't true?

Not looking at her, Rick said, "There are those who've never believed the philosopher's stone was a what—but a *who*."

This was not the moment for philosophizing. "Where are we?" Lucy demanded.

Please be hearing this, Ravi.

"A merchant's house. Once a big player in the opium trade," Rick answered, unhelpfully enigmatic.

"The Sophists were nineteenth-century drug dealers?"

"Narcotics can be medicinal." He lifted an eyebrow. "His descendants run a pharmaceutical company. And this home is now open to the public as a museum."

A *museum*? They'd broken into a freaking museum! The police were probably already on their way.

"Are you kidding me? There must be a million cameras in here." She pitted her cheeks. "Shouldn't we at least be wearing masks?"

"Not a million cameras. Only the one."

Rick pointed at a grandfather clock on the opposite side of the room.

"Take care of that for me." He waved at it with a grin. "You Americans say *cheese*, correct?"

Anger flared inside Lucy and the radius of the St. Elmo's fire grew. Rick wasn't concerned about starring in *America's Most Criminal Home Videos*. Meanwhile, Lucy could forget about college.

"Whatever you think I can do, you're wrong," she said, an edge to her voice.

Rick lunged for her and allowed the emerald flame to singe his jacket. She yanked her hand back instinctually, then cursed herself for not holding her ground.

"What I *know* you can do is send an electromagnetic pulse that disables the camera's circuitry. By the time anyone realizes the feed has gone dark, we should be gone."

"You're delusional."

Rick smiled at her, a hard smile, but the look in his eyes was strangely misty.

"I knew someone else like you. Long ago. You remind me of her."

Lucy rocked onto the balls of her feet. "Who? What happened to her?"

"That is also not a story for tonight." Any glimmer of tenderness vanished from his face. "Meet me upstairs in two minutes. We need to clear out before the guards do their next sweep."

"What if we don't?"

"That's what Meifen is for."

In three imperious strides, Rick had left Lucy to her own devices. She had no time to lose.

She eyed the grandfather clock. Weathered cherry wood, a swaying brass gong like a lolling tongue. It didn't look like a worthy adversary, but looks could be deceiving.

"Okay, Luce. You're back in your lab," she said aloud. "You need to create an electromagnetic pulse. What do you do?"

If Ravi knew the answer, he wasn't forthcoming. All she was getting was spitting white noise.

Of course!

Lucy was the source of the static. Her heightened emotional state must be jamming the frequency. She should have realized sooner. But she did have a pretty good reason for being stressed out of her mind.

She held the Tesla Egg in one hand and rubbed the tourmaline around her neck with the other. The stone stabilized her oscillations, but what Lucy needed was to be the opposite of stable. She glared at the egg. Theoretically she could amplify her electromagnetic field so that anything else using her frequency would couple with her and burn itself out.

Theoretically.

The question was how to focus the direction of the electromagnetic burst. She didn't want to fry everything in her immediate vicinity. Especially not her com device, the only link she had to Ravi.

Urgently, with shaky fingers, Lucy unfastened the necklace Claudia had lovingly crafted and laid it on the mantelpiece.

She hurried toward the clock and held out her hand. In the center of the gear that suspended the second and minute hands together she noticed a blinking red light. If the Order of Sophia didn't know about her before, they did now.

Lucy gripped the Tesla Egg and watched the emerald fire intensify, brighter and brighter. Like when she was back in her garage lab, she imagined the most distressing thing she could.

She pictured Claudia, blood leaking from her mouth, her throat split from ear to ear in a gruesome grin. *You were too late.*

Lucy swallowed a scream as a dull popping noise echoed throughout the room.

The red light had vanished. She had done it. Incredibly anticlimactic, barely a whimper, but she'd done it.

Swaying on her feet, Lucy doubled over and hugged her knees. The Tesla Egg dropped onto the floor. Icy sweat dripped from her forehead to her lips.

She glowered up at the clock. Not quite a dragon but she'd vanquished it all the same. Lucy snatched up the tourmaline and the egg and walked slowly up the stairs to the second floor. Temperance in one hand; excess in the other.

It was up to Lucy to choose. She brushed away a fresh drop of blood from her nose.

Now she understood why Tesla had hidden his laboratory within the New Yorker Hotel and protected it with a Faraday cage—because a Faraday cage was the only way to guard against an EMP.

He'd been protecting his research from people like himself.

And Lucy.

ANTIQUES ROADSHOW

Once upon a time, Lucy would have been enjoying her after-prom with Cole at the White Hart Inn instead of hanging out in the bedroom of some long-dead drug lord. She supposed the interior design must be what had passed for bling back then: silk draperies, gilded mirrors, Ming vases, and Persian rugs.

If she'd never activated—or reactivated—her lightning gene in Tesla's lab, Lucy would have gone off to college believing Cole's lies, none the wiser that he'd always been more in love with himself than with her.

"Come," Rick commanded Lucy.

She trudged to where he was crouched on the floor. His flashlight struck the planes of his face in the most menacing way possible. Lucy rolled the Tesla Egg between her fingers. Two could play at that game.

The tourmaline necklace had been tucked into her sneaker.

Stooping beside Rick, Lucy summoned the St. Elmo's fire. She couldn't deny she was getting better at controlling it. *Practice makes perfect.* She also couldn't deny the contented hum beneath her skin.

"Aren't you going to ask if I disabled the security camera?" Lucy said.

"I don't waste my breath on questions to which I already know the answers."

She guessed Rick didn't believe in thank-you notes either.

"What are you looking for?" She peered at the floor.

"Look closer."

Lucy lowered the Tesla Egg next to Rick's flashlight, rendering it superfluous. Beside the leg of the armoire there were fine scratches on the wooden floor. Squinting hard enough to make herself cross-eyed, Lucy realized they weren't scratches at all.

There, deftly chiseled into the floorboard, was another scarab.

Rick covered the beetle with his palm and pressed.

Click.

The scarab-decorated plank lowered farther and slid beneath the one beside it. Was the entire floor a false bottom? Just like a suitcase. Smuggling tactics hadn't changed much in two hundred years, it would seem.

Wait. Were they pilfering an opium cache? That could mean serious jail time.

Rick reached into the void, tipping forward under the weight of whatever he was hoisting from the darkness. "*Merde*," he muttered, panting a couple times from the exertion.

A safe thudded onto the floor at Lucy's knees.

It was approximately the size of a toaster, and it didn't look particularly ancient. The paint was matte gray. Spotless. Definitely not built two centuries ago. Lucy would expect to find it in a modern hotel room.

Rick's cheeks swelled in a deep breath as he lifted the safe once more, turning it to face them. There was no keypad on its door. No combination lock.

Lucy touched her hand to the door and St. Elmo's fire sparked on the raised image of a silver snake eating its own tail.

"I don't understand." Her voice hitched. Had the Order of Sophia stolen this from the Archimedeans? Would Professor T know what this was? Or Ravi?

Rick blew a thick layer of dust from the door. Whatever its provenance, the safe had been beneath these floorboards for a while.

"This is why I require your assistance."

He slashed Lucy's palm with a penknife before she'd even noticed the twinkle of the blade. The egg tumbled from her grasp and bounced. In its fading, eerie green light, her blood leaked black.

"*Ow!*" she complained.

Without an apology, Rick grabbed her wrist and flattened her hand against the Ouroboros. Lucy was too shocked to squirm or protest. He raised his flashlight and she watched her blood fill the lines between the snake's scales, red on silver. She could have sworn she heard the reptile hiss. The blood coursed unhurriedly, counterclockwise, through the serpent's body until it reached the head.

Glacier-blue beams of light spouted from its sockets and the Ouroboros spun twice to the left and three times to the right. It was a combination lock, after all.

Gasping, Lucy whipped her hand back as the door flew open. Just like the plasma lamp in the Tesla Suite, the lock responded to her blood—to the lightning gene.

Rick held out a white handkerchief but Lucy didn't mistake it for surrender.

"It's better not to know the pain is coming," he explained with a shrug.

Begrudgingly, she accepted the token. Lucy doubted he'd uttered the words *I'm sorry*—in English or French—in his entire life. With a huff, she bandaged her hand, tying a neat tourniquet to stanch the bleeding.

Lucy fumbled in the darkness for the Tesla Egg as Rick rooted around the safe, flashlight pinned between his teeth. She needed to see whatever he extracted. Not only to report back to Ravi, but for herself.

A sage-colored nimbus appeared as her uninjured hand connected with the egg. She lifted it like a lantern.

She couldn't believe her eyes.

Rick held a thin, three-inch square of blue plastic in his hand.

A floppy disk.

Lucy had never seen one in real life.

Curiously, she reached for it but Rick lurched back, guarding the metallic circle in the middle of the square.

"Stop!" he barked.

Lucy snorted. "You want a dial-up connection with that?"

"Look, but don't touch."

"Why *n*—" She broke off. She knew why Rick didn't want her to touch it. He was afraid Lucy was a giant magnet who could destroy the data contained on the disk.

Could she? More important, *should* she?

"What's on that disk?" she asked sharply. Lucy didn't think floppies could store more than a couple hundred megabytes of information. That was barely half a TV show.

The corner of Rick's mouth twitched and he stashed the disk under his shirt.

Lucy shoved the Tesla Egg in his face.

"I deserve to know. I deserve to know what's on the disk and why the Sophists stole it from the Archimedeans. I deserve to know what any of this has to do with me!"

"My client did not divulge the contents of the disk. Although one must assume the Sophists believe whatever it contains is best not in the hands of their rivals."

If Rick shrugged one more time, Lucy would sock him.

She inched the egg closer to his chest. "Tell me or I'll demagnetize the disk. You know I can do it."

He smiled a snowcapped smile.

"I want you to consider your options very carefully. Jessica is on her way to retrieve your friend from where she has been napping. What happens to her next is entirely your decision."

An orb of green light as large as a globe enveloped them as Lucy's frustration mounted.

"Who's your client? Who told you about me?" she said, voice laced with desperation. "Tell me that much." Her shoulders quaked.

"I wouldn't be very good at my job if I did."

Clearly, Rick didn't respond to threats. Lucy needed to try something else.

"You were a Sophist once," she said. "If they hid the files on that disk, it might have been for a good reason. Do you really think it's *wise* to sell the information to whoever is willing to pay the most?"

"Need I remind you the Order of Sophia would lock you up too? You're not the first carrier of the mutation I've met. Trust me, it's not a desirable fate."

Rick's words knocked the wind out of her.

"Go downstairs and wait for me," he ordered. Lucy was so dazed it barely registered as he shoved her toward the exit. "We're behind schedule. Unless you're eager for the Sophists to put you in chains."

She stumbled to her feet. "At least tell me where Claudia is."

His face softened a smidge. "There's a hotel near the High Line. We'll meet your friend and Jessica there." He paused. "We're not the real monsters."

Lucy didn't know about that. "*Merci*," she said softly.

The High Line was a public place. A defunct railway line converted into a park. Perfect for the Freelancers to dissolve into the crowd. She refused to feel guilty about doing what needed to be done to get Claudia back. Lucy didn't want the information on that disk sold on the open market, but if she had to choose between her own safety and Claudia's, Lucy would choose her best friend every time.

With a light step, she slipped down the stairs until she was out of earshot.

Lucy stilled her breathing, closed her eyes, and pictured the toy sailboats in Central Park. The sun in her vision caressed her face as she counted the ripples the boats left in their wake.

"Lucy?" Ravi's voice was panicked, yet it made her smile. "Lucy? Are you there?"

"I'm here. I'm accidentally interfering with the frequency."

A pause. "Right, right. I should have thought of that."

"We're going to the High Line. They're bringing Claudia. Can you track me?" She conveyed the information without taking a breath.

"I'll find you, Lucinda. Anywhere."

Then someone kicked in the front door.

BULLETS OVER BROADWAY

Not Ravi.

"We've been made." Amara's face shone with sweat, gun in hand. "Where's Rick?"

Unable to form words, Lucy pointed toward the stairs.

"Papa!" the other woman yelled, her accent thickening like syrup.

Two heartbeats later, Rick appeared and launched himself down the stairs.

"*Qu'est-ce qui s'est passé?*" he shout-whispered.

Lucy didn't need a translator to figure out he was asking his daughter what the hell was happening.

Amara scowled at him. "No time for tunnels."

Withdrawing a gun from an ankle holster, Rick grimaced in equal displeasure. "This wasn't the plan."

"This is the new plan," Amara said. Turning to Lucy, she commanded, "Stay behind me."

Like father, like daughter.

Seeing as she was the only one without a gun, Lucy did as she was told. She trotted at Amara's heels with Rick at her back, checking the neighboring windows and rooftops with owlish eyes. If Lucy didn't know better, she'd say the Freelancers were concerned for her safety.

"Pedro was hit," Amara called back to her father. "Meifen took down two of them. They must have gone on patrol early."

Rick didn't answer. Lucy could guess what he was thinking. She had been the one to cause the delay. To get one of his team wounded.

What if he punished Claudia for Lucy's insubordination?

Panic gushed through her, sweeping away her hard-earned calm—the calm she needed to keep the line of communication open with Ravi. Energy cascaded from her head to her toes. The static in her ears taunted her.

"I'm sorry. I'm so sorry," she babbled. Rick was close enough that Lucy could feel the heat from his body as they moved together down the cobblestone street. "Please don't hurt my friend."

"Now you understand the stakes," was all he said before a bullet whizzed past Lucy's ear. The storefront behind them exploded, jagged shards of glass like icicles tearing toward them.

"Run!" cried Amara as she took aim at a target Lucy couldn't see.

Gunfire exploded behind her.

Lucy ran. The next bullet set off the alarm of a parked car, its windshield shattering. The boom reverberated through her body, her heart thundering.

"Lucy?" Ravi gasped. The static made it sound like he was shouting through a wind tunnel. "Was that a shot? You're coming in and out."

"It's the Sophists," she managed between pants.

Amara gave Lucy a dirty look. "Brilliant deduction."

Tires squealed and the Freelancers' van sped toward them. Backwards.

Mikhail hung halfway out of the back as the door opened. He hauled Lucy inside; the rage emanating from him crushed the air from her lungs. Amara and Rick jumped in behind them while the van careened forward.

"Where to?" Meifen asked over the intercom. Tinted Plexiglas partitioned the front from the back of the van, but Lucy recognized her voice.

Rick growled, "Stick to the plan," and the intercom cut out.

ThankGodthankGodthankGod.

They were still going to meet Claudia.

Lucy collapsed against the cold metal interior of the van as the adrenaline drained from her. On the bench opposite hers, Amara inspected Pedro's wound. An aureole of blood spread from his bare shoulder. The other woman felt gingerly around the perforated flesh like someone who performed triage on a regular basis. Mikhail sat on Pedro's other side, gripping his forearm. He dipped his head to whisper something in the wounded man's ear and an unexpected look of tenderness swept across his face.

Lucy averted her eyes. She told herself she wasn't responsible for his injury. The Freelancers had kidnapped her friend and press-ganged her into service. And yet, she couldn't dispel the heaviness in her gut.

Amara lifted her chin at Rick.

"The bullet's still inside. We need to get it out. But he'll live." She showed her patient a teasing smile.

"*Gracias, señorita,*" Pedro groaned with a smirk.

Rick met his eyes. "We need to deliver the package." It was as close as the crew leader would come to asking permission, Lucy surmised.

Pedro nodded. Mikhail unrolled a bandage and began wrapping his colleague's shoulder. Like unscrupulous Boy Scouts, the Freelancers came prepared. For whatever it was worth, they did seem to care about one another.

Lucy's gaze dropped to her own bandaged hand. She rubbed her thumb across the center of her palm. Feeling Rick's eyes on her, she squared her shoulders at him, expression steely.

"You're in the big leagues now," he said.

"Yeah. *Merci beaucoup* for putting me on the Sophists' radar."

"It was only a matter of time." He leaned back, arm brushing her faintly. No surprise that she couldn't pick up on his emotions. "What is remarkable," Rick mused, "is that you've stayed hidden for so long."

"I wasn't in hiding," Lucy countered. "I was living a normal life." Okay, not quite true. "I had no idea. Neither do my parents."

"It's fortunate the Archimedeans found you before the Sophists did, I suppose."

Mikhail flung a dark look in Rick's direction, then returned to tending Pedro. Lucy suspected there was another story behind that look that she wouldn't hear tonight.

"I don't know what you mean," she hedged, jamming her hands flat against her thighs. The Freelancers must have discovered her existence from a mole within the Order of Archimedes, but she didn't want to provide any further details.

Rick laughed, an empty sound. "Don't insult my intelligence. We knew the instant Tarquin's protégé turned up as a new science teacher." Another mirthless snicker. Lucy swallowed. "*Pas mal.* Clever," he added with reluctant admiration. "The old fox will make you believe you have a choice."

"Sounds preferable to a bullet in the brain—which is what the Order of Sophia was offering back there," Lucy responded snidely as she shot a pointed glance at Pedro.

"You might be inclined to think so." Rick shifted to face her dead-on. "The Freelancers can protect you. We're the only ones who will put your fate in your own hands."

"Like you did tonight?" Lucy snorted. "This was *what*? Some kind of messed-up job interview?"

Rick darted a glance at Amara, whose entire body had gone rigid. "We could use someone with your skill set on our team," he said.

"No thanks. I don't need to pick a side."

"If you don't pick a side, a side will pick you."

"They can try."

Lucy was sick to death of playing by everyone else's rules all the time.

"Stubborn. I like that about you. But it's not the smart move here."

"So if I don't pick the Freelancers, you'll kidnap someone I care about whenever you feel like it? That's quite a sales pitch."

"I'm a businessman. I was paid for a job. The job is done. I have no further use for your friend."

Meifen's voice came over the intercom. "ETA two minutes."

Rick reached inside his pocket and handed Lucy a sliver of paper with the word LIBERTAS printed on it. The Roman goddess of liberty, the very same who graced New York Harbor.

"*Lib*—" Lucy began in a questioning tone, but Rick silenced her with a finger. "Someone is always listening."

Her body turned to lead. Rick knew. Had he known Ravi was listening the whole time? His true motivations were buried too far below the surface for Lucy to discern.

Doing her best not to let her voice falter, she asked, "Why are you giving this to me?"

Rick tapped a web address, a chat forum, listed on the second line. "You can find me here."

"Why would I want to find you?"

"When you want real answers."

Lucy lowered an eyebrow. "Let me guess, those answers come with a price tag."

"Nothing in life is free."

"Not even liberty?"

"Especially not that."

The van screeched to a halt.

"Amara and Meifen will escort you to the exchange point," Rick told her. "But I'll be needing the egg." Reluctantly, Lucy handed it over. Nothing mattered more than Claudia. "*Bonne chance*," he said blithely. "I expect I'll be hearing from you soon."

"Don't hold your breath," she said, but she tucked the scrap of paper under the elastic band of her leggings.

Lucy couldn't think about Rick's proposal right now. She couldn't think about the floppy disk that had been hidden in a safe that could only be opened with her blood. All that mattered was getting Claudia home safe.

HIGH LIFE

Her gaze lifted to the winding steel structure. Lamplight glinted off the elevated railroad, tangerine and pearl.

"Try to act natural," Amara cautioned as they ascended a steep set of stairs from the street level to the linear park that slinked along the West Side.

Lucy barely contained a snarl. "Like your dad didn't take my best friend against her will?"

Amara smiled. "*Precisement.*"

Lucy snorted, tightening her hands into fists. Meifen shadowed her more closely. Despite Rick's offer of protection, she couldn't forget he would do anything to achieve his goals. If he believed Lucy would ever voluntarily contact him, he was more deluded than she'd originally suspected.

As they reached the upper deck of the High Line, low beams of light traveled the length of the abandoned railway tracks, bringing tall grass into sharp relief. The pinpricks fluctuated as Lucy walked past. The closer she got to Claudia, the more Lucy feared she would slip through her fingers and the more violent her oscillations became.

The tourmaline in her shoe was no counterbalance for Lucy's outsized emotions.

Wildflowers sprouted between the tracks in a riot of muted colors, and Lucy counted each steel bar, stealing shallow slivers of air. If she wasn't careful, her feet might get stuck. There was altogether too much metal around.

Why had the Freelancers chosen this place for the exchange?

As if reading Lucy's mind, Amara said, "This railway was constructed in the time of Tesla. There is a certain symmetry. Rick loves to be poetic." Meifen laughed. Amara watched Lucy, gauging her reaction. "Did you know there were so many freight train accidents that this became known as Death Avenue?"

Lucy worked hard to blanket her face in a detached expression.

"Thanks for the history lesson."

Amara shrugged. "You know what they say. Those who ignore history are doomed to repeat it."

"I've had enough veiled threats for one night, thanks."

"It's not a threat. It's a warning."

Lucy threw her head back, and shifted her gaze to the dark waters of the Hudson River. Couples leaned against the railing together, flirting, kissing, taking in the vista of New Jersey now cloaked in velvety black. Amber city light spilled onto the flowing river. As her eyes focused on the obscured horizon, a voice crackled in Lucy's ears, her nerves interfering with the signal.

"We're here, Lucy. Hold tight."

We? Who had Ravi brought with him?

Surreptitiously, she scoured the faces of everyone they passed, scanning the Manhattanites lazing on wooden chaise longues, not that she would recognize any of Ravi's friends or comrades or whatever. *Oh no.* Her heart kicked. Lucy wouldn't recognize the members of Ravi's rescue party—but the Freelancers might.

Lucy's eyes landed on the one face she wanted to see more than anything else.

Clauds. The crowd had thickened around her friend, swaying to the alt-rock from a band located at the bottom of a terraced row of steps. It reminded Lucy of an ancient amphitheater.

Claudia was on her own, and she seemed unsteady on her feet. Most likely the effect of the sedative. Lucy's anger surged. Where was Jess?

Amara flattened an arm across Lucy's collarbone, holding her back, and eyed her sidelong. "Natural, remember?"

"Oh, I remember." She showed her teeth. "Has your dad told you what I can do?" A satisfying moment's hesitation tightened the other woman's face and Lucy waded purposefully into the crowd.

Her armed escorts followed at a small distance, fanning out farther into the throng, no doubt keeping watch.

"Claudia!" Lucy called over the din. Her friend's head jerked in Lucy's direction but she couldn't spot her. Lucy picked up her pace.

A line of people snaked away from the green-and-white umbrella of a beverage cart into a blue-washed tunnel. Lucy spied Jess among them. Her eyes were trained on Claudia, face wan. No hint of triumph in her stance. Maybe she really did love Claudia. It didn't excuse her actions tonight. No matter what she believed the Archimedeans had done to her brother.

The nearer Lucy drew to where her friend was standing, the more overpowering the music became. It became impossible to hear Ravi over the baying of the electric guitar. She kept her gaze focused on Claudia's headband, a slash of teal against strawberry locks.

"Claudia!" she tried again. Her anxiety spiked. She shoved a few drunken music lovers from her path. They jolted back, cursing, as if they'd received a shock. Which they had. Lucy was losing control, but she didn't slow down. She couldn't.

"*Clauds*," Lucy gasped as she threw her arms around her. "Are you okay?" Frantically, she patted down her friend's hair, stroked her cheeks. Claudia's eyes remained slightly dilated.

She rubbed them, shaking her head. "Luce?" Another rub. "I'm so confused." Her friend's voice cracked, parched. "What are you doing here? What am *I* doing here?"

Lucy squeezed Claudia into another hug.

Help.

The word rocked Lucy's world. Her fingernails bit half-moons into Claudia's bare arms. Like a still from an old-fashioned film reel, the room where Claudia had been held popped into Lucy's mind—from her friend's perspective. *Help*, Claudia had whispered it to the universe.

Help. Lucy plucked it from her frequency, replaying on a feedback loop.

Angry prickles rushed along her skin, her power demanding release. She should have done a better job at protecting her best friend. Lucy couldn't blame Ravi; all of this had been her fault.

"I'm so sorry," she whispered in Claudia's ear.

"Why are you sorry? And where's Jess?" her friend asked, tongue still sluggish. "She was just here."

Lucy pulled back to look Claudia in the eye. "What's the last thing you remember?"

"I . . ." She scrunched up her nose. "Prom. The lights blew. I don't know, it's all disjointed. Like a dream." Her eyes were gradually becoming less dilated. "Then I was here," she continued. "With Jess. She said to wait here." She frowned. "How much did I have to drink?"

Lucy was grateful Claudia didn't remember what she'd seen in her mind. She also couldn't believe Ravi had been right about the whole telepathy thing.

"Clauds," she began, voice heavy. "Jess isn't coming back."

"What are you talking about? Of course she is."

"I'll explain later, I promise. But we need to leave. Now."

Claudia planted her feet, regaining some focus, seeming more herself. "Not until you tell me why we're in Manhattan and where Jess is." She folded her arms, wearing the same expression as the moment before she'd decked Tony Morelli all those years ago. "And what happened to your dress?" Oh yeah, Claudia was back.

"Did someone call for a ride?"

Ravi appeared from nowhere, interrupting the best-friend showdown. He placed a warm hand on Lucy's shoulder. His question came out serious but, as she angled her gaze at him, she spied a quarter grin. A grin of relief.

"What is *he* doing here?" Claudia said, swinging her eyes between them. "You better start explaining what on earth is going on, Luce."

Ravi gave a deliberate shake of the head. He didn't want Lucy to reveal herself. But lying is what had gotten them here.

Claudia tapped her foot. "I'm waiting."

Jess emerged from the crush of people before Lucy had decided what to do.

"So am I," said the other girl.

Down below, the drummer decided to barrel into a relentless solo. Hoots and hollers rose from the audience scattered along the terraces.

"Jess?" Claudia said, her voice hitching up. "Where'd you go?" She took a step toward the person she still thought was her girlfriend, and Lucy blocked her path. "Luce, what are you *doing*?"

"Trust me," she told her best friend, but for the first time ever, Lucy wasn't sure if Claudia did.

"I'm sorry, Clauds," Jess told her. "I never meant for you to get caught up in this." Her eyes roamed Claudia's face, a deep crease cutting the bridge of her nose.

"Caught up in what? I don't understand."

Jess nailed Lucy with a hard glare instead of answering. "You were supposed to come alone. Throwing your lot in with the Archimedeans was the wrong call. You broke our agreement."

Lucy stepped out farther in front of Claudia. "Rick and I completed the mission. There's nothing for you here."

"What mission?" Claudia demanded from behind her.

No one answered. The beat of the music pulsed through Lucy as if the drumsticks were pounding the inside of her skull.

"Unlike the Orders," Jess said, slashing Ravi with a glare. "Rick doesn't own me."

Ravi scoffed. Jess pulled something from her waistband.

Claudia gasped as light gleamed off steel. Lucy's pulse skyrocketed. The streetlamp directly overhead began to flicker.

"I want answers," Jess said, and pointed the gun at Ravi.

"Jess!" Claudia exclaimed. "Why do you have a *gun*?" Thunderous applause all but swallowed the question.

Her friend rushed forward and, again, Lucy blocked her. She felt the hammering of Claudia's heart as if it were her own, her friend's energy a blaze of panic and confusion.

Lucy's eyes combed the mass of vibrating bodies for Amara and Meifen. A public confrontation wasn't part of Rick's carefully laid plans. What would they do?

Ravi walked toward Jess, brows drawn, unafraid.

"Put the gun down and we can talk," he said.

"Do what he says," Claudia pleaded, voice quavering. Jess regarded her with sheer misery.

"I can't, Clauds." To Ravi, she said, "I put the gun down, I'm as good as dead. I know how this works."

"What does she mean?" Claudia whispered, grabbing Lucy's arm.

Lucy had no idea, but, "Ravi isn't the one in the kidnapping or murder business!" she yelled at Jess.

Jess ignored her. "Tell the Initiates to show themselves," she said.

Initiates?

Ravi looked toward the sky. "Chaps?"

A cherry-red dot instantaneously appeared on Jess's forehead.

Snipers? Snipers! Ravi had brought sharpshooters! What the frak?

Jess caught Lucy's eye. "That's right. I told you, you don't know who you're dealing with."

Lucy swallowed, not wanting to admit she might be right. When Ravi had told Lucy he could take care of himself, she'd imagined some martial-arts moves for self-defense, not . . . this. Why *did* scientists need their own special-ops unit?

Still, the Archimedeans wouldn't shoot a twenty-year-old girl in cold blood. In a public place. This had to be a bluff.

Returning her focus to Ravi, Jess said, "I want to know the truth about what happened to Jeremy. Tell me why the Initiates killed my twin—what he found—and I won't shoot you before they shoot me. Make me believe it."

Ravi stood a foot in front of Lucy, back turned, so she couldn't see his face. And yet, from the way he flinched, she knew there was at least a shred of truth to Jess's accusation.

He dropped a hand to his waist. Ravi must be armed, but he didn't draw his weapon.

"The Sophists killed Jeremy like they killed my parents," he said in a level tone.

"The Order of Sophia make a rather convenient bogeyman," Jess retorted. "Tell me something more original."

"Well, they tried to take my head off tonight," Lucy snapped. "They're capable of anything."

"They did?" Claudia gulped. Fear surged through Lucy—Claudia's fear. Fear for Lucy. Lucy was no longer convinced she deserved it.

Another red dot appeared on Jess's shoulder.

"You're surrounded," Ravi said.

"So are you."

Lucy followed Jess's eye line. Meifen and Amara had circled closer. Other long-limbed, black-clad men were also closing in. Friend, or foe? And what did that even mean anymore?

Meifen reached Jess first, coming to stand shoulder to shoulder with her while Amara hung back.

"These odds don't seem fair to me," Meifen told Ravi, face blank. Lucy had no doubt she would carry out Rick's orders—whatever they were. Her stomach triple-knotted itself.

The nearby speakers went on the fritz. Frak. Lucy did *not* need a repeat of prom right now. Had that only been earlier this evening?

Claudia used the distraction to dart out from behind Lucy and put herself directly in the line of fire. "Clauds!" Lucy shouted, but she was too late.

Her best friend stepped between Ravi and Jess, shielding him with her body.

No! What was she thinking?

Claudia held up her hands. "Jess, I don't know what's going on here. What you think happened. But I know this isn't you."

The gun trembled in Jess's grip.

She took another step. "Please, Jess. I know you miss your brother. Just put the gun down. Nobody needs to get hurt."

"*Do something,*" Lucy whispered, praying Ravi could still pick her up on the com.

"Claudia's right," he said in a collected tone.

"Jess, look at me," Claudia said, voice stern, commanding her attention. "I love you, I love the way you put Sriracha sauce on pancakes. And the way you sing—badly—in the shower. And the way you kiss me awake. You're not a killer. That's not who you are."

Lucy held her breath. Without a doubt, her best friend was the bravest person she'd ever met.

"I love you too," Jess said. A tear sluiced through the glitter still sparkling on her cheeks. "But you never really knew me."

"I want to, Jess. I *want* to," Claudia pleaded. "You just have to let me in."

More tears spilled down the other girl's face. She shuddered a breath and, slowly, she began to lower her weapon.

Before Lucy could sigh in relief, the bulb overhead exploded, casting them half in shadow. It wasn't Lucy's doing, however. Someone had shot it out. The Initiates? A second later, someone shot at Jess's feet.

"Never trust an Archimedean," she spat at Ravi. Incandescent rage shone from her face. "Move, Clauds!" she shouted. Claudia stood frozen.

"Hold fire," Ravi barked at the Initiates, wherever they were.

"You think you're in charge, professor's pet?" Jess laughed in a broken way and started raising her gun as Meifen drew her own.

From where the other Freelancer was standing, she had a clean shot at Ravi.

"Ravi!" Lucy gasped. Meifen didn't get the chance.

A howl of pain rent her lips as blood spurted from her thigh. She cursed as she crashed to the wooden deck, dropping her gun and cradling her knee.

The Initiates had fired. They had fired first. Into a crowded public place.

They weren't bluffing. At all.

The lights at floor level burst. Those *were* Lucy's fault.

Ravi pulled his weapon. Jess held her ground and aimed.

Lucy heard another shot and Claudia let out a shriek. Blood welled from her friend's upper arm. "No!" Lucy hollered, and dashed to Claudia's side. Now both of them formed a wall between Ravi and Jess. "Ravi, call them off!"

Jess snarled a laugh. "Archimedeans don't play that way. Do they?" She kept her gun raised.

"Nobody is playing here!" Lucy screamed as she tried to cover Claudia's wound with her hands. Thankfully, it didn't seem deep, only a flesh wound. A bullet must have grazed her. Blood nevertheless streamed through her useless fingers.

"Oh God, Clauds," Lucy moaned.

Claudia tensed her jaw, tears leaking from her eyes. She'd gone pale, stunned. Lucy squeezed her arm tighter and her friend yelped from an unintended shock. She let go, fighting her seesawing emotions.

"See, Lucy?" Jess seethed. "They'll stop anyone who gets in their way."

Calm, Lucy. Shield, Lucy. Calm, shield; calm, shield. Who was she kidding?

Amara darted to where Meifen was slumped. Crouching next to the other woman, she glowered up at Lucy. "My father has too much faith in you."

"No one else has to get hurt," Ravi said to Amara without inflection. "Drop your weapons and you can all walk away."

Amara kicked Meifen's gun down the tracks. Then her own.

She pressed a comforting hand to Meifen's cheek. "*T'inquiètes pas,*" she murmured as she slung one arm around the other woman's waist and dragged her to her feet. Meifen let out a hiss of pain.

Amara nodded at Jess. "Time to go."

"They'll never let us walk out of here."

Ravi glanced from Jess to Amara. "You have my word."

"Your word means nothing," said Jess, scoffing, eyes filled with disgust.

"*Go,*" Ravi ordered. Lucy had never heard him sound so ferocious.

The Initiates fired another warning round just in front of the Free-lancers' feet. Lucy heard a few pings as some of the bullets ricocheted off the metal tracks and into the audience. Finally realizing they were in danger, their screams tore from the crowd. The deck began to rumble with a stampede.

Jess didn't move a muscle.

Amara, on the other hand, used the chaos to disappear with Meifen. Jess had disobeyed Rick, derailed the plan for her own personal ven-detta, and the other Freelancers evidently weren't sticking around to get shot. Jess lifted her chin, holding her gun on the three of them. Lucy couldn't let Claudia get caught in the crossfire either.

Working on pure instinct, she pushed her friend forcefully aside and lunged to where Jess stood opposite Ravi.

"Lucy, no!" he shouted as she barreled straight into the other girl, knocking her to the ground.

Their bodies slammed together as they landed between the railway tracks, wildflowers cushioning their fall. Jess's gun skittered a few feet away.

Terrified New Yorkers ran past them, nearly trampling Jess and Lucy as they fled for their lives; others dropped to the ground, scattering amidst the shrubbery, and pressing their bellies into the dirt.

"Jess!" Claudia shouted, charging straight for them. Ravi grabbed her around the waist, still holding his gun. She struggled in his arms but he held firm.

"You're going to get Claudia killed!" Lucy roared as she and Jess be-gan to tussle. "If you really love her, you shouldn't have put her in danger!"

"I'm not the danger. Your boyfriend is!"

Jess threw a livid glare at Ravi, who stood with his gun pointed at their entwined form. Another man in black had Claudia in his grip.

"Just stop, Jess! Ravi said you could go, so *go*!"

"I owe it to Jeremy to find out the truth. I had to try." She released a harsh breath. Sadness, guilt, and fury crashed over Lucy. "I'd die for the truth," Jess said between gritted teeth. From the desperation inundating Lucy, it was clear that the other girl really didn't expect to live through this.

Lucy struggled to breathe against the weight of her frequency. "You don't get to make that choice for the rest of us," she wheezed.

"No shot," Ravi said tersely into his coms. "I repeat, no shot."

"You're safe, don't worry," Jess told her. "You're too valuable. For now." She flipped Lucy onto her back, pinning her to the tracks. Jess was slight, but strong. Where Lucy's arms and legs connected with the metal, green flames erupted.

Using all her of strength, Lucy managed to wrest one arm free and her fist connected with Jess's jaw. Another streetlight went dark. Lucy had never punched anyone before. Her hand smarted.

"Don't make the same mistake I did," Jess warned. "If you care about Claudia, stay away from her." Then she returned the punch.

Lucy's head snapped back against the ground as Jess scrambled for the gun.

She had to stop her. Lucy reached out and a thin tentacle of white light streamed from her hand to the darkened streetlamp. *Holy* . . . That was new. She didn't have time to think about it.

High on adrenaline, Lucy wriggled across the tracks toward Jess as St. Elmo's fire licked her knees, surged across her torso and down her arms.

Jess got to the gun first. Seizing hold, she jumped to her feet.

She aimed for Ravi's head. "Would you die for the professor?"

"No!" Lucy howled and grasped Jess's ankle, trying to throw her off balance.

Jess's entire body spasmed the moment she made contact.

Her arms flailed and the gun clattered onto the steel slats.

Lucy ripped her hand away, but the other girl crashed against the tracks, unconscious. *OhmyGodOhmyGodOhmyGod*. Her limbs continued to twitch like a puppet on a string.

What had Lucy done?

The smell of burning filled her nose. Lucy recoiled in horror.

The flesh of Jess's right ankle and shin was *burned*. Burned! She stared down at her hands. They were covered with blood—Claudia's blood—and white sparks zipping from her fingertips to the metal bolts of the tracks.

Lucy gagged on her own bile.

Out of the corner of her eye, Lucy spied Mikhail racing toward them. The Freelancers hadn't left, after all. What if they tried to take Claudia again in retribution?

Jess continued to convulse.

Ravi was suddenly squatting at Lucy's side. "Lucinda, we need to move."

"Jess?" she croaked.

He lowered his face closer to the other girl's. "She's still breathing." Ravi turned back to Lucy. "You're bleeding. Again."

Lucy hadn't noticed the blood gushing from her nostrils. Nor was she worried about herself.

"Claudia?" She searched out her eyes, and then she wished she hadn't. If Lucy thought Cole had regarded her like a monster at the prom, it was nothing compared with what she saw now.

Her best friend's features were twisted in terror—and for good reason.

"*Jess*," she cried out, covering her face with her hands.

"Let's get out of here," Ravi told Lucy. He tugged on Lucy's arm and she skidded backward on the ground, out of reach.

"*Don't.* I'm not safe to touch."

"I'm not scared."

"You should be."

Lucy pushed to her feet without his help but she tottered, knees weak. Lightheadedness deluged her and she saw the Flower of Life, hovering above her. She watched as the petals became six bright emerald flames. A flower of flame. The flames were life. Energy, neither created nor destroyed. Lucy recognized the signs and she prepared for a fall.

"Get away!" Lucy warned as Ravi tried to catch her.

The entire length of the High Line burst into green flames.

Then everything went black, and she welcomed the darkness.

BLACK HOLE

Lucy's eyelids blinked open, her mouth as dry as cotton balls. The first rays of dawn wended across the wall. She was in bed. But she wasn't in *her* bed.

Lucy bolted upright, then rubbed her forehead with a groan. Her head throbbed and all of her muscles were sore.

"Morning." She glanced toward the voice. "Or almost morning," Ravi said. He sat at the counter in the kitchenette, his shoulders tense. The stillness was fraught with unasked questions.

Lucy was in *Ravi's* bed. And it was morning. Her parents were going to kill her. She'd never even broken curfew let alone stayed out all night.

Her gaze dropped to her hands, one of which was bandaged, and the horror that was prom night came rushing back.

"Claudia?" she forced out.

"Safe. Home," Ravi reassured her quickly. He rose from his stool and walked toward the bed. "You've been out for the count. I hope you don't mind that I brought you here." His tone was stiff but his dark eyes teemed with worry.

"No, no—" Lucy started. She couldn't imagine what her parents would have thought if she'd been deposited unconscious on their doorstep. "Thanks for looking after me."

"Of course." He stopped at the foot of the bed.

Lucy rubbed her thumb back and forth along the bandage. Ravi had washed her hands and face, but she was still wearing the black turtleneck and leggings the Freelancers had provided. Blood was crusted into the ridges of the turtleneck. She began to itch all over. She was dirty, she felt so dirty—what had she done to Jess? Lucy's breath hitched as she choked back a sob.

"Lucy?" Ravi said softly.

"*I*-I need to take a shower."

He nodded, pointing toward a door in the corner. "The towels are all clean."

"Thanks." She didn't meet his eyes. Her bones creaked as she got up and padded toward the bathroom. Pulling on a cord to turn on the light, she shut the door behind her.

"The hot water takes a few minutes," Ravi called from the other side. "Let it run."

Lucy didn't answer, but she followed his advice. The shower knob squeaked. She peeled off her turtleneck first and peered down the length of her body. Her bra was bloodstained. Lucy's chest constricted as she recalled the look Claudia had given her on the High Line. Steam obscured her reflection as she examined it in the mirror—Jess had given her quite the shiner—and the running water drowned out the sound of her tears.

Shucking off her leggings, a scrap of paper drifted to the floor. LIBERTAS. Lucy crumpled the word in her fist, shaking her head as she dragged herself into the shower. The chat room log-in imprinted on her memory as she watched the paper disintegrate. If only hot water could wash away what Lucy had done so easily—what she *was*.

She'd lied to her best friend for months, gotten her kidnapped, and then electrocuted her first love right in front of her eyes. The fact that Jess was still alive was only small comfort. Lucy had lost control and she didn't know what the long-term effects of that much voltage would be. She was basically living one of those epic poems her mother liked to translate so much. They never ended happily.

Lucy choked on another laugh-sob. Blood swirled around the drain.

After a few minutes staring at nothing, she shut off the water. She still didn't feel clean. Not even close.

Ravi rapped once on the door as she wrapped herself in a towel.

"Fresh clothes?" he asked.

Lucy opened the door a crack. Yesterday, having Ravi see her dressed only in a towel would have made her blush from head to toe. Today, all she felt was numb.

"T-shirt and *sweatpants*." He tested out a smile as he held them out, but Lucy couldn't muster one in return.

"Thanks." She accepted the offering and closed the door on his furrowed brow.

Both the T-shirt and sweatpants were emblazoned with the I ❤ NY logo, like something you'd buy at an airport souvenir shop. Which Ravi probably had. The irony pinched Lucy's gut. She wished she'd listened to her parents and never ventured into the Bad Apple.

She attempted detangling her wet curls with Ravi's flimsy comb for about twenty seconds before giving up. Exhaling a long breath, she scooped up the turtleneck and leggings from the floor.

Water dripped down the back of her T-shirt as she entered the main room.

Back at the counter, Ravi looked up with an electric kettle in his hand.

"Tea?" he said, pouring boiling water into two mugs. "It makes everything better. At least if you're British."

There wasn't enough tea on the planet to make Lucy feel better.

"Trash can?" she asked.

"Here." He stepped on a pedal and a can opened next to the counter. Lucy tossed in the bloody clothes. She never wanted to see them again.

Ravi slid a mug across the countertop toward Lucy as she slumped onto a stool. "How are you feeling?" he asked.

"How do you *think* I'm feeling?"

He raised his mug to his lips. "What about physically?" he said as he swallowed.

Lucy curved her hands around the mug, glowering at the light-brown water. The now-soggy bandage on her hand dripped onto the tile.

"Let me change that for you," Ravi offered.

"It's fine. I'm fine."

"I'm sorry you were hurt," he said, a new hardness to his voice. "It's my fault."

A small, stunned laugh distorted at the back of Lucy's throat.

"I'm not the one who nearly died. Or was kidnapped. I'm fine."

Ravi narrowed his eyes. "Fine might be an overstatement." He opened a drawer with some force and pulled out a first-aid kit. Rounding the counter, he pulled his stool closer to Lucy's and inspected the contents of the plastic box.

"Hand," he said. Lucy obliged, and Ravi carefully cut off the wet bandage.

"I guess I'm Internet famous by now," she said with a resigned sigh. "How many views do I have on YouTube?"

"Why would you be on YouTube?" Ravi sounded genuinely perplexed.

"Oh, I don't know, the shootout and impromptu electrical storm at the High Line, maybe? I know New Yorkers have seen it all, but surely that qualifies as unusual? And the NYPD probably has some questions, I'm guessing."

Ravi unwound the gauze methodically. It shimmered in the strengthening sunlight.

"You don't have to worry about the authorities or anybody else connecting you to last night's events," he told her. *Last night's events.* What a sanitized way to describe what had happened. What Lucy was capable of doing to another human being.

"How is that possible?" she demanded.

Ravi held her gaze as he tore open the antiseptic swab with his teeth. He brushed the alcohol swab across Lucy's cut and she hissed softly.

"How did you get this?" he asked in a low voice. He traced the line of the wound with his fingertip.

Lucy ignored the way her body reacted to his touch.

"Answer my question first," she said.

Ravi pulled the gauze taut between his hands. "Lucy, all traffic and security cameras in the vicinity of the High Line were remotely disabled as soon as you relayed your destination." He wrapped the gauze around her palm as he talked. "There will be no proof you were ever there."

"But there were witnesses."

"There were panicked people, and eyewitnesses are notoriously unreliable. The news is already blaming faulty wiring and kids playing with fireworks for starting the stampede."

Lucy's mouth fell open. Who *were* these people? Could it really be that easy to cover up? The lie certainly sounded more believable than the truth.

"But what about smartphones?" she insisted.

Ravi finished with the bandage. "The Initiates are thorough. You have nothing to worry about."

"I bet." Lucy couldn't help but snort. "Like they were *thorough* with the Freelancers? They could have killed someone! Why did you bring your own SEAL Team Six?"

"You saw what happened. The Freelancers are lawless. And the Sophists are fanatics." Ravi scowled. "The Initiates were necessary. If anything—*worse*—had happened to you, Lucinda . . ." He touched her blackening eye, then trailed his thumb over the tiny hills of her knuckles, and tingles pervaded her.

"Don't do that," Lucy rasped. She couldn't think straight with his energy flowing through her, and she was still too drained to block it out herself. Yes, Lucy had strong feelings for him, and *yes*, his energy still felt like a summer's day, but Ravi had shown her a different side of himself last night—a side she didn't know what to do with yet.

"Sorry. I thought I was shielding." Hurt crossed his face. He dropped his hands and walked to the other side of the counter. "Now answer *my* question. How did you injure your hand?" His tone became brusque, businesslike.

"Rick," she said, and Ravi swore. "He needed my blood to open a safe. That's why he wanted me." Ravi swore again, pounding his fist on the counter. The mugs rattled against the tile.

"Did you see what was inside?"

"A floppy disk."

"A floppy disk?"

"You heard me," she sniped, although she understood his skepticism.

Ravi pinched the bridge of his nose. "Do you know what was on it?" His mental calculations were practically audible, plotting possible answers in his mind. For the first time ever, Lucy didn't think an equation could solve anything.

Hopelessness coiled inside her until she was spoiling for a fight.

"That information was on a need-to-know basis," she replied. "Rick didn't think I needed to know."

Lucy decided to leave out Rick's job offer, although she doubted it was still on the table after the High Line fiasco. She just hoped he was too pragmatic to hold a grudge, or she'd have to count both the Freelancers and the Order of Sophia as her enemies.

"The Freelancers had the Tesla Egg," Lucy informed him. "They did steal it. Rick had me use it, but then he took it back."

Ravi released a frustrated breath. "It's okay. Professor T might have some ideas about the disk. You did well." He captured her gaze. "I'm proud of you."

"*Proud* of me?" she exclaimed. "How can you be proud of a monster?!"

"You're not a monster, Lucinda," he growled, even as his expression grew tender.

"I almost killed Jess!"

"It was an accident. And she didn't leave you much choice. You were defending yourself. Defending *me*." She heard the agony in his voice. "It should have been the other way around."

Lucy inhaled a sharp breath. Ravi was twisted up about this too. Part of her wanted to reach out—to comfort him—and yet she didn't. There were still big pieces of his puzzle missing.

"What Jess said about her brother—was she right?" she asked instead. "Did the Initiates eliminate him for asking questions?"

"*What?* No, Lucy. No. They're not assassins."

"They? You're not one of them?"

"I've gone through their basic training but no. My domain is research."

Lucy's shoulders curled in momentary relief. "And her brother?"

"I'd never heard of Jess or her brother before last night. Professor T briefed me very quickly when I phoned for backup. Her brother was an Initiate killed in an attack by the Sophists on one of our facilities. That's all I know." Softening his voice, he continued. "But she was out of her mind with grief. It wouldn't be wise to take anything she said to heart. I know . . . what that's like."

Lucy lowered her gaze to the floor. Jess was acting irrationally, no doubt, but there was so much Lucy didn't know about the Orders or the Freelancers or how everything added up. The other girl had been willing to exchange her life for the truth. What if there was even the smallest possibility that she was right?

"Yeah, probably," Lucy said to her hands. She heard Ravi move toward her again. "What am I going to tell Claudia? She must hate me."

"You risked your life for her. She knows that. I don't think she hates you. She's just scared. She's been through an ordeal."

"Ravi, what do we do if the Freelancers come after her again? Or my parents?"

He blew out a breath. "The best way to protect her is to keep her in the dark. It would be safest for Claudia—and for you—if she didn't remember what happened last night."

"How could Claudia ever *not* remember?" She swiveled on the stool and pinned him with a glare.

His fingers twitched as if trying to resist stroking her cheek.

"Ravi?" she prompted.

"There are new technologies, surgical memory extraction using precise voltages."

"Are you serious? You can't play with her brain! Claudia could end up a vegetable!"

"It's not the 1950s, Lucy," he said calmly, as if what he was proposing were totally standard. "The procedures we've developed at Chrysopoeia Tech are much more precise."

"*No*. No! You can't go around wiping people's memories! Cole saw my hands on fire but not burning—are you going to erase his memory too?"

Ravi's expression remained frustratingly sympathetic.

"Claudia might be relieved. The technique originated as a treatment for shell shock. She doesn't need to remember—"

"What I did."

"That's not what I was saying."

"Why should Claudia have to remember her best friend's a monster, right?"

"You know that's not true."

A caustic laugh. "Then what am I?"

"Last night I'd say you were a hero."

"If you truly believe that, Ravi, you're more misguided than Rick."

"*Lucinda*—" He reached for her and Lucy hopped down from the stool. "I need to go home," she told him. She would happily accept whatever punishment her parents deemed fit. It couldn't be worse than the black hole inside her, threatening to swallow her whole.

"I'll drive you," Ravi said.

"No. I want to walk."

"You're still recovering—we need to talk about the nosebleeds, and the seizure, and any other—"

"Not now," Lucy ground out.

Indecision pursed his lips. "Okay," he agreed after a minute. "Later. But here—" Ravi pulled the tourmaline necklace from his pocket. "This fell onto the tracks when you . . . collapsed." He said the last word quietly, and it filled her with foreboding.

Morning light winked off the silver starburst setting.

Lucy had a stop to make on her way home.

ANOTHER WAY TO DIE

Lucy shambled through the peaceful quiet of an early suburban Sunday morning. Her sneakers scuffed along the pavement—the only sound besides the occasional chirping of birds. She glanced at the phone Ravi had returned to her: barely six A.M. In an hour or two, the neighborhood would be a flurry of lawn mowers and kids playing in their yards. Not now. Now there was silence and all Lucy could hear were her own swirling thoughts and pounding heart.

She fingered the tourmaline pendant. Idly, she wondered whether Cole and Megan had enjoyed an after-prom party for two at the White Hart Inn. Lucy could only imagine the two of them swapping stories about flying staplers and volatile lighting systems. That night in the hot tub with Cole, Lucy had scared herself—but not enough. She'd still been in denial.

Until she saw Jess lying, almost lifeless, on the High Line, Lucy hadn't fully comprehended how dangerous she truly was.

Ravi said she didn't scare him. He was a fool. Lucy scared herself.

She stopped in front of Claudia's house.

Her friend's phone was doubtless still in the possession of the Freelancers so Lucy couldn't text her, and it was way too early to dial the landline and risk waking Claudia's parents. Lucy shuffled down the driveway toward the back garden, which Claudia's room overlooked. They never locked the gate. She scooped up a handful of gravel.

Lucy sucked in a breath as she swung open the gate. No pebbles required.

Claudia was slouched on the tire swing, head tipped back, gazing up at the big blue sky. The metal links twisted back and forth. It was going to be a beautiful day.

Lucy remembered when Mr. O'Rourke had installed the swing in the old oak tree. It took months of begging her mom before she agreed to let Lucy try it out and then only if she wore her helmet. As Claudia had pushed her higher and higher, Lucy hadn't minded about the helmet, thinking life couldn't get any better.

Slowly, Claudia pulled herself upright. She was wearing Jess's *Ceci n'est pas une pipe* T-shirt. A weight pressed on Lucy's chest.

"Clauds," she said in a hush. She weaved between Mrs. O'Rourke's prize rosebushes toward the swing.

"You're okay?" Claudia asked, expression drawn. Her gaze lingered for a moment on Lucy's black eye.

"Yeah." Lucy pointed at the bandage peeking out from beneath the sleeve of the T-shirt. "You okay?"

"Ravi patched me up. No stitches, even. Just Steri-Strips." She shrugged. "And I'd been hoping for a sexy scar. Ladies love scars."

Lucy swallowed a laugh. Claudia's tone was light but off-key.

She came to a halt in front of the swing, shoving her hands in her pockets to keep them away from the chains. Hanging her head, she said, "I don't know where to start, Clauds."

"I don't either, Luce." Her friend pushed her feet against the grass and began to swing. She looked Lucy up and down. "I take it you haven't been home yet."

Lucy pulled at the baggy sweatpants. "Not yet."

"I've been briefed on the cover story," she said. "You were with me all night. I'll confirm it with the Drs. Phelps."

The crater inside Lucy expanded. "What else did Ravi say?"

"Not much. National security may have been mentioned—although he's not American, so I don't know how that works. I gather he's not a college student or a teacher's assistant." Claudia arched an eyebrow. "Keeping my mouth shut was the general gist."

"I'm so sorry. So, *so* sorry."

Her best friend's face remained impassive. She kicked herself higher.

"I didn't mean—I didn't mean to hurt Jess. I need you to know that," Lucy said, because it seemed the most urgent of the things she needed to make her best friend understand. "I could never . . . on purpose . . ." Lucy's entire being recoiled as the other girl's twitching body flashed through her mind.

"How?" Claudia asked softly. "How did you do . . . what you did?"

Lucy exhaled. Ravi thought it was safer for Claudia not to know anything about the Orders, but that ship had sailed last night. Claudia deserved the truth. How could Lucy ever regain her friend's trust with so many secrets between them?

"Well, for starters, I don't have epilepsy," she said.

"But I saw you seize. On the High Line. I've never seen you seize that badly, I was *so*— I thought you were going to die, Luce." The broken quality in her friend's voice made something inside Lucy unravel. "Both you and Jess."

Lucy dared a step closer, wanting to touch her best friend, yet still too afraid.

"I'm sorry you had to see that." She could only imagine how terrifying it had all been for Claudia to witness. Even Ravi seemed torn up about what he had seen, although Lucy wasn't ready to discuss it with him yet.

"It *was* a seizure," Lucy explained. "But it wasn't caused by epilepsy."

"Then by what?"

"A different kind of genetic disorder. A mutation."

"Oh-kay . . ."

Lucy interlocked her fingers. "That's how . . . what happened with Jess."

"I may not be a scientist like you, but I'm pretty sure that's not possible."

"It shouldn't be." Lucy drew in a breath through her nostrils. Perhaps people like her *shouldn't* be allowed to exist.

"Have you always known?" Claudia raked a hand through her knotty curls.

"No. I only just found out. My parents don't even know." Claudia cocked her head at that revelation, and Lucy continued, "Ravi works with scientists who've been studying my mutation. He says they can help."

Her friend dragged her feet along the ground, stopping the swing.

"Scientists," she repeated. Lucy nodded. "Scientists with guns." Lucy nodded again. "Right." Claudia's shoulders hunched forward. "How does Jess fit into all of this?"

Lucy wet her lips. "Jess came to Eaton to watch me for the people she works for."

"The people who took me."

"Yes."

"So what was I?" Claudia rubbed a glossy sheen from her eyes. "What was I to Jess? *Bait?*"

"For what it's worth, I don't believe she wanted to hurt you."

"It's not worth much."

"I'm sorry."

Claudia frowned. "She's gone, isn't she?"

Lucy sure the hell hoped so. Wherever the Freelancers had fled, she didn't want them anywhere near Claudia, ever again.

"I do think she loved you." Despite everything, Lucy actually did believe that.

Claudia hiccupped a laugh. "I don't know what love means anymore."

The pain on her face broke Lucy. She grabbed for Claudia's hand and the other girl pulled back on the swing. Out of reach. Lucy's hand brushed the metal chain and a small green flame appeared. *Frak.*

Claudia's eyes went wide.

Flushing, Lucy shoved her hands back in her pockets. "Please don't be afraid of me, Clauds." Her lips trembled as her eyes began to water.

Maybe Lucy was destined to become untouchable, and maybe that was for the best.

"I'm not afraid of you, Luce—I'm *furious* about the fact you've been lying straight to my face. Over and over!" Claudia raised her voice at the same time she dissolved into tears. "All the trips to New York, all the excuses. I would have listened. I would have helped. I've known you my whole life, but I don't know you at all—and *not* because of your powers. You were my best friend!"

"*Were?*" Lucy yelped, staggering back another step. She clutched the tourmaline. "I'll do anything to make this right, Claudia. No more secrets. Tell me what you need. Anything."

"Some things you can't make right."

"I can, I swear. Let me try. Whatever you want to know, I'll tell you."

"I don't want to know any more." Claudia swiped angrily at her tears. "Both my best friend and my girlfriend were deceiving me for months and I had no idea. What does that make *me*, Lucy? Tell me that!"

"Trusting. Loyal. Better than I deserve."

"I'll keep your secret, Lucy, but what I need is for you to leave me alone."

"I love you, Clauds," Lucy rasped.

"*Please*, Luce. Just leave."

Lucy nodded, unable to speak. Sorrow burrowed into her bones. They had never felt so heavy. Silently she turned, barely able to force her feet to move.

Each of Claudia's soft sobs punctured her heart.

The swing resumed its squeaking as she walked away. She didn't chance a final look. She might not leave if she did.

After last night, nothing would ever be the same.

I, ZOMBIE

The walk home from Claudia's house was the longest of Lucy's life. She had the distinct impression of walking toward a firing squad for the second time in twenty-four hours.

Staring at the *Cave Felem!* door mat, she swallowed hard. The Beware of the Cat welcome mat had been a present from Claudia a few Christmases ago. *Oh, Clauds.* Lucy dug around the pockets of Ravi's sweatpants, feeling for her house keys. At least he'd kept her essentials safe while she was breaking into museums and dodging bullets.

The front door juddered just as her hand closed around the keys.

"Dad."

"Lucinda."

Her dad's face was drawn and haggard, as if he'd aged twenty years since Lucy had last seen him. And he was still wearing his suit. Nevertheless, wrath knitted his brow and Lucy did her best not to cower beneath his blazing eyes.

Her throat burned, unable to put together a greeting much less a defense—because her name had indeed been an accusation.

Lucy's father studied her like she was a stranger, examining her clothes, her bandaged hand, and settling on her bruised cheek.

Incredulity threaded through his voice as he said, "Were you in a fight?"

"Only with some A/V equipment." Lucy forced out the lie.

Her dad stroked the tender skin around her eye, and Lucy gasped not only from the unexpected gesture but also from the depth of the sadness that washed over her. Dr. Victor Phelps scrutinized his daughter intently, almost as if he could see his own sorrow reflected in her eyes, then retreated into the foyer. Lucy followed him inside.

They stood in the exact same spot where—what seemed like a lifetime ago—he'd been a proud dad admiring his daughter in her prom dress.

What if he never looked at Lucy that way again?

"Your mother's waiting in the living room," he informed her. "We've been worried sick."

Guilt clashed with anger. Lucy hated that she couldn't tell her parents that she hadn't broken curfew on purpose. But explaining that Claudia had been kidnapped and Lucy had to rescue her would only make matters worse. Maybe endanger her parents even more than they already were.

And yet, all of this had started with the photo in her father's office. Ravi said it hadn't been sent by the Archimedeans; the Freelancers had sent Jess to determine whether it was Lucy or Claudia who carried the lightning gene, so it couldn't be them either; and if the Sophists had known about Lucy, they would have locked her up and thrown away the key. On that point, disturbingly, the Archimedeans and the Freelancers actually agreed.

Who did that leave?

"Lucy!"

Her mom sprang up from the sofa and rushed to hug her. Not what she'd expected. Her mother wasn't much of a hugger under the best of circumstances. Lucy prepared for another wave of emotion, but none came.

"She's safe, Elaine," said her dad. Her mom pulled back, staring at Lucy as if she didn't believe her own eyes. Her hair was loose, yesterday's makeup cracked around her wrinkles. She'd already been burning the candles at both ends, and Lucy had only added to her stress.

"Prom ended hours ago, Lucy," her father said in a steely tone. "Where have you been? I nearly called the cops."

Lucy sucked in a sharp breath. That would have been bad. Very bad, indeed.

Watching her hesitate, her father's expression hardened. Between her parents, Lucy's mom had traditionally been the disciplinarian. She wasn't used to her dad turning his Wall Street shark glare on her. She squirmed where she stood.

"I was with Claudia," Lucy said to the carpet.

"We checked with the O'Rourkes," came his reply.

"We weren't at her house."

"We know. Where *were* you? And why didn't you answer your phone? And what are you wearing?" Her father's volume increased a notch with each question and Lucy realized he wasn't just angry—he seemed frightened.

The only other time he'd ever been this upset with Lucy was when she was six or seven. She'd deliberately disobeyed his instruction not to climb the monkey bars at the playground and proceeded to fall flat on her face. She still had a paper-thin scar on her forehead from the incident.

"I'm sorry." Lucy's voice grew very small. "We went to Jess's dorm and—"

"The Jess who came over last night?" her dad interrupted, dark eyebrows pinched together.

"Yeah. I spilled punch on my dress so she lent me these." Lucy tugged at the T-shirt. Her temples throbbed and she could sense her oscillations starting to go haywire. She touched the tourmaline to steady herself. "My phone was on silent. And we lost track of time. I'm really, really sorry."

"I can't tell you how disappointed I am in you, Lucinda. What if you'd had a seizure? How are we supposed to trust you to take care of yourself at college? It's not like you to be so irresponsible," he fumed.

"Victor," her mom said in a cautioning tone.

Fine. Better for her parents to think she'd stayed out all night in some age-appropriate act of rebellion than to learn the truth. Safer for them, safer for everyone.

Going on the offensive, Lucy charged, "Why are you so disappointed in me? Because I'm not perfect? Because I acted eighteen for once? Instead of like some retiree who loves early bird specials?"

Her father crossed his arms. "Don't be ridiculous."

"Ridiculous? *Me?*" She threw her hands in the air. "*I'm* being ridiculous because I wasn't totally in your control for thirty seconds!" Lucy had thought she was pretending, but the frustration rising to the surface was real. "You never ask me what I want. You just give orders."

She wheeled toward her mother. "*Both* of you! I don't even want to go to Gilbert. That's *your* dream. Not mine."

"I don't know who you are right now," barked her father.

Neither do I.

He clasped her around the shoulders. "Have you been drinking?"

She released a smothered half-laugh as desperation clawed through her—*his* desperation. Lucy yanked herself away, not wanting him to get trapped in her electromagnetic field.

"I'm still your father, Lucinda. As long as you live under my roof, you live by my rules."

"If you're ever here," she shot back.

Grief seized her father's face so completely that it mystified her.

"Everything I do, I do for you." He drew in another long breath. "One day, I hope you'll appreciate how much both your mother and I have done to give you a good life. A normal life."

His words pierced her like arrows.

"Because I'm not normal."

I'm a freak. I'm a monster.

"Don't turn this around, Lucinda. You're the one in the wrong here. Except for school, you're not to leave this house until you show some remorse for your actions."

"*Remorse?*" she squeaked. Lucy felt nothing but remorse: she had lost the trust of all the people who mattered in her life in a single night.

She flew up the stairs and dove under the covers, muffling her sobs in her pillow.

A few minutes later, a knock came at the door. When Lucy didn't answer, it creaked open.

The smell of peppermint prickled Lucy's nostrils. Her mother held a mug in one hand and a prescription bottle in the other.

"Did something happen at prom?" Concern underscored her mom's question. "Want to talk?"

Lucy tightened her arms around the pillow. She did, but she couldn't.

"Nothing happened, Mom. Can't I just be an irresponsible teenager for once?"

Her mother winced. Lucy had thought she couldn't feel any worse, but she'd been wrong.

"The most important thing is that you're safe, and you're home," her mom said, almost to herself. "Take your pills." She set them next to the tea on Lucy's desk. If only her mom knew how useless the medication actually was.

There was no cure for Lucy's condition. She wouldn't burden her mother with the knowledge that she'd birthed a mutant who could kill with a touch.

Instead, she said, "Go away," and as the door shut behind her mother, Lucy's heart begged, *Stay.*

THE CHOPPING BLOCK

Monday morning came and Lucy found herself squaring off with Principal Petersen.

He surveyed her barely brushed hair, barely brushed teeth, and the dark circles beneath her purpling bruise. She wondered if Jess had a matching one, wherever she was.

"Miss Phelps. I trust you've recovered from the excitement of prom," said the principal in monotone, Mrs. Brandon at his side, as he adjusted his horrid tartan tie. Lucy might never recover from the excitement of prom night. Her father could hardly stand to remain in the same state as her, decamping to his office in Manhattan immediately after their argument.

Lucy didn't reply. Principal Petersen didn't really want an answer. She focused on the principal's bald spot to avoid meeting Ravi's eyes. He stood next to Mrs. Brandon, leaning against a bookshelf, his gaze hot on her face.

The principal angled his chin toward the physics teacher.

"I hope we gave you some food for thought at our last meeting, Miss Phelps," he continued, focusing a laser-pointer stare on Lucy, "and that the weekend provided some clarity about your position. So, enlighten us. Who is responsible for circulating the physics exam among your classmates?"

If Principal Petersen had asked Lucy to tattletale at prom, she would have turned Cole in as the culprit with relish. Now, however . . . Lucy's high school problems seemed very small compared with everything else that had happened.

What Cole had done was wrong, and his threats were childish, but she didn't want to ruin his future. Involuntarily, Lucy's eyes slid toward Ravi. She and Cole had already hurt each other enough. She didn't need petty vengeance.

"Principal Petersen," she began, looking from him to Mrs. Brandon. "I wish I could tell you who distributed the exam, but I can't. What I can tell you is that I often left my book bag with the office keys inside in public places. Like the gymnasium while I worked on prom decorations." She cast her eyes downward. "So it's possible that someone else could have used my key to the science office without my knowledge. I realize this was irresponsible of me, and I apologize."

Principal Petersen steepled his fingers together. Mrs. Brandon's lips were pursed, eyes troubled.

"That is disappointing, Miss Phelps. And not the answer I was hoping for."

Disappointing: Lucy's new defining adjective.

"I'm sorry."

A nasal sigh. "Not as sorry as I am. I will have no choice but to fail the entire senior class and report your breach of the honor code to Gilbert College. In addition, you will be suspended from all graduation activities."

Lucy's chin wobbled. Hearing her sentence being pronounced turned her insides to jelly. Her parents would never get over this. She'd never win back her father's trust.

"Principal Petersen," Ravi interjected in his most formal BBC voice. "I believe I have another solution."

"I'm all ears."

Ravi crossed to Lucy's side. His hand brushed hers—just for an instant—and, although he was shielding, his touch was still reassuring. Perhaps more than it should be. He knew she was lying, he knew Cole had stolen the exam, but he was willing to back her up. Lucy's feelings for him were jumbled and thorny, no doubt, and yet she couldn't deny she was grateful he was here.

Ravi's chest swelled as he planted his feet, exuding that same quiet confidence he had on the High Line.

"I would suggest that the entire senior class takes a new physics final. Tomorrow morning. There will be no paper copies. I will write the exam questions on the blackboard. That will preclude any possibility of cheating."

"A very generous offer." The principal scratched his gleaming head. "Mrs. Brandon, what do you say?"

Expression pained, she said, "Lucy is a model student. My best."

"I believe in her," Ravi said, voice firm. He cast Lucy a charged look, and she felt heat flare across her chest. She wished his eyes weren't so damn mesmerizing.

Principal Petersen's steepled fingers slid together and interlocked.

"You agree, Cheryl?" he asked Mrs. Brandon.

Lucy held her breath. "I do," said the teacher with a small smile.

"Very well." The principal sighed. "Then it is, of course, your prerogative to administer another exam. I will have Mrs. White email the relevant students immediately."

"Thank you," Ravi told him.

"And you, Miss Phelps, ought to thank Mr. Malik for his steadfast support."

Mr. *Malik*. Lucy ground her teeth at Ravi's fake name. "Thank you," she said stiffly. Ravi rotated his torso so that only Lucy could see his mouth, *Always*.

Principal Petersen nodded in a satisfied fashion. "You may go, Miss Phelps."

"Thanks," she repeated as she backed out of the room.

"Mr. Malik, stay a minute," she heard the principal say, his voice becoming muffled as she closed the door.

Another exam. She'd gotten off easy. Ravi had saved her skin. She hurried toward the exit before she could rip any more lockers from their hinges.

The cynical part of Lucy told her Ravi was just under orders from Professor T to make the problem go away. She was his mission. His assignment.

But the Archimedeans had nothing to do with the way Ravi and Lucy had danced at prom. Remembering how his energy had subsumed her, a dart of lust traveled through her.

Lucy's powers told her she could trust him, and yet he could still lie to her—to everyone. What if she didn't pick up on any conflicted emotions in Ravi because he truly believed what he was doing was right. He believed he was helping Lucy. He cared for Lucy. But he could still be in the wrong.

Pencils scratched paper as the lowerclassmen finished up their exams in the classrooms on either side of the hallway. The sound reminded Lucy of scurrying insect legs. If she never saw another scarab again it would be too soon.

Her pocket vibrated just as she reached the exit.

Boats. 15 minutes.

There was both too much and nothing that Lucy wanted to say to Ravi, but she couldn't risk him turning up at her house.

She felt for the tourmaline at her throat and loosed a breath.

Time to face some more music.

THE FIFTH ELEMENT

Crunch, crunch. Lucy's ears pricked as a few twigs snapped beneath Ravi's loafers. His tread remained uniform, purposeful, as he approached. She dipped one foot over the edge of the cliff, swinging it above the Sunfish below.

Ravi circled a hand around her upper arm and pulled her toward him, away from the steep drop to the lake. With his shield firmly in place, Lucy could only guess at what he was thinking—but she had a pretty good guess.

"It's later," she said. When Lucy had walked out of his apartment yesterday, she'd figured he wouldn't delay their talk for long. "Thanks again for intervening with Principal Petersen."

"It was my pleasure." He released her arm. "That wanker Cole got off lightly."

"I've hurt enough people," Lucy said.

"Lucinda." Ravi spoke her name low and rough. She captured his gaze, daring him to deny it. "You didn't leave your house yesterday," he said. "I've been worried."

"I'm grounded until we land a manned mission on Mars. But why were you watching my house?"

"I was doing my job. Like I should have been from the start."

"I'm your *job* now?" Lucy retreated a step.

Anguish streaked his face as Ravi grabbed her hand and swung her well away from the cliff's edge. "You're much more to me than that," he said like it cost him, dropping her hand to cup her cheek. "Isn't it obvious? It's why I was too distracted to see the threat right under my nose. The Freelancers never should have been able to get so close to you."

His touch made Lucy feel so alive, and that was dangerous. Ravi meant something more to Lucy too—even if she didn't know how to quantify or qualify that *more*. What she did know was having these kinds of feelings—desires—for someone she couldn't completely trust was dangerous.

Jess's taunt on the High Line came rushing back.

You're too valuable. For now.

Ravi flicked his tongue across his teeth in response to her silence.

"Why?" Lucy asked.

"Why what?"

"Why do you care about me?"

He rubbed his thumb along her cheekbone. "Do you really have to ask?" Ravi said softly.

Lucy raised her chin. "Yes."

"All right." He inhaled. "Because you're fiercely intelligent. Brave. Selfless." Ravi tilted his face downward. "Beautiful." He wrapped his other arm around her shoulders. "Whenever I'm around you, all I want is to be closer."

Lucy really wished he didn't have the same effect on her.

"But how do I know you're not just telling me what I want to hear?" she said. "Seducing me to your side?"

"*Seducing you?*" Hurt flared in his eyes and Ravi straightened. "Falling for you was not part of the plan."

"You sound like Jess."

Lucy felt a pang of regret as soon as the words flew out of her mouth and, from the way Ravi's chest lurched, they'd hit their mark.

"I'm sorry you think so little of me." He stumbled back a pace. "I thought—I thought you knew me better than that."

"How could I possibly *know* you, Ravi? You haven't exactly been forthcoming!" Lucy fired back. Her unkempt curls began to rise with her pulse. "You showed up at my school all charming and British and talking about Replicants. I liked you from day one—even when I shouldn't have! When I still had a boyfriend!"

Lucy tried and failed to pat down her wayward curls. "Then I find out you're not who you say you are—"

"I made a mistake," Ravi said, almost guttural. "I thought you'd forgiven me."

"I'm not finished!" she shouted at him. He folded his arms. "We have this amazing kiss, which you say can't happen again, but you rent tails for my prom," she went on, the words pouring out of her. "My best friend gets kidnapped, we kiss again—a lot—and then I find out you've got snipers at your disposal. *Snipers*, Ravi!"

Lucy exhaled a short breath. "Every time I think I've gotten to the bottom of the mystery of Ravi Singh, I discover another secret. So you tell me, what would you think if *you* were me!"

Her chest heaved as she ended her rant, and Lucy had to admit she felt better for it.

"Are you finished?" Ravi asked quietly.

"Yes," she replied, trying to get a hold of her oscillations. She squeezed the tourmaline.

"When you collapsed on the High Line, my world stopped." His words were weighted, like they were dragging him down. "I failed to train you. I failed to protect you. And I've given you good reason to doubt me, and my motives." He pushed his glasses up the bridge of his nose.

"For that I'm more sorry than I can say." He took a step toward her, but his hands remained at his sides. "I asked you to meet me here because I don't want there to be any more secrets between us."

Lucy's breath hitched at the severity of his tone.

"I have things to tell you," Ravi continued. "Some of them will be hard for you to hear." He jammed his lips into a thin line, briefly closed his eyes. "The first is that, because my professionalism has been compromised, Professor T has tasked a pair of Initiates to watch you and Claudia," he said.

"What? Why are they watching Claudia?"

"At my request. I thought it's what you would want."

"Is she in danger?" Lucy asked breathily.

"Nothing will happen to her again. I swear. I hold myself responsible for putting you and the people you care about in danger."

Lucy placed her hands on her hips. "*I* put the people around me in danger, Ravi. Not you. In fact, I put *you* in danger."

"I chose this life."

But had he really? Lucy wondered. The Sophists killed his parents and he joined the Archimedeans to get revenge when he was fourteen. It was the only life he knew. Like Rick had said, eventually a side chooses you.

Ravi scrubbed a hand across his face and threw his shoulders back, posture becoming rigid. Sunlight danced on his finely whittled cheekbones. When his gaze met hers again, it was guarded.

"Professor T—" He coughed into his hand and started over. "Professor T would like me to reiterate his offer to intern at Chrysopoeia Tech. We could help you develop your powers so that you can't be used against your will."

"*Develop* my powers? Ask Jess if she thinks they need any further development!"

"Develop and *stabilize*. Besides, you acted in self-defense. But the Archimedeans can train you to control your powers. Use them with precision."

"Oh great. That way I can electrocute someone more precisely!"

"Lucy, your oscillations were off the chart when you fell unconscious. *You*— I almost lost you."

"What?" The look on Ravi's face filled Lucy with foreboding.

"Your heart stopped. It stopped, and then restarted itself—as if you had an implanted defibrillator. But you weren't breathing for thirty seconds."

Lucy sucked in a breath, almost to prove that she still could. No wonder Claudia had been so upset by Lucy's seizure. Her symptoms were getting worse.

Ravi dared to extend a hand and twirl one of her dark strands around his forefinger.

"My heart stopped when yours did, Lucinda. I never want to go through that again." He stared at Lucy with mounting intensity. "Sod it," he said under his breath, and his lips found hers.

Surprise was replaced swiftly by desire. She raked her hands through Ravi's short, soft hair, tugging him nearer. She devoured him with hungry kisses and he moaned against her mouth, pressing one hand into the curve of her spine. Lucy arched to meet him. She wanted to lose herself. She wanted to forget what she was, the damage she could do. The damage she could do to herself.

When Ravi broke away, they were both breathing hard.

"Work with us—with *me*," he pleaded. "We'll figure out how you can live a long and healthy life. There's so much good we can do together. So much potential for understanding the power of the mind. The way the universe works."

Lucy let out a desperate laugh. "No pressure."

The Freelancers had wanted Lucy's powers to benefit their criminal activities, the Order of Sophia wanted to destroy her, and the Order of Archimedes wanted her to, what, unlock the secrets of the universe? She laughed again.

"Have you heard of the fifth element?" Ravi asked.

She did a double-take. "The old Bruce Willis movie?"

"No." He smiled. "Quintessence. Newton believed it was the link between spirit and matter that comprises the other four elements. The invisible energy that breathes life into all things."

"That sounds like mystical hocus-pocus to me." Although it might explain how she'd heard Claudia's voice in her mind, grabbed a snatch of the hotel room from her friend's perspective.

"Newton didn't think so. He conducted many experiments to prove quintessence was a magnetic force that coaxed life from chaos," Ravi explained, tone patient. "Professor T has long asserted that the true philosopher's stone isn't a stone at all, but the ability to tap into quintessence, manipulate it even."

Lucy's mouth went dry. The Flower of Life smoldered in her mind. She had hallucinated it on the High Line, right before her heart stopped.

Could it actually mean something?

"If Newton proved the existence of quintessence," Lucy said, "then why aren't there any records of his experiments?"

Ravi exhaled. "The Royal Society suppressed the papers. They believed his association with alchemy would taint the public's view of his science. But the Order of Archimedes has kept them safe."

"And you think the lightning gene is what allows me to access quintessence," Lucy said, voice wobbly. "I suppose Newton also possessed the lightning gene."

"It seems unlikely. But from the records of his experiments we believe he must have had access to someone who did."

"So I'm supposed to become, what, your personal lab rat?" Lucy said, arching a brow. Then something occurred to her, something she should have realized before. "Your parents, Ravi—if they were researching the lightning gene, they must have had access to blood samples. And since there aren't that many of us around . . ."

Rick's remorseful tone as he'd told her he knew another woman like her echoed in her ears. "Your parents were collaborating with a female carrier of the mutation, weren't they?"

Hope lit inside Lucy that she might be able to find someone else with her condition. Someone who could understand what she was going through.

"Is she still alive?" she asked, breathless.

Taking in Ravi's crestfallen expression, Lucy instantly knew the answer was no.

"Did she die in the fire?"

He dropped his voice. "Not in the fire."

"The Sophists?"

A shake of the head. Lucy didn't want to know any more. This other gene carrier must have died from the condition. Lucy's condition. She was a ticking time bomb. "Why do you think I had such a violent sei-zure on prom night? The tourmaline had been helping," she said, try-ing to keep her panic in check. "I thought I'd been doing so well."

"I'm not sure. Perhaps because you were forced to use your powers so much in the space of only a few hours? Maybe it had something to do with the Tesla Egg?" Ravi fiddled with one of her curls. "But these are questions we can answer together. You won't be a guinea pig. You'll be a partner. A researcher."

"Even if I wanted to, my parents would never let me leave the country or take time off before college."

"You're eighteen, Lucy. An adult. You can make your own deci-sions."

Her parents' distraught faces wavered behind her eyes.

"I can't. I've upset them enough already. And I can't explain what I am to them without putting them in danger from the Order of Sophia, right?"

Ravi's eyes darkened a shade. "Come sit with me." He extended a hand and she allowed him to lead her to the boulders where he'd first demonstrated how to build a shield. Lucy's gaze tripped along the ripples on the surface of Lake Windermere.

They sat in silence for a few moments, listening to the wind stir the water below. He kept her hand tucked in his, absently tracing the ban-dage he'd tied.

Slanting his gaze to hers, Ravi said, "Tell me again why you chose Gilbert College."

Not a question she'd anticipated. "It was where my parents met. And they have a terrific physics department. It just made sense." *Gah.* Lucy had become a parrot. "It was their dream," she admitted.

"Not yours?" Ravi squeezed her hand. "Lucy," he began with his battlefield calm, "Gilbert College is a Sophist institution."

She almost swallowed her tongue. "Excuse me?"

"This all started with the photo in your father's office. You've been looking for a complicated answer but the truth has been staring you in the face."

"What are you saying?" Lucy tried to pull her hand away, but Ravi wouldn't relinquish his hold.

"Your father works for the Sapientia Group. What does *sapientia* mean in Latin?"

"Wisdom," Lucy choked out. From the Greek *sophia*. "But that doesn't make any sense. The photo was sent *to* my dad's company, which means they didn't know about me."

Ravi frowned. "You never told me that." There was a hint of regret in his voice.

Dammit. "And I wasn't going to—not after what I've seen the Initiates can do." She should have made the photo disappear. "I'm not involving my parents in this."

"But they *are* involved, let's look at the facts." A slight snarl infused his reply. "Your mother is a classics scholar. Not many homeschooled students are taught to be fluent in both Latin and Greek these days."

"She translates ancient poetry!"

He canted his head. "Is that all she does?"

The *Pharmakon of Kleopatra*. The secret to the philosopher's stone. Fools' gold, her mom had called it. But what if it wasn't? If Professor T was right, then Lucy *was* the philosopher's stone. Could the *Pharmakon* contain the key to understanding her condition? Or controlling her? Her palms grew sweaty.

"Your middle name—Minerva," Ravi forged ahead. "Who is she?"

Of course he knew Lucy's embarrassing middle name. Another Roman goddess. The goddess of . . . "Wisdom," Lucy said, voice shaking. "She's the goddess of wisdom. The Roman version of Sophia."

The horizon smeared.

"My parents are *not* Sophists, Ravi. They may be mad at me right now, but they've always loved me."

"Is it so impossible?" Ravi said gently.

"Of course it is! The Sophists shot at me the other night. My parents would never hurt me."

"They shot at the Freelancers after they raided one of their safe houses."

Lucy stared at him, disbelieving. "You're defending them?"

"Not at all." A muscle in his neck flickered. "I'm simply saying that you might not have been their target—that night."

"The Sophists are murderers, Ravi. My parents are good people. Overprotective, yes. But not killers."

"Haven't you ever wondered why you were homeschooled? Why they wouldn't let you enter any science fairs? Or apply to the best universities in the country?" he said, each question becoming more pointed. "You're too brilliant to be hidden away."

"Because of my condition. Because they want to keep me safe."

"No." The word was solid as a rock. "Because they didn't want us to know you existed. They didn't want us to find you."

"Find me?" Lucy croaked.

"Lucinda," he said, and traced the line of her jaw. "Your parents stole you from the Order of Archimedes. We've been searching for you for years."

Adrenaline made each one of her muscles spasm.

"Why would they steal me? They didn't know about my mutation— they still don't! You're not *listening*, Ravi. The photo was sent *to* my father's company. If my parents had kidnapped me, they would have already known!"

Launching to her feet, Lucy ripped her hand from his. "I can accept that I'm some kind of mutant, but not that my parents are kidnappers, Ravi. Kidnappers!" She backed farther away from him. "If you've known this whole time—why didn't you tell me sooner?"

"We had to be sure."

"And how are you sure now?" she charged, very close to hyperventilating.

"I performed a DNA test."

"With what?"

His cheeks colored. "The bloody clothes you left at my apartment."

"You're unbelievable, Ravi!" Lucy shouted. "Absolutely unbelievable! And I am *so* stupid. I was actually starting to trust you again!"

"I told you that you wouldn't like some of what I had to say, Lucinda.

But it's the truth." Ravi smoothed his face into a mask of calm. "The Order of Archimedes will never force your hand. However, I urge you to perform your own DNA test." He paused, inhaled quickly. "I will stay in town until graduation and wait for your decision. A good scientist should want to have all the facts."

"You're wrong," Lucy said as her knees trembled. "You're dead wrong, and I'm going to prove it."

A crack appeared in his façade. "Lucinda," Ravi said in a way that tempted her to remain exactly where she was.

"Stay away from me, Ravi. *And* my family."

She ran. Lucy ran down the hill, lungs burning, because it would also be a challenge for her to stay away from him. But she didn't have a choice. Her parents came first.

She would protect her family no matter what it cost.

DNA-4-U

As Lucy biked past the Gallery, her heart spiraled into a nosedive. The café was now off-limits. Claudia had effectively dodged Lucy in the exam hall yesterday after the physics retake, and Lucy was trying to respect her friend's boundaries.

Even if staying away stretched every fiber of Lucy's being like she was on a rack. Especially now. Claudia was the one person she could trust with Ravi's suspicions about her parents, but she didn't deserve her trust anymore.

All things considered, Lucy would prefer the medieval torture instrument.

Time to focus. Her gaze dropped to the package in her bicycle basket, concealed in a discreet brown paper bag, and pumped the pedals until her thighs burned. Who knew that peace of mind could be purchased for the low price of $39.99? Or so claimed the paternity-test kit she'd bought with her leftover birthday money.

The unassuming-looking contents of her basket had the potential to change everything. How dare Ravi accuse her parents of belonging to the Order of Sophia? Of not even being her parents?

Two geeky academics hardly fit the bill for *America's Most Wanted*.

If Lucy couldn't prove to the Archimedeans that Victor and Elaine Phelps were—without a shadow of a doubt—her parents, what would the Archimedeans do?

A light breeze stuck to the sheen of sweat covering her face. It did nothing to refresh her. *In. Out.* Lucy concentrated on her breathing to avoid any green flames sprouting from the handlebars. Her diaphragm tightened in response to her electromagnetic field supersizing itself with anticipation. If only she could shield herself from her own emotions.

Lucy swept the street with her eyes as her driveway came into view. No sign of the Initiates. Of course, they wouldn't be very good spies if she could spot them. No sign of her parents, either. Both of their cars were gone.

She slammed on the brakes and walked Marie Curie toward the garage. Inside was cool and dark. Only a few birdcalls punctuated the quiet. She drew in a heavy breath and removed the paternity kit, paper bag rustling like autumn leaves underfoot. She read the instruction leaflet three times as the magnitude of what she was about to do hit her again.

Easy as X,Y, Z! the manual proclaimed. Yeah, not so much.

Okay. Time to prove Ravi wrong.

Lucy didn't doubt her parents, she *didn't*, but climbing the stairs two at a time toward their bedroom, a chill worked its way down her body. Despite being alone, she crept along the carpeted landing. Schrödinger gave her a wide berth as static crackled at her feet. Damn Ravi for turning Lucy into a spy in her own home.

Her fingers cramped around the plastic vials into which she would be collecting the samples. Buccal swabs provided the most complete DNA profile, but it wasn't as if Lucy could ask her parents to sit still for a Q-tip to the cheek. She could venture a guess at how that conversation would go. Toothbrushes were the next best thing.

Tiptoeing toward her parents' en-suite bathroom, Lucy took note of the knickknacks and framed photos that littered her father's dresser and her mother's vanity. A lopsided pottery dish Lucy had made for her mom years ago now contained spare buttons and safety pins. Next to it, between the cluster of perfume bottles, sat a photo of Lucy and her mom by a waterfall. Must have been from one of their camping trips. Her mother was hugging her, a protective look in her eyes.

Her dad had a photo of Lucy in a white lab coat and goggles as well as her junior class photo on his dresser. Everyone else at Eaton High had dreaded photo day, but Lucy couldn't stop grinning, and it showed. She'd been elated to take part in a genuine high school class photo and had ordered enough copies to wallpaper the attic.

Beside the photo sat a crystal paperweight. Lucy tapped her lips as she glimpsed the inscription: *Dr. Victor Phelps, 10 Years of Service, The Sapientia Group.*

Lucy remembered the awards dinner had been right around the time she'd started at Eaton High. Which meant, if she was doing the math correctly, her dad would have started working at the Sapientia Group *after* the photo was taken of Lucy. But that wasn't necessarily significant; it was circumstantial evidence at best.

If her parents were stone-cold kidnappers, would they have been so invested in her, taken such good care of her for eighteen years? No, they would not. Ravi was too blinded by losing his own family to see this issue clearly.

Entering the bathroom, Lucy snatched her father's toothbrush, which had been casually strewn next to the tap. Her mother's was neatly placed in a brass-colored holder on her side of the sink.

Lucy would prove Ravi wrong and she would protect her parents from the Orders, the Freelancers—even herself if need be.

She uncapped the first vial with a deliberate motion. Attached to the inside of the stopper was a thin piece of plastic that resembled an elongated cotton bud. Keeping her hand steady, she skimmed the tool over the bristles of her father's toothbrush, then resealed it, ensuring it was airtight. She repeated the procedure on her mother's with clinical exactness.

Only science had no hidden agenda.

Lucy unscrewed the third vial and opened her mouth. The swab tickled the inside of her cheek. All that was left to do now was mail the samples, create an online account with DNA-4-U, and wait to be vindicated.

THE GRADUATE

Eleven days.

Eleven days with no answers.

Lucy's classmates had filled the countdown to graduation with end-less parties and sailing trips on Lake Windermere, or so she'd ascer-tained from the few pity invites emailed to the entire senior class. It didn't matter that she was still grounded, she wouldn't have attended anyway.

If Cate and Stew had managed to convince Claudia to come along, Lucy didn't want to be there to spoil her fun. She had ruined her best friend's senior year more than enough for one lifetime. Maybe, just maybe, after a summer away from her in Chicago, Claudia might be ready to talk. A long shot, but it was all Lucy had.

Her gaze drifted to the top of her dresser. The tourmaline necklace rested next to her phone. She willed an email to arrive from DNA-4-U confirming what Lucy knew to be true: she was the daughter of Drs. Victor and Elaine Phelps, lightning gene and all.

Zilch.

On-demand answers from the universe wasn't one of her super-powers.

With a sigh, Lucy fastened the tourmaline around her neck. A true touchstone. Given to her by Ravi and fashioned by Claudia, the neck-lace had a complex history but it grounded her—and not just her oscillations. She would need as much help as possible today. Besides Claudia, Ravi would be at the graduation ceremony and he would be expecting a decision.

Sometimes, joining the Archimedeans seemed like the only rational choice. They knew what she was and she didn't frighten them. Professor T seemed convinced she was the key to research that could help lots of people—as well as prolong her own life. Lucy tried not to think too much about the fact that her heart had stopped for thirty seconds. What secret to the lightning gene had Tesla unlocked that the Archimedeans had been unable to reproduce?

But going with Ravi and Professor T would mean abandoning her parents. And they might never get over it. Staying out all night was one thing. Not showing up for freshman orientation was quite another.

A knock startled Lucy from her thoughts and she whirled around.

"I can't believe it. My daughter, the graduate."

"*Mom*," she muttered, embarrassed, cheeks warming.

"Can't I be proud of my little girl?" Laughing softly, her mother strolled toward Lucy with her effortless grace. "Not so little, I know."

"Proud?" The question became a peep.

"Oh, honey. Of course I'm proud. So is your father." She stroked the tiny scar above Lucy's eyebrow from the stapler incident, and Lucy inhaled the faint aroma of smoke. It was pretty early in the day for her mom's one cigarette. Could she be stressed about graduation too?

Lucy fingered the tourmaline.

"You scared us to death on prom night," continued her mom, "but that doesn't negate everything you've accomplished."

"Tell that to Dad."

"Your father is all bark, no bite. Trust me, he adores you. I think what he finally realized is that you're not three years old anymore and that he can't protect you from everything—although he tries."

Lucy's breath caught for a moment. Her mother had never spoken so frankly to her about her dad before. "I don't need him to protect me," she forced out, almost reflexively.

"I know it's time for you to stand on your own two feet." Her mom cupped her cheek. "Just give your father some time to catch up. We're both going to miss having you at home."

Lucy's heart was in a tangle. "I'm not going anywhere for a couple months," she said, knowing it might not be true.

Sadness glinted in her mother's eyes so quickly that Lucy nearly missed it.

"I wanted to give you your graduation present early." She reached into the pocket of her cashmere cardigan. "I thought maybe you could wear them to the commencement ceremony?" Lucy's eyes widened, throat growing dry. "I've noticed you haven't gone anywhere without the necklace Claudia made you," her mom said, glancing at the stone. "When I saw these, I thought they'd match perfectly."

Her mom held out two tourmaline bracelets, like garlands of night. Lucy accepted them with a dagger-sharp breath. She reached out for her mother's energy as their fingers brushed but there was nothing. If only Lucy had an equally iron grip on her emotions.

"Do you like them?"

An expectant gaze drilled into her. The bracelets were exquisite. Cool. Smooth. Thick bangles an inch wide that sat heavily in her palm. Their potential meaning weighed even more heavily.

"Where did you find them?" Lucy rasped.

"I can't reveal all my secrets," she said. "I wanted to get you something special for this special day."

Lucy slipped them on either wrist and painted on a smile.

"They're beautiful. I love them." And the more grounded Lucy was today, the better.

"That makes me very happy, honey. Your father will be too. He had to go out early to run a few errands but he'll be at the ceremony." Her mom dropped her gaze to check her watch so she didn't notice the way Lucy's face fell. Her dad was still avoiding her. "Lucy, you should get going. Don't you need to pick up your cap and gown?"

Lucy tipped her gaze at her phone and her heart tumbled.

9:35 A.M. She would be late to her own high school graduation if she didn't leave soon—but that wasn't why Lucy couldn't speak. There was an email notification.

From DNA-4-U.

She snatched the phone from the dresser and pressed the screen to her chest before her mom could see.

"You're right." Her smile trembled at the corners. "I'd better jet."

She took two steps and her mom stopped her with an uncharacteristically tight hug. Lucy detected the scent of peppermint beneath the smoke. The embrace was warm and it didn't take a sixth sense to know the affection was real. Lucy squeezed the phone harder against her heart and guilt twisted like a knife. It was her secrets, her lies that threatened to tear her family apart.

"You'll always be my little girl." Her mom breathed against Lucy's temple. "Don't forget."

"I won't."

Her mom planted a swift kiss on her cheek. "See you at the school." As she exited, she enthused, "Break a leg!"

Nodding, Lucy cast her eyes to the floor. She didn't want her mother to see the tears threatening to spill over.

After she'd gone, Lucy spun around to look at herself once more in the mirror. On the outside, in her cheerful royal blue dress, she looked like any other American teenager on her way to her high school graduation. If her mom knew Lucy had almost killed someone and pulled off a heist with mercenaries, she'd never think of her as her little girl again.

Lucy wanted one last day being her mother's daughter.

Now that she had the answer at the press of a button, she didn't want it.

The truth could wait. At least one more day.

PARALLEL UNIVERSES

CONGRATULATIONS, GRADUATES!

The banner hanging from the first-floor windows rippled in the wind, the satiny fabric flowing like water. Lucy secured Marie Curie to the school fence for the last time. With everything going on, she hadn't yet changed the combination from the date of her first kiss with Cole. She grimaced at her pang of nostalgia.

The girl who started here two years ago would not be the girl taking the stage to accept her diploma today.

Excited chatter reached Lucy before she ascended the front steps of the school. It only grew louder the closer she got to the gymnasium where graduates-to-be were to pick up their mortar boards before lining up in alphabetical order and filing out to the football field for the ceremony. Lucy gulped as it hit her that she would never wander the halls of Eaton High as a student again. Compared with the other decisions bearing down on her, it was a small thing, but she had worked hard to be allowed the full high school experience and now it was over.

Lucy plodded toward her locker one last time to drop off her messenger bag. She hadn't wanted to leave her phone at home with the damning evidence it contained. Damning for her parents or damning for Lucy, the click of a button would tell.

The sound of rubber skidding on linoleum attracted her attention and an ultramarine gaze caught her, but there was none of the sizzle there used to be. Not on her part.

"Lucy." Cole smiled nervously. "Hey."

"Hey."

"You look really pretty," he blurted, then pushed his hair back in an awkward gesture, color rising in his cheeks.

"Um, thanks." Where was he going with this? She gave him a double-quick once-over: jeans and sneakers. "You look . . . underdressed."

His flush deepened. "I'm not graduating."

"Oh." Was he expecting an apology?

"Not today. I have to retake physics in summer school."

"Right."

"But UNNY is holding my spot on the track team—as long as I pass."

Lucy spun one of the bracelets around her wrist.

"I'm glad," she said, and she meant it.

He stepped closer, grazing her elbow. Lucy braced herself for that familiar seasick feeling but nothing happened.

"Thanks for not turning me in."

"I thought you deserved a second chance."

A sad grin. "You were always better than I deserved."

Before she could say anything, Cole added, "I hope the Brit makes you happy."

Lucy shrugged. The way Ravi made her feel was . . . more tangled than a Gordian knot, and she definitely didn't want to discuss it with her ex.

"I didn't expect you to talk to me after the prom," she said to Cole instead. "You seemed pretty afraid of me."

"Why would I possibly be afraid of you?" he asked.

"The fire around my hands?" Did he really not remember?

Cole burst out in a stunned guffaw. "You might've had smoke coming out of your ears, but you weren't *on fire*, Luce." Another laugh. "I was worried you might have been hurt when the lights blew. I couldn't see you." He gripped her shoulder and gave a little squeeze. "I did look."

"I was fine." Her heart stuttered like a car backfiring. At his wounded expression, she added, "But thanks."

He edged his lips slightly upward. Cole clearly wasn't afraid of Lucy now. Well, if he'd convinced himself that his eyes were playing tricks on him that night, she wouldn't contradict him.

When confronted with the unbelievable, most people invented a truth they could live with. Ravi had been right that no footage from the High Line had shown up online. Even the eyewitnesses seemed content to blame what they'd seen on faulty wiring and firecrackers.

"Anyway," Cole said, glancing at something behind Lucy. "I see there's someone else eager to congratulate you. I'll be cheering extra loud from the stands when it's your turn."

She returned his cloudy smile and a feeling of finality settled over her. "Bye, Cole. And good luck."

This was truly the end of Lucy's first love story.

From the way he dipped his head in response, Cole knew it too.

Lucy didn't have another second to process the goodbye before a small giggling torpedo knocked her sideways.

"There you are!" Claudia exclaimed, face beaming. "I've been looking for you everywhere!"

Lucy's entire body thrummed. "You have?"

"Duh. We're right next to each other—Phelps comes after O'Rourke. We'll take the stage together." She grabbed Lucy's hand. "Just like we'd planned."

That *had* always been the plan. Since before Lucy had convinced her parents to let her go to regular school, Claudia had promised her they would graduate together. Her best friend's confidence had given Lucy the boost she needed to take on the Drs. Phelps. But prom night had blown that long-standing plan out of the water.

"Are you sure?" Lucy asked, a frog in her throat.

"Of course I'm sure!"

Lucy could only stare. This was her Clauds—the friend who believed in her when she didn't believe in herself. But it couldn't be. That Claudia was gone. She had made it abundantly clear.

Something was so, so wrong.

Claudia scrunched up her nose, interlacing their fingers. Lucy couldn't get a read off of her. "Are you okay, Minnie Mouse?" she asked. "There's no need to be nervous."

The worry in her tone made Lucy's knees go weak. In the past Lucy definitely would have been nervous about walking onto a stage in front of hundreds of people, but that wasn't why she was anxious now.

"Have you forgiven me for Jess?" she forced the question out haltingly. "For . . . prom?"

"What are you talking about, Luce? There's nothing to forgive." Claudia's pupils became unfocused and she gazed briefly into the distance. "You tried to warn me about her. It's not *your* fault she stole the Mystery Minivan and ditched me at the prom." She rolled her shoulders. "I guess we both had shady first loves. But at least we have each other."

The earth shifted beneath Lucy's feet.

"I'm sorry," she rasped, everything inside her fracturing. "So, so sorry."

"Luce, what's going on?"

She crushed Claudia into a hug and took off without answering. This was one parallel universe she wasn't allowed to live in. She didn't get to have her best friend back—not like this.

"You're going to miss graduation!" Claudia called down the hallway.

Lucy didn't care. She had a score to settle with a certain Archimedean.

He had just made her decision a whole lot easier.

SIGNED, SEALED, DELIVERED

Not even the sight of Ravi in a smart navy pinstripe suit could put a dent in Lucy's fury. She could excuse him a lot, but not wiping her best friend's memory.

"How could you?" she demanded, stabbing him with an angry finger as he exited the physics lab.

"I'm afraid you have me at a loss."

Ravi's reply was glacier cold. Although the ridges forming between his brows told a different story.

"Oh, do I?" She jabbed him again. "Well, Claudia seems to have *lost* her memories. She thinks Jess dumped her at prom!"

Disbelief flattened his scowl. If Lucy didn't know better, she'd say he was genuinely shocked. But Ravi was a master at self-control and deception.

"It wasn't us," he said.

"Oh no?"

Hurt and irritation sparked in Ravi's eyes. "The Archimedeans aren't the only ones who possess the necessary technology to alter your friend's memory." He let the statement hang in the air for a moment. Then, in one continuous motion, he opened the door to the classroom, pressed his hand to Lucy's lower back, and shoved her inside.

The glass shook as it slammed closed behind them. Her messenger bag slipped from her shoulder, thumping on the ground. She spun around to face him.

"You have to reverse it," Lucy pleaded. "It's not right. I've caused her enough misery."

Ravi peered down at her, the muscles in his neck tight as cords.

"I respected your wishes, Lucy. Even if it made Claudia a liability—a danger to you, I did as you asked." Tension threaded through his words, and Lucy could tell Ravi still thought it was the wrong call.

"Then just change it back," she challenged. "If you really didn't do it, change it back."

"That isn't advisable."

Lucy latched onto his lapels. Ravi stumbled forward until their lips were nearly touching. "I don't care what's *advisable*. You robbed her of the truth. Claudia should hate me."

"You don't deserve to be hated, Lucinda." His voice grew softer. "But if Claudia's memory has been altered, it wouldn't be safe to attempt another procedure so soon."

"Why not?"

"I never said the procedure was without risk."

Lucy twisted his lapel. "You two-faced—"

"The Initiates have been keeping a close eye on your friend, as I promised," he interrupted. "The only suspicious visitor Claudia has received was your father."

"You're lying."

She shoved him viciously backward and edged out of his grasp. Fear and loathing curdled in her veins.

"You're lying," she repeated.

Regaining his balance, Ravi brushed off his lapels.

"Did you perform the DNA test?"

"And if I did? How do I know you didn't manufacture the results?"

He scoffed. "We're not Skynet. There's a limit to what the Order of Archimedes can do."

Under normal circumstances, Lucy would find his nerdy sci-fi reference charming. But normal circumstances didn't apply to her anymore.

Her gaze fell to the messenger bag that lay at her feet. Ravi's followed.

"You have the results," he said.

She didn't answer.

He scooped the bag from the floor. "You haven't looked," Ravi deduced, offering it to her. "Let's open them together. I'll be here for you. Whatever the results may be."

"I know what they'll be," she told him. The heat faded quickly from her retort.

"I hope you're right."

Lucy's hand trembled as she flipped open the canvas flap and dug into the bottom for her phone. Sweat stippled her brow and her fingers slid around the touch-screen. It took three tries to enter the code she knew by heart: Claudia's birthday.

Dropping the bag carelessly to the floor, Lucy gripped the phone with both hands. Such a small piece of circuitry shouldn't hold so much power over her fate.

Her finger hovered over the email app.

"I can look for you," Ravi said.

"They're *my* parents." Lucy turned away, showing him her back.

This was Lucy's future and she had to be the first to know.

"Okay," he said. Sympathy shaded his tone but Lucy didn't want his sympathy. She was going to prove him wrong once and for all, and then her parents would be safe from the Initiates.

Moment-of-truth time.

She planted her feet, breathed deeply, and pulled on her big-girl pants. *Tap.*

Subject: Your Confidential Results from DNA-4-U.com

Another tap. Her breath steamed up the screen.

Lucy wiped away the fog and the clarity she received made her head go fuzzy. The spreadsheet dissolved before her eyes. Numbers and percentage points ceased to make sense.

Alleles, chromosomes, kinship index. The terms might as well be gibberish. She wanted them to be gibberish.

Lucy the scientist wished she didn't understand precisely what they meant.

Probability of Paternity: 0%

Probability of Maternity: 0%

Lucy was alone, and she always had been.

JUDGMENT DAY

She hurled the phone to the floor as if it had stung her. She wished it had. That wound would be easier to heal.

"Don't you dare tell me I told you so," Lucy threatened.

Ravi dropped to a crouch, collected the phone, and scanned the cracked screen.

"I'm sorry." He straightened himself to standing, his expression grave. "I would've preferred to be wrong."

"Would you?"

"Of course."

"But now I have no choice other than joining the Order of Archimedes. Isn't that what you wanted?"

"Lucy," he said. "I would never force you into anything. Neither would Professor T. We're only trying to help. We care about you. *I* care about you—a lot."

Salty tears dripped onto her lips. Ravi extended a hand but she batted it away. He set her damaged phone on the worktop beside them.

For a long moment, the only sounds were Lucy's ragged breaths. Both of them jumped in place as the brass section of the marching band announced the arrival of the graduates.

The procession! Lucy was missing it. Her heart pounded. She didn't want to miss it. Not on top of everything else.

She lunged for the door. Ravi blocked her path. "Where are you going?" he asked.

"To get my cap and gown! Where else?"

He worked his jaw. "Lucy, think. It's not safe. If your father changed Claudia's memory, then your parents must know what happened on the High Line. They know you've discovered your powers. It's not safe for you to stay with them."

"You don't know that for a fact. What happened to not forcing me into anything?"

"I'm not. You don't have to join us—but I *do* want to keep you safe."

Her hands balled into fists. "If my parents were going to do something to me, they would have done it already. Maybe you're wrong about the Order of Sophia."

"I'm not wrong."

"You don't know my parents, Ravi." Lucy lifted her chin.

"Look, I can't begin to know how you're feeling right now, but we need to be smart. And the smart thing would be to slip away while everyone is distracted by the graduation ceremony."

Lucy closed her hand around the brass doorknob. No flames. Strange. She didn't feel in control at all.

"I'm going to graduate," she told him, "and I'm going to give my parents the opportunity to explain themselves—unless *you're* planning on kidnapping me."

"I would never hurt you," Ravi said, words clipped.

"Then get out of my way."

He stepped aside and Lucy nearly ripped the door from its hinges.

"I'm coming with you," he said into her ear, frustration obvious, at the same moment she exclaimed, "*Dad!*"

Lucy halted in her tracks and Ravi knocked her forward as they collided.

"What are you doing here?" she said in surprise.

"I could ask you the same question, young lady." Her father's fiery glare shifted from Lucy to Ravi. She had no idea which dots he was connecting, but none of them would be good. "Your mother was concerned when she didn't see you in the graduate procession and sent me to find you."

Regret seeped from every one of Lucy's pores. Her mother had been so proud of her that morning and she hated to let her down. But that woman wasn't her mother, was she? Her stomach plummeted. It must be the shock preventing Lucy from having a total breakdown.

Her father threw back his shoulders as he eyeballed Ravi once more, and the look he gave him could practically bend steel.

"And you are?" he said to Ravi.

"Ravi Malik." Stepping around from behind Lucy, he extended his hand. "Mrs. Brandon's teaching assistant." Her father waited a few beats before accepting it in a bone-crushing shake. Ravi grimaced.

A shrill arpeggio from a badly tuned trombone shattered the hush of the deserted hallway.

"Nice to meet you," her father said, though his tone implied the polar opposite. "What are you doing with my daughter?"

Ravi's mouth tilted up in a smile so natural it made Lucy blink.

"I'm sorry for delaying Lucinda. We were just reviewing her independent-study project." The lie slid easily from his tongue. "She did exceptional work."

"Lucy is exceptional."

The edges of Ravi's smile grew hard. "I couldn't agree more."

Turning to Lucy, her father said, "Let's get to the ceremony."

"I'll escort you," Ravi told him.

"No need to trouble yourself, Ravi. I've got it from here."

"Oh, it's no trouble at all."

Lucy's eyes pinged between the two of them, two apex predators preparing for a fight.

But there was no fight.

She didn't even see her father move. One minute Ravi was standing beside her. The next he sank to his knees, convulsing.

"Dad!" she shrieked. "What did you *do*!" Lucy lunged for Ravi, but a strong arm instantly wrapped around her waist, dragging her back.

"We need to go," her father said roughly. "It's not safe." He set Lucy back on her feet and holstered the Taser that his suit had concealed. He glanced at Ravi with disdain. "This place is crawling with Initiates."

Oh God. Her dad knew who the Initiates were. "You really *are* a Sophist," she whispered, edging away from him. Ravi had been right, and she hadn't listened to him, and now . . .

Lucy moved towards Ravi's prone form again and her father seized her shoulders. "*Stop*, Lucy. The *teaching assistant* will be fine," he said, and relief flooded her chest. "We need to be gone by the time he comes around. Your mother will meet us at the car."

"I'm not going anywhere with you." She struggled under his grip. "You tased my friend!" Whatever more Ravi might be to Lucy, he was at least that. He'd warned her. At every turn, he'd looked out for her. She watched as his body stilled and her breath buckled.

"Your *friend* works for some very dangerous people," said her father.

"And you don't? I've been *defending* you! I was going to give you the chance to explain. But you came to my graduation *armed*!" Lucy's bottom lip quivered. *Don't cry, don't cry.* "I guess that's all the explanation I need!"

Her father's expression softened. "The Archimedeans have no doubt told you many lies about the Order of Sophia, Lucy." Glancing up and down the corridor, he said, "I'll explain everything once we're on our way."

"On our way where?"

"Somewhere safe." Lucy snorted at that. She was getting pretty tired of vague statements and assurances. Her dad squeezed her upper arm. "I'm sorry you're missing your big day. Truly." Regret stained his words. "Your mom and I both wanted to see you get your diploma."

Indecision rooted Lucy to the spot. This man looked like the dad who'd invented Einstein Time, who'd tucked her in at night, and taught her to tie her shoelaces. But he wasn't. This man . . .

She didn't know what to think of him.

"Before I go anywhere with you, I think we should talk about the fact that you're not my father."

He flinched as if she'd sucker-punched him. "I'm your father in all the ways that matter, Lucy. I love you," he said, and pain glimmered in his eyes. But he had successfully lied to her for years. "So does your mom." And so had she.

Lucy spun one of the tourmaline bracelets, sorrow cramping her heart.

"She's not my mother."

"Elaine raised you. She would do anything for you."

"Except tell me the truth. Are you two really married or was it all an elaborate ruse? Were you ever going to tell me I wasn't yours?" she said, temper igniting.

"Goddamn Archimedeans!" Her father cursed. "You *are* ours, Lucy. We *are* a family. You're the most important thing in our lives. We've tried to give you a normal life."

"*Normal?*" She scoffed. "By hiding me away? Making me scared of my own shadow? You've always treated me like I'm broken. Damaged."

"That's never what we intended—"

"And all the time, you knew I had the lightning gene." Lucy's pulse continued to rise but strangely her hair remained in place, and the lockers didn't jangle. Not even a little bit.

Her father didn't need to say anything. The answer was written on his face.

"Dr. Rosen was in on it too," Lucy realized. "He's a Sophist, isn't he?"

He nodded. At least now she understood why Dr. Rosen had told her the EEG was normal. He'd been lying.

Which meant the Sophists had known her powers had been developing for months.

"You knew I'd decoded the photo, that I'd found the Tesla Suite. Why didn't you just tell me the truth? Do you have any idea how scared I was?" Lucy said, voice trembling. Her father's features tightened. "Families are supposed to trust each other."

Lucy's eyes darted to Ravi. He looked like he was sleeping. "At least the Archimedeans were honest with me."

"I very much doubt that. Honesty isn't their policy." Her father crossed toward her, and Lucy backed up against a bulletin board. "When we discovered you'd found the lab," he said, "we waited to see how you would react. Your mother and I were hoping the medication would be enough to keep you stable."

Like an experiment. They'd been observing her as if that's all she was. Lucy's whole life was one giant experiment.

"What was in the pills?" Lucy said roughly. "I'm betting the prescription didn't really come from CVS!" She wouldn't tell him she'd stopped taking it weeks ago.

"A formula the Order has been trying to perfect for years, to—"

"To suppress my abilities," Lucy interrupted. He gave a curt nod. Lucy had had more than enough of being *suppressed*. "And now that you know the meds weren't enough? That I'm . . . whatever I am. You're going to lock me up and throw away the key, is that it? At this undisclosed location?" she demanded, raising her voice. "You stole me from my real parents because you think my mutation makes me a monster, after all!"

His expression grew bleak. "We didn't steal you, Lucinda. It's complicated," he said. "And I've been working for months to convince the more conservative members of the Order to allow you to attend Gilbert in the fall."

"Because it's a Sophist institution?"

"Yes." Ravi had been telling the truth about that too. "All the business trips—that's what I've been doing. Negotiating. Believe me, kiddo, nothing matters more to me than your welfare."

Lucy swallowed a lump in her throat. Her father wasn't denying that a faction of the Order of Sophia *did* want to contain her. Possibly eliminate her. Why should she be surprised? They had murdered Ravi's family to achieve their aims.

"It would be easier to believe you if you and Mom hadn't been lying to me for my entire life," she retorted.

On the floor, Ravi groaned. Her dad spared him a glance, and then clutched Lucy's shoulder. "We can discuss my mistakes later," he said, gritting his teeth, "but I need to get you away from the Archimedeans. And the Freelancers. *Now.*"

Her lungs emptied of air. "You know what happened on prom night," she said as he yanked her towards the fire exit. "You *did* erase Claudia's memory."

"I had no choice. It was too dangerous for her to know the truth about you—about our world."

He'd admitted it. Her father was responsible for violating the mind of the person Lucy loved most. While part of Lucy would be willing to excuse her parents' lies, she'd never condone hurting Claudia. Ravi had also thought the memory erasure prudent, but he'd at least respected Lucy enough not to go through with it.

Because of her father, however, Lucy would never have the chance to earn genuine forgiveness from her best friend.

"And Cole?" she rasped.

"It was for the best."

If it was that easy to play with people's minds, how could Lucy be sure her parents hadn't altered *her* memories over the years? How did she know what was real and what wasn't? Her whole life might be a total fabrication.

Fear curled inside her and she felt sick. The Sophists were ruthless, and her *fa*—Victor was a Sophist. Was Victor Phelps even his real name? And did Lucy dare cling to the hope that her mother didn't know what he'd done?

Lucy tried to wrench herself from his grasp.

"Lucy, I swore to protect you with my life. You can hate me if you want to—but I'm getting you out of here." Victor's tone brooked no compromise. "Don't make me knock you out."

Her eyes went wide. He'd already tased Ravi; she had no reason to doubt he wouldn't make good on this threat. Ravi had said she needed to be smart, and she couldn't fight back if she was unconscious.

"Okay," Lucy agreed. She would pretend to cooperate until the opportunity to escape presented itself.

Victor kept an arm clamped around her shoulders and broke into a brisk pace. Lucy had to take two steps for each of his to match it.

"I keep having this dream," she began as they walked, partially to distract him, partially because she needed to know. "I'm in this tropical garden. Mom is there. I mean, *Elaine*," she corrected herself in a pointed tone. "It's like the garden in Kleopatra's *Pharmakon*. A storm is coming. There's lightning overhead."

She angled her head to stare Victor in the eye.

"It's not a dream. Is it?" The question came out hollow, which was precisely how Lucy felt.

He stopped short. Good. Lucy would keep stalling him.

"You were so young. I can't believe you remember that."

"Did you erase the memory?"

"*No.*" A harsh syllable. "It was when we first saw . . . saw that the lightning gene had expressed itself."

Anger filled the hollowness inside Lucy. Her younger self had been joyful, carefree. "So you started suppressing my powers," she concluded. Her impostor parents had taken that away.

Victor raised a hand to her cheek. "We've been looking for a cure, Lucy."

"Maybe I don't need to be cured," she said hotly. She almost added, *Dad*, but stopped herself. "The Order of Archimedes doesn't think I need fixing."

"They'll exploit you. It's what we've been trying to prevent all these years."

"Seems to me there's little difference between your protection and imprisonment."

Victor's chest contracted and he dropped his hand. She'd landed a blow.

From outside, the roll call of graduates blared over the loudspeakers. It was almost enough to blot out the noise of someone running toward them from behind.

Both Lucy and Victor wheeled around to see who was coming, and hope swelled inside Lucy that Ravi had regained consciousness.

But it wasn't Ravi. It was a woman with short auburn hair wearing a dark pantsuit. Lucy didn't recognize her. An Initiate?

She didn't wait to find out. She stomped on Victor's foot with all her might and ran for her life. He might be waylaid for only a second, but it was enough to give her a head start. Lucy legged it to the fire exit. Even if her parents truly believed they were protecting her, she couldn't trust the rest of the Sophists.

As she burst into the faculty parking lot, alarm bells sounded.

Over the high-pitched wailing, Lucy heard the distinctive sound of a shot from inside the school.

Who had shot whom? Her thighs throbbed but she didn't stop running.

"Lucy!" shouted Victor, not nearly as far back as she was hoping.

Glancing behind her, she barreled straight into the hood of a stretch limousine.

That certainly didn't belong to any of the teachers.

The door swung open and Professor T stepped out. He was dressed immaculately in a three-piece suit and leaned his weight against a walking stick topped by a golden ouroboros.

He trained his eyes on her pursuer.

"Victor Phelps, I presume," said Professor T. "You didn't expect me to miss my own granddaughter's graduation, did you?"

REMEMBRANCE OF THINGS PAST

Granddaughter?

Lucy searched Professor T's face for any trace of her own. Maybe beneath the bushy eyebrows and beard it would be easier to see herself.

Professor T met her questioning gaze. "I have longed for this day," he told her. "I had almost given up hope. And then you walked into the Tesla Suite."

"*I*-I . . ." Lucy stuttered. Thunderstruck didn't begin to cover it. *Oh.* So that was how Ravi had performed his DNA test—checking hers against a sample from Professor T.

In less than thirty minutes, Lucy had lost two parents and gained a grandfather.

Victor caught up to them and drew to her side, hands balled into fists.

"The infamous Professor Weston-Jones," he said with loathing.

"The very same."

The driver's-side door of the limo opened and a tall, freckled man stepped out. He held a gun with a silencer in his hand. Frak. Way more than a chauffeur, it would seem. Maybe another Initiate.

"Lucinda," Professor T said. "You remind me so much of Quentin. My son. Your true father."

Quentin. The name was like a relic from a lost world. Next to her,

Lucy felt Victor flinch. He began reaching his hand inside his suit jacket, and Professor T's driver raised his weapon.

"Be so kind as to leave your hands where I can see them," Professor T said to Victor as if he were beneath his contempt. "I'm speaking with my granddaughter."

Lucy's heart swelled with panic. Her first impulse was still to protect the man she'd called Dad until a few minutes ago. She looked between him and Professor T.

"You're nothing to her," Victor growled while keeping his hands at his sides.

The professor raised his eyebrows. "Do you deny that Lucinda is my blood?"

"That's all you share," Victor spat. Lucy had never heard such hatred in his voice.

Professor T took a step in her direction. "I was told you were stillborn, but I never believed it." He sneered at Victor. "The Sophists aren't nearly as clever as they think."

"Does Quentin have the lightning gene?" Lucy asked. "Do you?"

He shook his head. "You inherited the lightning gene from your mother."

Her mother. Her birth mother. "Ravi said you'd been working with a female carrier of the mutation, but that she died. Was that her?"

Her grandfather inclined his head solemnly. "I'm sorry. She died in childbirth." He paused. "She wanted to name you Nikola, after Tesla."

Nikola. That's what had been encrypted in the photo. But she'd never divulged that information to Ravi.

"And my father?" Lucy asked. Victor lanced her with an agonized look, and she sucked in a breath. "Quentin? Where is he?"

"My son was killed by the Order of Sophia," Professor T replied. "Your mother went into hiding when she learned she was pregnant. Quentin wouldn't give up her location. He loved her beyond reason." He drilled the walking stick into the pavement. "I will always regret that the Sophists found you anyway, and that I missed the first eighteen years of your life. But Lucinda, I promise you, I won't miss out on the next."

"Bravo!" Victor began to clap, slow and venomous. "What a performance. Encore!" He clasped his hands around Lucy's shoulders, rotating her to face him. She heard a *click* as the man with the gun released the safety.

"Listen to me, kiddo. Your father wasn't killed by the Sophists." His words were low, urgent. "He brought you to us—asked us to hide you. The photo you decoded was sent by your father."

Lucy's head swam. "You *knew* him?"

"No, Quentin sent it to one of my superiors. He'd been on the run with you, but it was no way to raise a child. And the Archimedeans were closing in. The photo—I didn't know that was how he'd communicated with the Order until recently."

"*Liber librum aperit,*" Lucy said in a hush, and Victor nodded.

"You're far smarter than me, kiddo." An almost-smile tugged at one corner of his mouth. "I never thought to scan the photo for a message."

"All alchemists know that motto," Professor T interjected. He was right. The phrase didn't prove it'd been sent by her father. Although the fact that whoever sent it had called her Nikola indicated they knew who she was, what her real parents had named her—before she became Lucy Phelps.

"But the photo was sent to the Sapientia Group *before* you started working there," Lucy said to Victor.

"True," he replied. "The Order funded my Ph.D. research and it was my professor who approached me. Your mom—Elaine—and I had been married a few years and we couldn't conceive." He brushed a hand against Lucy's cheek the way he had so many times over the years. "When he showed me the photo, I took one look and knew I would love you as my own."

His story sounded so convincing. "But *why*—why would he do that? Why would Quentin give me to his enemies?" Lucy asked.

"Because your father didn't want you to spend your life as a test subject in one of *his*"—Victor jabbed an accusing finger at Professor T—"research facilities."

"Professor T isn't the one who's treated me like a test subject."

"We've dedicated our lives to keeping you safe. To helping you."

"Help?" Lucy slapped his hand from her face. "That wasn't your decision to make. You never asked me what I wanted—because you don't care."

"Kiddo, you know that's not true."

"No, I don't. I don't know anything about anything, apparently. And that's *your* fault!" Lucy folded her arms. "Besides, you failed. My heart stopped on the High Line despite all of your attempts to *cure* me!"

Victor paled. "Lucy." She could see in his face that he hadn't been aware of that detail. He looked devastated. Haunted.

"Lucinda," said Professor T. "Your mother belonged to the Order of Sophia, and their experiments to suppress her powers hastened her death. She grew too weak to survive childbirth. The Sophists convinced Evangeline she was a monster and she believed them. They'll do the same to you—I won't stand for it." He pounded his walking stick on the ground.

Evangeline. Evangeline and Quentin. It sounded so formal, so Victorian. Were those really her parents? Rick had been a Sophist and he claimed he'd known another woman with the lightning gene. Was it her mother? Could Rick have been aware of Lucy's true parentage the entire time? She hated that there might actually be a reason for her to contact him.

Lucy's eyes traveled from Professor T to Victor. "Please," said the man who had raised her. "You can't believe a word that viper has to say."

She tore at her curls. "I can't believe anything *you've* told me." Lucy felt utterly paralyzed, and Victor was so adept at shielding that she couldn't read him at all. There was too much information. Lucy wished her powers included freezing time.

"Unlike the Order of Sophia, the Archimedeans make offers, not threats," Professor T told her. "Lucinda, you are my last remaining family. I would like the opportunity to get to know you better, to work together, but the choice is yours."

A new voice joined the fray.

"I understand your confusion, Lucy. But I can't let you go with the professor."

She flashed her eyes toward the intruder and found herself looking down the barrel of a gun.

"Mom?"

Lucy gaped, trying to reconcile the woman who smelled of peppermint and agonized over the precise amount of gluten in her organic banana bread with the woman aiming a gun at her.

"Mom?" she repeated. It was a cracked, jagged sound.

Her mother stood statue straight, her chignon pinned precisely to the top of her head like a crown. The breeze didn't dare ruffle the flyaways framing her face. She seemed equally at ease with the weapon in her hand as she did poring over manuscripts.

"The Initiates have been subdued," she said to Victor as she approached the limo at a measured pace from between the parked cars, her breathing even.

He nodded. Had her *mom* subdued the Initiates? Single-handedly?

"There's no cavalry coming to your rescue, Professor Weston-Jones. I suggest you get in your car and leave while I'm still inclined to let you go."

She kept the gun on Lucy as she issued her threat. This brought monastic composure to a whole new level.

"I'm afraid I'm not inclined to let you take my granddaughter against her will," replied Professor T. "Elaine, isn't it?"

Her lips parted in a brittle smile. "You don't have a choice in the matter."

Suddenly, Professor T's driver clutched his chest, trying to brace on the hood of the limo, and toppled to the asphalt.

Lucy's hands flew to her mouth, too stunned to scream. Lucy's mom didn't move a muscle. The shot had been silent, but it hadn't been fired by the woman in front of her.

Who had taken the shot?

"As I was saying," Elaine said to Professor T. Another scream died in Lucy's throat. How many life-or-death situations had Lucy's mom been in? Just this morning, she had told Lucy her father was all bark and no bite, and Lucy hadn't believed her.

"Sophists are always so quick to violence," Professor T chided. He didn't seem concerned about the man crumpled on the ground. Although Lucy suspected he'd never show fear in front of the Sophists.

"We have more discipline than the Initiates," Victor rebuked. "You nearly got Lucy killed after her prom."

"As did you." Professor T narrowed his eyes.

While the men argued, Elaine said, "Lucy, we need to go." Her tone was dispassionate. "I won't let the Order of Archimedes take you."

"And if I don't come with you, then what? You'll make sure no one else can have me?" Lucy's accusation rushed out in a hysterical jumble.

"I took an oath to protect you, and protect you I will."

Elaine Phelps spoke with conviction, never raising her voice. Victor might do menacing really well but Elaine's calm was exponentially more frightening.

Lucy's gaze zoomed in on her trigger finger.

"You can't protect me if I'm dead!" she yelled.

She thrust out her hands, screwing up her lips, and concentrated on attracting the gun in her direction and out of Elaine's grasp. Tears burned her eyes and yet she felt none of the exhilarating anger that had preceded the stapler flying at Megan's head.

Come on. What was wrong with her powers?

Elaine watched Lucy's efforts with no reaction. "I blame myself for not taking the threat to you more to heart," she said in an infuriatingly rational manner. "After all these years, I had dropped my guard." She cast a poisonous glance at Professor T, who stood immobile by the open limo.

"I blame myself for not destroying that photo. I blame myself for underestimating my daughter. Even when you caused a neighborhood blackout. Even when Dr. Rosen concluded that your abilities had begun developing at an accelerated rate."

The fine lines tightened around Elaine's eyes. "I ignored the warning signs because, like your father, I wanted you to stay my little girl a little longer."

"I was never *yours*." Lucy hurled the reproach as hard as she could, once more attempting to magnetize the gun. Nothing. "Our family is a lie."

Elaine exchanged a heated look with Victor and his muscles tensed as if preparing for a punch.

Before the bullet had a chance to hit Lucy, pain like she'd never known set her body alight. The pain of a betrayal like no other.

Elaine had pulled the trigger.

The woman she had called mother was willing to end Lucy's life as if she were nothing but a failed experiment.

With more strength and speed than Lucy ever imagined she could possess, she clawed her nails into Victor's forearm and levered him in front of her.

His mouth opened in a grunt of disbelief as the bullet hit him square in the back. His eyes went glassy and he collapsed on top of her. Lucy fell to the ground under his weight, his body banging against her rib cage. As Lucy braced her hands on his shoulders to roll him off, she realized there was no blood. Anywhere.

A sprig of silver stuck out from his scapula. It was a dart—a tranquilizer dart.

Relief—if it could be called that—washed over Lucy that Elaine hadn't intended to kill her, only render her unconscious, take away her free will.

Professor T arced his walking stick in a broad stroke and the ouroboros connected with Elaine's hand. Lucy heard a sickening crunch. The gun fell to her feet. Elaine howled in pain, cradling her injured—possibly broken—hand and lunged for Professor T. The older man lost his footing and crashed against the open car door.

The walking stick fell from his grasp, rolling under the limo.

"Lucy!" It was the lilt she would recognize anywhere. "The bracelets!"

Ravi was running at full speed across the parking lot. From the corner of her eye, Lucy saw another man in a dark suit sprinting toward him at a diagonal.

At the same moment, Professor T felled Elaine with a sweeping kick. They began to struggle on the pavement beside the limo.

The bracelets. Of course. She stared down at the black stone coiled around her wrists. A small piece of tourmaline grounded Lucy's powers. Too much must neutralize them.

Her skin crawled. Her parents had tricked Lucy into putting on her own handcuffs. If she hadn't seen Claudia, their plan might have worked. She would be halfway to some Sophist safe house—or prison.

Lucy removed the first bracelet and, almost instantly, Victor's frequency rushed over her. In his unguarded state, she saw a tall briar in her mind. Sunlight sparkled on the tips of its thorns. Was that how Victor saw himself? Was he guarding Lucy from the world—or the world from her?

She wanted to believe her parents, but they had never trusted her, never believed in her. All the rules and restrictions were meant to contain Lucy, not protect her. As she removed the second bracelet, she glimpsed several more black-clad figures weaving through the parking lot. Whatever the Sophists' equivalent to the Initiates were, she supposed.

Adrenaline jolted through Lucy's system, bitterness glazing her tongue, and she shoved Victor's drugged mass to the side.

Raising herself to standing, Lucy captured Elaine's gaze from where she grappled with Professor T, and pitched the ebony shackles toward the football field with all her might.

Claudia O'Rourke

Lucy had tuned out Principal Petersen's monotone announcing the graduates, but her ears caught on her best friend's name. This was her big moment. *I'm sorry. For missing it. For everything.*

Claudia was the only true thing about her childhood and the best thing about growing up in Eaton. But to keep her friend safe from the feud between the Orders, Lucy would have to give her up. Jess had been right.

If Lucy truly loved Claudia, she could never see her again.

Sorrow eddied inside her and she stretched her hands in the air toward the tranquilizer gun on the ground behind the struggling forms of Elaine and Professor T. Lucy squeezed her fists and concentrated harder. The gun began to quiver.

She heard another shot. Her eyes dashed in Ravi's direction. It looked like he was locked in an embrace with the man who'd been chasing him.

Then the man keeled over. *ThankGodthankGodthankGod*. Ravi seemed unharmed.

Lucy stalked closer to Elaine and Professor T. Metal rattled against the asphalt. She pictured the arc of the trajectory the gun would need to take in order to land in her hand and bit her lips until she tasted blood. Then the pain dissipated, swept aside by a raging elation.

Elaine bashed Professor T's head against the open door. He groaned. She moved toward Lucy, and Professor T managed to grab a fistful of Elaine's skirt, holding her back.

The gun flew through the air and landed at Lucy's feet. Professor T's eyes widened. She glimpsed pride there.

Ravi had just reached Lucy when Elaine spun back around toward the professor. He spotted something Lucy didn't, his features contorting with fury.

"Professor!" he shouted in warning. Ravi dove into the small space between Elaine and the car, leaping in front of his mentor, who remained on the ground.

Elaine staggered back a step, away from the limo, knife in her good hand. It was tipped with blood.

Ravi's blood. Hissing, he gripped the top of the car door to support his weight. Red blossomed across his abdomen.

"What did you do? What did you *do*!" Lucy screamed at the woman who had been her mother. "Ravi!"

Elaine rounded on her. "I *didn't—I* . . ." She swallowed. Ravi hadn't been her intended target, but this was not a woman who apologized. She stilled her shaking hand. "Protecting you is all that matters. You're my daughter."

Ravi released a painful groan, losing his balance and slipping toward the ground.

"I am no one's daughter," Lucy declared.

Lucinda Minerva Phelps.

Principal Petersen could keep his diploma.

She grabbed the dart gun from the ground and pulled the trigger.

WONDER WOMAN

Lucy watched as Elaine tumbled to her knees, sprawling next to Victor.

She blinked away her tears. There wasn't time to give in to the fear or sadness spreading outward from her heart.

Another shot rang out. The back tire of the limousine burst. This getaway car wasn't going anywhere.

"I *s*-see three . . ." Ravi forced out, struggling to drag down air. Lucy wheeled around. More Sophists. They were coming from the direction of the school.

On the other side of the parking lot lay the football field, where commencement was still proceeding without interruption.

Lucy rushed to Ravi's side. "Can you stand?" she asked. She wrapped an arm around his waist and he leaned against her as the blood continued soaking his shirt.

"Yes," he said through clenched teeth. But clearly he wasn't doing well. Ravi's shield had crumbled and a comforting warmth—like sitting by the fire on a rainy winter's night—filled Lucy. The affection jarred with the anger that was holding her together.

Professor T pushed to his feet and wiped the trickle of blood from his temple.

"Lucinda, help Ravi behind the car," he ordered in the tone of someone used to giving orders. "I'll hold off the Sophists."

"*H*-how?" she said. The Sophists were drawing closer by the second. Professor T motioned for her to follow him as he dashed around the back of the limo to the other side. "Let me take your weight," she said to Ravi. His eyelids were fluttering, his complexion growing pallid. Static crackled between them. Lucy's chaotic emotions were too much for the tourmaline pendant alone.

Ravi didn't speak, mouth set in a grimace, as he panted and leaned further into Lucy, using all of his energy to stay upright.

As they rounded the back of the car, Professor T lifted the gun from beside the fallen Initiate and fired. He motioned for them to get down.

"We have instructions to take the girl alive!" shouted a male voice. Lucy couldn't see exactly how close the Sophist was from where she cowered behind the barricade of the stretch limo.

Ravi's blood seeped onto her hands. *Oh God*. She couldn't lose him. She refused. Not like this. Not after all the things she'd said to him— but especially the things she hadn't.

Lucy looked from Ravi to Professor T: her grandfather. She'd just found him. She didn't want to lose him either.

The Sophists said they had instructions to take *her* alive. They didn't say anything about Ravi or Professor T. She had no reason to think they wouldn't kill them to get to her.

"I'm giving myself up," she said, resolved, slackening her grip on Ravi.

"No!" Professor T made a guttural sound as he grabbed Lucy's arm, eyes blazing. "I won't let them take you from me again."

Ignoring her grandfather, she propped Ravi against the limo door and began to straighten when Ravi squeezed her arm. "Wait, *Lu*—" he strained to whisper. "Help is . . . coming . . ."

He must be delirious. "It's not. My mom—*Elaine*—said she *subdued* the Initiates." Lucy shuddered, not wanting to know precisely what she'd meant.

"Look up," he said. The effort of speaking made him groan. *Look up?* Definitely delirious.

"I'm coming out!" Lucy yelled to the Sophists. "Don't shoot!"

Then she heard it. Whirring. The distinct whirring of—

A helicopter. A helicopter was heading straight for the football field!

Eyes closed, an almost-smile on his lips, Ravi said, "*Go*."

"Run!" Professor T urged. "We'll catch up."

Frak that. Lucy had already lost one family today. "I go, you go," she said to Ravi, using his words from prom night.

Lucy circled her arm once more around his waist and hoisted him to his feet. He hissed in pain. Professor T met her stare. "Just like Quentin," he said, realizing she wouldn't be dissuaded from her plan. "You two first. I'll cover you."

There was no more time to argue. Lucy nodded and began running, half dragging Ravi. He limped alongside her. Professor T had probably been training with the Initiates since the moon landing. He'd hold his own. He would. He *had* to.

Ravi's wheezes grew more labored, like wind whistling through a cavern. Each of his strained grunts tightened her own chest.

Lucy heard the shots behind her, as well as the glass of windshields exploding, but she didn't look back. She kept the dart gun clamped in her right hand as they reached the football field. "Just a little farther," she whispered to Ravi.

The whirring intensified as the helicopter began its descent at the opposite end of the field from the dais on which Principal Petersen was handing out diplomas.

From the corner of her eye, Lucy spotted a hundred caps and gowns turn to gawk. Shouts of surprise rose from the graduates and their families.

How would the local news explain away a helicopter landing in the middle of graduation?

Not Lucy's problem. She just prayed Claudia didn't come looking for her.

Ravi lost his footing on the grass, which was soft and muddy from last night's rainfall. He fell to his knees, bringing Lucy down with him. Dirt spattered her graduation dress.

"*Please*," she murmured. "Please, get up."

As the helicopter landed about twenty feet away, a shot bounced off the tail.

Lucy swiveled on her knees and released the trigger of the gun. A woman cried out as the dart struck her in the chest.

Professor T was on the heels of the Sophist. "Go! Go! Go!" he yelled at Lucy. Using all of her strength to raise herself to standing, she pushed Ravi up with her. Her thighs quivered.

Professor T checked that the woman Lucy had shot was unconscious, then sprinted to Lucy's side. He slung Ravi's other arm around his neck, and took the majority of his weight. Lucy let out a short huff of relief. They ran together toward the chopper.

The door to the main compartment slid open and a pilot with light-brown skin angled her head at Lucy from the cockpit. She took off her headphones.

"I'm Camila," she called over the roar of the blades. "Ready to get out of here, *chica*?"

Frak yeah.

"Get in!" Professor T commanded Lucy. Lucy stepped onto one of the landing skids and turned around, reaching her arms for Ravi. She looped her arms through his from behind as Professor T lifted Ravi's lower body off the ground.

Lucy pulled Ravi onto the floor of the chopper, scuttling backward, laying him flat. Professor T set Ravi's legs down carefully and hopped in. He pulled the door closed behind him.

"Move!" he yelled at the pilot.

Camila nodded. "*Vámonos*," she said as she replaced her headphones.

The helicopter lifted off the ground, and Lucy glimpsed her former classmates scattering across the football field, some running for the parking lot, others hiding behind their folding chairs. Talk about making a dramatic exit from high school.

Returning her eyes to Ravi, Lucy pressed her hands as firmly as she could against his wound. Blood continued to gush. She wished she'd been paying closer attention when Amara had treated Pedro in the back of the Freelancers' van.

Buttons popped as Lucy tore open Ravi's shirt. The gash lay between his ribs on the left side. He needed a doctor.

"There's a hospital about fifteen miles from here," she told Professor T at the top of her lungs. The noise from the rotating blades was nearly deafening.

Barely audible, Ravi said, "No *hosp* . . ." Obviously he wasn't thinking straight.

"We're meeting an excellent doctor at the airfield," came Professor T's reply.

"Airfield?" Lucy shot him a confused look.

"It won't take the Sophists long to regroup. We can't afford the diversion."

"He's losing too much blood," she hollered, more adamant.

"Ravi's a strong young man. He'll make it." Professor T smiled in a kindly way, a grandfatherly way, but it was forged from iron.

"You can't know that! *Please.*" In trying to protect Lucy, Ravi had been tased by her father, and stabbed by her mother. *Please don't let him die.*

"It's what Ravi would want." Professor T patted Lucy on the back but she couldn't read him.

Could he be willing to trade Ravi's life for hers? Well, she wasn't.

"Stay with me!" Lucy hated to do this but—she slapped Ravi open-palmed across the face. His eyes shot open, then his lids trembled. "No going to sleep!" Looking to Professor T, she barked, "Do you have a pen?"

He raised his eyebrows. "A pen?"

"A pen," she repeated, almost hysterical. "A metal one. Or anything metal."

Professor T reached into his suit pocket. Lucy wiped her hands on her skirt, smearing it with blood, then snatched the silver fountain pen from his grasp with desperate hope.

The initials monogramed in filigree were *Q.W.J.* For Quentin Weston-Jones? Had this belonged to her father?

She'd ask later. "Handkerchief?" she said to Professor T instead. If anyone would carry one, she figured it would be him. He immediately produced a square of paisley from his waistcoat. Lucy wrapped it around one end of the pen, barking, "Hold him down!"

Professor T's forehead creased in a V, but he used his weight to press Ravi firmly against the floor of the helicopter.

With a deep breath, Lucy tried to focus her erratic emotions, concentrate on the metal in her hand. She thought about all the small moments she and Ravi had shared, their jokes and mutual geekiness. An emerald glow began to emanate from her fingers. Lucy could summon her powers from positive emotions as well as fear and anger, she realized.

Control. She needed to heat the pen but avoid shocking Ravi. Hopefully it would also kill any bacteria. Exhaling, Lucy lowered the glowing silver to one end of Ravi's knife wound. *Sizzle.* He twitched but Professor T kept him secure. Her grandfather's eyes were unafraid as he nodded in approval.

Lucy scorched Ravi's skin again. The flesh fizzed. This scar would join the many others Ravi had received from the Order of Sophia.

Her stomach churned. Even if Lucy disagreed with some of his methods, Ravi had proven himself to be a steadfast ally. *Her* ally. His enemies were now Lucy's enemies—and that included the people who'd raised her. They hadn't loved her enough to tell her the truth.

She applied the pen to the last section of the cut. Heat rose from the blackened wound but the blood, the blood . . . was stopping.

Professor T's posture relaxed and Lucy's heart skipped a beat.

"Quick thinking," he said, panning his gaze over Ravi's chest. "Like a true Archimedean."

Lucy wanted to believe her grandfather and the Archimedeans were the white hats. So much. For now they were at least the lesser of two evils.

She let out a ragged breath and dropped the pen beside her. The emerald glow faded. Her right palm was singed, blistering, and she swore as pain replaced adrenaline. The handkerchief had provided meager protection.

"Just because I'm coming with you," she told Professor T, "doesn't mean I'm agreeing to become a card-carrying member of the Order."

"Understood," he said. "I will earn your trust, Lucinda. And I would expect nothing less from a Weston-Jones."

Was that who Lucy was? In another life, maybe. She might never know who had really handed her over to the Sophists. What she did know was, she was done living up to other people's expectations.

Until she had all the players in the world of alchemy figured out, the only side Lucy was on was her own. This was Lucy's body, Lucy's life, and whatever she did with it from now on would be on *her* terms.

"Lucinda?" Ravi choked out. His dark eyes opened, and they were beautiful. She tipped her head downward to hear him over the rumbling of the chopper, but said, "*Shh.* Don't speak."

"You healed me."

"I just cauterized the wound."

The shadow of a smile flitted over his lips. "My Wonder Woman." Ravi was in no state for one of their debates, so Lucy simply returned his smile.

He shifted his gaze to Professor T, who loomed above them.

"Rufus is awaiting our arrival," said the professor, bending down to shout in Ravi's ear. "Camila will radio ahead, tell him to have blood prepared for a transfusion in the air—just in case." Ravi nodded. Whoever this Rufus was, Lucy was glad an actual doctor could repair any damage she'd done with her field medicine.

Raising himself into a squat, Professor T said, "You did well, granddaughter." *Granddaughter.* Lucy wasn't sure if she'd ever get used to that. "Rufus will patch you up too," he added, glancing at her injured hand.

"You're hurt?" Ravi said, voice strained.

She shrugged. "Sadly, I'm not immune to burning metal."

"We'll be home soon," Professor T promised, his voice raised, looking between them.

"Home?" Lucy gasped. "As in *England*? I don't have a passport."

"We'll take care of it," Professor T said. No doubt forging a passport was the least of the strings the Order of Archimedes could pull.

Taking a shallow breath, Ravi said, "Do me a favor?" and motioned for Lucy to lean closer.

"I just saved your life."

"Besides saving my life."

He beckoned her even closer, reaching for the tourmaline pendant. Professor T cleared his throat and levered himself into the copilot seat. He slipped on a pair of headphones.

Ravi's gaze never left her face as Lucy lowered her lips until they hovered just above his. "Close enough?" she whispered, relief and exhaustion coloring her laugh.

"Not quite."

He kissed Lucy with infinite tenderness and a burning magenta sunset exploded in her mind's eye. Given his injured state—and the proximity of her grandfather, Lucy forced herself to show some restraint. But it wasn't easy.

She kissed his forehead, and Ravi smiled up at her. She would deal with the fallout and all the unanswered questions tomorrow. Today both of them were safe and alive, and she planned to keep them that way.

Maybe her powers held the key to mysteries that scientists and alchemists had been seeking for centuries. Maybe not.

The only person Lucy owed any answers to was herself.

She glanced out the window and watched the town of Eaton become a speck in the distance. Eaton was her past; Lucy was flying toward her future.

And when her enemies found her again, she would be ready.

ACKNOWLEDGMENTS

Publishing is a team sport and this has been especially true in bringing this project to fruition. My deepest gratitude goes to my agent, Sara Crowe, who continues to be a pillar of support. A hearty thank-you to my editors, Brendan Deneen and Kat Brzozowski, who oversaw the inception of Lucy's story and to Chris Morgan, who shepherded it through the final stages. Thanks also to Rachelle Mandik for your eagle eyes.

I am very grateful to have found a home at Tor Teen. Many thanks to Kathleen Doherty, Sumiya Nowshin, and everyone in marketing and publicity who work so hard to get books out into the world! Also a huge shout-out to Liane Worthington and the team at BookSparks.

There are many early and second readers to whom I owe a huge debt for lending their critical expertise in various domains and helping me to shape this story into something book-like. Thank you to Amy Carol Reeves, Teresa Yea, Elizabeth Fama, Alex Bear, Ellen Rozek, McCall Hoyle, Sangu Mandanna, Darshana Khiani, Kamilla Benko, Robin Talley, Misa Sugiura, Carlie Sorosiak, Ame Igharo, Deborah Mc-Candless, Georgina Cullman, and Suguru Furuta. My husband, Jack Mozley, is always my first reader at the end of a fevered day of writing and his Ph.D. in quantum physics came in pretty handy this time around. Any scientific or sci-fi errors are entirely my own!

I am also sincerely appreciative of the time my fellow authors have taken to give me blurbs and generally shout about my books online. An enormous thank-you to Stacey Lee, Taran Matharu, Laura Lam, Dan Godfrey, Rachel Lynn Solomon, Julie Cross, Royce Buckingham, Beth Revis, Amie Kaufman, Samantha Shannon, and Stephanie Garber.

Although publishing a book takes a village, the writing life can often be quite a solitary existence (especially in the depths of an English winter), which is why I consider myself lucky to have bookish friends in a plethora of time zones. Sending much chocolate and gin to Kaitlyn Sage Patterson, Heidi Heilig, Kelly deVos, Annie Stone, Karen M. McManus, Rebecca Denton, Melissa Albert, Sara Holland, Vic James, Sarah Nicole Smetana, Kes Trester, Somaiya Daud, Dhonielle Clayton, Melanie Conklin, Ali Standish, Lucy Hounsom, Julia Ember, Katherine Corr, Megan Bannen, Yamille Saied Méndez, Rhoda Belleza, Elsie Chapman, Alice Broadway, Elizabeth Lim, Zoraida Córdova, Natalie C. Parker, Samira Ahmed, and April G. Tucholke. I also owe the next round at the pub here in London to Laura Dodd and Stevie Finnegan.